W9-AYR-350

THE GIRL BEHIND THE RED ROPE

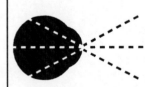

THE GIRL BEHIND THE RED ROPE

TED DEKKER AND RACHELLE DEKKER

THORNDIKE PRESS
A part of Gale, a Cengage Company

Farmington Hills, Mich • San Francisco • New York • Waterville, Maine
Meriden, Conn • Mason, Ohio • Chicago

Thorndike Press® Large Print Christian Fiction.
The text of this Large Print edition is unabridged.
Other aspects of the book may vary from the original edition.
Set in 16 pt. Plantin.

LIBRARY OF CONGRESS CIP DATA ON FILE.
CATALOGUING IN PUBLICATION FOR THIS BOOK
IS AVAILABLE FROM THE LIBRARY OF CONGRESS

ISBN-13: 978-1-4328-6986-1 (hardcover alk. paper)

Published in 2019 by arrangement with Revell Books, a division of Baker Publishing Group

Printed in Mexico
1 2 3 4 5 6 7 23 22 21 20 19

A12007 355235

THE GIRL BEHIND
THE RED ROPE

CHAPTER ONE

It was hot that day in the hills of Tennessee. I remember because the aged boards that made up the tiny church's floor creaked with every step. As if to say, *I'm tired of all you meat sacks treading on me. Be still.*

But we couldn't be still. Not on that day.

I was only a child, six years old, but my memories of what happened on that Sunday are clear. Or maybe hearing the retelling over and over has crystalized a distorted version of them in my mind. Either way, I remember.

It was late August in Clarksville, a small town along Route 254 in the hills west of Knoxville. I was seated on the third pew next to my mother, who cradled my newborn brother, Lukas, in her arms. From the first time I laid eyes on his tiny fingers and heard his soft cooing as he stared up at me, all I dreamed about was having a baby like Lukas of my own one day.

My older brother, Jamie, fidgeted to my left. The small, decaying building that housed Holy Family Church needed a new air-conditioning unit the congregation couldn't afford, so the windows had been opened. But without a morning breeze, the sanctuary felt like a sauna, slowly cooking the faithful as if extracting punishment for hidden sins — a helpful reminder of the hell to come for all who did not adhere to the dictates of a holy God.

It was the tenth Sunday since the flock of Holy Family had received the prophecy of the destruction that would soon visit the earth. We all accepted the word given to Rose Pierce as truth. She was a devout woman who loved Jesus and his church, a dedicated servant of Christianity. We had repeated the prophecy until it was etched first in our brains, then on our hearts, which is why none of us could be still that Sunday.

In three years' time, a great scourge would cleanse the earth.

We were a small community of the purest faith, the bride of Christ, the elect, ever diligent to obey the teachings of righteousness from the word and always on guard against the sinful ways of the world. Only seventy-two in that day, the Holy Family was seen as radical and fringe to many in our small town. *Fringe,* a word I only understood because my mother had explained it to me and my brother after we'd overheard her arguing again with our father.

Arguing because my dad didn't buy into all the fear-mongering, as he liked to call it. Billy Carter, a redheaded boy my age, called him *faithless* to my face, and it was clear the whole church thought the same. Half of me thought so too. Either way, my dad had stopped attending the services, so he wasn't there that hot August Sunday. If he had been, he would have become an instant believer in the prophecy Rose had delivered.

Because in the space of five terrifying minutes, everything about all of our lives was forever and irreversibly changed.

Our shepherd, Harrison Pierce, husband to Rose, had prefaced his sermon with a few remarks that I don't recall before pausing and holding the congregation in silence, eyeing us each with care. Then, in a gentle but gripping voice, he repeated the prophecy.

"In three years' time, because the world has turned away from holiness, the world's sin will rise up against them in monstrous form and destroy the wicked. But those with true sight will be shown what is to come and delivered from the great fury. The

9

chosen remnant shall seek refuge away from the world and wait until the ground has been cleansed of sin. For then those with eyes to see and vigilant of faith will be spared from destruction and inherit the earth as the pure bride under the law of a holy God. So be it."

"So be it," we all repeated.

Each one of us believed that we were those called to receive true sight, but none of us knew what that sight would show us. We only knew that an angel named Sylous had appeared to Rose and delivered truth, so we could remain true to the end and be presented as a pure bride to Christ.

Having spoken the prophecy, Harrison glanced at his wife, dipped his head once, and took a deep breath. He nervously scanned the flock. "Today, dearly beloved, is the day we have been waiting for. Today . . . Today we will all be given eyes to see what is to come."

I sensed Sylous before I heard the door at the back of the small sanctuary softly closing. I knew it was him before I saw him. Every hair on my body stood on end. For a moment, I couldn't breathe, much less turn to see.

It was as if my soul knew who he was before my mind could catch up.

I had expected an angel with wings and a choir, maybe because I was only six and naïve, but when I finally turned with the rest, Sylous was nothing like anything I had imagined.

There, standing at the back of the room, stood a man dressed head to toe in white. Pants, suit jacket, shoes, all pristine white. His skin was tanned, tight across a chiseled jaw. Red lips and warm smile, but it was the bright blue of his eyes that has always wandered into my dreams. Beautiful and terrifying at once. Intriguing and dangerous.

For a moment, I forgot he was an angel. Maybe he wasn't — no one really knew, not even Rose, because according to the Bible, even angels could show up as men and you wouldn't know the difference.

No one moved. No one dared speak. All eyes were fixed on the man standing at the end of the center aisle.

Rose was the first to kneel. I saw her from the corner of my eye, there on the end of the pew, sinking to the floor with head bowed in reverence. Her husband followed suit beside the podium, eyes wide, face white.

Without further hesitation the rest of us knelt, sliding off the pews to our knees. My heart was pounding. My eyes were fixed on the angel sent to save us. Then, without warning, my excitement shifted into something else. Fear. My brother Jamie must have felt the same, because he grabbed my hand, trembling. I glanced at little Lukas, who slept soundly in my mother's tight embrace.

Sylous started forward, his slick shoes clicking across the creaking wood. All the way to the stage, where Harrison knelt. He stepped up to the podium and turned to face us, eyes moving slowly across the pews.

When they met mine, I was sure he'd peeled back my skin and was seeing what hid inside me. I wanted to look away, but I couldn't. None of us could.

"The purity of your hearts has been acknowledged," he began. "You are ready to see what few have ever seen." His voice was gentle and kind, with unmistakable authority. "Will the bride say yes to Jesus?"

"Yes," Rose whispered from where she knelt.

Then others and all: "Yes."

"Then you are ready," Sylous replied.

A long beat of silence held us on edge.

"In three years' time, because the world has turned away from holiness, the world's sin will rise up against them in monstrous form and destroy the wicked."

The floor under our knees began to vibrate. The old wooden pews shook, knocking against the floorboards. I was aghast, terrified, but Sylous continued without a concern in the world.

"Today you will be shown a foretaste of the destruction to come so you might be delivered. Seeing what you see today, you will seek refuge away from the world and wait for that day of reckoning. When it comes, you will be spared in a safe haven as you wait for the world to be cleansed of sin."

Dust fell from the ceiling onto my shoulder, and a back pew rattled loose enough to slap against the floor. A shutter to my left fell from its hinges. Hands were extended everywhere, searching for something sturdy as the building felt like it was going to collapse.

"For then those with eyes to see and vigilant of faith will be spared from destruction and inherit the earth as the pure bride under the law of a holy God."

With the last utterance of the prophecy, the shaking stopped and, but for dust in the air, all was still again. My mother was breathing heavily beside me; Jamie's hand was clenching mine with enough force to leave a mark. Only little Lukas remained oblivious in his deep sleep — how, I have no idea.

"Now I give you eyes to see," Sylous said.

The sound of rushing wind filled the church. It surrounded us, behind and in front, to the right and to the left. What the rest of the world couldn't see, we saw.

And what we saw struck terror in our hearts.

Screams ripped through the chapel. Cries for protection, weeping from some. All in the blink of an eye, as what couldn't possibly be real closed in around us.

My bones rattled and my skin went numb. No one could experience what visited us that day and remain the same.

Through all the chaos, Sylous's words whispered through my mind.

Now I give you eyes to see.

And so we saw.

CHAPTER TWO

Thirteen Years Later

I took a deep breath and tucked my fingers into my palms. Anxiously glanced at the thin silver watch that decorated my wrist. The hands hadn't moved since I'd looked at it last. It felt as though time itself had slowed. Jamie should be here by now. I looked back at my watch and stared until the small hand ticked forward. Other than the simple wedding band that circled my finger, it was the only piece of jewelry I was permitted to wear.

Both pieces were new. Both received five months earlier on my wedding day as gifts. One from Andrew Marks, the man I now called husband, the other from Rose Pierce. Receiving a gift from her had humbled me. Rose loved me and I loved her for that love.

I often considered leaving the watch safely in my room, but I wasn't sure what Rose might think if she saw me without it. I feared disappointing her more than harming the watch, so I wore it and made sure to protect it, as I did with everything of value. My eyes, my mind, my voice, my body, my heart, my soul.

I was betraying all of that by being here now.

I shuddered, closed my eyes, and wished this moment was different. Harrison Pierce's words spoken from the pulpit filled my ears. *"To keep another's transgression in the darkness, never bringing it to the light, is to participate in transgression yourself."*

It was true, yet there I stood, participating in transgression by helping my older brother venture beyond the perimeter. I hadn't followed him past the boundary — God forbid — but I was definitely participating. So wasn't his sin my own?

A railway car stood against the edge of the forest fifty feet from me. We couldn't see the town from the abandoned tracks, which is why Jamie had me wait by them. But looking at the old cars only reminded me of the danger we were both facing. Jamie had always been headstrong, but now he'd lost his mind.

I heard a rustle to my left and turned, hoping to see Jamie. Nothing but the trees. The forest stretched for miles in every direction, protecting the valley we'd moved to after Sylous had opened our eyes to the truth.

The perimeter was marked by a thick red rope staked six inches off the ground. Staying behind that red rope was a matter of life and death. We all knew the terrible danger of being exposed beyond that line of safety. Hell. Death. The Fury.

We had all seen the Fury. Our eyes had all been opened thirteen years earlier on that hot Sunday, and we'd all seen exactly what the coming judgment looked like.

The words used to describe what we'd witnessed varied, but we'd seen darkness itself in form. We referred to them collectively as the Fury, a name that felt appropriate because they were what were left when God removed his hand of protection. They were death itself, and that death could ravage not only our minds but our bodies.

We'd all seen them, erupting from the air as if they'd been waiting for a thousand years to show themselves. No one could experience what we had and not be permanently altered.

Even as the rest of the world remained in blindness, we had been given true sight to see the evil coming to destroy the earth, straight from hell, unstoppable and more terrifying than one could imagine.

Three years after we'd been given sight to see the coming scourge, and only six months after Rose had led us to the safety of Haven Valley, the Fury swarmed the earth. We didn't see them this time, but the world had gone dark and lightning had ripped jagged tears in the sky. Crackling thunder punctuated the terrible howling and screams that echoed from the hills beyond our perimeter.

But we in Haven Valley were spared, as Sylous had promised.

They had come alright. For sure. And even now they were out there, beyond the red rope that kept us safe, hunting and feeding on every wayward soul, and they would continue until the whole earth was cleansed of wickedness. They had been present ten years, so maybe the purging would end soon, but not yet. Not until Sylous told Rose it was time to leave the valley and inherit a new, purified earth.

And yet Jamie had broken the law and ventured out already. And I'd helped him. What had I been thinking?

Again I glanced at my wrist, trying to push away the frightening thoughts. More of Harrison's wisdom echoed in my mind. *"To truly love someone is to hold them accountable. As God loves us with a fierce wrath, so we should love one another."*

I should have locked Jamie in his room. Or tied him to his bed. At the very least, I should have told someone. But I couldn't betray my brother. So what was I to do?

I turned away from the forest, took a deep breath, and let it out slowly through my nose. "What should I do, Lukas?" I whispered.

Lukas had died twelve years ago, just before his first birthday, and I'd cried for days. When I spoke to him he never answered me, but sometimes I imagined he did. He was my own little angel, always there in my mind when I became confused. With so much to worry about in Haven Valley, he was a bright light of innocence that gave me comfort. If he'd lived, he would now be thirteen, but I still saw him as the adorable one-year-old with blond hair and blue eyes, a much younger version of Jamie.

His death had crushed me. Jamie said it was why I was so obsessed with children. I was refusing to grow up, he said, clinging to fantasies of innocence. Maybe he was right, but I didn't care.

"I'm stuck," I whispered. "I think I made a terrible mistake. I think I betrayed Rose and now Jamie's in trouble." I swallowed. "What if he's dead?"

19

"Grace," someone whispered to my right.

I spun around and stared at Jamie, who stood at the tree line, grinning. He wasn't much taller than me, but his shoulders were wider. Both of us were thin, with long limbs and sharp features, as my mother would say. Our appearances favored our father, she'd told us, something we would have to take her word for since neither of us had seen him since we'd left for Haven Valley. We had no pictures of him and he wasn't to be mentioned in the house, which was fine by me because I hardly thought of him as my father any longer.

"Jamie." I exhaled, awash with relief as he hurried up to me. I forgot the rules for a moment and rushed forward to give him a hug, then caught myself. He noticed, and for a beat we stood staring at each other. The rules of purity forbade any physical contact between males and females over the age of ten unless they were married.

As quickly as my relief had come, it melted to anger. "You're late."

"Only by a few minutes," he said.

"Late," I snapped, tapping my watch. "I was terrified!"

He hesitated, then nodded. "I'm sorry."

His shoulder-length hair was free from the usual tie that held men's hair back at the nape of their necks. It was the same light blond color as mine, but much longer. Men were allowed to wear their hair as they pleased. Women over the age of fourteen were required to keep it very short — less than two inches in length — so as not to be unnecessarily attractive to men.

Beauty led to lust. Lust was a sin.

One thing was certain: if sin was allowed to enter Haven Valley, our purity would be lost and Sylous's protection would fail us even here. We all would suffer the same fate as the rest of the world. Our objective now was to remain pure as we waited to inherit the kingdom of heaven on a new earth. Some called that coming day "the new millennium."

Jamie quickly tied his hair back with the rubber band around his wrist, glancing past me to be sure we still hadn't been seen. "My hair came loose while I was running back," he said.

"You were being chased?"

"No. Though I wish I had been."

"What do you mean? You wish for death?"

"I wish for certainty and clarity."

"You've lost your mind, Jamie. This is all a horrible mistake!"

"On the contrary, like I told you earlier, I'm reclaiming my mind."

"Then you've lost your faith. Either way, it's terribly dangerous."

"Five times, Grace. Five times I've been beyond the border, each time venturing a little farther in search of my faith. Each time encountering not a single Fury."

"Jamie, please —"

"This time I made it to the end of the forest, where it breaks out into a clearing. Beyond this mountain, there's a large town. Who knows what's down there. People perhaps, others who weren't destroyed."

"If they haven't been, they will be. Never again."

"But what if I'm right, Grace? What if the time has come to claim our inheritance? What if we aren't alone in this heaven on earth? What if it's now!" The light in Jamie's blue eyes drew my own curiosity.

"Rose would know if it was time," I said.

"Would she?" Jamie asked.

I shook my head as outrage gathered in my chest. "How can you doubt her? Doubt Sylous? You're going to get us all killed!"

He fell silent for a moment, his eyes searching my face. There had been doubters in our community over the last ten years, but all had eventually come back to truth. Now my own brother was walking a similar path — so persuasive that I'd finally agreed to help him find out for himself. But I couldn't do it any longer.

"Why haven't I encountered the Fury?" His voice was low, and I shifted my eyes because it was a question I had asked myself more than once.

"You doubt the guidance of our shepherd and the existence of the Fury," I leveled at him. "Do you also doubt the existence of God?"

"Of course not."

"Just his laws?"

"They're the laws of Sylous!" he snapped.

"Sent to us by God! Isn't it the same, brother?"

He jabbed a finger into the air. "Remember who you're speaking to! Mind your voice!"

I recoiled from his disciplinary scolding. "Now Sylous's laws mean something?"

"Silence!" he shouted.

How dare he scold me after his actions? It was wrong for a woman to dishonor any man through tone or action, so he was in his rights. But who was he to leverage laws even as he was breaking them? I wanted to tell him as much, but I'd already broken too many laws to gather the courage.

A flash of remorse crossed his face. "Sorry. Just out of sorts, that's all." He paused. "I've been thinking . . . What if there never were any monsters?"

"Don't be ridiculous. We all saw them."

"Only that once, thirteen years ago."

"Once was enough for me," I said. "And we heard them when God removed his hand of protection ten years ago. How can you doubt what's so obvious?"

"What if it's all in our minds?" he pressed. "Like the make-believe stories you tell the kids all the time. Like Lukas and the imaginary world you disappear into all the time."

"Stop it —"

"What if Sylous is the real monster? What if this place is our hell with all the rules and fear and there's nothing out there but the real world? What if Sylous got us seeing something that wasn't really there? For that matter, what if the Fury are actually good and he's the devil?"

I felt my face flush. He was talking the kind of heresy that would get him banished! But he still wasn't finished.

"Even if they do exist," he continued, "we don't have any evidence they've taken over the world like Rose insists."

"Because we're in Haven Valley, protected by Sylous!"

"Really? So where is he? No one's seen him in ten years. At the very least we should wonder if the Fury are gone and all we have to do is go out and take what's ours."

"The great testing hasn't come, so we know it's not the end. Please don't talk like —"

"Yes, the infamous great testing. A wolf will come in sheep's clothing after all this time, because even now we still haven't proven our purity. It's nothing but a convenient teaching to keep us in fear, Grace! Can't you see? If there are Fury out there, why am I safe?" He spread his arms. "Do I look like a ravaged soul to you? Why would I need Sylous's protection from something that doesn't exist? Meanwhile, we waste away in our own personal little hell. Why?"

"Because there's evil out there," I snapped, thrusting a finger at the horizon. "Fear protects us. You know that as much as I do. If you didn't fear, you would just throw yourself off a cliff, and that's exactly what you're doing now. Please, Jamie. I'm begging you."

"Maybe I don't believe that anymore," he said. "Maybe I just want to be free now. What if we have it all backward? And even if we don't, there's still the question of who the Fury are. What are they? How does something like that just pop out of nowhere and then disappear for a decade? Please tell

25

me you've secretly wondered at least that much."

I hated the thoughts his questions brought to my mind. He was playing with fire, and I'd made the terrible mistake of playing along.

I ground my teeth, no longer willing to argue. He was too clever for me anyway. I was always the naïve one, like he said, too childlike for my own good, but that didn't matter to me now. What mattered was that we were still out in the open. The longer we stood out here, the more danger we faced.

Jamie opened his mouth to speak again, but I held up my hand to silence him, a gesture I wouldn't dare with any other man.

"We need to go," I said. Without another word I turned and hurried for the eastern section, which I knew would be free of guardians at this time. Jamie followed quickly, silent for now.

Though the perimeter wasn't walled, Haven Valley's guardians, seven men selected by Harrison and Rose to ensure our protection, conducted regular border sweeps. Different sections of the perimeter were checked at different times of the day. And those times changed regularly to discourage people from doing exactly what we were doing. Rose kept a copy of the schedule in her home office, an office I was privy to because I spent so much time in the Pierces' home. Keeper of their three young children when Rose was tied up with administrative and church duties was one of my roles because of my love of children, they said. Rose was mentoring me.

I couldn't count the number of hours I'd spent sitting in her office, listening to her teachings on the law. Now I was using that relationship to read the guardians' schedule to ensure my brother could break the law without consequence.

I was wrong to have come. I should confess. The whole thing made my stomach turn.

Pausing only twice to keep from being detected, we returned to the center of town within ten minutes, no one the wiser. But even Jamie knew his absences for several hours at a time would be noticed and called into question soon enough. This had to stop. I decided then that no matter how much pressure Jamie applied, I wouldn't be helping him again.

And maybe I really should confess to Rose. I would have to think about that.

We slowed our pace as we stepped into the alleyway between the single schoolhouse, currently unoccupied as evening drew close, and the town's general store, which closed at five p.m. each day. I took a deep breath when we reached the end of the alley and rounded the corner onto the town's main street. It was quiet this time of day — children home from school, chores and tasks completed, people preparing for the night. Tucking into their homes, doors and windows locked, as the law required.

Just because we were protected from the Fury didn't mean temptations weren't everywhere.

I tried my best to squash the uneasy feeling in my stomach as we walked openly down the sidewalk toward home, located south of Haven Valley's town center. A dozen buildings lined either side of the only main road. The tiny town had been built by a mining company in the early 1980s, complete with a stretch of train tracks north of town that were never completed. They'd abandoned the compound twenty years later, leaving most of the buildings, the tracks with several old cars, and some rusted equipment.

Following Sylous's visit, our community had purchased the land from the mining company, restored most of the buildings, and built new residences that suited our needs. The tracks and train cars were a good ways beyond the town perimeter and out of sight.

No building stood taller than four stories. All the structures had simple matching asphalt-shingled roofs, white trim, white shutters and white doors. Simple colors: tans, browns, a few shades of blue. Calming and familiar.

Everything besides the homes, the small farm, the fresh spring-water well, and the Chapel stood adjacent to the two-thousand-foot stretch of the double-lane paved road. A road that started and ended in unfinished edges. It looked as if the mining company had laid asphalt for one small chunk, then changed its mind. Not that it was of any consequence to Haven Valley. We had no use for roads. The sidewalks were nice though. They kept the dust off your shoes so they didn't need to be scrubbed . . .

Oh no! My shoes! They were filthy! If someone saw my shoes they might ask questions. If they asked questions I might have to lie. If I lied . . .

I couldn't heap sin upon sin by lying.

I hadn't even considered the possibility of being caught from the appearance of my shoes. How foolish of me. Hadn't I been taught to see the potential for danger everywhere?

I shifted my eyes to Jamie's shoes. His were even worse. Much worse!

"What?" Jamie asked softly.

"What if someone sees our shoes?" I whispered.

"Shoes?"

"We have to get home!" I said, fixing my eyes on our destination. Four rows of matching homes, several dozen in total, capped the south side of Haven Valley and housed the residents — nearly one hundred now.

Jamie said nothing as we picked up our pace. My thoughts tripped between running and the knowledge that running would be its own red flag. I was guilty. Terribly guilty. And in that moment, all of my guilt caught up with me.

I bit the inside of my lip to keep tears from collecting in my eyes. I couldn't be crying. I couldn't be running. I couldn't be covered in dust.

I could think of nothing else as the last several hundred feet to the second row of homes passed under my dirty shoes. Then my front door was in sight. Then the knob in my hand. But then a thought dropped into my mind and I released the knob.

I turned and headed back down the three simple wood steps. "We should go through the back and wash our shoes before Mother sees."

Jamie huffed. "Again with the shoes."

But he followed me, and seconds later we were at the back door, up three more wooden steps, and into the house. Relief washed over me the moment the door closed behind me.

Though married five months now, I didn't yet share a home with the man the council had picked for me. Newlyweds weren't permitted to live together until they conceived, because the purpose of marriage was to make a family, not to experience romance or gratification. Until a child was conceived, a new bride was allowed only scheduled conjugal visits to her husband's home. The rule reinforced Rose's insistence that all women must give the highest priority to bearing children and repopulating the earth. Truly, romance was almost a sin.

Alice, who was eighteen, had been married to David the same day I'd been married to Andrew, farmer and council member. She couldn't wait to conceive and move in with David, who was twenty-four. They did their best to hide their affection for each other, but I knew it all too well.

Me, I was grateful to live at home still, because I had no real attraction to my husband. The thought of having a baby thrilled me, but the idea of moving in with Andrew, more than twice my age, made my stomach turn.

The house was dark and silent, although I knew my mother was there somewhere. I kept my hand on the door behind me to steady myself for a beat, then proceeded to pull my shoes off.

"Grace! Relax, sister. You're seeing ghosts now. Let that simple mind of yours tell you better stories — you're good at that."

I shot him a glare, hoping he could see the fire in my eyes despite the dim light. He was probably right, but I didn't care if I was overreacting. I only wanted to get back to the way I knew things should be. I wasn't good at taking big risks. I was good at being innocent, like the children, and telling stories that made them laugh.

He exhaled as I returned to my task of purity. Each house had a cleaning room inside the back door, complete with a bucket of soapy water. It was required by law to shed the outside world before entering the main house.

My pulse eased as I washed away the evidence of my sins. Shoes clean, I grabbed a folded rag, removed my socks, and rinsed my bare feet, ankles and calves. Seeking a sense of absolution I couldn't find from the water, I felt like I needed to cleanse my whole body.

"Grace," Jamie said as he reached down and took the rag from my hand. "Enough."

He caught my eyes and for a breath we stood still.

"Children?" Stocking feet padded down the hall, and my mother, Julianna, popped her head around the corner toward us. "Oh goodness, you're here. I've been waiting. You had me worried!"

She flicked on the small overhead bulb, flooding us with light. Shorter than Jamie and me both, she stood just over five feet, with short graying dirty-blonde hair, worry-filled brown eyes, and a wrinkled face laced with shame. Anxiety had aged her by a decade, a constant reminder of her personal tragedy. Falling in love with a nonbeliever. Being too weak to convert him. Losing a child for her sin. Now the only single mother in Haven Valley.

Her failure had left her half the woman she'd once been.

"Why were you sitting here in the dark?" my mother demanded. "Is everything alright?"

When neither of us answered immediately her tone rose half an octave. "Did something happen? What's happened? Please tell me nothing's happened."

"Mother, please," Jamie said. "Nothing's happened. Everything's fine."

"Then why are you late?"

"It's my fault," Jamie said. "The evening was just so nice. I urged Grace to walk slowly with me. Please forgive me." He was always so good with Mother. No one calmed her so quickly.

He placed his hand on her shoulder, which was allowed since she was his mother, and gave her one of his famous charming smiles. "Forgive me?" he asked again.

She smiled slightly and nodded.

Jamie leaned down and placed a small kiss on her cheek. "Now," he said, "how can I help with dinner to serve my penance?"

"You may wash and peel the potatoes." She moved her eyes past him to where I stood. "And you, dear, will you not offer penance as well?" She was teasing, but it hit me like a boulder.

"I need to bathe," I said.

"Now?" she asked.

"Yes, I seem to be dirtier than usual, and it wouldn't be appropriate to eat without being clean."

"Very well," she said, "but please hurry."

I quickly excused myself and hurried

down the hallway to the staircase, pattered up the steps to the second floor, and slipped into the first door on the left that held the bathroom my mother and I shared. A second bathroom downstairs belonged to Jamie, which neither of us women would dare use.

Inside the small washroom, I turned on the warm water and stripped. It took some time to remove the required layers of clothing, all of which were naturally white. The long-sleeved dress that hung only inches above my feet. The thinner undergarments and the compressor, which every woman over the age of twelve was required to wear. The corset ran six inches in length and pulled the breasts closer to the chest. Uncomfortable at first, it was something you got used to after a while.

Women's clothing was designed to hide the body from the eyes of men. We wore white to symbolize our purity as the bride of Jesus. Stains of any kind were a sign of waning devotion. But I'd begun painting simple designs on my white undergarments when I was sixteen because I missed wearing color and I didn't think Jesus would mind. No one could see the red and yellow flowers I'd painted. In fact, I'd convinced myself that they were a gift to him as much as to me.

But seeing the simple designs painted on my undergarments now, I felt a pang of guilt. The smallest sin was as black as the greatest sin — plenty of sermons using many Scriptures had made that utterly clear. Black was black. Whether lust or dust, sin was sin. And I was covered in it.

Stepping under the flowing water, I grabbed the bristle brush, harsh but necessary, and scrubbed. My hands, my arms, my legs, my shoulders, every inch. My skin turned pink from the agitation and scalding water.

I treasured the absolution of that pain. Slowly I washed my sins down the drain. Tomorrow would be a new day.

But still . . . still I knew that inside, both Jamie and I were dirty. Guilty. And the guilty had to be punished.

Dear God, what was happening to me?

CHAPTER THREE

"Grace! Wait a second."

I was hurrying to the Chapel the next morning after a disturbing sleep when Alice's voice called to me from behind. I stopped and turned to see her holding the hem of her dress off the ground as she approached me with bright eyes.

"Good morning, Alice. We're going to be late."

"We have a moment. Please, just a moment."

She was pregnant, I thought. I could see the light in her eyes. And for Alice, being pregnant meant that she would be allowed to move in with her husband, David.

"You're pregnant?"

Alice pulled up, blinking. "What makes you say that?"

"Just a guess. You look like the sun." She was a redhead and reminded me of women who might have modeled back in the days when we had at least some magazines to read and approved television to watch.

A daring smile revealed Alice's perfect teeth. "I think I might be!"

"You're late?"

"Three days." She whispered it like a great secret. I couldn't help but be a little jealous, not of her pregnancy as much as for her affection for David. Why couldn't they have found someone young and handsome for me, like Samuel, who was twenty-three and single? Not that I was drawn to Samuel, but at least he was my age and we might figure life out together with our child.

"You're not thrilled for me?" Alice asked.

"I am." I forced a smile. My stomach was still in knots from the previous day, but I was happy for her. "Very much so. But you can't know after only three days."

"Of course not. I'm going to the clinic this afternoon." Her eyes darted over my shoulder. "David is over the moon."

"I'm sure he is." I took her hand, getting over my selfishness. "I hope it's true. I really do."

"Me too." She blushed. "It is true, I can feel it. It's as though the whole world has shifted. A woman was made to live with a man, don't you think?"

A squeal sounded behind me before I

could answer, and I turned to see little Bart from the Hansen family rushing up to us.

"Miss Grace, Miss Grace!" The four-year-old boy collided with me, wrapping his arms around my legs.

"Well hello, Bart!" I grabbed him under his arms and swung him up to my hip, Alice momentarily forgotten. "My, aren't you getting big," I said, poking his side.

He threw his head back, giggling.

"Soon you'll be tall enough to reach the moon and go on wild adventures with me."

"Mommy says adventures aren't good."

"Then we'll just laugh in joy as we fly around the moon with our animal friends and look at the beautiful world God made. And maybe eat strawberry ice cream, because maybe the moon is made out of ice cream."

"What's ice cream?"

"A sweet dessert that is cold and tastes like a little bit of heaven on earth. But you have to grow another inch first. Deal?"

He grinned wide. "Deal!"

"Don't tell a soul," Alice said to me over her shoulder, hurrying for the Chapel.

"My lips are sealed."

I set Bart down and stooped, my thoughts back on the troubles that had kept me tossing and turning through the night. "Hurry to Chapel, Bart. It's about to start."

He ran up the slope, arms spread like a bird, mind no doubt lost on flying around the moon. I followed him quickly.

The entire flock had already gathered in the small Chapel perched on top of the hill north of town when I entered. Early morning rays cast strips of light across the wood floor and illuminated Harrison Pierce's strong face where he stood at the pulpit. A required daily activity for every member, seven a.m. Chapel was typically one of my favorite moments of each day, because I often was allowed to take the children outside to play while the rest prayed. It was my special role and I was good at it.

But today I was so torn by my indiscretion that I walked straight for my assigned pew and took my seat between Andrew and Jamie. I was still dirty inside. I had to get clean, and getting clean required confession.

But I was afraid of what might happen to me. Even more, to Jamie.

"Good morning, Grace," Andrew said.

"Good morning, Andrew."

My eyes swept across the familiar faces of the flock. Margaret Holden, a middle-aged woman often chided for her inability to keep her mouth shut, sat in the row across from me with her silent but stern husband, Daniel, and their three young boys. Tanner Rifle, a gray-haired guardian with a military past, and his teenage daughter, Megan, sat in the next row. His plump wife, Sandra, whispered to Rebecca Teller, an elderly woman who occupied one of the seven council member seats. Her quiet grace and wisdom were respected by all.

The following row was filled with the Martin family — six children aging from seventeen to one, and their parents, George and Lucy, who were perfectly behaved but rarely seemed to notice each other as far as I could tell. In front of me sat Tyler Smith and his wife, Veronica. They ran the general store with their three children — an irony since the Smith children were allergic to nearly everything they sold.

So many faces, stories, and histories, all of which I knew nearly as well as my own, gathered here. And they knew me just as well. Every time I caught an eye I wondered if they could sense my guilt.

"Good morning, dearly beloved," Harrison began. "I see we are all here and in good spirits. Let us begin with a prayer."

I closed my eyes and heard the prayer, but my mind quickly moved to other things. Alice. David. Jamie.

I felt Andrew's elbow brush mine, so I withdrew. Touching, even for the married, wasn't permitted in the holy house, and for that I was grateful because I didn't like being touched by Andrew in any way, at any time.

I'd accepted my place at his side in public but still couldn't imagine living with him the way Alice and David could be together. He still lived in the house he'd occupied with his first wife, Bethany, before her tragic death two years earlier. Her cancer had since increased the community's vigilance to follow all laws regarding food to the letter.

I'd been told that the council deliberated our pairing for some time. Still in his late forties, Andrew had plenty of healthy life left, and unable to have children with Bethany, he felt lacking.

Rose had assured me that I would grow to love him, but until then it was more important that I honor and respect him. Not only was he a man, he was an elder in the community, and he'd picked me, so for that I should feel blessed. Maybe I would get pregnant and have a son who looked like Lukas. I could hardly imagine anything as wonderful.

Submitting to my role as Andrew's wife

by spending two nights a week with him was a price I really had no choice but to pay for such a blessing. So maybe I should be grateful.

"Remember, family, the trickery of evil," Harrison was saying. His voice was rich and comforting. His wife, Rose, and their three children listened attentively from the front pew. "It masquerades in sheep's clothing and hides its fangs behind alluring lies. It makes promises to entice your flesh, and if you believe lies and give in to falsehoods of the world, you too become like the world, subjecting yourself to the ravages of sin."

He paused, his words sinking into my brain and igniting my shame.

"Remember always that the thief comes to steal the hearts of the bride. Soon a wolf will come in sheep's clothing to test us, as Sylous has spoken through our sister Rose. A Fury dressed as a friend will arrive when we least expect it. The darkness of its heresy will masquerade as light to plunge us into punishment. The Fury will come, but when it does, we will not yield!"

He slapped the pulpit hard and I jumped. A chorus of *amens* filled the sanctuary, punctuated by a handful of *nevers*!

"We will throw that evil out and stand firm in our inheritance as the bride," Harrison continued. "An inheritance we earn by believing the truth and submitting to the one by whose blood we are saved into our holy calling. And so we protect our hearts from the evil of the world. We must never forget the danger that comes for us. Fear it, beloved saints. Use that fear to be vigilant. When you feel afraid, run, for surely you are getting too close to the evil of the world. Safeguard your hearts. Only then will we be faithful when the time of great testing is upon us."

We knew all too well that Haven Valley would endure a great test before the end. A final attempt of evil to gain entrance into our hearts by coming to us as an angel of light. If our guard was down, we would never recognize it.

I hoped Jamie was listening. For his sake and mine, I hoped he was even now seeing the foolishness of his defiance.

Even as I thought it, Jamie shifted on my right. A sign of guilt. Good.

And then he was standing.

"What if the evil of the world's already gone?" he asked.

The entire room stilled. I felt the blood drain from my face. He was committing suicide!

"What if we've already been tested and

passed that test and we sit here without knowing? I think it's time to leave this place and find out for ourselves."

The congregation was too shocked to react.

Harrison's right brow arched. "And what would cause you to believe this?"

I knew what he would say. And a small piece of me knew that as soon as he said it, Haven Valley would forever be changed.

"Because," Jamie said, "I've been out beyond the perimeter, and there are no more Fury."

CHAPTER FOUR

Ben Weathers watched as the flames of the fire he'd built inside the small rock pit lapped against the night. He leaned back in the squat folding chair and stroked his thick, unkempt beard. Refining fires, he thought, were the kind he'd been walking through the last several months. Turning what he thought he knew to ash so that something new could grow in its place.

A beautiful thing indeed. A single tear slipped from the corner of his eye. The thought of his transformation stirred his emotions. He hoped to never get *used* to the way it felt, but he knew it would surely happen. This was, after all, still the world of up and down.

Ben chuckled at himself and wiped the tear from his cheek. A smaller laugh joined his, and Ben raised his eyes across the fire to where Eli sat.

"Something funny?" Ben asked.

"I'm laughing because you're laughing," the boy replied.

"You think my laugh is funny?" Ben teased.

Eli grinned and gave Ben a grin. How he loved the boy. The sheer expansiveness of the emotion caught him off guard at times. He had the same love for his other children, the one gone too early, the two stolen and taken off the grid to live separate from him. Or at least that's the story his mind always wanted him to believe. The story he was still letting go of.

It didn't matter if they'd been taken or if they'd gone willingly. It only mattered that, with any luck, he would see them soon and share with them the gift he'd discovered.

Eli.

Eli, the orphan boy Ben had adopted as his own. In a world ravaged by the darkness, this child had been his saving grace. Without him, Ben would have succumbed to the great scourge of fear.

"Are you afraid?" Eli asked. Even in the dark, Ben could see the brightness of the boy's blue eyes. The rest of him — dark brown hair, freckled cheeks, short frame for his twelve years of age — was different from his other children. But those blue eyes reminded him of them constantly. All three had those beautiful blue eyes.

"Yes," Ben said.

Eli was drawing circles in the dirt at his feet with a long stick he'd collected when they'd arrived at the campsite. They'd been on the road for several days. After months of searching, Ben had finally narrowed down the likely location of the valley Rose had taken his children to. But it had been over ten years ago now. There were no guarantees.

A familiar stab of shame filled his gut and he didn't fight it. The only way to be free of shame was to let himself feel it. Shame for not seeking out his surviving children earlier, for letting them leave at all, for not protecting them the way a father was supposed to, for failing them according to the standards of the world.

Shame was just a feeling, he thought, and it was okay.

Ben shifted and exhaled. A wave of coughing overtook him and he bent over, fist at his mouth. The disease was progressing quickly. Intensifying. The headaches, the heat spells, the nausea — all getting worse with each passing day.

"We could stop at a doctor on the way," Eli said.

Ben shook his head. "I don't want to

waste time."

Eli didn't argue. "Do you need me to get you anything?"

Ben smiled. "Nah, I have all I need."

Eli thought about this for a moment before a sly grin pulled at his mouth. "Except powdered donuts. We ran out of those yesterday."

Ben chuckled and Eli's smile widened.

"We'll get some in the morning," Ben said. The two fell into silence, the space in which they normally operated. Simply being together without needing to speak, each one was occupied with his own thoughts. Eli had never really been much of a talker, which suited Ben fine. And when the boy did speak, it was best to listen.

Ben's thoughts returned to the distant past. To the moments that had redirected his life. Falling in love with Julianna, getting married, having three children, joining the Holy Family, the pain of their misalignment, the day she was given what they called *true sight,* the way he'd cursed her for believing such nonsense, the death of little Lukas, the day she'd vanished with the others, bent on following Rose Pierce to a glorious end.

He'd let them go, not realizing then what regret and loneliness would follow. It had launched him onto a path of self-

49

destruction. The world had fallen apart. Then Eli had come to his rescue.

"It's okay to be afraid," Eli said.

Ben looked at his face through the flames. "Are you ever afraid?"

Eli looked up at the stars that hung over them and let the question stand. The fire crackled and popped. He looked back at Ben, the fire dancing in his eyes. "Not really, no."

Emotion rose in Ben's throat. "Then I will try to be more like you."

"You already are," Eli said.

For long minutes they sat, lost in their own thoughts, until Eli playfully toppled from the small stump and sprawled to his back by the campfire. "I wish we had donuts now," he said with a dramatic sigh.

Ben began to laugh. Encouraged, Eli stretched his arms toward the sky and cried, "Will this night never end?"

Then they laughed together, lost in the wonder of what they knew and where they were.

That night Ben dreamed of Jamie and Grace, as he always did, and of the time when they would all be laughing together once again.

CHAPTER FIVE

Rose Pierce watched the entire Chapel still as Jamie Weathers's words filled the air around them. *I've been out beyond the perimeter, and there are no more Fury.* She felt the vein behind her ear pulse, and she swallowed her panic. *That can't be,* she thought.

A sharp whimper broke the silence. The boy's mother, Julianna. The frail woman had paled and held her palm over her mouth. And for good reason, Rose thought. Her son dared to stand on holy ground and speak blasphemy. Rose felt the urge to stand and defile the sinner herself but knew better.

The Chapel began to stir back to life. Whispers, murmurs of disbelief, silent prayers, confusion. They hummed around her like static. Rose glanced at her three perfectly controlled children and gave them a nod. *Stay where you are.* She glanced at

51

her husband.

Harrison's face remained stoic, but she knew his mind better than anyone. Behind his stone expression his brain was churning, uploading the information being presented. He wasn't easily subjected to his emotions but bound himself to faith and belief above all things — the perfect, incorruptible partner for the radical journey that many couldn't handle.

Which was why Sylous had picked Harrison for her.

She felt the energy in the room suddenly shift, and the familiar change nearly took her breath away.

Sylous was here.

She closed her eyes to let her heart settle. He always had this effect when he came. The hairs on the back of her neck rose, and for an extended moment Rose relished her private encounter with him. It was as though he pulled her from reality for a long breath before returning her mind, body, and heart back to the room.

She opened her eyes and saw him standing behind Harrison at the far back corner of the stage, dressed in white. No one else in the room reacted to his presence because no one else knew he was there. He was there just for her. He always was. She was his disciple, his voice to the people of Haven Valley, the one he'd picked to be in communion with.

She'd been a child the first time she'd seen him. Battered by a father who demanded unattainable perfection and neglected by a mother too weak to save her children, Rose had been in terrible suffering before Sylous rescued her. He'd given her the gift of sight, whispered promises for a future outside the hell she was trapped in.

All she had to do was follow him and he would keep her safe. Sylous was her heavenly guardian, sent to set her free, and his promises had come true.

Her skin always tingled at the sight of him, at first in fear of his staggering power, now in longing to be near him. The thought of losing his protection, his presence, made her chest ache.

Fear me alone, and I will always protect you from evil. His words filled her mind. Their communication was like a melody only they shared, a song sung that only they could hear.

I will never stop fearing you, Rose responded silently.

Need my truth alone, and I will always watch over you.

I will never stop needing you.

Listen to me, and I will always guide you.
I will listen.

Peace settled over her.

Sylous shifted his gaze to Harrison. She did the same. Her husband had moved out from behind the pulpit and was silencing the congregation with a raised hand. He stood at the front edge of the carpeted stage, hands tucked calmly behind his back, eyes on Jamie.

"Going beyond the perimeter is against our laws," he began. "How do you explain yourself?"

"It's against our laws because of the danger," Jamie said. "But what if the danger's gone?"

This drew more hushed questioning from the flock, and once again Harrison raised his palm to quiet them. Jamie continued before Harrison could answer.

"I've ventured deep into the forest, miles beyond the edge of the surrounding hills." He stepped out from the wooden bench and into the main aisle. "There's a large town on the other side of these mountains. It looks normal, not caught up in the fiery hell you'd expect if the Fury were still —"

"Did you venture into the city?" Harrison interrupted. "Did you see any people?" Rose could sense a hint of fear in her husband's voice, and she flicked her gaze back to where Sylous watched, motionless. At ease.

"No," Jamie said. "But I believe we should see for ourselves."

"Oh, son, how could you?" Julianna said, her cheeks wet with tears.

"Could it be time to leave this place?" Jamie asked, ignoring his mother. "Maybe the world's different than we believed it would be. Maybe it wasn't destroyed. Or maybe it's been cleansed for us already."

Colin Peterson, another member of their high council, stood from the pew behind Rose. "I've heard enough of this!" he thundered. "The Fury still haven't attempted to penetrate our valley, which can only mean the end is not here. I won't stand by and let you mock the faith that's saved us from damnation!"

A murmur of agreement rippled through the auditorium.

Unmoved, Jamie looked at the taller man. "And what if our faith is only saving us from phantoms?" he said. "For that matter, what if the Fury have always only been phantoms?"

Several members gasped; others whispered hurried prayers. Still, Sylous showed no sign of concern, which stilled Rose's heart. If he wasn't worried, neither should she be.

"How can you even say such a thing?" someone demanded.

"I've been in the woods for hours at a time and the Fury aren't there," Jamie said. "That's why. But you are all too full of fear to actually see for yourselves."

"They only deceive you," Colin snapped. "They lure you into their trap by hiding themselves. But make no mistake, they prey on a world full of sinners, offering only a painful death for all who haven't committed their lives to righteousness. Or don't you remember?"

"Then where is the evidence of all that death and destruction?" Jamie asked. "The town I saw showed no sign of decay."

Beside Grace, Andrew stood and spoke. "It's not for us to know but to believe and follow. This is the meaning of faith, boy."

"Even if we are following blindly?" Jamie asked.

"Blindly?" Harrison challenged from the stage. "You were there when the Fury made themselves seen. Did you not see as the rest of us did?"

"Maybe what we saw wasn't real," Jamie said. His voice had dropped a level, as if he himself couldn't believe he was questioning the foundations of their faith.

"He's lying!" Andrew faced Harrison.

"How could he have ventured beyond the perimeter and not been destroyed?"

"No," Jamie said. "I'm telling the truth."

"He wouldn't have survived," Andrew said. "His mind must have been poisoned, and now he's trying to shake our faith. This is the darkness masquerading as light to deceive us all."

This theory brought Tanner Rifle, one of our guardians, to his feet. "From among our own?"

"Are we all in danger?" his wife, Sandra, asked.

"Lord help us," George Martin muttered, clutching his youngest daughter in his lap.

Then cries were piling up on top of others. All the while, Grace sat with her head bowed between Andrew and her brother. Did she know something?

Rose returned her gaze to Sylous, who was now leaning back against the wall, watching the show with arms casually crossed. His brilliant green eyes shifted to her and held her gaze. She could feel her cheeks flush.

Rose felt the room drift away for a moment, and in that space of disconnected calm, Sylous gave her a reassuring nod. Just that single nod before she returned to the room and all its chaos.

But now she knew: there was nothing they

needed to be concerned with. Jamie and his silly thoughts were nothing compared to the real power in this room. Doubt was a foolish venture for foolish minds. Rose knew the reality of what they had built here; Jamie just needed to be reminded.

And if he was indeed the wolf in sheep's clothing, he would be easily dismissed.

"This boy needs to be cleansed from the evil in his mind," Colin was saying.

"I'm telling you the truth!" Jamie insisted over the cacophony. "Why would I lie about this? Bring myself under fire for what purpose?"

"The enemy comes dressed as one of our own and tempts us with alluring theories of a beautiful world," Colin retorted. "You seek to confuse us, that's why."

"I seek to understand, not confuse!"

"Enough!" Harrison snapped. Her husband rarely raised his voice. The room immediately stilled.

But the councilman Colin couldn't hold his tongue. "We cannot delay on this," he said, voice trembling. "Actions must be taken immediately. Punish the boy's sins. Cleanse the devil within."

"There is no devil within," Jamie ground out through his teeth. "I'm only speaking truth."

For a brief moment, no one spoke. And then one did. The soft voice of his sister, Grace, whom Rose loved dearly.

"He's not lying," Grace said, rising to her feet.

Every eye in the Chapel turned to her. A familiar warm buzz nipped at the back of Rose's skull as Sylous spoke to her mind.

Are you prepared to speak for me?

Always.

His voice filled her mind with instruction, and it was clear what needed to be done. So she would do what he commanded.

Always.

My mind had considered and discarded a dozen ideas of how to help Jamie before I knew that defending him was my best option. I couldn't stay silent as the room started to lean with Colin. You could see it on the faces of onlookers. With nods of agreement, faces stricken with fear, people were quickly buying into the theory that my brother might be a source of evil among them. Possessed even.

My movement from sitting to standing felt slowed. Voices in my head urged me to stay put. What would my poor mother think? What would Andrew say? How would people perceive me? What would Rose do to me?

My knees knocked together and my stomach did flip-flops. But then I was standing, and speaking, and everyone was watching.

"He's not lying," I said again. Louder. I sensed Andrew stiffen, but I kept my eyes forward.

"You've been with him beyond the perimeter?" Harrison asked.

"No," I said.

"So you're defending his good character then?" Colin scoffed. He addressed Harrison. "Her word on his behalf means nothing. She is his sister."

"I helped though," I said.

Again, all eyes were on me.

"Grace, don't," Jamie whispered. It was too late for that.

"I helped him cross the perimeter unseen," I said.

The room was deathly quiet now. I knew I was throwing myself into terrible trouble, but I was confessing. The shame and fear I'd been carrying around eased as I spilled my guts in front of the entire flock.

"I used my access to the guardians' rotation schedule to help Jamie move in and out of the town without being discovered." A beat. "He isn't lying. He's been out beyond the border for several hours at a time."

"Impossible," Rebecca said. I couldn't bear to look at her.

"This is nonsense!" Colin objected. "She could be lying for him. To save him."

"Grace wouldn't lie," Colin's wife said.

But several others were murmuring in agreement with Colin, wanting anything but what I said to be true. I didn't blame them. In fact, I agreed with them. Jamie was delusional, but I couldn't let him take the fall alone. I had played a role, and for that I would accept responsibility.

"Holy Family," came the voice of our prophet. The room fell silent. Most sat back down as Rose stood and stepped up to the platform beside Harrison.

"Husband," Rose said, looking into his eyes. He offered her a gentle nod and stepped aside.

Rose stood behind the podium, scanning the flock. When her eyes reached mine, they paused a moment longer than I was prepared for. Guilt swallowed me again.

But my shame was mine alone. Instead of offering me or Jamie scalding looks of disapproval, Rose stood with grace and poise. Even with her red hair kept as short as required, she was striking. Light unblemished skin, hazel eyes, petite nose. She was beautiful, even dressed in white, leaving only her hands, neck and face uncovered.

Rose spoke with an authority that commanded the room.

"It is important to remember that these two," she started, lifting her hand toward Jamie and me, "are chosen, as are we all. They're not strangers. They're part of our righteous family. We can't sweep them aside as evil without that evil proving itself in them."

I half expected Colin to respond, but even he had nothing to say against the prophet.

"Did they break our laws? Yes. And we understand that punishment is essential to holiness. But we have always respected each other. Respect has shaped our laws and made our community safer. No one here is higher than another. We were all given the same gift of sight. We have all agreed to follow the path of righteousness. We all hold faith in God's holiness. And we all understand the danger of grace without judgment."

Rose had us cradled in the palm of her hand. Her words soothed rough edges and brought us into alignment with each other. They always had. It was a gift.

But I was wondering what she intended

with her remark about grace.

"So," she continued, "a brother believes that maybe the world outside is different now. Could the devil have implanted such an idea? Perhaps. But maybe he's right." Rose let the thought marinate for a moment. "Who's to say exactly how claiming the earth for our inheritance is to happen?" She waited. "Anyone?"

No one responded at first. Then Colin spoke what was on everyone's mind. "But we haven't been tested yet. The end comes only after —"

"Or maybe we have been tested without knowing," Rose interrupted. "Maybe our purity made any Fury's appearance among us so fruitless that it vanished without showing itself. It matters not. What does matter is that we've been faithful, diligent, and vigilant in our pursuit of purity. Jamie and Grace as well. So then, family . . . maybe Jamie is showing us the way. Maybe this is our time."

No one dared speak. Even I was lost in confusion. She was suggesting that Jamie might be right after all. How could that be?

"I've been given direction," she said, stepping out from behind the podium. Her eyes rested on Jamie. "Send them out past the perimeter with our blessing. Let them see what is really out there. If they return with glorious news, then, friends, we will join them."

Her words settled into my mind. Send *them* out, she'd said. Jamie and me. Fear stabbed at my heart.

"But," Rose continued, lifting a finger, "if the boy's sensibilities are wrong, the Fury will deliver swift judgment to both of them."

The silence in the Chapel was thick enough to slice. I could feel Jamie's eyes on me, and I knew he could sense my terror.

He shook his head. "I'll go alone."

"No," Rose said. "Grace will join you. She already has."

"But I'm the one who —"

"Sit," Rose said.

Jamie barely hesitated before taking his seat. He wouldn't dare confront Rose as she prophesied. Some boundaries were never crossed, even by Jamie.

"Grace," Rose said.

I feared my legs might give out from underneath me.

"You willingly assisted your brother as he broke one of our fundamental laws, yes?" Rose asked.

My voice was trembling. "Yes," I whispered.

"Was it because you too are unsure of

what lies beyond? Are you now also questioning what you believe?"

I wanted to say no, because I wasn't really. But a tiny part of me was. Looking at Rose, I knew I dared not lie.

"Yes," I said.

"Do you trust your brother?" she asked.

"He's my brother."

"Then there should be nothing to fear."

Her words were the nails in a coffin from which there was no escape.

Rose moved her gaze back across the congregation, and I knew she was finished with me. I slumped to my seat, stunned at the events unfolding. Andrew was staring forward, jaw fixed. I could read the anger in the shallow lines in his face and longed for him to send me a signal that maybe he would save me. But I knew that was foolish thinking. Maybe if I'd been with child, but until then I was only someone who met certain needs and held the potential to mother his offspring.

"We will trust our holy brother as his dear sister does," Rose announced. "We will send them out with our blessing. May they find truth and faith. May we all benefit from whatever they discover. And all God's children replied?"

"Amen," the flock spoke in one accord.

And with that word, our fate was sealed.

Two hours later, I stood staring at the tall wooden gate at the mouth of Haven Valley. A tall fence extended nearly fifty feet in either direction from where the red line that ran the full perimeter of the town began. The gate was more symbolic than a deterrent. The forest and the Fury, not a fence, were our guards.

The council had affixed a wide wooden sign above the gate long ago. The same inscription that we'd all burned on our hearts had been burned into that sign. *The righteousness of the upright delivers them, but the unfaithful are trapped by evil.*

A cold chill filled me with dread. Ahead of me stood the seven council members. Andrew, Rose, and Harrison were part of the group. Beside me, Jamie. Behind us lay the rest of Haven Valley, now silent except for my whimpering mother.

What felt like only moments earlier I'd been confessing in search of absolution. And now I was being cast out of my home and tossed to the Fury.

They had given us enough supplies for the night. These were strapped inside a pack over Jamie's shoulder. My brother's only words to me had been "Don't worry." They provided no comfort. We were facing certain death.

I tried to hold to the truth that maybe Jamie was right after all. That beyond the gate was nothing but a Fury-less world. But my skin was crawling as imaginations of the Fury crowded my mind.

Rose stepped forward. "We send these two out with our blessing," she said, addressing the crowd and repeating her earlier words. "May they find truth and faith."

The doors began to open and the woods beyond them came into view.

"May we all benefit from whatever they discover," she continued.

"Where is Grace going?" a little voice asked behind me. Bart, speaking to his mother, who hushed him. "But isn't it dangerous?" he pressed.

I looked back at him and offered a re-assuring smile. "Don't you worry, Bart. I'll be safe. I promise."

But my voice was thin and his round eyes were filled with doubt.

Tanner approached me, as did Marshall Flint, another guardian with kind brown eyes and a booming laugh. They urged us forward. I wasn't sure my legs could move. Tanner gave me a soft shove, and I stumbled forward after Jamie, through the open gate and into the wild.

"And all God's children replied?" Rose finished.

"Amen," came a chorus behind us.

The gate closed with a soft thump that might as well have been a terrible crash. We were on our own to face the Fury.

Fear filled my chest like wet cement.

Chapter Six

I can not begin to express how I felt as I followed Jamie into the woods beyond the perimeter that had kept me safe for so many years. The only way I was able to move one foot in front of the other was by resigning myself to my certain fate.

I was going to die.

True, Jamie had gone past the perimeter and come back without a scratch, and I kept telling myself that. But deep inside I knew: God would punish all who strayed, and at any moment the Fury would streak out of the forest and rip us both limb from limb.

I was so consumed with this thought that I didn't even think of looking for re-assurance from Jamie, who walked with an eager gait just in front of me. He glanced back several times that first fifteen minutes, but I didn't speak. Maybe I was afraid my voice would bring unwanted attention.

Instead of reaching out to Jamie, I silently

called out to Lukas, my little brother. *I'm so sorry, Lukas. I tried my best. If I get back to Haven Valley alive, I'll be perfect, I promise. I'll always be there for you. Please, just let me live.*

I'm not sure why I felt the need to apologize to him. Or why I thought he might be able to save me. Maybe I was just talking to myself. Or to whatever angels might be listening.

Either way, with each passing minute I began to gain just a little more hope. Nothing had happened to us. No Fury. Not yet.

Jamie stopped on a small rise and spun back, eyes bright. "Well? You still don't believe me?"

I pulled up, glancing around.

"See?" he asked, arms spread. "Nothing but trees. No Fury. What did I tell you?"

I finally dared to speak. "Not yet."

"Not ever, I'm telling you. It's all in our minds. Like Lukas."

His mention of my speaking to Lukas as if he were still alive irritated me, but maybe he had a point. Lukas was real enough to me because I believed in him. Maybe the Fury really were like that. But then I threw the thought away. Rose couldn't be wrong after all this time. We'd all seen the Fury even before we believed in them.

70

"Follow me, sister," he said, turning back to his march. "Follow me and see for yourself. There's nothing to fear out here, not unless you're afraid of trees."

I had no choice but to follow. And I did, staying close. For an hour. Then two, settling just a little bit more with each passing minute. But that didn't mean everything couldn't change in a moment.

The forest was vast, filled with thick trunks that reached up to fully leafed treetops. It was like a maze, but Jamie had marked trees and boulders on his previous outings.

My legs ached from crossing the uneven ground, up and down, around impassable thickets, through heavy brush, even across a small river. We removed our shoes and socks to ford it. Every distant sound drew my ear. The rumble of a stone, the snap of a twig, the rustle of a small woodland creature.

Rather than court constant thoughts of being attacked by the Fury, I found my thoughts drifting to the world beyond this mountain. What did it look like? It had been over ten years since I'd seen cars on streets. Would I really see that? What about clothes, like jeans and T-shirts and pretty shoes? Did they still exist?

And movies. I used to love watching

71

Disney movies before we'd moved to Haven Valley. *The Little Mermaid* had been my favorite. So many of the stories I told the children in Haven Valley came from those memories of wild cartoon adventures. *Mary Poppins* too. And *The Sound of Music*. And books. What I would give to steal away and read a novel filled with adventure and romance!

How many times had I imagined the dangers that awaited anyone who dared cross the perimeter? But all I saw now was beauty growing from the ground, from the treetops, from the sides of cliffs. Not a monstrous thing could be seen.

The lack of death and destruction was so surprising to me that I began to embrace the wonder of it all. After three hours, that wonder gave way to a kind of jubilation.

"It's going to be okay, Lukas," I muttered, forgetting that Jamie was with me.

"Yes it is, Lukas," he said. He skipped ahead and jumped up on a rock. "It's going to be more than okay, little brother!" Then to me, eyes wild with excitement: "Just think, Grace! All those things you used to love, they're waiting for us just over this rise."

"Really? We're that close?"

"Closer than you would guess." He

jumped down. "Strawberry, right?"

"Strawberry?"

"Your favorite ice cream flavor. Before coming here."

I couldn't help but grin at the thought. "Yes."

"So imagine eating as much strawberry ice cream as you like. And staying up all night watching movies. And falling in love with someone you choose."

The thought carried me away. It sounded both scandalous and wonderful at once.

"You could do other things too!" he said, spinning in a circle. "The world would be our oyster. Cars and video games and girls —"

"Jamie!"

"What? Don't tell me you don't think about it. What would you wear if you could?"

I didn't have to think long, and no one could hear us. "A red dress?"

"A red dress!" He swayed like a dancer in a dress.

"And red lipstick!"

He made the motion of painting makeup on his face. "Made up like a peacock with as many colors as you can imagine. You could be the peacock writer, spinning a hundred stories that everyone would line up

73

to read."

"You think?" I was grinning now, caught up in the fantasy.

"Why not? It's what you're good at, making stuff up. Put your wild imagination to good use. Have it turned into a movie."

It was almost too much to consider. A wilder fantasy than floating around the moon with Bart. A hundred thoughts battered my mind. Wouldn't all that upset God? Surely. The thought tempered my enthusiasm, but only a little because so far Jamie had been right.

No Fury. Not yet.

"Come on!" he cried and raced up the path. "The city's just ahead."

"It is?" I hurried after him, alarmed. "The city?"

"Not the city, but a cliff from where we can see it, like I said."

The plan had been to reach that precipice before nightfall and cover the rest of the distance tomorrow. I followed him to the edge of a high cliff that fell away to a vast valley.

I pulled up, gasping. "A city!" I whispered.

"Of course. Just like I said."

It was too far away to see anything clearly, but the outline was there. Tall buildings rose from the right side of the landscape, and shorter structures ran out to either side — homes of all sizes. Roads stretched out between the structures, and a wide green square I thought must be a park sat almost directly in the city's center.

It was startling to see with my own eyes. Just as Jamie had said, the city shimmered under the afternoon sun, permanent. Present. When we taught children who were born in Haven Valley about the world outside the gates, we spoke of monsters and evil. We told tales of destruction and war. Stories where the Fury had been allowed to invade the earth and bring all sinners to a bloody justice.

From this place atop the cliff's high edge, nothing looked as I would have imagined.

"Beautiful, isn't it?" Jamie said. He dropped the pack he'd been carrying. "Can you imagine what it must be like?"

Seeing the city sitting far away, I suddenly felt anxious. We had no business being here. We were being lured. Something was wrong.

"Well?" he pushed. "Can you?"

"No," I said. "I'm not sure I should want to."

He looked stunned. "How could you not? You imagine everything else."

"But this is . . ."

"Real?"

"Is it?"

"Of course it is! More real than Haven Valley, I think."

"And dangerous," I said.

"And maybe that's just an idea too. What if all of our fears are only fears of ideas?"

"That's the most ridiculous thing I've ever heard," I said. "How can you tell from standing here that there's no danger?"

Jamie sighed and said nothing.

"Don't you feel any fear at all?" I asked.

Again, no response, which was a response in itself.

"Fear helps keep us safe. When you feel afraid, run, because something's not right. How can you be ignoring your nature?"

"Fear isn't my only instinct," Jamie said.

But my fear was making a quick comeback, and with it, anger. Something was wrong. Very wrong.

"Those other instincts might get us killed."

He turned to me with apologetic eyes. "You're angry with me." It wasn't a question.

I held my tongue despite my anger, yielding to the conviction that raising my voice to him was inappropriate. Even miles from Haven Valley I could feel the comfort of the laws that tucked me safely into bed each night. I longed for that safety and comfort now.

"Grace." Jamie reached for my shoulder.

I pulled back and turned away from him. "We were called to a different life," I said. "A purer life, separate from the world filled with evil, however intriguing or beautiful it might seem." I thrust my arm at the valley. "I don't *want* this city with its newness and uncertainty. I want to be worthy of our inheritance. Why couldn't you just leave well enough alone?"

"Who's to say our inheritance isn't now?" Jamie demanded, face reddening. "As Rose said, maybe my sensibilities led us here for a reason."

"You said maybe what we saw wasn't real. Do you really believe the Fury never did exist? Are you really willing to pretend we didn't see what we saw?"

Jamie looked past me, easing. "I misspoke."

"Misspoke?"

"I was caught up. Desperate to understand."

"So you do believe?"

Another beat of silence passed between us. "I don't know."

At least he was being honest.

"You always tell me that I use my stories

to escape reality," I said. "Well, maybe you're doing the same thing. Maybe your imaginations about cars and girls and all that are just your fantasies. Did you ever think about that?"

"We're alive, aren't we? Is this a fantasy?"

"We're alive, but for how long? You know we can't go back."

"Of course we can. As soon as we can prove that the Fury are gone."

"Or never, because we'll be dead."

He frowned. There was that.

I settled and stared at the city. "Do you still have nightmares?" I asked. "See their faces in the dark corners of your bedroom?"

Jamie lifted his eyes. "Often."

Something snapped loudly behind me, and my heart leaped into my throat as I spun around. Jamie took two quick strides to place himself in front of me. I peered around his broad shoulders at the trees and thick brush beyond. The bushes rustled; another twig snapped.

I could see the tension in Jamie's shoulders and back as we stood waiting for whatever approached. The world seemed to still and my mind raced too quickly for me to pin down a single thought.

Nothing came.

More moments of waiting, watching,

primed both of us with fear. Still nothing came. Jamie's shoulders dropped as he began to relax, and my nerves settled.

"See?" he said, stepping back to his pack at the cliff's edge. "Nothing."

I took a few breaths, working to get my lungs and heart back to normal rhythm, and turned to meet my brother's eyes. "When you feel fear, run. Something isn't right," I said. "This isn't right."

Jamie held my gaze before turning and heading along the edge of the cliff. "This is as far as I've gotten. We need to find a place to camp for the night."

I followed reluctantly but with new clarity. Jamie was afraid too.

We found a place to make camp within half an hour. We didn't have shelter, but after assessing the sky, Jamie assured me it wouldn't rain. So we unrolled the thin sleeping mats we'd brought and worked on starting a fire. It took us little time to get the flint to spark a flame and coax it into a healthy blaze. Fire that brought a little comfort as dusk darkened my mood.

"Maybe they only come out at night," I said, staring into the flames.

"Why would evil wait for night? Is it that limited?"

But I wasn't convinced. At least we had a fire and some food. Eight buns, some peanut butter, a packet of smoked jerky, and four apples. Enough to last for two days, we thought. But Jamie had already pointed out a variety of edible berries along the way.

Other than our exchange at the cliff, we hadn't spoken much. There wasn't much to say. Jamie might be eager to reach the city, but I was far less so. What if the Fury kept to that place, where they had plenty of souls to feed on?

Jamie's thoughts were elsewhere.

"I know you're frightened, Grace. I was sweating the first time I came out. But you have to trust me. No one would have guessed that we could make it even this far without being crushed. Even if the Fury are still out there, they're not as aggressive as they once were. It's worth the risk to find out if we're mistaken, living in fear the way we do in Haven Valley."

His words confused me, because we all knew how valuable fear was in keeping us safe. But at the same time, I had always trusted Jamie with my life. So I was caught between opposites and didn't see a good way out. Maybe he was right, maybe he was wrong, but either way he was still my brother.

Maybe I really was just a naïve girl who followed whatever came along.

"I'm sorry for dragging you into this," he said softly, watching the flames dwindle. "I didn't mean to put you in this position."

Well, you did, I thought.

"It's okay," I said.

And then neither of us said anything for a while.

Jamie finally pushed himself off the ground. "We need more firewood. Need to keep this fire going."

"Do you want me to come with you?" I asked mostly for my own benefit. I wasn't sure how I felt about being alone, even for a few minutes.

"I won't be gone long," he said, then disappeared into the trees.

As if his parting had sent a signal to the sky, dusk quickly faded to darkness. I inched closer to the fire, regretting I'd let him out of my sight.

I'd never liked darkness much. Andrew preferred it pitch-black when he slept, and nights in his bed left me tired. Truthfully, I wasn't comfortable sleeping next to him, so the dark protected me from seeing him. But the darkness itself was as much of a problem, so there was no way to find peace in his house.

I wondered how he would treat me when I returned to Haven Valley. Would he scorn me? Divorce me? Maybe that would be a good thing. I would rather have a baby with someone my age whom I loved, like Alice had.

Assuming I survived the night.

I tried to meditate on things that made me feel peaceful. The Scriptures, the promises for the holy and faithful. But I no longer met the criteria for those promises. So where was I now? I finally pulled my hood up over my head, grateful for the many required layers I donned each morning to hide my figure. They lent me warmth now.

Out here, I could dance around in my long slip with the red and yellow flowers I'd painted on it. Actually, the undergarment I'd put on today had blue flowers as well. I could hardly imagine wearing a red dress. Well, I could, but even the thought of it made me nervous.

What was taking Jamie so long? Maybe it had only been a couple of minutes and I had lost all sense of time.

As if on cue, I heard him in the thicket, approaching from my left, and I released a small sigh of relief. "Finally. What took you so long?"

He didn't respond. The brushing of leaves

drew closer as a hot breeze picked up and swirled around me.

"Jamie?"

I froze where I sat, straining my ears for a response. The leaves were now rustling all around me, and I stood as panic edged into my mind. I desperately hoped it was only the wind kicking up.

"Jamie!" I screamed.

A thin, mournful cry, like the death moan of a ghost, rose from my right. I spun, heart in my throat.

But now it came from my left, a longer cry, piercing and terrifying. I wanted to cry out, but my throat had frozen shut.

The sound was now behind me and I twirled around, but it was still behind me, shrieking like a wounded animal. Or was it coming *from* me?

The wind howled and the terrifying sound rushed me and all I could do was throw my hands over my eyes and scream. I was sure in that moment my end had come.

My scream ran out of air and I gasped, mind lost to terror. Only then did I realize the wind was gone and the night was still. And I hadn't been touched.

Slowly I removed my hands from my eyes and stared across the fire. What I saw chilled my bones and stopped my heart.

There, staring at me with white eyes that peered from a hooded, black, swirling shroud, was a Fury.

It hung in the air, feetless. Its thin tattered cloak drifted around its body, if it even had a body. What it did have were arms with long gray fingers and sharp nails. And it had a black head under its hood. Or at least eyes and a mouth. I couldn't actually see a head. Only white eyes that shifted as if fueled by a fire within its unseen skull. And a round, fanged mouth. No lips, just the mouth.

I saw it all before my heart stopped, and I knew I was going to die.

If it had been a werewolf or any other monster, I might not have lost myself to such terror, but this creature, the same kind we had all seen thirteen years earlier, pressed a wicked chill deep into my bones. It was the kind of fear that made me want to beg for death.

But I couldn't beg. Nor scream. Nor breathe.

Its fangs parted and a low phlegm-popping growl cut through the silence. Its jaws snapped wide and it released a bone-rattling roar. And then it was rushing, and even though I saw it coming straight for me, I still couldn't move.

The Fury was no more than three feet

from me when a white streak from my right slammed into it broadside. With a yelp, the Fury slammed into a tree ten feet to my left.

I stared in disbelief as it fell to the feet of its attacker, jerked once, then turned to vapor.

The attacker stood with feet planted firmly, fists low, staring down at the wisps of vapor as if to make sure the creature really was gone or dead or whatever.

Satisfied, the attacker turned around and faced me. A woman.

Tall and thin, she was dressed in white pants and blouse with a striking black silk jacket. Her platinum blonde hair flowed down past her shoulders and framed pale, gentle facial features. High cheeks, full lips, a symmetrical nose, vibrant brown eyes.

My mind struggled to understand what my eyes were seeing. The woman held my gaze, her eyes flashing in the firelight. Or was it something else I was seeing in her eyes? They were white, like the eyes of the Fury she'd just killed.

I scurried backward and slammed into a tree trunk.

"Careful," the woman said with a gentle smile. "You'll hurt yourself."

She could speak! My mind was numb.

The woman took a step toward me. I lifted my arm as if to ward her off. "Please," I begged. "Please don't hurt me."

"I would never hurt you, Grace."

She knew my name.

"I know many things," she said.

I didn't remember speaking out loud, but she'd spoken as if I had. I forced myself to take deeper breaths. I'd never heard of or seen such a creature. Was she a Fury disguised as a woman?

"Personally, I never much liked the term *Fury*," she said. "But I can assure you I'm not what you think."

Again, I hadn't spoken and yet she'd known what I was thinking. How?

"Do you really need me to answer that question?" she asked.

I opened my mouth in wonder. Shook my head. No. My body was still trembling. I couldn't process what was happening.

A terrible cry, pained and full of terror, echoed through the night, and I knew immediately the wail belonged to Jamie. I jerked my head in the direction of the sound as another scream ripped through the air, followed by a thunderous roar.

Fury! More Fury!

I had to save him! I had to find Jamie!

"That's not a good idea," the woman said.

Jamie's distant screeching tore a hole through my heart. What were they doing to him? I couldn't just stand there.

"I can protect you," she said.

"I can't just leave him," I managed to whisper.

"You have to," she said, and took a couple steps toward me.

"They'll kill him."

"They'll kill *you*."

She was only a couple feet from me now. The dancing fire illuminated a beautiful face. Her eyes were clear and confident.

"If you want to live, come with me," she said.

Hearing a Fury offer me life filled me with confusion. How could that be? She was lying to me, she had to be.

More cries flew overhead, cutting off my words. Suddenly she had closed the distance between us and held my wrist in a firm grasp.

"Remember, we run away from the cliff, not toward it, Grace. Fear keeps us safe."

The familiar words snapped me out of my confusion. She was speaking truth. Rushing after Jamie would get me killed. Would staying with her also get me killed? Maybe she was an angel. Or a Fury deceiving me.

"I would never hurt you," she said. "I can

keep you safe, but to do so, I need your permission. Let me protect you."

A chorus of low growls pricked my ears, and I knew two things: first, there was more than one Fury out there; second, they were closing in. My brother's cries had stopped.

"We have to go now," she said. She yanked on my wrist and I surrendered to her. I stumbled behind her through the darkened forest, scraping against bark and branches, nearly tripping over my own feet. She moved swiftly and without fault, pulling me behind and keeping me upright.

Within the minute, we arrived at a large rock overhang. Before I could object or consider, she was dragging me under the rock, into a cave.

She released my wrist and turned to leave.

"You're leaving me here?"

She faced me, silhouetted by the gray light beyond the cave's mouth. "Under no circumstance should you leave until I come for you."

And then she was gone, out of the cave, into the forest.

I wanted to cry out for an explanation. I wanted to rush from the hole where she'd hidden me. But I knew if I did, I would face the full wrath of the Fury she'd sworn to protect me from.

A screech split the air and I knew it was Jamie.

I sank farther into the darkness of the cave and slumped to the dirt, mind lost on Jamie. Poor Jamie. I desperately prayed he was still alive.

You were wrong, brother. The Fury are real. They are more real than we could ever have imagined.

CHAPTER SEVEN

My mind stirred before my body. I could hear the chirping of birds and smell the strong aroma of wet grass as my eyes slowly opened. The cave was dim around me, filled with shadows. A chill ran through my bones. A brief beat of curiosity pounded at the back of my mind before the memories of last night came rushing back.

Startled, I jerked up, bumped my head against a rock, and grunted. I grasped my head with both palms, disoriented. I couldn't remember crawling so far back into the cave, nor falling asleep. Pulling myself forward, I carefully struggled to my knees and then to my feet. I stumbled from the cave, momentarily blinded by the bright sun.

"Heck of a way to wake up," someone said behind me.

I turned and saw her — the beautiful woman who was either a Fury of a totally different kind than any I'd imagined, or an angel.

I took a misguided stride backward into a log that sent me crashing to the ground. My arms caught the brunt of the fall. Pain shot up through the heels of my hands.

The woman stepped forward to help, and I held up my hand to stop her. I pushed myself back to my feet, a wave of nausea coursing through me, and I swallowed to calm my stomach.

We stood there two paces apart. Seeing her clearly in the light as the morning breeze lifted her hair off her shoulders, I struggled to reconcile this beautiful woman with any of my notions of what a Fury was.

"Thank you," she said.

"How can you hear my thoughts?" I asked.

"We can all hear thoughts," she replied.

"We, as in the Fu . . ." The word caught in my throat and I swallowed.

"Like I mentioned, I'm not what you think."

Then she had to be an angel, like Sylous. But she could still be a Fury who was deceiving me. She looked far more like an angel than a Fury, but I knew I couldn't trust what my eyes were seeing.

"I guess seeing *isn't* believing," she said.

"Stop it," I said.

"Stop what?"

"Reading my thoughts."

A beat of silence passed between us.

"Please," she said.

I shot her a curious look.

"Stop reading my thoughts, *please*," she said.

I stared at her for a moment, a tad stunned. "Please. Please stop reading my thoughts."

She returned the stare for a long moment. "Not possible. But I can pretend."

I felt like I was in a game of sorts. She was the cat and I was the mouse, and that game never ended well for the mouse.

When you feel afraid, run, because something isn't right. The idea played through my mind, and even though she'd saved my life, I was afraid. I should be running. But I had questions.

"And I have answers," she said.

"I thought you weren't going to read my mind."

"Sorry. I'll try to do better."

I looked at her from head to toe. "So, you're an angel?"

"Some might say."

"What would *you* call you?"

She gave me a small grin. "My name is Wisdom, but you can call me Bobbie."

"Bobbie?"

She nodded. "Better than Wisdom, don't you think?"

"So you're real."

"Think of me as your guiding light. But you must also know that what you call the Fury are not all the same."

I wasn't sure I could trust her. I had to be careful.

"You saw what you saw last night."

"I saw you kill a Fury."

"I saved you."

I hesitated, wondering what else she could tell me.

"Who are the Fury?" I asked.

"You saw one last night. There are many kinds."

"But you're not one of them?"

"As I said, I'm the guiding light who keeps you safe."

"But what are you? What are you made from? What, *what*?"

She winked. "The answer to that, dear Grace, is beyond your pay grade. Maybe one day you'll understand."

"Okay, then tell me how you know my name."

"I've known you your whole life."

"You have?"

"Of course. I've been guiding you. Wisdom, remember?"

The way she spoke gave me some comfort.

"But it's true that the Fury have taken over the world?" I asked.

"In more ways than you can ever imagine. I think Jamie learned that last night."

Jamie!

"I have to find him! Can you help me?"

"He isn't my concern," Bobbie said. "Only you."

I didn't know what that meant, but I knew I had to find him. Assuming there was anything left of him.

I turned away from Bobbie and only then saw I was standing in a clearing. Pockets of little white flowers popped their heads above the green blades, bending with the grass at the wind's command. The clearing gave way to a thick forest that looked impassable.

How was I going to find him in there?

"Stick to the path," Bobbie said.

I glanced over my shoulder at her. She was reading my mind again. She gave me an apologetic shrug and thrust her chin forward slightly. My eyes followed the direction she indicated and I saw a break in the tree line. A path.

"Is he alive?"

"Like I said, he's not my concern," she replied. "Only and always you."

"Then can you help me find him? That's me too."

"I am helping you. Stick to the path."

I didn't glance back. My only thought now was for Jamie. I started forward and within seconds I was running.

"Don't wander off the path, Grace," Bobbie called after me. "You never know what's still hiding among the trees."

I stumbled into the thick foliage, feet pounding on the dirt as I moved up the path. I had no idea how far I needed to go or if Jamie would even be here. But Bobbie hadn't been wrong yet and she'd told me to follow the path. So I did.

After a full minute of running, I slowed to a jog. My lungs heaved painfully at the high altitude. I gasped for air, looking in all directions, trying to keep my thoughts off images of Jamie bleeding out or torn in half.

Something moved in the bush to my right, and I jumped to the other side of the path, crying out. Then I settled as a small fuzzy creature scurried out from the brush and hurried back into the forest. I clamped my eyes shut and shook my head.

What are you doing, Grace? What are you expecting to find? Jamie couldn't have survived. You should go back to the cave.

When I opened my eyes, tears blurred the

path before me. My thoughts continued to batter me, draining all the false confidence I'd used to get this far. Rooted to the ground on that path, I stared straight ahead. And it was that stare that rewarded me.

I caught sight of a slight movement in the forest ahead. A couple yards down, on the right side, just breaking the plane onto the path, lay a small heap of something. Something that was twitching. A dying animal was my first thought, but the way it moved was unusual.

I took a step forward, squinting to focus, and thought the lump was more fleshy than furry. Several more steps and it started to take a more pronounced shape. A heel, toes, half covered in a torn wool sock. One I had washed, one I knew.

I was in a full run then, reaching the foot quickly and finding the rest of Jamie attached to it. He was stretched out along the ground on his left side, one leg elongated while the other was bent closer to his middle. Arms cupped up around his head, his shoulders shaking, his mouth muttering incoherently.

I fell to my knees beside him. "Jamie!"

He gave no indication that he'd heard me. His clothes were torn, body bloody under a tattered shirt and slacks. Several large gashes ran the length of his curled leg. His blood had soaked the ground.

How much had he lost?

"Jamie," I said again, and reached out my fingers to brush his shoulder.

He shrank away, face tucked in the crook of his elbow as though deeply ashamed.

I grabbed his shoulder, keeping my touch tender. "Jamie, it's me. It's Grace."

He was shivering and mumbling. I took his wrist and gently pulled at his arm, needing to see his face, hushing him when he objected.

"It's okay, Jamie, it's all going to be okay. I'm here now." I spoke through sniffled tears.

He was stiff, but he moved. The moment his arm cleared his face, my heart dropped. The right side of his face was deep purple, swollen and badly bruised. A gash ran the length of his other cheek. Dirt and dried grass stuck to bloody areas. Dried mucus and saliva caked his swollen, trembling lips.

"Oh, Jamie," I whispered.

He squinted up through puffy eyes. Recognition flashed in his gaze, and he began to weep. Deep and mournful sobs shook his whole body. He reached for me and pulled his head onto my thighs, clutching me like a frightened child.

The rules of what constituted proper contact between a man and a woman, woven into the very fabric of my mind, meant nothing to me in that moment. This broken brother laying his head in my lap stirred a powerful instinct that I refused to fight. So I wrapped myself around him and held him close. I whispered kind words as he wept and trembled in my arms. And in his muttering a single phrase came through. A phrase he repeated over and over.

"They're real. They're real. The Fury are real."

CHAPTER EIGHT

Jamie and I remained on the forest floor, tucked behind the trees, for a full hour. He finally started to calm, and as he did I helped him into a sitting position.

His injuries seemed primarily external — dozens of minor cuts and bruises — but he'd also received two gashes. We needed to get back to Haven Valley.

Considering Jamie's condition, I doubted we could cover the distance in less than two days' time. This was a problem. A big one. He needed medical attention sooner.

Still, Jamie insisted we try.

He was speaking clearly again, telling me where things hurt, helping me as I packed the serious wounds with sod. I tore the rest of Jamie's slashed jacket into strips to form primitive bandages. Neither of us spoke a word about the Fury. His own horror was still too real, and I didn't have a clue how to talk about Bobbie. I wasn't sure I ever would.

Was she still nearby? I didn't know. I kept a watchful eye, naturally, but if she was near, she was out of sight. Which made me wonder if she had the power to vanish at will.

Eventually I helped Jamie stand, then limp out onto the path. "You sure you can do this?" I asked.

"Yes. Anywhere but this place. We just need to get to the path I marked."

He was far too slow on his own, so he draped his right arm around my shoulders and I lent him support. My legs were already burning from our exertion the day before, but I ignored the pain and tried to keep us moving at as steady a pace as we could manage. Finding Jamie's marked path was a relief — at least we knew where we were going.

We stopped frequently so Jamie could rest, once at a creek. There I helped him to the water so he could drink and wash his face. The splash bath rejuvenated him for a while, but as the sun reached the highest point of the sky, he started to lose his strength again. Still, we pushed on. Two more hours at least, but by then Jamie was so pale and wheezing so hard that continuing was impossible.

I escorted him to the base of a large tree and helped him sit. Leaning back against the trunk, Jamie took slow and labored breaths. He looked down the path in the direction we were heading, then back up at me.

"You're going to have to go without me," he said.

"Not a chance. I'm not leaving you here."

"I'm not strong enough."

"Neither am I! I'm not going out there alone."

"I'm not going to make it."

"Stop that, of course you are. We just need to rest."

He shifted and his face twisted in pain. Tears sprang to my eyes. I couldn't leave him again. I just couldn't.

"Listen to me," Jamie said. "You're going to have to get to Haven Valley and bring help back."

He couldn't be serious. He was the one who knew these paths and was leading me. I couldn't go alone.

"We'll never make it if you just keep dragging me along," Jamie said. "This is going to kill me."

I nearly scolded him again, but I knew he was right. I wasn't a nurse, but I knew it wasn't just pain that was slowing him down.

He'd lost a lot of blood.

"Just follow the markers," he said. "They'll take you all the way back to the gates."

I looked down the path, wondering where Bobbie was. "And if I meet the Fury?"

He grabbed my hand and gave it a squeeze. "Maybe you're right. Maybe they only come out at night. Which is why you have to leave now before it gets dark. You can still make it, Grace. You have to."

Tears swam in his eyes. He was shivering, so I took off my coat and draped it over his body. I pushed back the fallen strands of hair from his forehead and held his gaze for a long moment. He was as afraid as I. But he was right — I had to get help.

"I'll be back," I said. "Even if Rose refuses to send help, I'll return. With medical supplies and whatever we need to get you strong enough to make it."

"Promise?" he said, forcing a grin.

I returned his smile. "Promise."

He nodded.

And then I was off, bunching up my thick skirt so I could run. As fast as my legs would carry me over rough, uneven ground.

Hold on, Jamie. Just hold on. I'm going to save you. I promise.

Jamie awoke with a start, gasping at the

afternoon air. It took a moment for his whereabouts to sink in. He was leaning against a thick tree beside the path he'd marked. He was alone. Injured and in pain. Grace had gone ahead for help.

The Fury were real.

How long had it been since Grace left him there? His throat was on fire, his vision blurred, every inch of his body ached. He was dying.

But he wasn't ready to die. Or was he? After his encounter last night, he wasn't sure falling asleep and waking up in heaven would be such a bad thing. The thought of facing the Fury again was unbearable.

But he couldn't die now. Grace would make it to Haven Valley and be back with help. He just needed to hold on a bit longer. Even so, he could feel the call to let go whisper like the breeze across his shoulders. It really would be so much simpler to fall back asleep and never wake up.

He swallowed and leaned his head back against the tree. Maybe he deserved death. He'd brought this upon himself. His memories of the Fury came into full focus and he shivered.

One moment he'd been alone in the woods, the next surrounded by Fury. Three of them. Terrifying creatures without heads

103

or feet. Death hiding in black shrouds. But the death called Fury had teeth and claws, and they'd tortured and toyed with his mind and body for hours. Manipulated and exposed his deepest fears and doubts, broken his mind and his body.

Trust us and we will leave you alone. Surrender to us and we'll keep you safe from harm. We are friends. We are you.

But he'd resisted them, and the more he did, the harsher their attacks became. During the worst of it, he'd begged for death.

Death is too small a price for your sins, they'd whispered.

They wanted him alive for the final showdown. For the day Haven Valley was destroyed from within. Jamie didn't understand what it meant, but their haunting words filled him with a deeper fear than he'd ever known.

The Fury were real. What they were was still an enigma, but his injuries proved their power beyond doubt. Could they be defeated?

Jamie closed his eyes and took a deep, calming breath. Rose had been right all along. The Fury were destroying the wicked, and nothing would stop them. You could only avoid it by believing the right things and following the right path. It was the only thing that made any sense.

"You really are in bad shape."

The voice was low, and Jamie jerked his head toward it, half expecting to find himself face-to-face with another Fury. But the speaker wasn't a Fury. It was a man dressed in white. A man he'd seen only once before, a long time ago.

"Hello, Jamie," Sylous said.

Jamie blinked, stunned by the man's casual nature. Nothing about him had changed since he'd visited the Holy Family thirteen years ago. Not his age, not his suit, not a hair on his head, as far as Jamie could see. Because he was more than just a man.

"I don't think we've been properly introduced," Sylous said, placing a hand on his own chest. "My name is Sylous." He shoved his chin at Jamie. "And you look like you're in a bit of trouble."

Jamie lay propped up against the tree, frozen.

"What do you say?" Sylous pushed. "You're in trouble, yes?"

"Yes," Jamie finally croaked.

"Clearly."

Sylous flicked a smooth white pebble he'd been holding into the air, then caught it in his palm.

"I help with trouble," he said. He took a

single step forward, eyes on Jamie. "I can help you with your trouble." Again he flicked the small stone into the air and caught it. "Do you know what your trouble is, Jamie?" He didn't pause to let Jamie answer. It was that kind of conversation. "Doubt," he said.

Flick.

"Doubt's a terrible kind of trouble. It leads to thinking and ideas. Ideas that make you wonder if maybe the world could be different. Maybe you could be different. Maybe there's a great deception brewing."

Flick.

Sylous took two more steps toward Jamie and stuck his free hand inside the pocket of his slacks. "I'm gonna tell you a secret, kid, just between you and me. There is more deception in the air than you can possibly know."

Jamie felt the man's presence stir his fear. It was as though Sylous was surrounded by a force field and that field was pressing against Jamie. The tree bark dug deeper into his back.

"There are really only two paths in life," Sylous continued. "One of safety and one of terrible danger. The first with protection and the second without. Safety has its requirements, naturally, and some might say those requirements compromise your freedom, which is true in some ways. But last night you saw just how dangerous freedom can be. The great deception is that you can have a little of both. Not true. You can't serve two masters. You have to pick a path."

Sylous grinned. "I promise you, freedom is a much harder path than safety."

Flick.

"I offered you protection. A safety net. An escape from the world and the monsters that threaten it. And I offered that protection without asking for much in return, yes? All you have to do is follow the law. A law that keeps you good and pure and holy. A law that ensures you're worth protecting."

Sylous dropped the white pebble into his pocket, closed the gap between them, and squatted so his face was only an arm's length from Jamie's.

"You look like you could use some protection," he said. "But you have to choose, my friend. Which master will you serve?"

Jamie's bottom lip began to quiver as the fear of facing another night alone with the Fury coursed through his veins. "You," he whispered.

Sylous took a deep breath and let it out slowly. "I'm inclined to help you with this dying-in-the-woods situation you've found yourself in," he said. "But I need assurances."

"Anything," Jamie croaked.

"I need you to kill your doubt. Fear me alone. Serve me only and fully. Do that and I will save your life and protect you from the Fury. What do you say?"

For a moment, Jamie wondered how this was different from what any of them had already done. Sylous seemed to be asking something more of him. But he was in no condition to question the man.

"I say yes," he said.

Sylous nodded. "Wise choice. Don't waver from it."

"I won't, I swear."

"No. No you won't."

Without delay, Sylous reached for his hand and gripped it tight. Energy surged up Jamie's arm and he gasped. The power buzzed over his skin and rippled down to the soles of his feet, a biting charge of raw current that felt like electricity.

"Receive my strength," Sylous said. "Let me protect you."

Jamie's back arched under the increasing energy.

"Say it!" Sylous said. "Receive me!"

"I receive you!" Jamie rasped.

Jamie felt the power mushroom inside his

chest, then rage up his neck and into his brain. For a moment, he was sure it had actually lifted him off the ground.

The world around him began to dim. Sylous's final words sounded far away as Jamie's consciousness faded.

"I need you. I need all of you."

CHAPTER NINE

My legs ached as I ran, but after hours of pain, I first accepted it, then ignored it. I used pictures of Jamie slumped against the tree to motivate me as I raced. The thought of him dying before I could get someone back to him pushed me past any concern for myself. My lungs were on fire and felt as though they would burst, but still I plunged forward.

I was forced to stop twice, both times to vomit, before quickly catching my breath and moving again. Keeping my eyes ahead, watching for markers, praying I was still going the right way. The air cooled as the sky dimmed. Dusk already. There was no way I was going to make it!

But somehow I did. Standing like the gates of heaven, the tall wooden doors to Haven Valley came into view. I nearly collapsed from relief the last hundred paces.

Daylight gone now, I reached the gates

and pounded. "Help me. Please! Open up!"

It occurred to me that I could just as easily run along the short wall and enter over the red perimeter, but I had been cast out. Didn't I need permission to enter again?

"Help!" I slammed my fist against the wooden door. "Please!"

Two large spotlights attached to the top of the wall blazed to life, and I backed away, squinting up. I had been heard and found. Now I would beg them to listen.

The doors creaked and slowly swung inward. Ralph, the oldest of the guardians, poked his head around, joined by Morton, his twenty-year-old son. They saw me drenched in sweat, panting, and exchanged glances.

"Tell Rose I'm back," I gasped. "We have to hurry, Ralph! Jamie's —"

"Wait here," Morton interrupted. Without further explanation, they closed the door. I hoped they'd been instructed to find Rose in the event either of us returned.

Overwhelmed by fatigue, I dropped to my knees and rested my palms on the dirt, head hanging, trying to get my lungs to fill with air.

The door opened again minutes later. Harrison and Rose walked out accompanied by Ralph and Morton, both armed with

111

powerful flashlights.

"You've returned," Rose said.

"Jamie's still out there," I blurted, staggering to my feet. "He . . . he needs help."

"And what have you discovered?" Harrison asked, ignoring my plea.

They stood and waited, watching me. An image of the Fury that Bobbie had killed filled my mind, and I shuddered. But I couldn't tell them about Bobbie. She hadn't made another appearance during my return, and I wondered if she'd left me altogether.

"They're more terrifying than we could have imagined," I rasped.

Harrison motioned to Morton. "Bring her. We shouldn't be outside the gates in the dark."

"Jamie's still out there," I objected. "We have to save him!"

"It was his choice to leave," Harrison said. "And his choice not to return." And then, as an afterthought, "You're saying he's alive?"

"He's wounded. He'll be dead if we don't get to him soon. Please, I'm begging you. You have to help him!"

"Calm down, Grace." Rose stepped forward. "You know very well that there's nothing we can do for him outside of Haven Valley."

"He won't make it without help!"

Her eyes shifted to the dark forest over my shoulder. "How was he wounded?"

"The Fury," I said. "He was attacked."

Her lips flattened. Not a cruel expression, just one that said *I told you so.* And so she had.

"I understand why this is upsetting," she said, "but let's not forget why he finds himself in this situation. The prophecy gave him ample warning."

"He'll die!" I shouted, forgetting myself.

"And now you ask us to risk our lives to the same Fury who took his?" she demanded. "Jamie gave up his life the moment he crossed the perimeter. It's a wonder you aren't dead as well."

"He's not dead!"

"Watch your tone, young lady." Her voice was soft, even apologetic. "Just be thankful you made it. There's grace on you, my dear. The next time you might not be so fortunate." She glanced at Ralph. "Bring her to my house. I need to know why Sylous saved her."

I wanted to object again, but I knew she was right. I would have to find another way, though the prospect of going back out tonight on my own was terrifying.

Morton and his father reached either side

of me quickly, their strong hands gripping both arms. My legs wobbled as they hurried me forward.

We were already inside the gate when a soft cry reached us from the forest. "Help!"

As one, we stopped.

The cry came again, distant but unmistakable. "Help!"

Jamie?

Pushed by adrenaline, I spun around and tore free from both guardians. "Jamie!"

"Stop her!" Harrison snapped.

Morton reached me before I'd taken three steps and jerked me back.

"Help me!"

"Jamie!"

A beam from a powerful flashlight cut through the darkness and lit the figure staggering from the forest. Even at this distance I could see that Jamie was a mess.

I struggled to free myself from Morton's grasp, but he was far too strong. Jamie stared into the bright light, took another unsteady step forward, and collapsed.

"Bring him," Rose ordered. Then to me, "It's alright, Grace. He'll be safe now. Please come with me."

Relief cascaded over me and tears slipped down my cheeks. We'd made it. Both Jamie and I had encountered the Fury and lived to tell about it. Rose would honor that.

I stepped back to where she stood as Ralph and Morton hurried to Jamie, hoisted him to his feet, and dragged him through the gate.

"Now you know," Rose said softly beside me. "Now we all know." Then, "Go home, Grace. I will see to Jamie's needs and speak to him first."

I lay on my bed, lost in my thoughts. Unnerving ones that kept me awake despite my exhaustion. My small side-table lamp gave off just enough light to cast most of my bedroom in shadows. My eyes wandered around the room — simple furnishings, one twin bed, one wooden desk and matching chair, one tall dresser, one nightstand and lamp, walls nearly bare except for the painting of red roses that hung over my headboard.

Everything was tidy and in its place, as required. The few clothes I owned were neatly folded inside drawers or hanging in the closet across from me. Apart from some personal items — a few devotionals, a journal, and a small box under my bed where I stored my paints — I owned nothing. Idolizing things was a sin, so the community at large attended to only what it needed for survival.

Every inch of my room was familiar, yet now it all seemed different. I knew the difference was really in me, but how?

I lost track of time. They'd taken Jamie to the medical clinic immediately and I'd asked to go with him, but Rose had refused. News of our return had brought my mother to tears of joy. She'd been allowed to go to Jamie's side. Ralph and Morton had been positioned at the front and back door of my home to "protect" me. From what, I didn't know. Rose and Harrison would want to speak with me, but not before morning. Until then I should rest and pray for my brother.

I was still unsure how he'd made it to the gates so soon after I had. It was only one of many questions I couldn't answer. Where had Bobbie gone? What was she? Had the Fury destroyed the people in the city we'd seen? Why hadn't they attacked us until we stopped for the night? How many were there and how close were they to Haven Valley? Was Jamie okay?

The questions swirled through my head, making sleep impossible.

Something creaked downstairs, and I glanced at my door, slightly ajar. My mother must be home. Or maybe it was one of the guardians.

Another creak and I sat up. Someone was moving through the house.

"Mother?"

The movement stopped. That was odd. I stood and walked to the door, opened it a tad farther. Stuck my neck out and twisted to look in both directions. The house was eerily quiet. A sudden wave of uneasiness hit me and I strained to hear.

"Hello?"

Again, nothing.

I swallowed my anxiety, shook off my discomfort, pulled my head back into my room and shut the door. Whatever it was, it no longer mattered. I was safe in my room. Right?

"Being safe is important," a familiar voice behind me said.

I jerked around, heart in my throat. There, standing in the far corner, was the woman who'd saved me on the mountain.

"I thought we agreed that you're going to call me Bobbie," she said.

Dressed in white and black, she casually leaned her right shoulder against the wall, arms crossed over her chest, watching me with bright beautiful eyes. Fury couldn't cross the red rope. They couldn't be inside Haven Valley. So she couldn't be a Fury.

"Like I said, I'm Wisdom, here to protect you." Bobbie smiled. "Unless you think this is a dream."

Could it be? How many times had Jamie told me my wild imaginations got the better of me?

"Look at your hands and feet," she said. "They say you can't see your hands and feet in dreams."

I lifted my hands. But I already knew it wasn't a dream.

Part of me wanted to run from her, the part that knew I was probably breaking a law even by talking to her. Any sighting of anyone or anything not part of the community had to be reported immediately. But there had never been an intrusion.

Until now.

"Until now," Bobbie said. "But that's not entirely true either."

"There are others like you inside Haven Valley?"

She just stared at me.

"You have to leave!" I snapped. "Or I will." I grabbed the door handle, thinking I would report her.

"Before you do that, you should know a few things," she said.

I hesitated. "Know what?"

"For starters, you're the only one who can

hear or see me. Like I said, you're my only concern. I won't reveal myself to anyone else."

I turned back around, heart still hammering. "And?"

She pushed herself off the wall. "You have to believe that I didn't come to hurt you, Grace. If I wanted you dead I could have let the Fury kill you or done it myself many times over by now." She spread her arms. "I appear to you in this form to make you feel comfortable, not so I can trick you into some elaborate scheme. I need you to trust me."

"Why?" I asked.

"Because, Grace, you're going to need my help."

"I'm afraid of you."

"Fear can be good for you. It helps you make wise choices. Don't touch the flame or you'll get burned. Don't run with scissors. Guard your eyes, guard your ears, stay away from anything that can harm you. We do all these things in fear of harm, which is wisdom. And trust me, Grace, evil is most definitely trying to harm you."

"Not in Haven Valley," I objected. "We're safe here."

"Are you sure?"

"Of course." Even so, I felt doubt tug at me.

Bobbie smiled. "Can I ask you a question?" She continued before I could respond. "What will they say when you tell them about what happened in the woods? How will you explain the fact that you didn't get a scratch? Because you were saved by a strange creature and willingly followed that creature into a cave? A creature that then followed you into Haven Valley?" She tilted her head and grinned. "That'll ruffle a few feathers. They'll assume I'm a Fury in sheep's clothing."

"And maybe they'd be right."

"Maybe, but I can assure you that without my guidance, you're going to face a terrible fate. You know how concerned Rose is with the safety of this little heaven on earth."

She was right about that. I didn't respond, but then she already knew I was agreeing with her, because she could read my thoughts.

"Be careful, Grace. Even here, in a place with perfect laws to keep you safe, there is danger," Bobbie said. "And more is coming."

"More? Wolves in sheep's clothing, you mean? Like the prophecy warns?"

"For now you just need to accept my offer

to help keep you safe. Like I said, you're my charge. I've waited a long time to reveal myself to you."

And yet she could still be the darkness masquerading as light. A Fury who had tricked her way into the gates to sow destruction.

"Really? Me, darkness masquerading as light? It could be anyone, but I promise you it's not me. My only purpose is to keep you safe. It's why I saved you from the Fury that would have mauled you and left you to die."

I was torn, but she made a strong argument.

"What do you mean, the coming threat could be anyone? Do you know who the wolf in sheep's clothing is?"

She shrugged. "I only know that it could be anyone."

"That's absurd! You're saying it could be my mother? Or Rose? Or Sylous for that matter? Impossible!"

"Not impossible. It could be anyone. My job is to keep you safe. Trust no one or you'll be in for a very rude awakening when the truth is finally revealed."

A wave of panic chilled my bones. I couldn't live this way!

"Ask me to leave, and I'll go," Bobbie said.

"Leave," I said.

Bobbie nodded. "Very well. But if you need me, and you will, just think of me. I'll be close." She started toward the door and I gave her clear passage, never taking my eyes off her. She reached for the knob and pulled the door open. It made me wonder why she needed to use the door at all. She'd seemed to appear at will when making her entrance.

She looked at me. "Take care with what you say about me, Grace. There are forces beyond your control at work in Haven Valley. Don't expose your only true lifeline or it may be taken from you."

Then she stepped out past the threshold and out of my line of sight. I waited for a couple beats, listening for her footsteps on the stairs, but heard nothing. So I crossed to the door and carefully peered around into the hall. It was empty.

She'd simply vanished, leaving nothing behind but dread.

CHAPTER TEN

Ben drove down the long, isolated highway while Eli slept soundly in the passenger seat beside him. The sun was climbing the sky, streaking the road ahead with early morning rays. He'd been driving all night. Motivated partially by wanting to get to their destination as quickly as possible, and partially because sleeping had become so difficult.

It was mostly the nausea that kept him up. And the aching of his body as the disease ate away at his muscles. Ben knew his time was running out. He'd known it before he'd finally managed to land on a diagnosis. His body had been losing the fight against human frailty for a while now.

He warred with moments of depression, when he lost sight of the truth he'd come to know well. The world had become obsessed with survival. Ben had as well, spending most of his energy avoiding death. He'd always attributed so much power to death, as if it were a god. And in doing so, he'd given the prospect of death all the power it held over him.

He was seeing things differently these days. It was a blessing to know his days were numbered. A blessing he wasn't sure he would trade for more days. They said hitting rock bottom was required for one to let go. True in his experience.

Eli stirred beside him, the new day's sunlight bright on his cheeks. He straightened in his seat and rubbed the sleep from his eyes. Ran his small fingers through his disheveled hair and yawned. "Are we close?" he asked.

Ben adjusted his grip on the steering wheel and nodded. "Only a couple of days, I imagine."

Eli slid down in his seat and propped his stocking feet up on the dashboard, letting the sun warm his toes. "Who knew Tennessee was so far away from California."

"Anyone with a map or GPS," Ben teased.

Even though he was the butt of the joke, Eli giggled. A welcome change to the steady silence that had accompanied Ben while the boy slept. He could feel Eli's gaze on him but kept his eyes on the road.

"Yes?" Ben asked.

"How are you feeling?" Eli replied.

Ben took a deep breath and, though he wasn't sure why, tried to mask the ever-present discomfort. Eli knew he was sick, knew he was dying. There was no reason to hide it from the boy.

"The same," Ben said. "But before you suggest it, I don't want to stop yet. I can go a few more hours before I need to rest."

"Not even to pee?"

"Well, okay. You gotta go, you gotta go."

"I gotta go."

"Then we gotta stop. Soon as we find a spot."

Eli stared at him a moment longer, then turned his attention forward and out the windshield.

Ben's mind wandered to his lost children. With any luck, he'd see them both in two days' time. A good thing, considering the fact that his own days were numbered not much more than that. Only a few minutes, that's all he needed with them. It might be all he'd get.

"She calls her Bobbie," Eli said.

"Who calls who Bobbie?"

"Grace is calling the one who's trying to protect her 'Bobbie,' " he said.

Ben thought about that. Eli rarely spoke about the particulars of the world at large, enslaved to darkness as it was. And Ben had long ago realized that it wasn't his place to ask for particulars. So much was beyond his understanding. All he knew was to trust in simple truths and leave the details alone. They did little but tie his thoughts into knots.

That Grace was calling someone who was trying to protect her "Bobbie" might be good news.

"Interesting," he finally said.

"Yup."

And that was the end of it.

A familiar melody broke through his thoughts. He glanced at the radio. The words *Kansas — Carry On Wayward Son* scrolled across the digital screen. Eli began to hum in tune, grooving his head back and forth with the notes. He pressed one of the buttons on his door, and the window dropped, letting in the cold morning air. His humming turned to soft singing that quickly became loud.

Ben turned the volume up, cruising down the lonely highway, letting the promise of peace sink all the way into his weary bones.

Yes, he thought, *carry on.*

CHAPTER ELEVEN

I eventually fell asleep, only to be woken by my mother a couple of hours later. She told me to clean and dress quickly. I was to speak with Harrison and Rose at their house posthaste. No time to delay.

She was in a foul mood, but I expected nothing less.

I was scheduled to stay with Andrew that evening, so cleaning and grooming took more effort than usual. It was important to be clean, but mostly I was eager to be cleansed of the day before. The least I could do was offer a little penance before standing in front of Rose.

Exhausted from too little sleep, I dressed. Nausea knotted my gut again, likely from all the stress. Properly covered by undergarments — a slip without any colorful flowers that Andrew might see and object to — and my long, white dress, I made my way down to the kitchen, where my mother had fixed breakfast and was busy over the sink. The smell of food made me a bit queasy, but I knew I had to eat.

"Thank you," I said, taking a seat before toast and eggs.

She didn't respond, but that didn't surprise me. Jamie and I had put her through hell. She looked as if she'd been up for hours.

I ate quickly and in silence, knowing that any discussion would bring some form of disapproval. Rose would likely give me all I could handle.

I forced down the eggs and stood to carry my empty plate to the sink. Wasting was prohibited, but the toast would keep.

"How's Jamie?" I asked, no longer able to keep silent.

My mother turned to look at me. Disappointment and anger flashed behind her eyes.

I dropped my gaze and placed my dish in the empty sink. "Please tell me he's okay."

Her response was lifeless. "They'll be monitoring him closely for the next couple of days, but Dr. Charles says he'll recover."

I closed my eyes and swallowed. "Thank God," I whispered.

"At least someone's looking out for him."

Meaning I hadn't been. His injuries were

my fault.

"I talked with him this morning," my mother said, vigorously wiping down the counter.

"You did?"

"He woke up for a bit, but his mind is still jumbled. He lost a dangerous amount of blood, was extremely dehydrated, suffered a concussion." She stopped short and closed her eyes.

I knew the scolding was coming before she turned glaring eyes on me.

"He nearly died, Grace."

I looked at the linoleum flooring, wallowing in shame. This was more Jamie's doing than mine, but I accepted guilt in full. It was always my fault. My mother had rose-colored lenses when she saw her son and dark lenses when it came to me. I knew that and accepted it. Better too much guilt than not enough.

"What happened out there?" she snapped.

I was about to give her an accounting with as little detail as possible, but she cut me off before I could speak.

"Actually, I don't want to know." She tossed the rag she'd been wiping the counters with into the sink and turned to leave the kitchen. She made it a couple of steps before turning back toward me. "Your brother asked for you when he woke."

"He did?"

"He wanted to make sure you are protecting yourself from what's coming. Do you have any idea what that means?"

What's coming. Her words dropped like rocks inside my brain. *There is danger, and more is coming.* Bobbie's warning.

I shook my head.

"Harrison and Rose will want answers. For the love of Haven Valley, Grace, no more lies."

And with that, my mother stormed to her bedroom.

Ten minutes later I was seated alone in Rose's office, the place that had once been my home away from home. It was here I'd been instructed in my role as a woman of the Holy Family, instructed by Rose and some of the books that lined a tall bookcase next to the desk.

Now I felt like an unwelcome sinner, because it was here I'd also copied the schedule that helped Jamie avoid detection each time he ventured out past the perimeter.

The room was cold and clammy, and the ticking clock became a countdown to the judgment that awaited me.

For the love of Haven Valley, Grace, no more lies. My mother's words haunted me still.

But the warning from my brother and Bobbie haunted me more. Something was coming. What? Or who?

If only they'd let me talk to Jamie before being interrogated. I felt utterly alone in my confusion, without a lifeline or clear understanding.

The door behind me creaked and I stilled. There was no escaping this. Rose stepped in and crossed to the large leather chair behind her cherrywood desk. I sat in one of two smaller chairs opposite the desk. A glass of water sat on the small round table beside me, but I hadn't touched it.

Rose scooted her chair underneath the desk and placed her palms on the surface. She looked at me as I absently bit the inside of my lip.

"Hello, Grace."

"Hello," I said.

"Did you get any sleep?"

"A little."

She gave me a small smile. I didn't deserve her kindness.

"Harrison isn't going to be joining us. I thought it might be better for just us to talk.

131

I've always felt we had a connection, you and I."

"Yes."

"That's one of the reasons this has all been so heartbreaking. You betrayed me, Grace. You used the trust I placed in you to undermine me and our community."

I dropped my eyes to her shoulder, unable to hold her gaze. "Can you ever forgive me?"

Rose considered before she spoke. "Your greatest mistake was trusting your brother instead of the law. I know the sins here are largely attributed to your brother's curiosity. That doesn't excuse your behavior, but it does give it a different tone. And yes, we are taught to forgive. But forgiveness is hard and must be earned."

"Of course," I said.

"I must admit I care for you a great deal, Grace. I've always seen you as part of my family. A daughter of sorts."

I wanted to weep there in her office. To fall at her feet and beg her to see me as she once had. To swear I would never betray her again. But I wasn't sure that would be in my best interest. Rose preferred strength over weakness. It was in part why she disliked my mother, I thought.

"It will take time and work," Rose continued. "All of Haven Valley will need to be reassured of your commitment to them. You *are* still committed, aren't you?"

"Always," I said, looking back up at her.

"Good. Now tell me what happened beyond the perimeter."

Be careful, Grace. Bobbie's words filled my head. *Even here, in a place with perfect laws to keep you safe, there is danger.* Again, I thought of what Jamie had said to our mother about protecting myself from what was coming.

I cleared my throat. "It took us most of the day to reach the cliff from where we could see the city Jamie spoke of."

"Most of the day? And no danger along the way?"

"Not that we saw. We knew it would have taken us at least another day's walk to reach the city, so we stopped for the night. Jamie left to get more firewood." I looked down at my hands in my lap. To lie or not to lie about my encounter with Bobbie? The moment had come.

Be careful, Grace.

And I made a choice.

"I was waiting for a long time and I started to get worried. That's when I heard his cries."

"Jamie's cries."

"Yes."

"And you were alone?" Rose asked.

I nodded. Tears stung my eyes as my memory of those awful cries returned to me. "I should have gone out to find him, but I heard movement in the trees, and I just knew they were out there."

"You saw the Fury as well?"

"No," I said quickly. Maybe too quickly.

"Why would they attack Jamie and not you?"

"I don't know." Another lie. "Maybe because I ran. I found a cave and I hid there till morning. It was terrible. The screams went on all night." More lies.

Rose leaned back in the leather chair, eyeing me. "You were lucky."

I nodded.

"Maybe it's a sign," she said.

"A sign?"

"Maybe you were meant to return and be the witness. How did you find Jamie?"

"He was on the main path," I said, going with her theory.

"Where he could easily be found. And how did he get back to the gate?"

"I don't know," I said, relieved to be telling the truth.

Rose nodded, keeping her eyes glued to mine. "So you never once encountered the Fury?"

"Never."

Another pause. She'd always used silence as carefully as her words.

"You shouldn't feel ashamed for running, Grace. Fear saved your life. Let's hope Jamie has learned from this as well."

"I should have done a better job keeping him accountable," I said.

"True. And you will continue to pay for that sin. Again, I hope you understand that the road to restoration can be long."

I nodded, knowing that the stain of my indiscretion would always discolor me.

"You'll continue to contribute to the Holy Family as before, but know that everyone will be watching you. If there's a silver lining to this betrayal, it's the confirmation you and Jamie offer our community. There's absolutely no more room for doubt in that pretty little head of yours."

"None," I said. Another lie, because there was Bobbie, and she'd put some new questions in my mind. What if her claim that I would need her was true? Did I dare rely upon her?

"You were chosen, Grace. Brought into our Holy Family and given the gift of salvation from the Fury along with everyone else. Please do not forsake it. What God gives can be taken away."

"I understand," I said. "I'll never do it again."

She gave me a shallow nod. "I know how much you love the children, but you won't be watching them today. You'll remain at home until it's time to see Andrew tonight. Use the time to reflect on your denial of God and seek his mercy."

"I will."

Rose pushed her chair back and sighed. "This life can be hard on all of us, Grace. But we press on, knowing the inheritance that awaits us. We all learn from our mistakes." She looked off, thinking, then spoke in a soft voice. "I pray your path is easier than the path I had to take to bring me to obedience."

Eyes back on me, she wore a gentle, compassionate smile. "You may leave."

CHAPTER TWELVE

The day moved at a snail's pace as I kept to myself in our house, rehearsing Rose's words of warning. Whatever consequence I would suffer was of my own making because I'd broken the law, plain and simple. Purity came at a cost, and I would have to pay that cost.

Little things led to bigger things, which led to terrible things. God could see even a small amount of selfishness, like painting flowers on my undergarments. Even my stray thoughts of wanting things I didn't have would cause me suffering. Getting away with those things had emboldened me to help Jamie break the law. And look how that had turned out. What had I been thinking!

I would work extra hard to stay in line. I would show everyone that I was sorry for the danger I'd placed us all in. I would love the children and be a pure example for them

— the thought of any harm coming to them because of me made me sick. I would show honor and respect to every member of our holy haven and be a shining example that made Rose proud.

They were keeping Jamie isolated at the clinic. My mother said he'd had a rough morning, and they wanted to keep visitors to a minimum. He'd asked for me again, which only made my desire to see him grow. But I wasn't in a position to question Rose's decision to deny any visitors.

The afternoon was the worst for me, because normally I'd be caring for the children. I used some of the time to bathe again and take special care to prepare myself for my visit with Andrew. I would be the perfect wife for him, even if I didn't care for being with him. Who was I to say what should or shouldn't be? Especially now.

Near dusk, sparkling clean and resolved to be the perfect bride, I told my mother I loved her, then headed out to my husband's house, where I would prepare dinner and fulfill his needs.

It was then, crossing the south side of our small town, that I became aware of my place as the shunned woman I would be until I regained the trust of the community. Mary Hansen was hurrying home with little Bart, passing by the supply store, when I stepped onto the main street. The boy immediately brightened as he always did when he saw me.

"Grace!" He started toward me, but his mother grabbed his hand and jerked him back, speaking to him in a hushed voice. She didn't acknowledge me with her customary greeting or smile. I was off-limits to her son.

And rightly so, but the rejection was a knife to my heart. Only a handful of others were out at that time of day, but they all avoided me. They weren't cruel or angry, but I could hardly have felt more conspicuous.

There goes the woman caught in sin. Best not go near.

Even Alice, as she stepped out of the hardware store, glanced in my direction before quickly turning her head and heading the opposite way.

I walked faster, wishing I'd taken the path behind the houses. It was okay. I was only paying the price I had asked to pay. And that price was supposed to hurt.

But it made me want to cry. For the first time since my marriage, I could not get to Andrew's house fast enough.

His home was similar to all the homes in

Haven Valley. Two stories, the main bedroom and bathroom on the bottom floor, with two small additional bedrooms upstairs. A simple kitchen, living room, and mudroom. The layout was almost identical to my mother's home, but even after spending two nights a week here for the last five months, the space felt new and strange.

It was the smell, I thought. Musky and dank. And Andrew liked to keep the drapes closed. But tonight I would embrace all of that.

He was a simple man with few strong preferences, so cooking for him was easy. The same was true of his house. Although style and design weren't encouraged, most people added small personal touches.

Andrew had nothing personal on display. Nothing on the walls, no rugs, nothing on the coffee table. Not even a knickknack to be seen. He'd packed all of his first wife's belongings in a box and stored it away. I had been upstairs once when first shown the house, but not since, because the rooms were empty.

He'd told me once over dinner that I could do whatever I liked with the home when I moved in. I had often tried to imagine what I might do, but the thought of living with him made my gut turn.

Not tonight. Well, yes, it did make me a bit queasy, but I tried my best, humming as I quickly prepared the meal, forcing myself to imagine making the house my own. Not so difficult, really. The first thing I would do was add color. Flowers. I wanted our child to imagine a world full of life and wonder.

I remembered the tiny jeans and red shirts that my mother used to dress little Lukas in. He'd been such an adorable boy.

What would you wear today, Lukas? Remember that Spider-Man shirt you used to waddle around in?

The thought made me stop in the middle of clipping the beans. If Lukas and my child deserved color, didn't I as well? I had accepted the laws that discouraged displays of beauty in fear of losing my purity, but would I wish such a thing on my own infant? Was it so wrong for me to want a red dress if I longed to dress my innocent child in red?

But it was exactly those kinds of thoughts that had led Jamie into disobedience. I had to watch my thoughts!

Dinner was to be green beans, boiled potatoes, and chicken, all of which I set in serving dishes on the table, ready for Andrew as always. Normally I'd be watching the time, waiting for his arrival at six o'clock on the dot.

Today I was distracted by Jamie. I prayed he was okay. How would he be after such a terrifying ordeal?

And Bobbie. Could I trust her? And my mother, who was still upset. And Rose, to whom I'd lied.

The last couple of weeks, Andrew had taken to placing his hand on my shoulder and kissing the top of my head when he arrived. Tonight he opened the door, walked straight past me, and sat at his place at the head of the table without so much as a word.

I quickly took my place at the table, bowed my head as he offered prayers, and started in on my food, hoping he would show me grace.

For long minutes, neither of us talked, though I could feel him glancing at me on occasion. I knew I should beg his forgiveness and offer him a renewed vow of obedience, but I couldn't bring myself to speak it aloud.

I heard him lay down his silverware, and I looked up to see his elbows perched on the table's end, fingers intertwined and resting just in front of his mouth, eyes contemplative but kind. They were always kind.

"I want to understand what you were thinking, Grace," Andrew said in his low, calm voice. "But I'm struggling."

"It was a terrible mistake," I said, lowering my eyes to my plate.

"I've been sick to my stomach all day."

"I didn't mean to cause any problems. It was wrong of me."

Andrew often struggled with stomach issues, particularly when he was upset. He rarely showed his frustration, but I saw it in him every time we were together. There was a ticking time bomb of fear in him that he'd found a way to control with great effort.

But that was true for all of Haven Valley. How else does one live, knowing that evil lurks to prey on the impure?

"You could have come to me when Jamie first asked for your help."

"I should have."

"I wish you would look at me," Andrew said.

His comment caught me off guard. I raised my eyes. Not to his eyes, but rather to the line of his jaw. As girls we were taught this was the appropriate place to look at an interested man when speaking with him. The eyes were much too personal. As my husband, Andrew was an interested man.

"I am your husband." His tone was gentle.

I shifted my eyes to his. They were light brown, flecks of darker brown patterned throughout. I lowered my gaze again, unnerved by the extended eye contact.

"I had hoped that after five months you would feel more comfortable with me," he said.

I felt a stab of guilt. I had been a horrible wife. "I'm sorry."

"You don't have to apologize. You're safe here with me. I care for you."

His words should have warmed my chest, but they made me uneasy. At times I thought it would be easier if he disliked me. That would be something I could deal with. But my failure to return his affection only filled me with more guilt.

"I was worried about you," he continued. "Terrified for you." He cleared his throat and picked up his fork. "I will continue to pray for your brother's swift recovery."

"Thank you."

"Please remember that you can always come to me. I'll never turn my back on you."

"That's kind of you." Far kinder than I deserved.

Those were the last words spoken at the dinner table.

That night I joined Andrew in his bed as expected. But he knew I was in shame, and he made no attempt to touch me. Even in that he was being the best husband he knew to be.

Or maybe his apparent disinterest in me was the result of his cramping gut and repeated visits to the toilet. Either way, I had to find a way to feel differently about him. One day I would be carrying his child.

Rose stood in the basement underneath Haven Valley's Chapel, drawing deep breaths of anticipation. Soon. Any moment now.

As the daughter of a conservative minister, she'd grown up in churches with basements and sanctuaries similar to this one. Her experience with the church had turned ugly when a brutal man, sick with power, stole her innocence and replaced it with terror.

That man was her father, though he made his children call him Pastor. Unlike other clergy who were kind and gentle, her father was a beast who only taught about the dangers of sin and the hell that awaited those unwilling to repent from their wickedness. Naturally, he expected perfection from his children.

Rose was no stranger to the wrath and punishment of God. It had been pumped into her brain from the moment she'd been born. Both she and her older sister, Lily, worked their fingers to the bone trying to obtain the perfection required to live in the

Pastor's home. Their silent and weak mother, Ethel, another subject of the Pastor's wrath, stood by and watched as he constantly ridiculed his daughters for their weaknesses.

The punishments for broken rules were severe. He used to say, "This hurts me more than it hurts you." A mockery of sorts, it amplified the pain, as if Pastor were suffering as he dealt out wrath according to the laws of raising a child in perfect righteousness.

The only relief Rose found was in Lily. They secretly whispered to each other of the day when they would escape the house to see the world in all of its wonder.

But they never escaped together, because Lily had become sick with pneumonia and died.

Actually, it wasn't the pneumonia that had killed Lily; it was the vile threats of Pastor, who demanded she repent of whatever sin had caused the illness. He wasn't about to be seen as a leader whose own children failed to attain the holiness required of them.

Or maybe it was the pneumonia, but Rose blamed her father for robbing Lily of the will to fight the disease.

Rose was sixteen, and the only light in her

dark world had been extinguished. She'd tried to kill herself with a rusty nail that night.

Sylous had come to her for the first time then. Whispered to her about how he could protect her, save her, and set her on a different path. A chosen path on which she would be safe from all the cruel people who lived in sin.

All she had to do was agree. Would she?

She had. And as his first show of power, Sylous had killed her father in his home office as Rose looked on. He showed Pastor monsters terrifying enough to send him into cardiac arrest.

It was the first time Rose had seen a Fury — the true wrath of God, not the manipulated version Pastor used to justify his violence.

Her mother mourned the loss of her husband, oblivious to how the heart attack had occurred. Despite her compassion for her mother, Rose couldn't stomach another day in the house with a woman who still treasured the monster she'd married. So she left with Sylous.

In the wake of such oppression, living homeless proved to be a blessing. For several years Sylous guided her as she blossomed into a young woman with strong character and beauty that turned heads. Sylous appeared and vanished at will, but whenever she needed him, he was there.

She was twenty-three and single, still living on the streets in San Francisco, when Sylous first promised her true sight and a community that would follow her. They would find a place in the hills of Tennessee, hidden away for them alone. A terrible tribulation was coming to the world, he'd said, but he would protect them from that Fury if they followed him.

Rose smiled as she recounted the events that had delivered them to Haven Valley. She'd moved to a small town in Tennessee, married Harrison at Sylous's instruction, and begun the process of assembling the faithful. Ten years later, Sylous had shown them all the Fury.

Three years following that day of true sight, they'd moved to this valley so far off the beaten tracks that even if the world hadn't succumbed to the Fury, no one would pay them any mind.

She scanned the basement, eager for his presence. It was a small square room — wall-to-wall brick with exposed pipes and cement for a floor, several storage rooms, and a root cellar, all off-limits to the others.

A single staircase led up to the narrow hall

that ran behind the main sanctuary and ended in the only office in the building. The whole Chapel was quite small. The sanctuary, one short hall, one little office, and the basement.

It was the perfect place for them to meet. He would, if needed, come to wherever Rose was, but he called her here.

She felt Sylous the moment he entered the room, like an electric charge that drew every hair on her skin. One moment she was standing in cool, damp air, the next she was enveloped by a force much greater than herself.

In that moment Sylous was all she felt. Then she was herself again, rooted to a lesser reality, awash in his presence.

"I can feel your worry from here," Sylous said.

She turned to face him as he stepped into the light of the single shaded bulb that hung from the ceiling.

"Should I not be worried?" she asked.

"Have you lost your faith in me?"

"No, of course not. Never."

"Then try not to worry so much. It will age you, darling."

Rose took a deep breath and tried to settle her nerves. "Maybe we should shut these two out of the community. They've disrupted everything."

He offered her a kind smile. "All were chosen for a reason."

"They shouldn't be allowed the glory of reclaiming the earth, not after their sins against us."

"They will stay."

"Even if they place all we've built at risk?"

"Are two so dangerous? You're assuming they don't play a role in delivering you to the glory you wait for. All things work together for good, at least for those in the narrow way."

"They doubt that narrow way," Rose snapped. She knew she'd spoken too harshly the moment the words had left her mouth. "Forgive me, I misspoke."

"The truth of how you feel is written inside your heart. I can see it clearly," Sylous said tenderly. "There's no need to raise your voice."

"I'm . . ." She was exposed before him, as always. Naked. It was she who doubted as much as Jamie had. Not doubted the Fury, but that they would survive the Fury.

Sylous moved closer, holding her gaze. "They've handed you the opportunity to reignite faith."

"They make others uncomfortable."

"Good. Perhaps some have become a little

too comfortable in this safe haven. It needed a good shaking. You might even say it was by design."

"You knew the boy was sneaking beyond the perimeter?"

Sylous said nothing, which was answer enough. How could she have doubted after so many years under his guidance?

"I wish you would tell me these things," Rose said. His enigmatic way sometimes bruised her heart and cracked her ego. Why didn't he trust her?

"I've offended you," he said.

Rose swallowed and dropped her eyes to his feet. She watched his shoes cross the distance between them, stopping only a foot from her. She felt his warm fingers brush her chin, and she closed her eyes as the touch sparked new life inside her chest.

"I never intended to hurt your feelings, my love," Sylous said as he drew his fingers along her cheek and back behind her ear. Rose inhaled desire as he traced the outline of her face. Her heart beat out of rhythm. Her skin tingled. Awe of Sylous had quickly turned to love long ago. He was her truest companion, the one she dreamed of and longed for.

Next to God, Sylous had become her everything.

"Everything I do is for you and this safe haven you've built for me," Sylous said. "Do you doubt that?"

"No," she whispered.

"Have I not always come to you in your time of need?"

"Yes."

"Did I not provide you with enough power to change the world?"

"Yes."

"Did I not commit myself to your protection?"

"Yes."

"Have I not always been faithful to you?"

"Yes."

"And yet you still doubt me. What you don't fully understand is that I need you as much as you need me. I live to see you safe. Your destruction is my destruction. I have given myself over to your salvation."

Rose looked up, taken aback by his confession. She reached up and wrapped her fingers around his where they lay on her neck. "You have?"

"Yes. Nothing matters except your safety. I could see the Holy Family's faith waning after so many years, and I saw an opportunity to reaffirm their certainty of the terror beyond these protective borders. Even the most faithful need to be reminded of what's at stake."

"Jamie said he went beyond the perimeter many times without encountering the Fury at all. How is that possible?"

"He did encounter them. Just not when expected. The Fury are far more clever than you might guess."

She hesitated, daring to ask what had been bothering her all day, though he undoubtedly already knew. "Is it possible the Fury have already penetrated the perimeter?"

He studied her as if trying to decide how much to tell her. She knew from previous discussions that he couldn't control the Fury beyond the valley, but he surely knew the situation within their perimeter.

"Obey the law and you will be safe," he said.

Why no direct answer? Was he withholding something?

His brow arched. "If I told you all I know, you would melt with fear," he said. "Trust me."

"Then it's possible that the wolf in sheep's clothing is already among us?" she pressed.

"It's always been possible. Like I said, they are clever."

His words did nothing to calm her fear.

"How will we know?"

"Evil cannot remain hidden for long. It

will be plain to me if not to you."

Sylous slowly lowered his hand from her face and she felt his power withdraw. She longed for him to touch her longer, be with her longer, stay with her always.

"And now Haven Valley needs to become more vigilant than ever," he said.

Nothing was clearer to her now than this. They could not waver.

She looked into his eyes. "Jamie speaks of something imminent. Something coming."

"He lived to tell a tale, so let him tell it," Sylous said.

He bent forward and gently placed a kiss on her forehead. She closed her eyes, feeling the warmth of his lips wash over her head and shoulders.

"You are so beautiful to me," he said.

Rose knew he was gone without needing to open her eyes. The familiar song of the sacred communication they shared whispered through her as she stood alone.

Fear me alone, and I will always protect you from evil.

I will never stop fearing you.

Need my truth alone, and I will always watch over you.

I will never stop needing you.

Listen to me, and I will always guide you.

I will listen.

Rose opened her eyes and stared at the empty basement, filled with new resolve. The end was near. So very near.

Rose opened her eyes and stared at the
empty basement, filled with new resolve.
I'd end now, but I'd go very soon.

CHAPTER THIRTEEN

My stomach was in knots as I knocked on the front door of the Pierce home the next day. I watched over the three young Pierce children four days each week, a privilege for which I had always been deeply grateful. Rose had relieved me of my duties yesterday but said nothing more than that. So I'd come, hoping I wasn't overstepping. But what if I was wrong?

The door opened and little Stephen's small, sweet face stared up at me. Their youngest son was just five years of age, with lighter skin tones and reddish hair. The tiny boy embodied joy itself.

I smiled as he gave me a little wave. "Hi, Stephen."

"Hi, Grace!"

Rose entered the hallway behind him. "Stephen, what are you doing?"

"Grace is here."

Rose pulled her son back and stepped in

front of him. She eyed me for a moment and opened the door wider for me to enter. Then she turned back to Stephen, dropped to his level, and spoke firmly. "You know the rules about opening the front door. Only an adult can answer when someone knocks. Are you an adult?"

"No, I'm a boy," Stephen answered proudly, as if he'd solved a riddle.

"It's dangerous," Rose continued. "You never know who will be on the other side. Okay? Do you understand?"

Having heard Rose issue similar warnings to her children in the past, I'd always wondered how anyone in Haven Valley could be dangerous. Now I knew.

Anyone, Bobbie had said.

Little Stephen nodded and waited patiently to be released. Rose sighed and nodded for him to go, and he rushed back down the hallway.

"No running!" Rose shouted after him. "You'll trip and fall."

I stepped into the house and shut the door slowly behind me. Rose stood and, without looking at me, headed to the kitchen. Her coldness was unpleasant, but I followed quickly.

The Pierce twins, Evelyn and Levi, sat at the dining table. The ten-year-olds both had light brown hair and light brown eyes, unlike their mother. Both had finished breakfast and were working through their required daily reading, a curriculum designed for the young children growing up in Haven Valley.

Evelyn sat on the right, her shoulders pulled back, eyes on the book. She paid me no mind. Even she was shunning me.

Levi sat on the left, book propped on the table, chin resting in his hand, legs swinging back and forth gently. The moment he saw me, his face brightened. "Hi, Grace. Can I show you how my airplane model is coming?"

"You haven't finished your reading," his sister snapped without removing her eyes from her book.

"How do you know if you can't read my mind?" Levi said.

"Have you finished your reading?" Rose asked from where she stood at the sink.

Levi hesitated. "Almost."

A small, satisfied grin pulled at the corner of Evelyn's mouth.

A knock sounded at the front door and Rose glanced at me for the first time. "Can you get that?"

I nodded and returned to the door. It was Megan Rifle, a quirky girl with hair nearly orange as a carrot.

"Hi, Megan. Is everything alright?"

"I was called for."

I eyed her curiously and opened the door so she could step inside.

She offered me a forced smile. "Thank you."

Rose looked up at us as we entered the kitchen. "Ah, Megan, so happy to see you."

"You too, Mrs. Pierce," Megan said.

"You're in my home, Megan. You can call me Rose." She turned to me. "Megan will be joining you today as you watch the children."

Megan might not have known it herself, but I understood immediately she was actually there to watch me. I reminded myself that this was an outcome of my own making. How could I blame Rose for not trusting me with her children now? Or ever again, for that matter.

"We are diligent in our home, so please pay attention," Rose said to Megan, reaching for a leather-bound book in the cabinet. I could see uncertainty spark in the girl's eyes. The book contained a long list of rules that Rose would expect her to memorize immediately. I only half listened as Rose read through each rule and gave detailed examples.

Rules about what they could eat, what they could drink: Particular snacks would be prepared for the children. The water must be boiled for purity and then cooled in the fridge. They weren't allowed anything outside the home that wasn't approved.

Rules about the weather: There were approved times of day, depending on the strength of the sun, when the children could be outside as long as specified amounts of sunscreen were used. If it looked like it might rain, the children were to stay inside until any chance of a storm passed. In the event of rain, the children could not be taken outside until the ground dried.

Rules about activities: Approved playtime activities were listed, but they could only play after all required reading and chores had been completed. Running, roughhousing, teasing, tickling, screaming, and too much pretend play were not encouraged, either inside or outside the house.

Rules about how they should appear, rules about how they should speak, rules about how they should interact with others, rules about their daily schedules. On and on, the leather book revealed the rules I knew too well. Rules I'd made sure to enforce, rules I myself considered instilling in my own children in order to provide the safest care possible. Rose loved her children fiercely and showed that love by making sure they were always protected from anything that might harm them.

That potential for harm now included me.

Nausea rolled inside my gut, not the kind spawned by nerves but by illness. I hoped I wasn't catching whatever afflicted Andrew.

"I understand it's a lot of information," Rose said, "so if you have any questions, ask Grace." She offered Megan a perfunctory smile. "Are we clear?"

Megan clearly had many questions, but she nodded. "Ask Grace."

"If you must." Rose faced her three children, all now seated around their kitchen table. "Walk your mother to the door, will you?"

Megan and I remained in the kitchen, avoiding eye contact as the children obliged their mother. Their tones were hushed, but it wasn't a very big house and I could hear every word clear as day.

"Are you sure you have to leave us?" Evelyn asked.

"Yes, sweetheart, you'll be fine."

"But she broke the law. I don't feel safe with her."

"Then stay close to Megan, sweetie. That's why she's here."

161

"Can Grace give me her sin?" little Stephen asked.

"No. Sin is a choice you make. Just follow the rules and you'll be safe."

A moment later I heard the front door close. All three children returned to complete their studies at the kitchen table.

Evelyn refused to look at me.

The afternoon sky was bright blue with large puffy white clouds, the breeze warm and welcoming — the perfect afternoon for a short walk. So I gathered up the Pierce children with Megan's help, packed approved water and food, and set out to walk along the approved paths that led toward the farmland east of town.

Though at first annoyed and hurt to have Megan watching over me, I was now thankful she was near. She really was good with the children, laughing and singing with them, showing interest in their interests, being cautious and following the rules.

I loved the Pierce children as if they were my own. I'd cared for them when they were sick, put them to sleep, made them laugh. I couldn't pretend I wasn't deeply wounded by Evelyn's total disdain for me, but I knew it was my own fault. More than the other children, she was sensitive to anything remotely close to breaking the law. When her siblings broke rules she suffered just as much as they did.

Nausea rolled through my stomach again, and for a passing moment I was sure I'd throw up my lunch. I tried to keep my focus ahead, breathing deeply, letting the fresh air fill my lungs.

The path we traveled behind the main stretch of town was marked clearly. Mowed grass grew along the left side of the path; to the right was a wild field that stretched out to the forest a hundred feet away. Forbidden ground.

Another wave of nausea washed over me, and I knew I wasn't going to be able to hold it back. I placed my hand on Megan's shoulder. "I'm not feeling very well. Let's stop here for a moment. I'm going to run up to the bathroom inside the market, okay?"

"Sure." Megan nodded and announced they would sit along the path for a little while and look for shapes in the clouds. That seemed to appease the kids.

I hurried toward the street and made it around the corner of the brick market building before the nausea overtook me.

Bending at the waist, I threw up on the ground along the building's wall. It burned coming up, making my eyes water and my head pound. Again I heaved, then once more, vomiting up all I'd consumed in the last couple hours. Still bent, both palms on the brick in front of me, I placed my forehead against the wall between my hands and took shallow breaths.

I couldn't remember the last time I'd thrown up or felt so sick. It made me wonder if the Fury had infected Jamie with something and he'd passed it on to me. Or maybe I had caught something sleeping in that cave.

A small cry of alarm reached my ear — one of the children — and I hurried to the corner of the market where I could see Megan and the children. Evelyn was standing in the middle of the path, pointing at Stephen, who had wandered out into the tall uncut grass.

Oh no!

I threw a glance up the street, hoping no one was watching. No one I could see. Megan was rushing out into the tall grass to collect Stephen.

She had scooped up little Stephen and was coming back, face white with fear, by the time I reached them. Evelyn was staring out across the grass, tears gathered in her eyes, small hands trembling.

I knelt beside her. "Evelyn?"

"We aren't allowed off the path," she said. "The grass isn't safe! It's tall and full of dangers."

"He's okay, Evelyn."

"No, no! He isn't allowed."

And if Rose found out there would be consequences. Especially now, after all the trouble Jamie and I had caused.

"It's going to be okay. No one is hurt. We can pretend nothing even happened."

I reached up to touch her shoulder, but she pulled back from me. "That's lying."

And just like that, I'd boxed myself into a corner. But I was desperate to get out.

"I would never lie," I said. "I just meant we can pretend for now. Until we tell your mother."

Megan stepped back onto the path, set Stephen down, and began checking him over, brushing off stray blades of grass. She looked up at me, searching for redemption and guidance. "I thought he was sitting right beside me," she said, voice strained.

"He wanders," I said. "I should've told you."

"We aren't allowed off the path!" Evelyn cried. "There are chiggers in the grass! He's going to get sick and then we'll all get sick."

165

Megan frantically looked Stephen over for bites.

"I got bit by bugs?" Stephen asked, fear mounting in his thin voice. "I don't want to be sick."

"You won't get sick," Megan assured him, but she didn't sound convinced.

"He was bitten!" Evelyn insisted. "He'll get sick and then get us all sick!"

Outbreaks of a rash had visited Haven Valley on a number of occasions, never with any clear explanation. Allergies, some said. Something in the air from the Fury, perhaps. No one seemed to know, but rashes had spread like wildfire and lasted for a few weeks before passing.

Evelyn was mixing up this incident with those outbreaks.

"No, honey, he wasn't bitten," I said, reaching out to touch her again.

"Don't touch me!" she screamed. "This is all your fault!"

I yanked my hand back. Her words were like a slap across my face.

"We have to get him home and bathed now!" Evelyn yelled.

"He wasn't bitten," Megan echoed.

"He has to be stripped and bathed." Evelyn itched her arm as if she'd been bitten herself. "They could be everywhere!"

I nodded at Megan and we quickly steered the three children back toward the Pierce house. We needed to get them home where they would at least feel safe.

Evelyn scratched at her skin the entire way.

CHAPTER FOURTEEN

Ben splashed cool water over his face from
the faucet they'd found in a long-abandoned
gas station, gripping the sink's side for support. It was the kind of bathroom that
required a key from the cashier inside, when
it was in order. This one had no door.

He glanced up into the broken mirror.
Seeing him, no one would be surprised to
hear he was dying. He coughed into his
hand and grimaced at the pain in his chest.
His head was pounding. Blood speckled his
hand when he pulled it away from his
mouth. He placed it under the running
water and watched the red wash down the
sink.

Eli was in the truck waiting. If the boy
saw the blood he might insist they stay the
night somewhere close, or worse, go to a
hospital. They were close now. One more
long push and then he could rest.

The lyrics from "Carry On Wayward Son"

hummed through his brain. He and Eli had heard the song half a dozen times over the last two days, as if it were playing just for them.

Yes, Ben thought, *there will be peace when I'm done. But not yet.*

He scooped water into the palm of his hand, swirled it around in his mouth, and spit it back into the sink. Turned the faucet off. It was a strange thing to know that once he completed this task there was nothing left for him.

His brain filled with images from the past. The time he'd first seen Julianna. Long blonde hair, golden-brown eyes, a world of excitement waiting to be explored in her smile. He'd been spellbound instantly.

Julianna had stolen his heart at a time when he was searching for worth and significance. Both young and uncertain about the world, they'd built their lives around one another. They'd become each other's missing part, an idea the world dressed up in beautifully poetic language. In reality their dependence on each other had become a kind of slavery, bound by a knot.

But that knot failed to deliver the promised bliss. So they'd pressed on, desperate to be saved by each other. When that knot finally unraveled, they were left with threadbare souls.

He'd spent so much time being angry with Julianna for taking the children. And yet now, even after so many years and such distance, his heart skipped a beat when she crossed his mind. He longed to tell her how precious she was.

Eli was reading a newspaper when Ben climbed back into the driver's seat. The boy's bare feet were perched on the dash, ankles crossed, newspaper opened like a book in front of him.

"Where'd you get that?" Ben asked, closing his door.

"At the free news box," Eli said.

Ben glanced out the boy's window to see a dispenser with "Free" and "Take One" plastered across the glass.

"Anything good?" Ben asked.

Eli looked up out the windshield. He scrunched his nose and laughed at something only he was thinking, then returned his eyes to the newspaper. "I think everything is good," he said.

Ben nodded and turned over the engine. The truck roared to life. Before shifting into drive, he reached into the plastic bag of goods he'd found inside and pulled out a round package. He playfully tossed the package into Eli's lap. "Look what I found."

Eli squealed with delight, dropped the paper, and grabbed the gift with both hands. "Powdered donuts!"

"I thought you might like that."

Fl squealed with delight. Dropping the
purse and grabbed the girl and held both
hands "Kansuma! dear."
"I guess someone the rear."

Chapter Fifteen

I walked through the back door of our
home, hoping to escape to my bedroom.
My body was exhausted. Rose's sharp
reprimand still echoed in my mind. Even
after Evelyn was safely home, her panic
continued to escalate. We sent for Rose, and
by the time she arrived Evelyn's forearm
had broken out into a bright red rash.

Stephen, who'd gone into the grass, was
fine. Not a mark on him.

The look of anger in Evelyn's teary eyes
as I left the Pierce home haunted me. I was
scheduled to care for the children in two
days, but I wasn't sure Rose would allow it.

I could hear my mother's soft voice in the
kitchen. She was talking to someone? I
stooped to remove my shoes, wiped them
clean, and hurried down the hall.

Jamie was sitting at the kitchen table,
listening to my mother as she cooked dinner. My surprise melted to joy, and I flew

across the room to embrace my brother.

He pulled back before I reached him and I remembered my manners. We were back in Haven Valley and he wasn't bleeding to death. I should know better. Regardless, I'd never been happier to see him.

"Jamie!"

"Hello, sister."

His hands were wrapped around the water glass on the table, fingers still bandaged. His face was covered in bruises, mostly purple, but some orange and yellow, which meant they were healing. He wore a simple black shirt, but it didn't fully hide the lumpy bandage strapped around his chest where he'd been gashed. They'd taped another white bandage across his left cheekbone, underneath a swollen eye. He looked as if he'd been dragged through a field by a horse, but he was alive and on the mend.

I sat across from him and tucked my hands into my lap. "I didn't know you were coming home."

"Of course he was coming home," my mother said, placing a large bowl of soup in front of Jamie. She laid her palm on Jamie's healthy cheek and smiled. "Soup?" she asked me.

I nodded, even though I had no appetite and still felt a bit queasy. I studied Jamie as he picked up his spoon and began to eat. He looked different. More than just all the bruising. Something new filled his eyes. An eagerness.

"Is it silly to ask how you're feeling?" I asked.

"Like I've been dragged across a field by a horse," he said, and I laughed.

"You look like it."

He chuckled, then grimaced. "Ouch!"

"Sorry."

Mother set a bowl of soup down in front of me, and I pulled away from the pungent odor. It made my stomach turn. I sat back, hand over my chest.

"Are you alright?" my mother asked.

"Yes, sorry. Just a bout of queasiness."

"Odd." She placed the back of her hand against my forehead and held it there for a long moment. "Are you coming down with something? I can't even remember the last time you were sick."

"I'm just tired."

"You don't have a fever." She returned to the stove and walked back with a bowl for herself. "If you really aren't feeling well you should go to bed early. Tomorrow's a big day."

"It is? Why?"

Mother stole a look at Jamie and beamed

174

with pride. "Your brother's been asked to speak in morning Chapel."

I looked to my brother, stunned. "What for?"

Jamie swallowed a spoonful of soup and set his spoon back in the bowl. Patted his lips with his napkin. For a long second we all just sat there in silence, waiting for him to speak.

Jamie cleared his throat and shifted in his chair, then drilled me with clear eyes. "I understand the truth in a new and terrifying way," he said. "I came face-to-face with evil and survived to tell others how threatening the darkness really is."

"Rose agrees," Mother said. "She spent the afternoon with Jamie."

"Neither of us should have survived," Jamie continued. "We were sent back for a reason." He paused for a moment, holding me with that piercing gaze. "Do you know what your reason is, dear sister?"

I sat stunned, frozen, unable to formulate my next move. His words set my nerves on edge. We'd always been the best of friends, watching over each other, but now he'd accepted a greater purpose and I didn't know where I stood with him. He wasn't shunning me, but he might if I didn't fall in line with him.

He broke off his stare and picked his spoon back up. "I suggest you find some clarity," he said, then took another spoonful of soup.

My mother reached out and set her hand on mine. She gave me a gentle squeeze, smiling. "Maybe you should go to bed, honey. You do look tired."

I took a shallow breath and nodded. She was right. Every inch of my body was drowning in exhaustion.

I reached up to grab my soup bowl, but my mother tapped my wrist. "I'll take care of that, you just go."

"Thank you." I hesitantly turned back to Jamie. "Good night."

" 'Night," he said. His air of grandeur was gone, but his words played back in my mind, clear as day. *I suggest you find some clarity.*

I stood and left the room. A part of me wanted to rush back in, shake Jamie, and demand to be told what he knew that I didn't. But I'd faced enough drama for one day.

I'd finished dressing for bed, drawing my sheets back, and turning the lights down low when a soft knock sounded at my bedroom door. My mother walked in, then closed the door behind her. Her eyes were shining as she walked to my side and sat on my bed. She patted the place beside her and I sat as well.

"Grace, I was thinking just now . . ." She paused, choosing her words carefully. "How long have you been feeling nauseated?"

I thought about it. "Couple days?"

"And you're exhausted, which makes sense considering all you've been through."

"Yes."

"Do your breasts ache at all?"

I knew immediately where she was headed and I clutched my chest, gasping.

"Well?" she pressed.

"Yes, but . . . You . . ." I wasn't sure how to put it. For several seconds we sat there caught up in the wonder of what she was suggesting.

She reached her hand up and lovingly placed it on my face. "Sweetheart, I think you might be pregnant."

Word of Jamie speaking had spread, and all of Haven Valley eagerly waited for what he might say at morning service. The idea of news from beyond the border was both terrifying and intriguing. I could feel their eyes stealing glances at the pew where we sat, Andrew on one side of me, my mother and Jamie on the other.

But half of my mind was on a different matter entirely.

I'd needed to sleep, but hardly had. Every couple hours, dreams stirred me awake. Thoughts of the child that might be growing inside me, of the pleasures and happiness the small life would bring, the adventure that would be uniquely mine. I was a bundle of nerves.

To be honest, I was struggling with some fear as well. How could I be a mother in such turbulent times? What kind of world would my baby grow up in? What if something was wrong with the baby? What if there was darkness in Haven Valley masquerading as light? There was no backing away from Andrew now. I only hoped he was pure and would make a good father.

My mother had stolen into my room as I woke to see how I was feeling. Her joy was contagious. The way her eyes sparkled when she looked at me, the way she gingerly touched my shoulder and held my hand. It was a different type of love than I'd ever felt from her. She'd suggested we see Dr. Charles that morning after Chapel to confirm the pregnancy.

But I already knew. Once the idea had been brought to light, an inner knowing had taken over. I could feel it in my bones. I was pregnant. Andrew was the father and I didn't know what to think about that, but I was going to have a baby! For now it was a secret between my mother and me. I didn't even feel the need to talk to Lukas about it. In fact, now that I was going to have a baby, thoughts of Lukas seemed a little irrelevant.

Lukas was only in my mind. My baby was flesh and blood.

Rose's movement caught the corner of my eye as she and her children walked up the center aisle to their places on the front bench. My gaze followed them as they moved, little Stephen glancing my way and offering a tiny wave, which I returned. Evelyn walked beside him, and there was no hiding the bandages peeking out from the edge of her long sleeves. Her rash must have worsened. That wasn't good. My heart broke for her.

How would I be if my child broke out in a rash? Probably a basket case.

The family sat, and Harrison appeared from the small doorway to the right of the stage. The shifting congregation settled as he stepped up to the podium and spread his arms to open with morning prayer. We joined him, our voices rising as one.

"With true sight and pure hearts, we come before you, God of righteousness, and we commit ourselves to your laws. We ask that you lead us away from sin as we fend off the evil that threatens our holiness. Let the earth be ravaged by your perfect wrath, and let us stand apart, your chosen flock and faithful servants. Amen."

The Chapel fell silent. Rose stood and made her way to stand beside him at the front of the stage. With a nod at him, she turned to face us.

"As you all know, the foundation of our community has been shaken to its core in the last several days. It would be reasonable to assume many of you have questions. I asked that we trust the sensibilities of Jamie Weathers as he wandered out beyond the perimeter. I would ask that you trust his voice now. His survival is not without purpose."

She nodded at Jamie, who stood, stepped into the main aisle and walked to the stage. A curious hush held the people of Haven Valley, but I could almost hear their concerns.

Jamie faced the gathering, face flat, eyes bright. "I have seen the face of darkness released on this world," he began. "It spoke to me, whispering its vile hatred, and told me the worst is yet to come. We've wondered if the Fury have finished their purge of the earth and left it in peace, but I'm here to tell you that they feed on souls still and are more vicious and monstrous than we could have imagined."

Every eye was glued to Jamie. I could see the pain and fear that now filled my brother's eyes, and my pulse quickened.

"We have to be more careful than ever. Darkness masquerading as light seeks to steal our holiness. We have to resist the temptation to look for hope in anything but what Rose has taught us. We must maintain purity and vigilance until the last day."

The crowd stirred as he spoke. Fear spread over them as the idea of what he was suggesting sank in.

"Are you saying we aren't safe inside Haven Valley?" Colin asked, breaking the silence. "I thought we were protected inside the perimeter."

"The perimeter keeps us safe from the Fury as long as we remain true," Jamie said. "As long as we are pure, they're powerless." He hesitated. "But that doesn't mean they aren't among us already, whispering their temptations even as they whispered them to me."

Many gasped.

Rose held up her hand to still the auditorium, and Jamie continued, eyes flashing a

181

certainty I hadn't seen from him. "I'm telling you, the temptations I gave in to are no less damaging than the Fury itself. Evil is evil, however it shows itself. And I can tell you that the great testing that's been foretold is coming as the end draws close. Evil is desperate to own us, and only through submission to the laws that keep it at bay will we survive and receive our inheritance. Watch your heart, watch your neighbor, watch for the demon who appears as an angel."

People murmured questions among themselves, many nodding in agreement. Jamie stood silently, having said what he'd come to say.

Colin stood and spoke above them all. "After you betrayed us once, how can we trust you?"

Jamie took a moment to consider, then nodded once. "Because I yielded to the temptation of doubt. I'm ashamed to admit that I questioned our ways. I longed for a different life. I was given the opportunity to live outside of the law, and it nearly killed me." His eyes roamed the audience. "I should have died out there. But I was spared to deliver a message against doubt. I know now that the rules we follow and the fears that help us see the right path are what guide us. If we stray from the path, we will suffer a greater hell than the hell I encountered."

What about me? I wondered. What were they thinking of me? Why was I spared? What was my purpose in this? I dared not look, but I could practically feel the stares of others on me. Would they forgive me after Jamie's confession?

An image of Bobbie filled my mind. She'd said the worst was to come and that I would need her.

"Be ever vigilant," Jamie continued. "Take every precaution. When you feel fear, know it's your discernment instructing you to run away. Avoid and protect your hearts against anything that might compromise the law."

Without another word, he left the podium and walked down the steps. Whispered concerns filled the auditorium as Harrison took center stage again, urging all to pray and seek only goodness.

Jamie walked back to our pew and sat down beside me. Our eyes met for a moment, and in his I saw a darkness that I could not fathom. My palms were sweaty.

Whatever Jamie had experienced beyond the perimeter had changed him.

It was just me and my bedroom walls as the

light of day faded into night, calling me to rest. But it wasn't just me, I thought as my hand instinctively moved to my stomach. Dr. Charles had confirmed what I had already known in my heart. I would tell Andrew the next time I saw him. The thought gave me butterflies.

Echoes of what Jamie had said hung in the air. An unspoken cloud of caution and suspicion had settled over the entire community. I hoped they would forget my part in Jamie's indiscretions, but I hadn't returned to warn them as he had. If anything, they were even more suspicious of me now. At least that's what I imagined I saw in their eyes as they quickly diverted them from me after morning Chapel.

Maybe I really would need Bobbie. She was an angel, right? She had to be.

Watch your heart, watch your neighbor, watch for the demon who appears as an angel. On repeat, Jamie's words whispered through my mind. I felt their urgency acutely, as I would now have to ward off evil for both myself and my baby.

"I can help you with that."

I spun around and she was there. Bobbie, standing in the same corner she had before, with the same startling beauty and glimmering eyes.

I glanced at the door. Still closed.

"Congratulations," she said, her eyes cutting to my stomach and then back to my face.

She knew. Of course she knew. She heard my thoughts, saw my fears. I was completely vulnerable around her.

Bobbie took a step forward, and for the first time since meeting her, I felt some comfort. She noticed and smiled. "Good. You should get comfortable with me."

"I asked you to leave," I said.

"That was before you knew what you now know."

"You said you wouldn't come back unless I asked for you."

"But you did ask for me. Not with your mouth but with your heart. With everything coming, do you really want to be alone to fight for yourself?"

There it was again. The idea that something was coming. A warning to be on the defense against the invisible force that would crush us all.

"You need me," Bobbie said. "Especially now." Again she dropped her eyes to where my unborn child grew.

I put my hand on my stomach, as if I could somehow protect my baby.

"Sooner or later you'll realize that I'm

here to keep you safe," she said. "Both of you."

"Why?"

"I already told you. You're my only concern." She flashed me a grin. "Don't you feel important?"

I didn't know how to answer that.

Bobbie spread her arms wide. "Think about it, Grace. You were chosen, set apart. Maybe not in the same way you think, but definitely chosen. Now you carry a child who longs to be born in light and beauty." She lowered her arms. "For all you know, that child will change the world."

I said nothing, but her words filled me with new hope.

"Invite me to stay, Grace. Claim me, and I will stand by your side in the face of what's coming," she said.

Watch your heart, watch your neighbor, watch for the demon who appears as an angel.

"Which is why you need me," Bobbie said. "I can help you, but you have to let me."

"So I should invite you to stay."

"Yes."

"Claim you."

"Yes."

"You'll protect me."

"And your baby," Bobbie said, walking

186

toward me. "Let me help you. Let me ensure the safety of your child."

My pulse surged with a deep knowing that what she said was true. And with that knowing, I began to awaken to a new purpose. Jamie had found his, and there in my room I found mine.

I was in Haven Valley to bring a beautiful new baby into a beautiful new world. And Bobbie was my guide. Suddenly I wanted nothing more than to have her by my side. I decided right then and there that Bobbie had to be an angel.

"Then I invite you to stay."

My angel's eyes grew bright. "Now you're talking."

Chapter Sixteen

Ben pulled the truck to a stop and placed it in park. The engine died and he sat for a long moment, listening to the machine ticking as it cooled. All the time spent searching, sitting behind this wheel, working through his demons to finally end up at this small town, this tiny hidden corner of the world.

Haven Valley.

The road in had been overgrown and riddled with potholes — anything other than a four-wheel-drive truck wouldn't have stood a chance. But they'd made it. At least to within a hundred yards.

He felt all his emotions at once. Terror, joy, desperation, guilt, love. All the emotions that had been with him along the journey here. He was trying to release his expectations of what might happen when he entered the town, but it was proving difficult.

A small hand reached for his, and he turned to see Eli looking at him proudly. "We made it," Eli said.

"Yes, we made it," Ben replied.

As if to object, his body shivered and he hacked into his hand. The world spun and he closed his eyes to regain composure. He took several breaths, deep as he could, though each draw brought pain.

"You going to drive up?"

"I think we'll walk from here."

"Walk? It's a long way."

"A car might seem more threatening. We'll walk."

"Okay."

Eli shifted to climb from the truck.

Yes, Ben thought, *we'll walk.* He stepped out and made his way to the front of the truck where Eli was standing, staring at the compound nestled in the depression of the earth.

Dated buildings, constructed close together, stood on either side of a single paved road that went nowhere beyond what appeared to be a perimeter of sorts, marked by a thick red rope. Gardens and fields to the east swayed in a gentle afternoon breeze. Some livestock grazed — a few cows and goats. Chicken coops stood nearby. All that was required to support a small community.

It looked peaceful. Inviting even.

A collection of matching houses occupied the far south side of the town; a small white church with a tall cross steeple stood north, on a small mound that couldn't really be classified as a hill.

They'd built a wooden gate on the west side. Symbolic, by the looks of it. The rest of the town was open to the surrounding land, partitioned off by the red-roped perimeter.

Hacking coughs shook his body again. Ben buckled under their intensity, chest aching. Gaining control, he straightened, spit blood to the side, wiped his mouth with the back of his hand, and forced a deep breath.

A hand touched his arm and he turned to see Eli's comforting gaze. "We can rest here," the boy said.

He returned Eli's smile and ruffled the boy's hair. "I made it this far. I'm not about to give up now."

Eli smiled.

"Ready?" Ben asked.

"Ready."

Ben pointed to the south. "We go in there where we won't be seen. Sound good?"

"Sure." The boy started forward.

Ben followed, taken aback by how weak

he'd become. For a moment, he wondered if not driving up to the gate had been a mistake. What if he was too weak?

Images of guards taking shots at an approaching truck washed away that concern. It was safer for the boy this way.

They stopped twice before reaching the southern perimeter, both times so Ben could kneel and rest. He suppressed his coughs as much as possible, hoping they didn't carry into town. But he was beyond even that now. His only purpose was to reach his family while he still could.

They crossed the red rope and stepped into Haven Valley without so much as a lark announcing their arrival. So far so good. But they couldn't go unnoticed for long.

The first to see them was a young boy, maybe twelve, just as they stepped past the last of the homes and headed for the main street. The boy stared at them for a long time, then spun around and fled without a word.

To announce the news, no doubt. There were strangers in town.

"You good?" Ben asked Eli.

Eli stared ahead, apparently curious but unconcerned. Ben let him be.

Like mice emerging from their holes, people began to appear. Women in white, hair short; men in brown, hair mostly long. All walked carefully or stood rigid. All had their eyes on him and Eli. All looked like they were watching two ghosts walking through their town in broad daylight.

For all Ben knew, they were the first strangers to set foot in the town in a decade.

None of this mattered to him. His eyes were for one of three people. Julianna, Jamie, or Grace.

A wave of nausea overtook him and he bent over, hacking into his fist. Eli stood beside him, studying the people. People who now knew that the one who'd violated their perimeter was ill.

He spat blood in the dirt, ran his sleeve over his mouth, and slowly straightened. Many were backing away, eyes wide. Others were appearing around buildings, curious.

Ben was about to take another step when he saw a young woman staring at him in disbelief, no more than twenty paces away. The world around him stilled. It had been ten years, but he knew her face — beautiful and grown, her eyes bluer than he remembered.

Tears blurred his vision. The name he'd given her described her perfectly. Grace.

CHAPTER SEVENTEEN

One of my duties as Andrew's wife was to stock his pantry and refrigerator once every week, usually on Wednesday afternoons when I was mostly free. I was walking to his home the back way to see what was needed, doing my best to avoid drawing any attention, when I noticed Clair, Colin's wife, hurrying toward the town center, clutching her long dress so she could move quickly.

Strange, I thought. *It isn't like her. She's baring her stockings!*

Then I noticed others heading the same direction and I knew something was happening. Too curious to mind my own business, I hurried around the Martins' house and saw what they were seeing: a man and a boy walking along the main street toward the town center.

Strangers.

I nearly turned and ran, but the sight of the boy, so young and innocent, stopped me. Without knowing why, I found myself walking toward them.

The man suddenly doubled over and began to cough, which concerned me. Others were pulling back, but I was pressing forward. The boy's eyes were on me now, blue eyes that drew me.

"Where are you going?"

I twisted to see Bobbie standing to my right. My heart leaped. It was the first time she'd shown herself in public.

"No one can see me. Where do you think you're going?"

"Who are they?" I asked.

"Strangers," said Lucy, who stood a few paces from me. She'd heard my question to Bobbie.

"No need to use your voice in public, Grace. I can hear your thoughts. It doesn't matter who they are, only that *you* don't know who they are. It's not safe. This is the kind of thing that will get you in trouble."

You don't know who they are? I thought.

She looked in their direction and frowned. "No, but that's not the point. Your only concern is keeping your baby safe."

I looked back at the visitors and saw the man was straightening. Then looking at me with kind eyes.

For a moment, he held my gaze as I took

in his face. Something about it pulled at my curiosity. A distant memory, something I might have known once and had long forgotten. But it captured me. And then the old memory sharpened, and recognition surged through my mind.

"You know him?" Bobbie asked.

The round shape of his face, soft jawline and light brown eyes. The same shaggy hair. Wide shoulders, tall and thin, like Jamie. The man before me hadn't always been a stranger.

Ben. My father.

But I didn't really know my father because he'd abandoned us when I was young. What I did know of him was from my mother, who resented him for his drinking and faithlessness. I was a little surprised I even recognized him.

Still, I did. And I had no idea what to think, much less feel. This was the monster whose name my mother forbade us from speaking in her house. I'd always assumed he was dead, taken by the Fury along with everyone else.

His eyes grew wide and filled with tears, and I knew that he recognized me. After thirteen years he still knew my face. It was a simple thought, and it filled my heart with confusion. Should I like that he seemed to care about me? Part of me wanted to, especially now.

The other part of me was angry at myself for wanting to like him.

Then he was rushing toward me, leaving the boy to stand alone. His eyes were filled with only joy and love, palpable enough to reach out and touch me.

I stood still, lost in confusion and anxiety. What was I supposed to do?

Casting a glance to my right, I saw that Bobbie was gone. Which meant what?

When I faced my father again, he was only a few paces away, wheezing and dropping to one knee, wide eyes on me, beaming with pride.

"Grace," he said. His voice was warm and full. "Honey, it's me."

I didn't know how to respond. The others were looking at me, connecting me with the stranger who'd come into town.

He pushed himself up and stepped forward, still wheezing. A part of me wanted to back away if only to avoid his disease, but my legs wouldn't move.

He reached into his jeans pocket and pulled out a short braided band. Yellow, purple, and green, knotted at either end of the braid with extra strings dangling.

"Do you remember this?" he asked.

The memory of making it washed through my mind.

"Do you remember?" he asked again.

"It's the bracelet I made," I said.

"You made two, actually," he replied. "One for me and one for you. They matched. I always carry this one with me."

Strange, conflicting emotions crowded my throat.

He held the colorful band out to me. "I want you to have this one. Something to remember me by." More tears slid down his cheeks.

I said the only thing that came to mind. "You're leaving?"

The reality of our situation in Haven Valley suddenly broke through my confusion. Of course he was leaving. Rose would never permit him to stay.

"I don't have long," he said. "I had to see you and your brother." A beat passed. "How is your mother?"

I inched back, unsure how I could have blindly exposed myself the way I just did. Jamie's words softly echoed in my ears.

Watch your heart, watch your neighbor, watch for the demon who appears as an angel.

I glanced at the small clusters of people looking at us. He was an outsider, invading our way of life. In the wake of Jamie's warnings, word would travel to Rose quickly. It wasn't safe for me to be here.

"You shouldn't be here," I said, shifting farther back.

He nodded, undisturbed. "It's okay, Grace. It's okay that you're afraid. But you don't have to fear me. And mostly you don't have to fear Eli."

Eli? My father was looking back at the boy who had started walking toward us.

"He's your brother," my father said. "No harm must come to him. I beg you, keep him safe."

Brother? Lukas? He had the same hair and eyes and looked about the same age. But that was impossible. Another brother, then. The sight of him transfixed me. Such a beautiful boy!

My father began to cough again, jarring me back to the present. Several deep, crackling hacks spawned a few more. He buckled at the waist, his shoulders shaking with each blow. Then he dropped to one knee.

The boy reached us and knelt beside my father, hand on his shoulder, face filled with concern. But he said nothing.

Another deep hack and my father sat hard, propping himself up with one arm as he coughed up blood. Murmurs ran through the onlookers at the sight, but I stood my ground, locked in indecision. Was I supposed to help him? Turn my back on him?

He'd abandoned me, but I couldn't turn away from him.

"I have so much I want to say before . . . ." he rasped, but then a terrible wheezing cut his words short. And I could see the truth in his eyes.

He was dying, and he knew it.

"Hey," someone shouted from behind us.

I turned to see three guardians headed our direction. Their eyes were fixed on my father, faces stricken with fear and confusion. "This is a private community! You're trespassing."

When I turned back to my father, he was looking up at me. Reaching up, he took my hand, and for a moment the world around us faded.

"My sweetest daughter," he whispered, "in whom I see no fault, know the depths of love. A love that knows no fear. A love that formed you and named you and gave you to me. A blessing beyond my understanding."

His fingers trembled. "Eli is the gift I bring you. Hear him. Keep him safe. He knows the way out of this great deception."

He drew my hand to his face and kissed my knuckles. "I love you," he said.

And then the guardians were on us. Tanner, Morton, and Claude, who was leading them. Claude yanked my father away from me. The moment my father's touch was gone, the momentary warmth I'd allowed myself to feel was gone as well, replaced by the fear of what would happen to him now.

"Where did you come from?" Claude barked at my father. "What are you doing here?"

Before my father could answer, he fell into another wave of vicious coughing, so heavy that all three guardians stepped back. They exchanged worried looks as my father collapsed. Blood dripped from the corner of his mouth. He couldn't seem to get a breath.

"He needs help," I said, ignoring the voices in my head that warned me to stay out of it. "Please, he needs the doctor."

But Claude had stepped back, put off by whatever disease had ravaged my father, and he showed no sign that he'd even heard me.

I made a move toward my father, but Claude stepped up and held out his arm, face red. "What do you think you're doing? He could be contagious!"

"He's my father."

"Your father?"

"He needs a doctor."

After a moment of hesitation, Claude told Morton to find Dr. Charles.

My father lay on his side, wheezing heavily. I watched as his eyes rolled back into his skull. Then he went still. Either dead or unconscious.

I stood trembling, torn by impossible conflict.

"Move," a voice boomed. I twisted to see Dr. Charles rushing forward, followed by his wife and nurse, Sherrie, and two more guardians, Marshall and Ralph. They hadn't been far. Half the town seemed to have gathered.

I backed away to give them space, praying my father would live.

"We need to get him back to my clinic now." Dr. Charles motioned for help from the guardians.

"He's not contagious?" Tanner asked.

"Just don't touch his blood. Hurry!"

The guardians quickly lifted my father off the ground, one on each leg and one on each arm. He hung like a sack between them as they hurried his body toward the clinic.

Claude jabbed a finger in my face. "You stay here." He turned to Marshall, who'd remained by his side. "Take the boy to Harrison and bring them up to speed."

The boy!

I glanced back over my shoulder. The blue-eyed boy stood a few feet away, tears trailing down his cheeks. *Eli is the gift I bring you. Hear him. Keep him safe. He knows the way.*

Marshall grabbed the boy's arm and led him away.

A terrible urge to protect the child surged through me, but I knew there was nothing I could do for him in my position. I watched as he was escorted off. Nausea swelled in my stomach and I swallowed to keep it at bay.

My thoughts turned to the life growing inside me. The life I had just endangered by interacting with my father. How many laws had I broken because I allowed myself to be swept up in my father's drama?

Be careful, Grace, Bobbie's familiar voice warned. An echo in my mind alone. And then she was there, standing across the street, hidden in shadow, invisible to others because she was there only for me. To protect me, I thought. Against things coming. My father had come and brought the boy, Eli.

Protect your heart.

Even from the boy?

From everything.

Yes, I thought, *protect my heart from everything.*

CHAPTER EIGHTEEN

"The patient fell into a coma several minutes after we began to administer care," Dr. Charles said. "His vitals are stable, but there's no telling when or if he'll wake."

I looked through the glass window that separated the clinic's waiting room from one of three patient care rooms. My father lay alone and motionless on the white bed inside. Several monitors stood around him, reporting his steady vitals.

My mother stood beside me. She was still in shock over seeing her husband for the first time after so many years. Her eyes were glazed, her body rigid. I was a little surprised she'd rushed to the clinic after hearing he'd come. Maybe he hadn't been as bad a man as she'd insisted.

Jamie lingered in the far corner of the waiting room, arms crossed, eyes pointed downward. He hadn't said anything since arriving and had hardly looked at our father.

I could only imagine the internal war taking shape in his mind. If Rose and Harrison hadn't been in the room I may have asked him about it.

"Do we know where he came from?" Harrison asked, staring through the glass.

"We found his truck beyond the western border, recovered it and moved it to a secure spot inside the perimeter," Claude answered. The first guardian on the scene, Claude was normally gentle and as loyal as they came. But when threats loomed, he knew his role. "The truck was clean. Mostly camping supplies and what you might expect from a long trip. Probably on the road for a while."

"And the boy?"

"He's under guard in my office," Rose said. "Refuses to talk. Evidently, the only one to speak with either of them was Grace." She cast me a suspicious glance.

"I didn't speak with the boy," I said. "Only with my father."

"I would hardly say he is our father," Jamie said from the corner. The room stilled for a long moment.

Rose broke the silence. "What did Ben say to you, Grace?"

Eli is the gift I bring you. Hear him. Keep him safe. He knows the way.

Should I tell them? If I did, Rose would immediately see the boy as a threat. I couldn't bear the thought of putting him in greater danger. I had to find out more. Evil would or had come to Haven Valley, but I didn't yet know who was good and who was evil masquerading as good.

Then again, who was I to declare any such thing?

"Why did he come here?" Rose asked impatiently.

"I don't know why he came."

"You must know something. People saw the two of you interacting before he collapsed."

I searched through my muddled mind and pulled his words from the corners. "He said it was okay to be afraid. Something about a great deception."

I saw Jamie shift. He pushed himself off the wall and stepped forward. "He said that?"

"And that the boy is our brother."

Jamie's eyes flashed curiously, then darkened. "This is precisely the kind of trickery a monster would use. It's obvious. He's dangerous. So is the boy."

"He didn't seem dangerous," I said.

"Then you're blind. He's a stranger among us, for heaven's sake. Isn't this exactly what Rose foretold?"

"The same could be said of any of us," I dared to say. "What if the boy is our brother?"

Jamie considered this for a moment, but the cold expression on his face didn't change. "I want nothing to do with either of them. They should both be thrown out."

Rose and Harrison exchanged a knowing look, and the room fell quiet again. My mother still said nothing as she continued to stare at her husband.

Rose wasn't done with me yet. "Please, Grace. Try to remember. Did Ben say anything else? Anything at all?"

What if Jamie was right? What if Eli was the wolf in sheep's clothing? What if Ben had been infected by the Fury and sent to deceive us all? But I just couldn't bring myself to condemn the boy. He reminded me too much of Lukas. And of what my own child might one day be.

"No," I said. "I only spoke with him for a moment."

Rose didn't seem convinced, and I suddenly wanted to be anywhere but here. I felt sick.

"I'm sorry," I said. "I'm not feeling well."

Rose reached out to steady me. Her expression softened. "It's alright," she said.

"Maybe you should sit."

She gave my arm a tender squeeze, and I was certain she knew I was pregnant. My mother must have told her. Which made sense, because no one cared as much as Rose did about creating new, pure life and raising up a generation of faithful. Protecting the children was her sacred calling.

I took a deep breath and let it out slowly. "I'm okay."

The door opened and Andrew was escorted inside. He found me and walked to my side. "You're okay?"

"I'm fine."

"She's healthy," Rose said. "And so is the baby."

And just like that, she'd stolen my thunder.

"I thought he should know immediately," Rose said. "This makes two pregnancies this week. Alice is also with child."

Just as she'd hoped. I moved my gaze back to Andrew, who was staring at me as if unsure what to think.

"You . . ." He glanced at Rose. "She's with child?"

"Ask her."

To me: "You're pregnant?"

"Yes."

His upper lip quivered. "Praise God," he

breathed. He put a hand on my shoulder. "Praise God."

It was too much for me. I no longer knew who I should give my loyalty to. Rose, yes, but what about the boy? Andrew, yes, but would I really have to move in with him now? My father, but he'd abandoned us and was an outcast. Jamie, but he was bitter. Bobbie, but Bobbie was warning me about everybody.

In that moment, I identified more with my mother than with anyone else in the room.

Rose placed her hand on my other shoulder. "You can move your things to his house next week. We're all very happy for you, Grace." And then, maybe sensing my apprehension, "Do you and Andrew need a moment?"

"No," I answered quickly. Maybe too quickly. I cleared my throat. "We can discuss it later."

I looked back at my father, unmoving inside the care room. Silence settled over us.

"The boy is key here," Rose said after a few seconds. "He must know something."

My mother spoke for the first time, voice frail. "Let me care for the child in my home. He's only here because of me and my children. And if he is Ben's son . . ." Her voice faded as she considered her own statement. She looked over at Rose. "I'll shoulder the burden of caring for him until we know more." She paused, and I watched the right side of her mouth turn up slightly. "He favors Ben, don't you think?" she asked no one in particular.

"You saw him?" I asked.

"Only for a moment. He looks like Ben looked in old childhood photographs."

"The boy will be placed in custody," Rose said matter-of-factly. "Don't you understand, Julianna? Jamie has spoken the truth. Evil is among us. Please don't let sentimentality compromise your better judgment."

My mother quickly returned her eyes to Ben. "Of course."

She would never argue with Rose, but she couldn't hide her disappointment and I couldn't fault her. If the boy was Ben's son, then he was our family.

When I looked back at my father, Bobbie was standing by his bed, arms crossed, looking at me through the glass. I gasped.

"What is it?" Rose asked.

None of them could see Bobbie, but they'd clearly heard me. I went with my gut. "I just remembered something else my father said."

"And?"

"Eli." I faced Rose. "The boy's name is Eli."

She searched my eyes. "Does that mean anything to you?"

"No. Should it?"

Rose held my gaze for another moment, then turned for the door and left without saying another word.

"Do you trust them, Grace?" Bobbie's voice reached me through the glass.

I jerked my head to stare at her. Blinked. Should I?

"You should trust no one."

And then she vanished.

Rose hurried to the chapel, desperate for counsel. Her children were still in school and the town was distracted by the strangers who'd appeared out of nowhere.

She remembered Ben well. He'd questioned their faith at every opportunity and tried to convince his wife to leave their church, to abandon her belief in what he called *nonsense.* He was a drunkard with a foul mouth who cursed God openly.

And now he lay comatose inside the very safe haven he'd spoken against. They were keeping him alive, a kindness he hardly deserved but one she would extend in good grace. He had already paid a steep price at his own hand.

Then again, what if he *was* overtaken by the Fury? How else could he have survived all these years?

She needed to see Sylous. He would know.

Rose unlocked the single door that led to the Chapel's basement, stepped onto the landing, locked the door behind her, and descended the staircase. She flicked the small light to life and walked to the center of the room.

She'd waited less than ten seconds when the atmosphere of the room shifted. A shift she never tired of. A shift she would never get used to. He had come. Her body tingled with relief and satisfaction.

"Sylous," Rose whispered.

He moved into the light, his white attire crisp and his face draped in shadows.

"You called for me," Sylous said.

"Yes," Rose replied.

"You're concerned about the trespassers?"

"Yes."

"You should be." His eyes were dark. He clasped his arms behind his back and took another step toward Rose. "They don't belong here."

"The man is unconscious," Rose said. "We're safe."

"You are never safe from the evil that lurks in darkness."

She hesitated, not sure how to feel about his tone. "He's their father."

"He wasn't chosen. The blood that runs through his veins doesn't change what he is."

"And what is he?"

"Ask yourself how he came to be inside Haven Valley. How has he survived so long? And why is the boy unharmed? Then you will know what he is."

A Fury. But she couldn't see the Fury in the boy. How could something so innocent be so evil?

"I don't think you understand the way evil works, dear Rose."

"I do," Rose said. "But he's a dying old man."

His eyes narrowed. "If you knew how evil worked, righteous rage would replace your pathetic human sentiments."

"The boy is just a child who . . ."

His hand flashed, slapping her cheek with an open palm before she saw it moving. The force of his blow snapped her head sideways. Tears sprang to her eyes.

She stood stunned for a long moment, fingers trembling, trying to understand Sylous's actions. He'd never dealt a blow to her before. She wouldn't have even considered him capable of such a thing.

He reached up, slid his hand behind her neck, and pulled her ear close to his lips. She could feel his hot breath against her skin.

"Have you become so full of yourself and the power I've given you that you think you understand better than I? That you could see better than I?"

"No . . . No, please."

"I realize this show of force is unsettling to you, but the wrath of God is designed to get your attention. Do not forget that you're alive today because of me. Do not think you can survive without my protection and guidance. Doubting God and his servant will seal your fate."

He released his grip and calmly clasped his hands behind his back. Rose stumbled back, gasping. She was afraid to look him directly in the eye, but also afraid to tear her eyes away from him.

"Fear me alone," Sylous said in a soothing voice, "and I will always protect you."

Rose swallowed, bottom lip trembling. "I will never stop fearing you."

His face softened and he spoke in the gentle voice she'd grown so accustomed to. "I'm sorry I had to do that to you. But fear has its reward."

She tried to calm her breathing, mind still reeling.

"Try to understand, my love," he said, reaching his hand up to gently wipe away her tears.

The moment his skin touched hers, the terror building in her chest began to ease, sedated by her deep longing for him, her desire to feel him close.

"I must protect Haven Valley from the deception that would consume it, however loving or kind it might appear at first," Sylous said. "The fate of humanity depends on it."

"And I am your servant," Rose replied, melting into his touch.

"The intruders must be dealt with."

"How?"

"After five days the sheep will show themselves as wolves. If you don't kill them both before they reveal the truth of what they are, Haven Valley will be lost."

Her pulse quickened. Five days . . . It was a new revelation.

Rose glanced up and met Sylous's gaze, only inches from her face. She didn't want to doubt him again, didn't want to feel his wrath replace the warmth that now held her. But she couldn't imagine murdering anyone, much less a boy.

He knew her mind. "Was the destruction of Sodom and Gomorrah murder?"

"We could send them away," Rose dared to say.

"To return in yet another masquerade of light? You still underestimate the power of the Fury."

Rose searched her mind for a solution that didn't require violence, but nothing came to her.

"Can *you* kill them?" she asked. "The way you killed my father?"

"Fear doesn't work against the Fury. Even if it did, God seeks your obedience, dear Rose. Pleasing him is all that matters now."

Sylous reached up and held Rose's face in his large warm hands. His deep green eyes pulled her in. "The bride looks to you for guidance," he said.

For a few moments, Rose stood in his presence, torn by conflicting emotions. "Kill them," she whispered, as if saying the words out loud might give her courage.

Sylous leaned in close and placed his lips against hers. Tender and warm, his kiss buzzed inside her mouth. He held her there, caught up in a perfect moment, and when he released her, a new resolve had flooded her chest.

"Don't be deceived by their show of innocence. If the Holy Family allows the boy to live, all of heaven will weep for your souls."

"Yes," she whispered, closing her eyes, her body still caught up in the pleasure of his mouth.

Listen to me, and I will always guide you, his mind sang to hers.

She felt him leave, felt the dankness of the room return at his departure, but she didn't move.

I will do as you say, she sang back.

And so she would.

CHAPTER NINETEEN

I stood inside the Pierce kitchen the next afternoon, watching the children, but my mind was on my father, dying in the clinic not far away. And on Eli, who'd been secluded somewhere, and on Jamie, who was hardly the caring brother I'd once known, and on Bobbie, who told me to trust no one. Rose would sense if I was distracted, so I tried my best not to show any concern. I was beginning to see what Bobbie meant when she said I would need help, because my whole world had been turned inside out in the last few days and I didn't know where to turn.

My father had told me he'd come to bring Eli. The boy was his gift and I was to keep him safe. A gift in what way? Where was he? What if he would be the undoing of all that was sacred in Haven Valley? What if he'd been sent to save us?

I felt like I was walking on thin ice, and it

was already cracking.

My father had called Eli my brother. *Brother.* I'd brought it up to Jamie the night before as we sat silently for dinner, and again he'd cut me off. But I pushed.

"Do you know where they're keeping him?"

"In the deepest hole, where he belongs," he snapped.

"Really? Where's that?"

"For all I know, they've already sent him packing. Forget him, Grace. You're in dangerous waters already."

And with that, he'd pushed away his plate and left.

Mother had said nothing, though I suspected she wanted to support me. She just couldn't bring herself to upset Jamie.

The news that Rose needed me to watch the children for a couple of hours that afternoon had come as a relief. She'd welcomed me into her home ten minutes earlier. Now I stood in their kitchen as Levi worked on his daily reading at the table and Stephen finished his lunch.

Rose was attending to Evelyn upstairs, where she'd been sequestered. The poor girl's rash was continuing to spread, and cooling ointment had to be applied several times a day to give her relief. Rose was terribly concerned that the rash would spread to others in the community.

Strange, I thought, how Evelyn had contracted the rash even though she hadn't left the approved path, while Stephen, who had, showed no sign of it. I hoped Dr. Charles would be able to identify what might have caused such a mysterious outbreak and the way to cure it before it spread.

Footsteps sounded behind me, and I turned to see Rose descending the last few steps to the main floor. She walked past me and placed Evelyn's dirty lunch dishes in the kitchen sink before staring out the small window above the sink.

"I shouldn't be gone long," she eventually said, turning. "Keep the children inside."

"Of course."

Rose held my eyes, offering nothing but a flat face. Something was eating at her mind. The children picked up on her heaviness and remained stone still.

She crossed to a small side table along one of the kitchen walls and picked up a piece of paper. "I made a list of required vitamins you should be taking now that you're expecting. They're important for the baby's development and overall health as much as yours."

I took the list from her hand and scanned

the items.

"You need to start taking these today — do not delay on this. Every moment is critical in an infant's development. Do you understand?" Rose asked, tone harsh.

Her foul mood was palpable. I nodded.

"It's important that we follow the law to the letter," she snapped. "Not just when it's convenient or when we agree."

"Yes, of course."

She gave me a curt nod and headed to the front door. "I'll have Dr. Charles put these items aside for you. You can retrieve them after I return. They must be picked up today. You're responsible for everything that happens to that life inside you. You must be vigilant."

And then she was out the front door, closing it firmly behind her, leaving me and the children in silence.

A semblance of normality had settled over the home within a half hour of Rose's leaving. Stephen and Levi peacefully occupied different spaces in the main front room, each lost in their own activities. Levi was tucked into the folds of the large couch, reading a newly approved youth novel, while Stephen sat on the floor beside the couch, coloring. He hummed softly to himself, a habit he'd started a couple months ago that usually had Evelyn up in arms. How could she possibly concentrate on reading while he made so much noise? His humming was sweet and made me smile, so I allowed it.

For a few minutes, I almost forgot how upside down my world had become. Maybe I would sit the children down and tell them a tall tale. We could all use some good laughter. Maybe I would set them outside of Evelyn's room with the door open so all three could hear the story.

The grandfather clock dinged as it did every hour, and Levi glanced up at me. It was time for Evelyn's next salve treatment. Rose had left written instructions: *Apply a thin layer over all affected areas, wearing gloves to protect yourself from infection. Don't allow the other children to see the rash or they might catch it too.*

"You two stay here," I said. "I'm going to check on Evelyn."

"Okay," Stephen replied without taking his eyes off his work.

I hurried up the stairs and into the bathroom next to Evelyn's room. On the counter, Rose had laid out several pairs of blue surgical gloves beside a jar of salve. After taking what I needed, I made my way down the hall.

I knocked on Evelyn's door, heard a soft call from inside, and poked my head in. The room was cast in natural light streaming in through the two large windows on one wall. Evelyn was perched on her twin bed, one of two that matched. Matching nightstands, a dresser, and a single closet rounded out the room. A gathering of large sunflowers was blooming in a tall glass vase and sat on the small nightstand beside Evelyn's bed. Not a speck of dust; everything was in perfect order.

"Beautiful flowers," I said.

She was frowning, staring at the wall.

I stepped into the room and softly shut the door behind me. "Your mother picked them for you?"

She hesitated. "Father."

"That's kind of him."

She was wearing a simple sleeveless dress so the itchy red blotches that ran the length of both her arms could be free from the uncomfortable fabric of sleeves. The rash had spread all the way up her neck to the underside of her jawline. It was no wonder she was in such a foul mood. Maybe this explained Rose's as well.

I set the salve down on the nightstand beside her sunflowers and slid the gloves over my hands.

Evelyn watched me dip into the salve, then held out her right hand. "Not too thick," she snapped.

"Right," I replied.

"If you make it too thick then it could get worse — my mother told you that, right?"

I looked into her worried eyes and tried to sound certain. "Yes. I just apply a thin layer."

She finally nodded for me to continue. So I did, taking extra measures to make sure the salve covered her entire arm, but not too heavily. We were silent as I worked, her eyes on every movement I made.

"Does Dr. Charles have any ideas as to how you got this rash?" I asked, trying to reconnect with a girl who used to trust me fully.

"No," Evelyn said, "he says it's probably a combination of things."

"Oh?"

"But I think he's wrong."

"Why do you say that?" I moved up under the collar of her dress, along her shoulder and throat.

"I know why this happened to me," Evelyn said.

"Why?"

"It's punishment for my sins," the girl said quietly.

She was staring out the window. We all knew how impurity could indeed manifest in all kinds of bodily ailments. Following the law benefited not only God but ourselves.

"But Evelyn, you didn't do anything wrong."

Her jaw flexed. "I'm the oldest. My mother always says I have to lead by example. Stephen wouldn't have disobeyed if I'd been a better example."

I wanted to offer her some sort of comfort, but I knew it would be of no use. She believed every word she was saying and so did I.

Didn't I?

Something about that belief disturbed me. Or maybe the disturbance was that a small part of me was questioning the belief, which was itself an infraction of the law. So would I contract the rash as well?

"I'll have this rash until I'm a better example," Evelyn said. Her bottom lip started to quiver slightly, and she dropped her voice to a whisper. "But I'm afraid."

I gently held her arm, hoping my touch offered her some comfort. "Afraid of what?"

"Afraid that I'll never be good enough to be clean." Tears welled in her eyes, and I wanted to hold her close. But when I placed my arm around her back, she pushed me away. "You can't touch me that way," she snapped.

I withdrew, embarrassed, and finished my work in an uncomfortable silence. I removed the gloves, recapped the ointment, and stood.

"Do you need anything else?" I asked. "I could make you some of that peppermint tea you like so much."

She looked at me hesitantly. "Do you think Mother would approve?"

"You're sick, so of course she would."

A small sparkle ignited in the corner of her eye, and she gave me a half smile. "That would be nice," she said.

"I'll be right back."

After returning the ointment to the bathroom, I hurried downstairs to put on the teapot, satisfied by the small smile I'd coaxed out of Evelyn. Then I headed into the living room to check on Levi and Stephen. But Stephen was gone.

"Where's your brother?" I asked Levi.

He looked up from his book and shrugged. I glanced around the room, moved to check behind the couch and curtains, then Rose's office. No sign of him.

"Stephen?" I called. No reply. "Levi, when did your brother leave?"

"I don't know," he said, annoyed. I gave him a warning look, and he put his book down on his knees. "I didn't even hear him leave."

I was moving then, full of trepidation, down the hall, past the staircase to the first-floor bathroom, dining room, and back mudroom. All were empty.

My heart was racing as I rushed back upstairs to check his bedroom. "Stephen?" I pushed open his bedroom door. No sign of him.

Evelyn's worried voice came from her room. "Everything alright?"

"Yes, don't worry, I'm just going to go get your tea," I lied.

My pulse was thundering as I raced back downstairs, worst-case scenarios now screaming through my brain. He knew better than to wander outside, right?

I was moving toward the back door when I came around the corner and noticed the basement door slightly ajar. I pulled up.

I'd nearly forgotten Rose's home had a lower level, because I'd never been down there. The door was always closed and locked. But here it stood, open just enough for a small person to sneak through.

I pulled the door open. An overhead bulb lit the unfinished wooden stairs. "Stephen?

Are you down there?"

A tiny laugh echoed up in response, and I released a sigh of relief.

"What are you doing?" Bobbie asked. I twisted to see her standing in the hall, arms crossed. "Getting into more trouble?"

Why was she suddenly here? What prompted her to come and go? I glanced around. Levi was still in the living room.

"I have to get Stephen," I said.

She walked toward me and looked down the stairs, arms still crossed. "I show myself to you when I'm needed. Like right now. You know that going into the basement's prohibited."

"Stephen's down there."

"Then call him up."

I hesitated, suddenly very curious as to what dangers might lurk in the basement.

"That's none of your business," she said quickly. "Your business is to keep your nose clean. Stay away from any appearance of wrongdoing. For the sake of your baby as much as your own."

"What's in the basement?" I asked, curiosity growing.

"Trouble. Wolves in sheep's clothing. Everything you should be avoiding. Don't go down; call him up."

Trust no one, she'd said. Trust no one.

And I wondered if that should include her. The thought confused me.

"Confusion is the devil, Grace. My only concern is to keep you safe."

"I know, but there's too many things pulling me in too many directions," I blurted. "Stephen is my responsibility. I have to get him!"

"I can't stop you, but don't say I didn't warn you." She shoved her chin at the stairwell. "Be my guest."

I looked down, then back at her, but she was gone.

I descended the stairs to a concrete floor and glanced around a mostly unfinished basement. Cold walls with exposed pipes above. Limited lighting and plenty of shadows. A single small window stood high on the far wall. Neatly stacked boxes and a row of steel shelves filled with odds and ends lined another.

I didn't see any danger.

Against the back wall was another door, also opened slightly, to the only finished part of the basement. A voice drifted from the room, then a tiny laugh that I recognized as Stephen's. See, no danger down here.

"We aren't supposed to be down here," said a voice from behind. It caught me off guard and I spun around to see Levi stand-

229

ing halfway down the stairs.

"Levi! Go back upstairs right this minute."

"Is Stephen with him?" he asked.

"With who?"

"The new boy. He lives down here, but we aren't allowed to play with him. Mother said he's wicked."

Eli!

My heart caught in my throat. Rose was keeping Eli in her basement!

I turned back to the door, knowing I was in a terrible predicament. In spite of Rose's warnings, I was desperately curious about the boy. This was what Bobbie was warning me about.

But now I had to know.

I hurried forward and pulled the door open. There was Eli, sitting on a thin mattress in the corner of the room. A simple space, no windows, a little table, a single lamp, no sheets, no pillows, no bed frame.

Stephen was sitting beside Eli. They both looked up at me.

Stephen held out a small bowl of grapes. "I wanted to share my snack."

"Mother told us not to come down here," Levi said just behind me. I glanced back, horrified to see that he'd disobeyed my instruction.

"But he was hungry," Stephen said.

"How do you know?" Levi asked, peering around me.

"I was hungry, so I knew he must be too."

"You're going to get us in big trouble," Levi said.

I knew I should rush Levi and Stephen back upstairs, but my eyes were glued to the blue-eyed boy sitting before me. He really did look so much like I imagined Lukas would have. The boy was watching me, maybe waiting for me to say something. He flashed me a small smile and I blinked, caught up in his sweet innocence.

"Hello," I said. "I'm Grace. You're Eli?"

"Yes," he said.

"It's a nice name." A beat passed between us.

"Thank you," Eli said in a sweet voice. His bright eyes drew me in like a deep well that could transport you to a different place if you stared for too long.

"He's a magician," Stephen announced excitedly. "He does magic tricks."

"Magic is a sin," Levi said.

Be careful, Grace.

Bobbie's warning echoed in the back of my mind. *This isn't safe, Grace. Get out.*

What had a moment ago felt like wonder quickly transformed to caution. I would face consequences if Rose found out we'd come

231

down. What was I doing here?

"We need to go back upstairs right now."

"Can Eli come too?" Stephen asked.

"No." I glanced back at Eli's face. "No, he has to stay down here."

"But why?"

Seeing his face now, I struggled to wrap my mind around how such an innocent child could threaten us all.

They come in sheep's clothing. Get out, Grace. Think of your baby.

"Because Mother said so, that's why," Levi scolded.

"That's right," I said. I reached a hand toward Stephen, not daring to go to collect him. "Come on, Stephen. We have to hurry."

"Strangers are dangerous," Levi said. "Mother's going to punish you."

Again the tiny whisper of doubt popped to life. Was Eli really a stranger? He was my brother, right? A brother could be a stranger, but . . .

"What is going on here?" a fearful voice asked from behind.

I spun around to see Rose standing at the bottom of the steps, her face pale, eyes wide with horror. Her gaze shifted to Levi, then past me to the room. Her face darkened with rage.

"Rose, I —"

"Silence!" She strode for us, yanked Levi away from me, and brushed me aside. "How dare you come near my son!" she snapped at Eli, storming into the room.

I opened my mouth to interject on Eli's behalf but felt a hand on my shoulder. "Not now, Grace." Bobbie stood beside me, shaking her head, finger on her lips to silence me. So I kept my mouth shut.

Rose reached down, grabbed a trembling Stephen by his arm, and jerked him to his feet. Flung him at me.

"Upstairs," she yelled. "Now!"

We responded in unison as if we were all three her children, running for the stairs and rushing back up to the main level. The door to the room below slammed shut and Rose clopped across the concrete basement, hard on our heels.

A high pitch whistled through the house, and it dawned on me that I'd forgotten the teakettle. Before I could move, Rose was rushing past me into the kitchen. She yanked the steaming kettle from the stovetop and clunked it into the sink.

She paused a moment, collecting herself, then swung around and dropped to a knee in front of Stephen, who'd followed us in. "Are you okay?" She ran her arms over him, twisted him either way so she could make sure he hadn't been hurt.

"Yes."

Rose stood and glared at me. "How dare you take the children down into the basement! Have you lost your mind?"

Before I could defend myself, Levi set her straight. "Stephen went into the basement."

Rose glanced at Stephen. "What do you mean? You went down on your own?"

His lips were trembling as he stared up at her, near tears.

"What were you thinking?" she demanded.

Her son opened his mouth, but Rose didn't actually want a response.

"Do you have any idea how dangerous that boy is? The basement is off-limits!"

Large tears filled Stephen's little eyes.

"How did you get down there? The door's locked."

Stephen reached his hand into his pocket and pulled out a set of keys.

She snatched them from him. "Where did you get these?"

"In your desk?"

"You are never to touch anything in my office! You know how important it is to follow the rules. They're for your protection and safety. If you break them, there are consequences!"

"I'm sorry." Stephen sniffed.

"Sorry's not good enough. You directly disobeyed me!"

"Mommy, I didn't —"

"Go to your room," she snapped, shoving a finger at the hall. "You will spend the afternoon dwelling on your sins until your father gets home to decide on the right correction."

"I'm sorry," he cried.

"To your room!" Rose barked. She flicked her eyes to Levi. "And you as well. Both of you, now!"

They hurried away like frightened mice, pattering up the stairs.

"How could you let this happen?" Rose demanded of me.

I opened my mouth to speak but couldn't find the right words. Rose was looking to place blame, not find answers.

"I trusted you with my children's care. That means you watch them! This is the second time in the last few days you've placed them in danger!"

"I went to check on Evelyn," I started. "She —"

"I don't want to hear your excuses! I hold you responsible."

"Rose, I'm so —"

"You've formed a bad habit of letting me and this community down, and I'm running

235

out of patience." Rose stepped closer, dropping her voice to a harsh growl. "There's no more room for failure, Grace. If not for the child growing in you, I would have you subjected to correction! This is outrageous!"

Her words cut me deeply and filled me with dread. She might be overreacting, but she was right.

"I tried to tell you, Grace," Bobbie said behind me. I glanced back and saw that she was leaning against the kitchen door frame, then quickly returned my eyes to Rose.

"Do you understand?" Rose said.

I remained silent, body rigid.

"Do you understand?" she shouted.

"Yes," I whispered, then swallowed and spoke louder. "Yes."

She stared at me for a long, hard second. "Go home, Grace," she ordered.

Without hesitation I turned and fled down the hall and out the front door. This was bad. I should have listened to Bobbie.

But what about Eli?

CHAPTER TWENTY

I was lying on my bed when I remembered the pills.

Gasping, I sat up, reached into the pocket of my white dress, and pulled out the list Rose had given me several hours earlier. The items I needed to start taking for the health of my unborn baby. In the wake of Rose's outrage, I'd forgotten.

I spun to the window. The sun was starting to hide behind the hills, marking the end of the day, and with it, curfew. No woman was permitted outside without a male escort after six.

Rose had insisted that I start taking these vitamins today. She'd been firm. But she'd also insisted I go home. Had she expected me to go home via the clinic? I could go first thing in the morning, but Dr. Charles would know and might report it.

I stood from my bed and paced the worn rug. In my state of exhaustion, the idea of facing my mother for a solution seemed insurmountable. Jamie would be home by now, but I didn't trust him to keep a secret in his newfound loyalty to the law.

My only sane option was to wait till morning and risk another scolding.

"Do you really think that's a good idea?" Bobbie asked.

I glanced at my bed where she sat, legs crossed, leaning on one arm. Her shimmering hair was pulled to one side across her shoulder.

"Do I have no control over you?" I demanded, but I was glad for her attentiveness, however sporadic.

"Do you want me to leave?"

"I didn't say that."

She shrugged. "I show up when I think I can help, which isn't always. If I'm not welcome, I have no power to help."

"How do you know when you're welcome?"

"Am I?"

I hesitated, then nodded. "Yes. Yes, you are." Then, "What do you mean, waiting until morning isn't wise? I can't get out and back by curfew. I have no choice."

"You always have a choice," Bobbie said. She stood gracefully and walked across the room to my window. Using two fingers she separated the blinds and gazed out. "If you hurry you'll have enough time to get back before dark. No rules broken."

"I could never get past my mother or brother."

"Who said anything about getting past them?" Bobbie yanked the blinds up, unlocked the window's latch and opened the bottom panel. "Slip out, tread carefully, slip back in. Easy."

I shook my head in disbelief. "I couldn't possibly do that."

"Why not? Then you avoid dealing with your family, and you follow Rose's instructions."

"Sneaking around feels like I'm doing something wrong."

"More like avoiding wrong." She turned back to face me. "You could wait till morning, but that means disobeying Rose."

Made sense. Maybe she was right.

"I usually am," she said. "I promised to keep you safe. But I can only do that if you let me."

I considered what she was saying, weighed my options, and started pacing again. The harsh, hurtful words of Rose echoed through my mind as they had all afternoon. *You've formed a bad habit of letting me down.* She wouldn't accept another excuse from me. And there was also my baby to consider.

I stopped and looked toward the window. Bobbie reached out and pushed it all the way open. Slip out, tread carefully, and slip back in. Easy.

Bobbie smiled. "Easy."

Rose slipped into the quiet clinic through the back entrance. Harrison had come home when he'd said he would, giving her enough time to deal with Ben before returning home to take care of the boy. Her husband didn't know what she would do, naturally. It was better that way.

The events of the afternoon had left her shaken. The boy had come off as innocent in the eyes of her children, likely in the eyes of Grace as well. And under the guise of innocence, he'd already influenced her children and Grace to disregard simple, firm rules.

Sylous was right about the boy. She only prayed she had the strength to do what was necessary. There was no other way.

She knew that by this hour Dr. Charles and his family would be upstairs attending to dinner in the attached apartment where they lived. But she wouldn't have long before they returned to check on their patient.

Sylous hadn't offered any instruction on how to kill them, which meant he didn't care. After much deliberation through the night, she'd settled on poisoning them. She didn't think she had the stomach for violence. Poisoning seemed safer, more disconnected. There would be no autopsy, naturally. No one would be the wiser.

She'd prepared earlier under the guise of researching rare causes of rashes like the one Evelyn had. It hadn't taken long to do a quick inventory of the medications the clinic had on hand and the lethal doses of those medications.

Supply was limited, but potassium chloride was available. Used to treat low blood pressure, enough injected through an IV would stop the heart. The boy's would have to be administered through his food with a side of thiopental, which would cause him to relax into an unconscious state while the potassium chloride killed him in his sleep.

Rose reached the doctor's personal office, opened the door and walked into the dark room. She went to the desk, slid open the top right drawer and reached into one of the back compartments for the keys to the medicine cabinet.

Making her way back to the door, she carefully peered around the corner to make sure the clinic was still empty. The front door wouldn't be locked until midnight, but most of the lights had been turned off, and with darkness fast approaching, few if any would be out at this time of day.

Taking a deep breath, she hurried to the supply room and entered. Using a small flashlight she approached the medicine cabinet, quickly unlocked it and scanned the labels. She withdrew a syringe and both medications, then locked the cabinet.

So far so good.

Thirty seconds later, Rose was standing outside the patient's room. The door stood wide open. She hesitated for a moment. Once she crossed the threshold there was no going back. A slight shiver worked through her fingers. Chasing away her doubts with a final breath, she quietly stepped up to Ben's bedside.

The room was cast in shadows, but there was enough light from the small window to guide her. Beeping from the monitoring device punctuated the patient's steady breathing. Ben lay still, tucked under white sheets and a blue blanket that were pulled up to his shoulders.

She studied the older man for a few seconds. Peaceful, lost to the reality of where he was or what was about to become of him. Perfectly ignorant. She felt a tinge of envy. While she'd been battling doubts and fear since agreeing to Sylous's guidance, he'd been at peace, oblivious to the problems of the world.

He would never even know she'd aided in his passing.

That burden was for her to carry, and she would carry it for the good of the world. A price she was willing to pay, she'd told herself a handful of times. Sylous had called her to walk this path, and she would always follow where he directed.

Even so, her hands shook as she held up the syringe and vial. "Forgive me," she whispered. "I have no choice." She looked back at Ben's still face. "I'm protecting your children, you understand? I've always protected them." She kept her voice low but felt the need to speak the words — a kind of absolution for what she was about to do. "Your sacrifice will eliminate the threat against your children."

It was true. Though she spoke it for her sake, not his. And her speaking seemed to calm her somewhat.

She uncapped the needle, lifted the vial, and pierced the cap. Three cubic centimeters of the amber fluid was all she needed, and it flowed into the syringe with ease.

It would be simple: inject the potassium chloride into his IV and, without any suffering, his heart would cease to beat. Easy and painless.

But she was hesitating. Her hands were still trembling.

Murder is a sin, an offense against God. But so was failing to protect his bride, the faithful few of true religion who'd come out from among the world. Could she commit one sin to justify not committing another?

Was wiping out Sodom and Gomorrah a sin? Was killing Jesus a sin? Even slaughtering children wasn't beyond God. In truth, Ben was now a Fury. Killing a Fury was a good thing.

So why was it so hard?

Rose swallowed as the shake in her hands worsened. "I am only doing what has to be done," she whispered to Ben. "Sylous commands it."

She reached for the thin plastic line of his IV. "You won't suffer," she said, silencing the opposition in her mind and placing the needle into the IV line. "You won't feel any pain, and I promise the same will go for the boy. But you have to understand, I must do God's will and protect Haven Valley."

Rose pressed the plunger, releasing the heavy dose of potassium chloride that would quickly find its way into Ben's bloodstream. A ball of tension rolled through her gut, yet she held steady. She was doing this for her people, for her children, for Sylous, who was the voice of God.

"To protect Haven Valley," she said, "you and the boy must die."

I didn't encounter anyone on the way to the clinic. Most people were already inside for the evening, and I walked in the buildings' shadows, trying to stay out of sight. I had to get back quickly before anyone knew I was missing.

I knew the clinic's doors would be unlocked but decided using the back door would be safer. I would rather not announce my late arrival. If someone was inside, I would slip back outside. Easy.

Rose had said she asked Dr. Charles to pull what I needed and put them aside for me. I hoped he'd done so. There was a pickup box in the front room. They should be there. Simple.

I reached the back door and eased it open. Made hardly a sound as I eased inside and softly closed the door behind me. I stood for a moment, letting my eyes adjust to the dark hallway, listening for sound. As far as I could tell, I was alone. All I had to do was get to the front, find the medications, and get back out. Then it was a straight shot home. Easy and simple. But I had to be quiet so as not to alert Dr. Charles and his family, who were on the floor above me.

I was four or five strides down the hallway when I heard a voice. Soft and indistinguishable, but there. I pulled up, flattened myself against the wall and strained my ears.

The voice was coming from up ahead, around the corner. A corner I had to cross to get to the pickup box. I considered heading back out the way I'd come.

The voice came again, a woman's voice, from one of the patient rooms around the corner.

An image of my father flashed through my mind. He'd been the only patient in the clinic yesterday when I'd left. Who would be with him now? Not Dr. Charles. A woman. His wife? Unlikely. Didn't sound like her.

I had to know, and there was no sign of Bobbie to tell me I shouldn't know. Besides, she was the one who'd suggested I come.

Creeping with caution, I eased toward the corner and the voice came clearer. A familiar voice.

"I am only doing what has to be done," the voice said. "Sylous commands it."

Dread mushroomed in my chest. I knew I should get out before I was discovered, but I also had to know what she was saying to my father. What had Sylous commanded? So I stood as still as a mouse and held my breath.

"You won't suffer," the voice said, and in that moment I knew it was Rose. "You won't feel any pain, and I promise the same will go for the boy."

The boy. Eli. Certainty crashed into my skull like a hammer. Rose intended to do something terrible to my father and Eli.

Terrified by that certainty, I craned my head around the corner and saw Rose standing over my father.

Her back was half turned to me, but I could see that she was holding something in her fingers. A syringe. And she was injecting the contents of that syringe into my father's IV.

"To protect Haven Valley, you and the boy must die," Rose said. Her words cut through the confusion gathering in my mind like a blade.

You and the boy must die. Her words echoed through my mind and the world around me seemed to stand still. *Die.* The word was in my mind, but so unsettling that it didn't offer me meaning.

And then it did.

Die, I thought again. Rose was killing my father. And Eli was next.

I lost my mind to fear and retreated without thought, hurrying on tippy-toes, not daring to breathe. Then I was outside and the cool evening air hit me like a wall of bricks.

The back door shut behind me, and a small part of my mind wondered if the sound had been too loud. But the thought didn't linger long because I was already around the clinic's corner, then pressing against the wall, hidden for the moment. If Rose came out, I would run.

You and the boy must die. Rose's final statement ravaged my thoughts, tore them into pieces and devoured them. Rose was murdering my father?

No, I must have misunderstood. An image of Rose standing beside my father's bed, syringe in hand, filled the space behind my eyes. *You and the boy must die.*

A wave of nausea rose through me and I fought to keep from emptying the contents of my stomach on the ground, but it was no use. I vomited at my feet, desperate to remain as quiet as possible. Between waves I took several harsh drags of air and tried to steady my breathing.

With that violent retch, clarity came to me. Sylous had told Rose that my father and Eli had to die because they were wolves in sheep's clothing. They were the darkness masquerading as light. It was the only thing that made any sense.

Rose had just killed my father.

Eli, the boy with the beautiful blue eyes, the child my father had called my brother, would be subjected to the same fate. How could killing him keep Haven Valley safe? Surely there had to be another way.

I straightened as a sudden urge of my own worked its way up my spine. I couldn't let Eli die. He was my brother. He was just a child. I had to protect him.

"Don't be crazy, Grace."

Bobbie appeared on my left, face firm, eyes sharp. But I wasn't interested in her advice now, so I turned away.

"You'll be declaring war on Rose," Bobbie snapped, her voice low and afraid. "There's no way to get to him without exposing yourself. It's a terrible idea."

My father had asked one thing of me: keep Eli safe. Maybe my desperate need to follow his dying request was a temptation, which confused me because I really didn't know Ben as a father.

What I did know in that moment was that

I had never wanted something so badly as to protect Eli. He was being held in the Pierce home, but it was a home I knew as well as my own. With schedules I knew intimately.

And Rose wasn't there. Not yet.

"This is insane, Grace," Bobbie cried. "Think of the danger you'll be putting yourself in. And your baby!"

That gave me a moment's pause. But only a moment. My need to save my helpless brother had taken root. And the branches were sprouting with each passing thought.

"And if Rose is right about him?" Bobbie demanded.

"You don't know?" I asked aloud, spinning to her.

She blinked. "No."

"Then please shut up."

And then I was running.

CHAPTER TWENTY-ONE

I raced along the outskirts of the town, angling for the Pierce home, moving as fast as my tired legs would carry me without making a ruckus. The sun had just set over the far mountains, and I knew within half an hour the sky would be dark. I didn't have much time.

Bobbie appeared and disappeared at will, stepping out from behind a tree or a house just ahead of me as I ran. Her voice of warning was insistent and constant.

"You shouldn't do this, Grace."

"Think of what they will do to you if you're caught!"

"You're running toward danger, Grace."

Every word she said was true, and my mind screamed at me in agreement. This was insane and dangerous. If Rose would kill a dying man and a young child, what would stop her from killing me? Even more, for her to go to such extremes could only mean that a true and terrible threat against Haven Valley had made itself known, at least to Sylous and her. Rose had always been a gentle and pure woman, and murder wasn't something I thought her capable of.

The fact that she'd been pushed over the edge meant I should be terrified of whatever had done it.

Determination like I'd never known pulled me forward. It filled my legs with strength and blocked out the cries from my brain. Eli needed to be saved, and there was no one else to help him. There had to be another way. My father knew he would need protecting.

Bobbie was relentless. "You can't trust anyone, Grace, and that includes the boy."

"It also includes you," I snapped, breaking my silence.

"I saved you from the Fury once. I will do it again."

"And what if *you're* a Fury?" That was unfair. "This is my choice!"

Bobbie hesitated. "Then at least be careful," she finally offered me. "And be quick. Rose will return soon." With that, she left me.

I rushed behind the houses, keeping my head and shoulders low, avoiding windows, trying to remain within the shadows that grew with the fading sun. Slowly a plan began to take shape in my mind.

Harrison and the children would be home. When the weather permitted it, he often enjoyed a sunset devotion with his children on the front porch in plain view of all who might pass by. Which meant they wouldn't be in the house. Rose usually accompanied them, but I knew she wasn't back yet. If she'd left the clinic only moments after me, she wouldn't be far behind. If she'd delayed for any reason, I'd have a couple minutes longer. Either way, I assumed I had less than ten minutes.

Getting into the house would be as simple as using the back mudroom window, which would be open, allowing the evening breeze to cool the home. The screen was loose in the bottom right corner, which would make it possible to pop out. The basement door would be locked, but I thought I knew from Stephen's confession where Rose kept the key.

If she'd hidden it elsewhere, my entire plan would be foiled. My stomach churned as I prayed with each breath that I would find it.

By the time I reached the Pierce home, I was panting hard and my dress was drenched in sweat. I brushed my arm across my forehead as I pulled up to listen.

Harrison's low, soothing voice carried on the wind — they were outside as I'd hoped. I hurried for the mudroom window, afraid that if I hesitated I would lose my resolve.

The window was about six feet from the ground. A firewood chest sat beneath it. I stepped onto the chest, eased my fingers through the broken screen and popped the right corner out. Then popped out the left corner with a sharp tug. With both bottom corners free, the screen came loose. I placed it inside and leaned it against the wall.

Placing both palms onto the sill, I hoisted myself up until I could swing my right leg up and into the open space. I stopped half in and half out, listening. What was I doing? It was insane! But I was committed, right? And my legs were dangling in the breeze for anyone to see.

Rolling over the sill, I found the floor with my right foot, and I was inside, crouched, breathing too hard, listening for any sound from the front.

The house was still quite dark. They hadn't turned on any lights yet.

I considered putting the screen back in place, but Eli and I would need to leave that same way, so I left it and tiptoed into the hall, hurried to the corner, and poked my head around.

Empty. Rose's office was down that hall beside the front door. The basement door was halfway between where I stood and the office. Warning bells were still screaming in my head, despite Bobbie's absence. I clung to her last words: *Be quick.*

I headed straight for Rose's office, covering the fifteen paces on the balls of my feet as quickly and quietly as I could. Harrison's soft voice carried to me from the porch just outside.

Rose's office was dark, but I knew it like the back of my hand. Knew where to find the key that opened the bottom desk drawer. Knew that she likely kept the key to the basement locked in that drawer.

With trembling fingers, I pulled the top drawer open, withdrew the desk key, lowered myself to one knee, and unlocked the bottom drawer. It took some fishing around in the dark to find the key ring in a tray at the back of the drawer. Relief flooded me. But Rose could be home at any moment.

I left the drawer open and hurried to the basement door, fighting off panic. At any moment the front door could open. At any moment I could be caught.

So I ran now, on my tiptoes, thankful I was wearing shoes with soft rubber soles rather than my Chapel shoes. They padded loudly in my ears. I desperately hoped the sound didn't carry outside.

Pulling up in front of the basement door, I shoved the key into the lock, twisted, and let out a breath when the knob turned. Open.

To buy myself some time in the event Rose returned while I was in the basement, I thought to return the key to the office and lock the basement door behind me before I descended. It would take an extra fifteen seconds, and for a moment I hesitated, thinking maybe I should just rush to grab the boy now. But I would have to return the key even after I got him — I didn't want to leave evidence of a break-in.

At least that was my plan.

I followed it, hurrying back to the office, replacing the key where I'd found it, closing and locking the bottom drawer before setting the desk key back in its upper-drawer tray. Now all I had to do was get Eli, get out of the house, replace the screen and be gone, leaving no evidence. Hopefully, they would conclude the boy had found a way to escape by himself and run away into the mountains. They would never search for him there.

I was at the basement door, ready to

descend, when Bobbie appeared next to me. "Would it be quicker and safer to exit through the basement window rather than return to the mudroom?"

I thought through her suggestion. Yes. But what if the basement window wouldn't open?

"Then you can return to the mudroom. But you need to replace the screen in the window now to make it look like the boy escaped on his own down below."

Made perfect sense. I followed her guidance, feeling the seconds stretch. Rushing with less stealth than I'd used to this point, I returned to the mudroom and quickly replaced the screen to cover my tracks.

The moment I stepped into the basement stairwell, closed the door behind me and secured the dead bolt, relief washed over me like a gust of morning air.

Still no sound from the main floor. I rushed down the stairs and spun into the unfinished basement. The high window let enough light in for me to see the door to Eli's prison was closed, locked from the outside with a sliding bolt lock high on the frame.

Now on concrete and under the main house, I didn't care about sound, so I sprinted to the room, slid the lock open, and flung the door wide.

Eli's head came up from where he lay on the thin mattress. He didn't look surprised to see me, and for a breath I just stood staring at him. I swallowed and took a step into the room, my hand still on the door handle.

"I need you to come with me," I said.

"You do? Why?" he asked.

"Because you're in danger here."

His expression didn't change. He was clearly too naïve to understand his predicament.

"Now?" he asked.

"Quickly! We have to hurry."

He pushed himself up and stood, grinning. "Okay."

We stood gazing at one another. I really had no idea who this boy was, yet I was risking everything to save him. Was I making a terrible mistake?

It was too late to second-guess myself. We had to move.

"Follow behind me closely, and stay quiet," I said.

Eli nodded and I turned to the window. But that was as far as I got before hearing footsteps overhead.

My pulse skyrocketed. Someone was in the house! I glanced over my shoulder at Eli, whose face remained unconcerned, and held a finger over my lips.

My mind was tumbling over itself, my flight instincts screaming for escape, knowing that at any moment Rose could open the door into the basement. Unless it wasn't her. And even if it was, she would have to get the key. I was glad I'd replaced the screen in the mudroom.

All these thoughts raced through my mind, silenced by the sound of more footsteps above.

We had to get out!

The window was too high to reach without something to stand on. I quickly scanned the basement, the boxes, and some old furniture, which included a small writing desk under a stack of boxes. It would take some time to get to that desk, but I didn't see any other alternative.

"Help me," I whispered to Eli, running for the desk. "We have to clear this desk and get it under the window."

"So we can get out," he whispered behind me. I wondered if he thought this was a game. Surely he wasn't that naïve.

"Yes."

Rose smiled as she approached her family home. She'd been terrified to do what Sylous asked, but now having followed his leading, she felt nearly jubilant. This was how it felt to surrender to God's will, even in the most difficult of circumstances.

She was smiling, but her fingers were still trembling. It was the quiet that had filled Ben's room when the toxins had finally stopped his heart. And that last death rasp. Now it was the boy's turn. But his death would be easier.

Her husband and sons were reading their nightly devotion together on the front porch. Evelyn was still safely tucked away in her bedroom. The sight eased some of Rose's tension. She was doing this for them. Keeping the valley safe, serving Christ and his kingdom. When it was finished all would be well.

Stephen jumped up and waved. She returned the gesture and collected her thick skirt in one hand while steadying herself on the handrail that guided her up the front steps.

"What are we reading today, dear husband?"

Harrison looked up from the book in his lap and smiled. "We're reading about the first time God cleansed the earth."

"I think drowning would be awful," Levi said.

"We wouldn't drown," Stephen said, picking at his nose. "We'd be on the boat because we're pure."

"That's correct, son." Harrison looked back up at his wife. "Will you be joining us?"

"Not tonight," Rose said, stepping past her children to her husband, who was sitting in his self-crafted rocking chair. The chair was a source of pride for him, even though he was careful not to show it. She placed her hand on Harrison's shoulder and leaned forward to kiss his cheek. "I'm going to check on Evelyn and put some soup on. Take your time."

"Sounds yummy, boys." Harrison looked up at her, brow arched. "Potato soup?"

"That's what I had in mind."

"Even better."

Rose pushed the screen door open and walked into the house. She removed her shoes and washed her feet, careful not to spill any water on the floor. After drying her feet then removing her overcoat, she walked to the kitchen to put a pot of water on for the soup.

The house was quiet, only her husband's soft voice shifting on the breeze outside. Rose took a deep breath, mind buzzing with the task set before her. She'd assumed that the boy would be easier than the old man, but facing that prospect now, she wasn't so sure.

She had to remind herself that the boy wasn't really a boy, but a deceiver in a cloak of innocence. A Fury in a lamb's coat. She was actually killing evil, not a child.

She'd poke her head in to check on Evelyn, then take some leftovers to the boy. Leftovers dosed with enough potassium chloride and thiopental to kill him peacefully in his sleep. She would have to figure out how to dispose of the body. Beyond the perimeter seemed like a natural solution. Sylous would know.

In the end, the community would conclude that the old man had died of his illness and the boy had escaped to be taken by the Fury.

The stairs creaked under her feet as she ascended to the second floor to check on Evelyn. She found her daughter reading in bed, curled up under blankets. Poor child. She really didn't deserve such pain, surely.

"How are you feeling, honey?" Rose asked.

Evelyn shrugged as Rose crossed the room. The rash had deepened in color and spread up Evelyn's left cheek. This wasn't good.

"Let me see," Rose said.

Evelyn slowly raised her hands to show

her mother that the rash had also spread down across her fingers. She sniffed, her bottom lip tucked under her teeth, tears shimmering in her eyes. "I'm sorry, Mother."

It occurred to Rose then that the rash might well be the effect of evil — not on Evelyn's part, but a sign of the darkness encroaching on Haven Valley. It made perfect sense. The rash had come on as Ben and Eli had neared.

Perhaps her daughter had a gift. Maybe she was a prophetic siren of evil. The rash would be healed as soon as the boy was dead.

Rose sat on the bed beside her daughter, comforted by the thought. "Don't you worry, sweetheart. This is all going to go away soon, I promise you."

"You're sure?"

She kissed the top of Evelyn's head. "Yes, I'm sure. I'll be back up in a few minutes with dinner. We'll reapply the salve later to help you sleep. I have a very good feeling that this will all be gone in a day or two at the most. Okay?"

Evelyn nodded.

"That's my girl." Rose stood. "Do you know how much I love you?"

"As much as the sky," her daughter said,

allowing a slight smile.

"That's right. And the sky goes forever."

"I love you too."

Rose left the room, descended the stairs, and hurried to the kitchen, eager now to be done with the task at hand.

Harrison and the other children were still on the porch, but they would be in soon. She fixed a bowl of leftover soup, poured some hot water in it so it wasn't so cold, and removed the vials from her dress pocket. She checked over her shoulder to ensure her family's voices remained outside the screen, then carefully measured the right dosages of both medicines.

Rose dumped the poisonous concoction into the warmed soup and stirred. She took a deep breath.

The time had come.

CHAPTER TWENTY-TWO

It took us way too long to clear the desk and manhandle it over to the window. I wondered if it was plausible that Eli could have done it by himself and decided yes, with enough time, he could have. It had to look like the boy had managed to jimmy the lock on his door and get out through the window on his own. At least that's what I wanted Rose to conclude, which meant I had to wipe the dust off the desk so I wouldn't leave prints.

But the desk wasn't tall enough.

"We need a box or a chest!" I whispered urgently.

"Like that one?" He was pointing to an old chest across the room.

"Yes," I said, running. "Like that one."

Once again Eli helped me. Thankfully, the chest was empty and we handled it easily. We carried it across the room, hefted it up on the desk, and set it down with a clunk.

A loud clunk.

"Hurry!" I whispered, wiping the dust off and clambering up. When I turned to help him, he was already kneeling on the desk beside me, staring up at the window. I followed his gaze. Then stepped up on the chest to get a closer look.

The windowsill, now at my chest, had a single rusty latch that looked as if it hadn't been used in decades. I twisted it as hard as I could but it refused to budge. My fingers were shaking, my hands sweating, and I couldn't get a good grasp.

More footsteps pounded overhead from several sets of feet, shaking free ceiling dust that fell over my arms. I glanced back at the door, certain it would fly open any moment.

Heart in my throat, I spun back to the lock and yanked as hard as I could. Still nothing.

Something tapped my leg and I glanced down to see Eli holding up a wrench. He smiled and my mind stilled. I didn't stop to consider where he'd found it or how he'd retrieved it so quickly. I just grabbed it from him, maneuvered the mouth over the lever, and jerked as hard as I could.

With a snap, the latch squealed open.

I placed the wrench on the windowsill and pushed the window open. Then I reached back for Eli. "Up, hurry. Hurry!"

He clambered up on the chest, reached for the window, which was just above his head, and jumped. I grabbed his waist and pushed him up. With a few kicks of his legs, he shimmied through and was out.

Holding my breath, I yanked myself up, pulled myself through the small opening, and made it about halfway before getting stuck at my waist without leverage. Eli grabbed my hand and tugged.

And then I was out and rolling free of the window, dress flying over my head. Eli fell to his rump and laughed as I jumped to my feet.

"Shhh!" I hushed, finger to my mouth. "Quiet."

I stood in a crouch, scanning the area. We'd emerged along the right side of the Pierce home. Anyone looking out the window of the house next door would see us. We had to move, and I already knew where we were going.

I grabbed Eli's hand, dropped my shoulders, and ran.

Rose had taken three steps toward the hall, soup bowl in hand, when the front screen door squeaked. The children were coming in.

She quickly returned the bowl to the counter. The patter of little feet sounded behind her, and she turned to see Levi and Stephen entering the kitchen.

"Call me when dinner is ready," Harrison's voice boomed from the living room.

Rose smiled at her children. "How would you two like to help Mommy with dinner?"

Levi pulled a stool over to the sink. "Should I peel the potatoes?"

"Too dangerous. But you can scrub them, and you can help, Stephen. Each of you scrub five potatoes, okay?"

"Okay."

"I'm going to take this food downstairs, then I'll return to cut them up for the soup," she said.

"Okay."

She ruffled Stephen's hair. "Good boy."

Careful not to spill, Rose hurried to her office, retrieved the key, made her way to the basement door, and opened it. She stepped in and locked the door behind her.

She tried to gather the full resolve she'd felt only minutes earlier, but uneasiness returned as she took the stairs down. Then again, no one said doing the right thing would be easy.

The moment she turned the corner into the main basement, she saw the desk and above it, the window. Open.

Still uncertain of what she was seeing, she looked to her right. The boy's door was open. She lost her grip on the bowl and it fell to the ground, smashing into a dozen shards. Still not daring to believe, she ran to the room.

Empty. The boy was gone!

Just to be sure, she hurried around the room, heart pounding, searching every nook and cranny. There could be no doubt, the boy was gone.

She rushed up to the desk, on which sat a chest. He'd somehow picked the lock on his door, slid the desk over here, gotten the window open, and climbed out.

Could a twelve-year-old boy do that alone? Maybe.

No. There was no way. Even if there was a way, she refused to accept it.

Someone had helped him.

Harrison was calling to her. "Honey, is everything alright?" He'd heard the shattering bowl.

"I'll be right up," she shouted, but her mind was on Sylous now. She'd betrayed him!

No . . . No, someone had betrayed her.

Who would do such a thing for a stranger? Who had anything to gain from freeing the boy? Who would be so bold as to do so from her home? Someone who had betrayed her before, Rose thought. Someone who believed the stranger had meaning.

Only one name came to mind.

Grace.

The abandoned train cars sat on rusted tracks to the north of Haven Valley. Only a stone's throw beyond the perimeter, the cars were out of sight except from the top of several boulders at the red line. When I was much younger, Jamie and I would climb those boulders and make up tales about how much gold and jewels the cars could carry.

That was before approved paths had been staked out. Before the laws to stick to those paths had been introduced and enforced. The only time I'd seen the train cars lately was with Jamie, when we'd broken the law so he could go check the Fury for himself.

Breathing hard, I pulled up just short of the red rope. I looked around to make sure we weren't seen by anyone doing a perimeter sweep. No one in sight. I glanced down at Eli, who'd matched me the whole way, two of his strides for each of mine. We hadn't spoken; I'd been focused on getting here without being detected.

He smiled at me.

"You good?" I asked.

"Good."

"Let's go."

"Where are we going?"

"To those cars," I said, and stepped over the red rope. Images of what had happened to me last time I'd been past the perimeter flashed through my mind. I'd tried to think of anyplace to hide Eli inside Haven Valley, but I knew once Rose discovered he was missing, they would search every house. There were a few abandoned buildings to the east that had once been used by the mining company, but they might be the first place the guardians looked.

At least for the night, the train cars were probably safe. The safest place I could think of anyway.

True, the Fury were out here. Part of me wondered if rescuing Eli from Rose only to put him in the reach of the Fury was doing him any favors. But he'd lived among the Fury for years and survived.

My body tensed every time I heard a sound. I was alone and vulnerable, even with Eli walking beside me. *Especially* with Eli beside me. He was just a boy.

Bobbie was absent. I took some comfort in that, because if there was any immediate danger, she would be around to warn me. At least, that's how I hoped she worked. Or maybe she'd become tired of my strong head and abandoned me. Like she'd said, she wouldn't force herself on me.

Either way, I missed her.

We reached the cars quickly. Three in total, linked by large rusted hooks. The sliding door on the one in front of us was open a couple feet.

"Go ahead," I said, turning to Eli. "Up inside." I offered my hand and helped the boy through the opening. With a final glance behind me, I hoisted myself up and in.

The inside of the car was nearly dark, but we could see well enough. The right side was empty; the left was strewn with stacked crates rotted by time. The ceiling was half rusted away, but the back half looked solid enough to stop rain. Best place I could see was the back right corner.

"Here," I said, stepping toward it. The floor was covered in a layer of leaves — I wished I had something to offer the boy to lie on. Something to keep him warm if the night became too cold. Maybe a light to give him some comfort, though a light would draw attention. But all I had was my dress, and I needed that.

I hadn't had any time to think through

this plan at all. And I had no more plan. I only knew that if I hoped to help Eli, I couldn't be caught myself.

He was checking out the dried leaves on the floor, seeing if they were free of snakes or something. Satisfied, he looked up at me.

"You're leaving," he said matter-of-factly. I was surprised by his calm.

"I need you to stay here tonight," I said, studying him. "Do you know why I took you away from the basement?"

"You thought I was in danger."

"Yes," I said. "And I have to return before they know I left my room. But you'll be safe here."

It was a lie, because I didn't actually know if he would be.

"Promise me you'll stay inside this car tonight," I said, hoping the urgency in my voice was clear. "I'll be back as soon as I can in the morning. Okay?"

"Okay."

"Promise me, Eli," I repeated. "Stay in this car tonight."

"I promise."

I nodded. "I'm sorry I have to leave."

His apparent lack of concern continued to surprise me. I should be relieved he wasn't afraid, but it didn't seem normal to be so unaffected. Maybe there really was something wrong with him? Again I was reminded how little I knew about this boy I had risked everything for. I wanted to ask him a hundred questions, but there wasn't time now.

"I will be back," I said.

He smiled. "Good."

Chapter Twenty-Three

I reached my house without being detected. The stars were out overhead, and the skyline was finally void of sunlight. Bunching up my skirt I climbed the small oak tree that stood outside my bedroom window. Then shimmied along the thick branch adjacent to the roof overhang, and in through the window I'd left open. The moment my feet hit the carpeted floor I felt a rush of relief.

I stood in the darkness, trying to calm my breathing, listening for any sound that might spell trouble. The house was quiet.

Rose had murdered Ben. The horror of it flooded me again, conflicting with thoughts of what I'd just done in defiance of Rose. I could hardly hold on to both ideas at the same time. I was sure Rose had her reasons, just like I had my reasons. Was I wrong, then? Was she?

I couldn't imagine Rose being wrong.

I forced the questions from my mind and

focused on the fact that I had a brother named Eli who was depending on me. He might be dangerous, but so was everything in my world right now.

A gust of cool night air reminded me my window was still open and got me moving. I closed it tight and yanked the curtains together as though doing so would conceal evidence of my betrayal. Then I removed my shoes and shoved them into the back corner of my closet where they wouldn't be discovered. But my dress was the worst — dusty and dirty from the basement and train car.

It took me less than a minute to undress, hide my clothing, and shrug into a clean dress.

What about my hair? And my hands! I could see several dark smudges across my palms and mud under my nails. I needed to wash before I was collected for dinner!

A hard, rapid knock on my door made me jump. My heart stopped. I dropped to my bed and crossed one leg over the other. "Yes?"

The door opened, and I did my best to appear as nonchalant as possible. And I would have pulled it off if it had only been my mother.

But it wasn't only her. Rose entered my

room behind her.

"As I said" — my mother indicated me — "she's been here all along."

I flicked my eyes from my mother to Rose, slowly tucking my fingers in toward my palms and moving them into the folds of my thick skirt to hide the smudges. Rose was here, in my home. *She knows. She knows it was me.*

Rose brushed past my mother, face drawn. "When did you get home?"

I think I would have answered well enough, but Bobbie appeared over Rose's shoulder, staring at me, and I was so taken aback by her sudden entrance that I struggled to speak.

"Tell as much of the truth as you can, but say nothing of Ben or Eli," Bobbie said. "It'll get you killed."

"Grace?" Rose said, and I shifted my gaze back to her eyes.

I cleared my throat. "Sorry. I came straight home from your house this afternoon." Truth.

"And you haven't left since?" Rose asked.

"No." Lie.

Rose was taking me in carefully. "You've been here? In your room?"

"Shift the conversation to your guilt regarding Levi and Stephen," Bobbie said.

277

"Speak some truth."

I spoke quickly, allowing guilt to swallow me. "I did exactly as you asked after letting you down at the house," I said. "Please . . ." I could feel my lower lip quiver. "I know it was wrong of me to leave the boys alone, but I didn't think to take them up to Evelyn's room. She was so distraught. I wanted to take care of her as best I could."

Rose blinked. For a moment, no one said anything. They were likely trying to follow my logic. But Rose knew what I was talking about.

"She hasn't left her room all evening, Rose," my mother said, answering Rose's original question for me. "Jamie and I have both been here."

Rose kept her gaze on me as my mother spoke. I could practically feel the heat rising from her shoulders. She took a step toward me. I wanted to flee, but I remained on the bed. She was only two feet from me now, drilling me with her glare.

"Would you lie to me, Grace?"

"No," I answered, my voice barely above a whisper.

"But you have lied to me before."

"Careful, Grace," Bobbie interjected. "She's trying to trap you."

"Yes," I said. "And I'm horrified by it."

"You aren't hiding anything from me now?" Rose pushed. "Not a single detail?"

"What do you mean?" I tried to appear confused. "No. I don't understand what you're talking about."

Rose hesitated. "Lies always come to the surface, Grace. Promise me I won't discover any more of yours."

"Never," I said. And I meant it. Eli was now my secret and my secret alone.

We stood there, holding one another in locked gazes, as the rest of the room stilled. Then the intensity in her eyes eased a tad, and she broke the hold with a nod.

"Good," she said.

"What's this all about?" Jamie asked from the door, arms crossed. Bobbie was gone.

Rose took a deep breath and let it out slowly. "Ben Weathers died earlier this evening, and the boy traveling with him is missing," she said.

My mother gasped, snatching her hand to her mouth. "No!"

"I'm afraid so."

For a long moment, my mother stared at Rose, unbelieving. I watched as she surrendered to the simple truth. Her husband had come back from the dead only to be snatched away again before she could make sense of his return.

"How?" she whispered.

"His heart apparently gave out. He was terribly ill."

My mother let out a gut-wrenching sob.

Rose gave her a gentle nod. "I know this must be difficult for you, and for that I am sorry."

As pain twisted my mother's face, anger rose in my chest. *Yes,* I thought, *my father's dead because Rose killed him.* I pressed my fingernails deeper into my palms.

Rose continued. "I believe the boy may have had help in his escape."

That shut the room down.

"And you thought it was Grace?" Jamie asked, looking at me.

My mother recovered enough to express outrage. "That's absurd!"

"Is it, Julianna?" Rose snapped. "Didn't both of your children recently betray this community? Do I not have good reason to question their loyalty?"

My mother stared at her without offering a defense. Because Rose was right.

Jamie was looking at me with suspicion, just as Rose had done moments earlier. He thought I could be guilty as well. Little did he know how right he was. He, perhaps more than Rose, might be my greater challenge now.

"I have to ask the hard questions," Rose said, pacing to her right. "But it appears Grace was here. And I suspect that you will attest to that, Jamie?"

He hesitated, then offered a reluctant nod. "She came home this afternoon."

Rose nodded. "Which means that either the boy did escape on his own or someone else helped him. We will begin home searches at first light tomorrow."

"Tomorrow?" Jamie interjected. "Why not tonight?"

"If he's being held in someone's home, he'll be there in the morning. If he escaped on his own, he's likely gone to the wind."

"Or hiding in one of the abandoned buildings," Jamie said. "For that matter, he could have found a way into any of our public buildings. Let me take a team out tonight and search everything but the homes. If he's on his own, we'll find him."

She eyed him, impressed, I thought. Surely he wouldn't go to the trains, not so far out at night.

Rose gave him a nod. "Alright. Take Claude and any guardians he recommends. Search every vacant building, every storehouse, every nook and cranny of the farm — everything but the homes inside the perimeter. We start with the homes at first light."

She stepped past Julianna and paused at Jamie's side. "You were right to be concerned. We're not safe as long as that boy is at large." She glanced back at Julianna and me for a moment. "Stay inside, and be on guard." And then she was gone.

We stood there as her footsteps clopped down the stairs, across the main floor and out the front entrance. The sound of the door closing echoed up the stairs.

Jamie dropped his arms to his sides. "Promise me there's no truth to her accusations," he said, looking directly at me.

"How could you even think such a thing?" our mother demanded.

"What accusations?" I cut in, wanting to deflect him. "Rose was just looking for clarity and I told her the truth. I failed her this afternoon, and I'm willing to pay for that, but I don't think she actually believes I helped the boy now. That's ridiculous."

"Is it? You think he's your brother."

"He's your brother too," I snapped.

"Says who? A man who abandoned me?"

Our mother turned and left us, crying into her hands.

Our time beyond the perimeter had divided my brother and me and built a wall between us. It was almost as if all the years we'd had before didn't exist.

What had the Fury done to him?

"I've done nothing wrong, brother," I lied, suppressing my frustration.

"I pray for your sake that's true, sister," he bit back, and stepped out of sight.

I spent half the night praying that Jamie wouldn't take his search beyond the perimeter in defiance of Rose's instruction to stay within. Claude was with him, and I knew the guardian would be loath to venture beyond the red marker at night. But still . . .

I finally fell asleep and dreamed of Eli. In my dream he was a Fury. A kind one at first, but at the end of the dream, he grew fangs and destroyed Bobbie and then went after my mother.

I woke with a start and hurried downstairs to find my mother drinking tea, dark circles under her eyes. She brightened and asked me how I was feeling. Hugged me and told me she was proud of me. When I asked her why, she smiled. "That's Ben's grandson inside of you," she said. "I think he would be as proud of you as I am. Not just because you're carrying our grandbaby, but because of who you've grown up to be."

I think I found a whole new love for my

mother in that moment.

But my mind was mostly on the boy.

"Did they find Eli?" I asked.

Her eyes drifted to the window. "No sign of him, Jamie said. They're already going house to house."

I nodded, trying not to sound too interested. "I hope they find him. I can't imagine him being alone out there."

"No. But I'm not sure being found will be good for him. Or whoever helped him." She looked at me. "These are dangerous times."

"The worst," I said. And then, after a pause, "Do you think he really is my brother?"

She hesitated. "I don't know, but I don't think Ben would lie." She looked away, eyes misted. "Sometimes I wonder if I was a fool to resist him the way I did."

She gathered herself and nodded at me. "With everything going on, you're free today. Take this time and rest. Stress isn't good for the baby."

"I will. What about you?"

"I have a prayer meeting," she said, rising. "I'll be back in a few hours."

I would be alone. Which gave me the window I needed to see to Eli.

My heart was already beating hard. I had to figure out what to do, but for now he needed food and some basics. And then we would see.

My mother left twenty minutes later, and I immediately began collecting items I thought Eli could use. Fresh clothes, older and smaller items that didn't fit Jamie anymore. A blanket, a flashlight, some matches, and a canteen of water. I carefully stole pieces of leftovers here and there, so that not too much of one thing was missing, then packed it all in a backpack and zipped it shut.

Odd as it sounded, I was thankful that the community was steering clear of me, because it gave me reason to stay clear of them. I was just the girl who was spending time alone in her room, repenting of her sin.

"What's the plan here, Grace?"

Bobbie. Behind me as I stood at the back door.

I gripped the backpack and shut my eyes. If I turned, I'd see her beautiful and worried expression. The wise voice that continued to remind me of the reality I was facing.

The reality that I didn't really have a plan here.

"You know as well as I do that Eli can't survive in a train car indefinitely. And he'll never be safe in Haven Valley."

I faced her, jaw set.

"You have to send him away," Bobbie said. "Give him enough supplies to make it to the city."

"It would take him days, and you know better than I what lies in wait out there," I said.

"What other choice do you have? You can't keep him here."

"I know," I said, shifting the pack on my shoulder. "I just haven't figured out what comes next."

Bobbie frowned and crossed her arms over her chest. "Well, you need to, and quick." She took a couple steps toward me, her dark eyes holding mine in place. "The longer you protect him, the longer you place yourself in danger. If he stays close to Haven Valley, they'll find him. And when they find him, they'll find out you've been helping him. Imagine what Rose will do then."

I knew she was right. I knew the threat against me had only begun, but there had to be a way out where I didn't risk Eli's life any more than I already had.

"What about your life, Grace?" Bobbie asked.

I dropped my eyes.

"What about the life inside you? You're

playing with fire."

"You don't have to stay if you don't want to," I snapped.

"Don't be foolish." Bobbie took another step forward. "You need me now more than ever. If I left you'd be facing this completely alone. Is that what you want?"

As I had multiple times before, I felt the warmth of having her near. The sense of security she offered, a companionship that I still didn't fully understand but longed for.

"No," I said.

"Then don't forsake me," she said.

I had always viewed our relationship as protector and victim. But maybe we were more alike than I'd first seen. Partners who needed each other's cooperation. Without my agreement, she was powerless to help, which was her purpose.

"I won't forsake you," I whispered.

"Then you'll never be alone," Bobbie said with a gentle smile. And I knew she wanted our partnership as much as I did.

We shared a final moment of knowing, a silent oath that tied us together. Then I slung the backpack over my shoulders and opened the back door.

Be careful, Grace, her voice whispered.

I glanced back over my shoulder to see that she was gone.

CHAPTER TWENTY-FOUR

It was midmorning by the time I reached the northern perimeter. It had taken me longer than expected, weaving between the buildings and avoiding being seen by anyone, especially the guardians who were sweeping the town. My stomach was in knots when I finally reached the train.

I quickly crossed toward the car in which I'd left Eli, praying he was still there and safe. I hauled myself up and scanned the car, expecting to see the boy.

"Eli?" I whispered, hoping he'd pop out from the darkness. But nothing. I scanned the entire train car as I moved to the corner where he'd been the night before.

"Eli," I called louder. Nothing.

There was an imprint left on the dried leaves against the far wall, as I'd expected to find, but the train car now sat empty. He'd left? Or been discovered! No, I would have heard.

A whole new possibility crashed through me at the thought. The Fury!

I hurried to the door and jumped down, glancing in the direction of the town. No sign of anyone. Good. Scurrying along the tracks, I checked under the cars.

"Eli?"

The day was utterly quiet. He was gone. Just . . . gone.

I reached the last car and crossed the tracks to the backside of the abandoned train. No sign of him anywhere, not along the tracks, not in the grass leading up to the trees. In that moment I felt completely lost. What now?

"Now is when you head back to the safety of your house."

I jumped at Bobbie's voice. "Stop sneaking up on me."

She shrugged. "Sorry. But you've had your little adventure, and now it's time to get back to safety."

"I have to find him!"

"Do you? He's managed to survive all this time out in the wild without your help."

"He had my father to help him."

"Or maybe he was helping your father. Either way, you're not in a position to help him now."

I heard a faint sound then, just as I was

289

about to tell Bobbie how wrong she was. A human voice, soft and distant. Singing?

I strained to hear again, but the breeze had died away and only the sounds of nature reached me.

"Did you hear that?" I asked, staring at the forest.

She was listening as well. "Be careful. Trust nothing. You have to get back, Grace. Now, before you're lured into terrible danger."

"It sounded like singing."

The bushes and leaves swayed with the breeze. Yellow and white flowers grew in clumps that were scattered here and there at the base of large tree trunks. It was quite beautiful. Was I being lured by the Fury, or was it Eli?

"You're assuming he's not a Fury," Bobbie said. "The worst of them come as angels of light, whispering of love and wonders in a fearless world. Give your heart to them and they will ravage you in the deepest imaginable hell."

The distant voice came again and I held my breath, turning toward the sound. Then again — a faint song — and this time I knew the voice had to be Eli's.

"Be careful, Grace."

But I was already moving toward the forest, drawn by that faint, sweet voice. My brother's voice. Eli couldn't be the kind of Fury Bobbie was warning me about. And I wouldn't give my heart to him or anyone anyway. Right?

A stick cracked under my foot and I jumped, nerves on high alert. Instead of slowing down, I surged forward, suddenly desperate to reach him. I couldn't abandon Eli, and I was certain that voice belonged to him.

The voice became clearer as I rushed through the trees. The soft and playful melody drifted on the wind and filled the air around me. The trees suddenly ended, and I pulled up in a clearing that ran up to a small cliff. The singing came from the ravine beyond. Either Eli or a Fury that sounded like Eli, luring me into its trap.

I hesitated only a moment, then crept up to the edge. Peered over.

There was a small stream running through the ravine. Squatting beside the sparkling brook was Eli, fingertips dipping into the water.

"Eli?"

He jerked his head around, saw me, and smiled. "Hi, Grace."

I looked in either direction. The descent into the ravine wasn't much, only eight or ten feet, but it was steep.

"How did you get down there?" I asked.

"I jumped," he said matter-of-factly.

Jumped? That was a long jump for a small boy.

"You were supposed to stay in the train car," I said, hoping he heard the edge in my voice. I wanted to be out of the clearing and back inside the safety of the train cars. "You made me a promise."

"I promised to stay in the train car for the night," Eli said. "But now it's daytime."

I opened my mouth to scold him but stopped. It didn't matter right now. "We need to go back. It's too dangerous for you to be out here alone."

He stood and turned around to face me, eyes bright and haunting. "What's so dangerous?" he asked, shaking the water from his fingers.

"How can you not know about the danger of the Fury? You've lived out there your whole life."

"Exactly," he said. "That's why I asked what's so dangerous."

"You're saying they aren't real?"

"That doesn't mean we have to be afraid." He looked around curiously. "Looks safe to me."

"It's not," I said. "The forest's full of

danger."

"But the train car's safe?"

"Much safer."

"Why?"

He was just a curious boy who didn't understand the world he'd stepped into, I tried to remind myself. Or a Fury trying to trick me. But looking at him, I couldn't believe that.

"Because it offers us protection."

"And you think you need protection?"

What a childish thing to say, Bobbie's voice whispered in my mind.

I glanced around but didn't see her at first. *Careful, Grace. This boy isn't who he seems. Foolishness will get you killed.* Bobbie emerged from behind a tree several yards to my right. She was half tucked out of sight, eyes glued to the boy, communicating with me but focused on him. *He doesn't know the danger he faces.*

I turned back to the boy, who was still staring at me, waiting for me to answer. I felt vulnerable in his gaze, as though he could see through the barrier of my skin.

"Why do you spend so much time and effort being careful?" Eli asked. "Living afraid sounds awful hard."

I couldn't answer. I knew the reasons, of course: Because darkness was everywhere and always coming for us. Because we had been called to guard our hearts from sin so we could be made worthy to inherit the earth. Mostly because without protection we would be killed by the Fury.

I knew all the reasons, but I couldn't deny that he was right. Living a life watching for danger was hard. Almost impossible. How had he and Ben survived beyond the perimeter? If he wasn't a Fury himself, he knew something I didn't.

Before I could respond, Eli walked to the cliff and scrambled up, using rocks and roots for hand- and footholds. He stood up beside me and brushed his hands on his pants. "See, simple. You can just jump down and climb up."

"Okay, but we need to go now," I said, starting to turn.

"Can you imagine what it would be like if you didn't have to protect yourself for even one day?" he asked.

I glanced over and saw that he was looking back at the brook in the ravine.

He twisted around, eyes daring, smiling. "I take it back. Imagine you didn't have to protect yourself for one hour." He lifted his finger. "Imagine that for just that one hour there was nothing to protect yourself from. Nothing to fear. Can you even imagine it?"

I tried, but I couldn't. And I couldn't because the very idea of living without fear was like trying to live without truth. Fear was a constant friend that protected me, so why would I try to imagine living without it?

"Then you could be like this beautiful brook, flowing without a care," Eli said, motioning to the water. "Wouldn't that be something? Try it, just for a few seconds, right now."

I followed his eyes and for the first time wondered what living in such freedom would be like. For a moment, I could actually imagine not having any fear at all. It would be like heaven on earth.

Careful, Grace, Bobbie's familiar voice whispered. *Don't let him trick you into trouble.* I could see her in my peripheral vision, hidden in the shadow of a tree. Her words snuffed out my calm.

Eli glanced in her direction, but when I followed his eyes, she was gone. Had he seen her? Impossible. Only I saw her. Hadn't that been proven?

"Oh, I almost forgot," he said, digging into his pocket. "Look what I found." He held out his palm. Perched in the center of his hand was a small golden stone, catching the light of the sun and shining as bright as the blue wonder in his eyes. "It was hidden in the muddy water. Ben and I used to search for buried treasure. Usually in the darkest places. Isn't it amazing?"

My heart ached at his mention of my father. I blinked. Did Eli know Ben was gone? No, he couldn't. I should tell him, but I didn't know how to say it.

The boy was turning the stone in his palm, smiling at its beauty. But the moment he looked up at me again, his face fell. Tears welled in his eyes.

He knew, I thought. It was as though he'd read my mind the way Bobbie did. We stood there for a moment, heartache filling the space between us.

But looking into his eyes, I saw more. I saw a certainty and peace that defied his sorrow. That calm seemed to reach out to me and hold me. For several long beats my fear fell away and I just stood there, strangely comforted.

"He knows now," Eli said.

I blinked. "Knows what?" I asked, assuming the *he* Eli was referring to was my father.

"Everything." He stepped up to me and held out the golden stone. "It's going to be okay," he said, dropping the stone into my hand. And then, with a nod, "I'll stay in the train car if you want."

I wanted to say something but found no words. What had just happened?

"I would like that," I finally said. "I just want you to be safe."

"Protected," he said. "So that evil doesn't get me."

"Yes, protected." Although my concern felt less acute now. Even a bit silly.

But then my sanity returned and I chided myself for letting my guard down. Imagined sentiments were one thing, but this was reality, where danger hid in every dark corner.

Without a word, Eli walked past me, headed back in the direction of the train tracks. And then he was running and I was hurrying to catch him. The backpack bounced on my back, slowing me, and part of me wished I didn't have it so I could run past him. It was all a game to him. Another part of me wanted to call out and tell him to slow down, but my more cautious side knew how far sound could travel in these mountains.

We reached the train car winded, I just a few steps behind him.

Eli stepped up onto the thick wooden beam that lined the rusted tracks and spun around to face me. "I beat you."

"You got a head start!"

He laughed. I started to join him but stopped myself. Had I lost my mind? The thought filled me with a moment's dread. Hadn't Bobbie warned me of just this?

But I still couldn't fear Eli. My father had insisted I keep him safe. I could do that and keep myself safe as well. But to do that, I had to get back before anyone knew I'd gone.

I shrugged the backpack off my shoulders and handed it to him. "Here's some things to keep you comfortable through the night."

Eli stepped off the track, sat on the wooden rail, and opened the pack.

"It's not much, just the basics," I said, watching him comb through the bag. "Food, water, a blanket. And a flashlight in case you need it. Promise me you'll be here when I come back. I just need a little more time to figure out what to do. I'm so sorry about all this, but they're looking for you, you understand? It's safer here for now than anywhere I can think of. Right?"

Eli looked up at me. "Right. But don't worry about me. I'm okay."

I stared at him, no longer able to hold back my curiosity. "Are you Ben's son?" I asked.

"Yes," he replied without a beat. "He adopted me."

"You're not a Fury?"

His brow arched. "Do I act like a Fury?"

"I don't know."

"You should. They're everywhere."

"But are you one?"

"No."

That's what a Fury would say. Bobbie again, whispering in my ear.

But for now I wanted to believe Eli, so I did. "Okay. Just one more night, I promise."

"And then what?" he asked.

"And then I'll find someplace safer for you inside the perimeter."

"One more night, then." He stood, hefted the backpack over one shoulder, and gave me a nod. "Let's go."

CHAPTER TWENTY-FIVE

Rose stood at her kitchen sink. The house was silent, her children asleep, her husband quietly tucked away in his office. She'd cleaned the kitchen twice with hope that the activity would distract her mind from the trial at hand, but nothing seemed to help. The kitchen was dark, with only a faint light streaming in from the hallway. She stared out the window above the sink, looking at the darkness that blanketed Haven Valley.

Sylous had given her five days to kill the intruders. But the boy was now missing. The thought made her cringe.

The guardians had spent the entire day searching and had come up with nothing. Every home and structure in the community had been overturned and shaken out. Not a trace of the missing boy anywhere. He'd either vanished into thin air or escaped into the forest. Either way, she'd failed Sylous.

Rose had gone over yesterday's events a hundred times. She'd left her children with her husband, gone to the medical clinic to deal with the old man, and come home to find the boy missing. Neither her husband nor the children had seen or heard a thing.

The boy had obviously left through the basement window, but how could he have managed without help? Yet there was no sign of a break-in. The key to the basement was in its place, the door to the basement locked, the windows and screens all intact. But she refused to believe he'd escaped on his own. He was too naïve a boy to attempt, much less pull off, an escape.

Then again, Sylous said he was a Fury. She shivered.

Even so, he was no longer within the perimeter, surely. Maybe Sylous would leave well enough alone. Maybe her nerves were more about having been violated in her own home, the sanctuary under her most rigid control.

She dropped her eyes to the sink, closed them and exhaled. Beyond the perimeter, the boy didn't present an immediate threat to Haven Valley. Sylous would know what to do.

The room's atmosphere shifted, and it

caught Rose so off guard that she gasped. She spun around and saw him standing there in her kitchen. Green eyes and white suit, his face clear even in the darkened room.

"Sylous," she whispered.

He was in her home, without warning, in the place where her children slept. They always met in the church. Yet here he was, standing before her, cold and consuming. Her stomach turned.

"The boy must be found," Sylous said, taking a step toward her.

She placed both palms on either side of the sink behind her, feeling his seduction pull at her mind.

"We've searched everywhere," Rose said, keeping her voice just above a whisper.

"Search further, search again." His voice was low and deep, the anger in his tone barely contained. "Haven Valley will suffer if he isn't found in time."

Three days. Less now. There had to be another way!

"The old man's dead," Rose said. "The boy's not inside the perimeter."

Sylous glared at her, eyes sharp and accusing. "I don't think you appreciate what we're dealing with here."

"Surely there's a way you can kill him

beyond . . ."

Sylous closed the distance between them in one movement, one hand on her chest, pinning her against the sink. He gripped her neck from behind and held her face close to his own. She could smell his sweat, feel his breath.

"Haven't I made it clear that I have no control over the Fury except to protect you from them?"

"Then protect us from him!" she cried, aware that she'd crossed a line.

"I am," he thundered, and she winced, hoping no one had heard. "I am protecting Haven Valley from the boy through you! Are you no longer my worthy servant?"

Rose couldn't answer. Fear had closed her throat and stolen her words. Sylous's anger seemed to be reaching into her chest and squeezing her heart.

He eased his grip on her neck and spoke in a soft voice. "This Fury comes as a boy feigning innocence and wonder to compromise your holiness. You must know by now that even my survival depends on your holiness."

His assertion confused her. He depended on them? She'd always seen it the other way around.

"It goes both ways, like any relationship,"

303

he said, calming. "The bride's holiness is the air I breathe. By following the law of God, you've established a well of righteousness in this valley that is deep and rich. Its aroma rises to please the divine. But if that purity is compromised in this last hour, the world falls to the Fury. Trust me when I tell you, my love, that as long as the boy lives, the final remnant of God's bride are in grave danger. The demon must be killed."

Sylous reached up and gently stroked Rose's left cheek, his fingers running down the length of her chin and neckline. "If you fail God the whole world will be lost."

Rose wanted to cry there in his arms. Wanted to beg for his forgiveness as the warmth of his touch flowed through her blood. She would rather die than lose the thing she craved most. Sylous's communion. His loyalty. His love.

"Find him," Sylous whispered.

Rose swallowed and nodded. "I will find him."

"Gather the faithful. Press them. Search beyond the perimeter. Find him."

"I will."

"And?" Sylous said.

Rose inhaled his scent and let the fear of losing him sink deep into her bones. She would use it as her fuel.

"And I will kill him."

An emergency meeting had been called at dawn. Every member of Haven Valley occupied the creaking pews as bodies shifted nervously. Word of the missing boy was well known. Every home had been thoroughly searched the day before. The fear was palpable, and for good reason.

Evil threatened to crush Haven Valley. And yet no one suspected that I was complicit.

The rash that had taken to Evelyn's body had spread to others. They were already calling it an outbreak. Colin and Rebecca had red blotches on their faces — the only members of the council thus far. But at least a dozen others were absently scratching at their arms and sides. Still, with the boy at large, the rash was of little concern. In fact, the boy's disappearance was the cause of the rash, many were saying.

I sat in the pew, mind numbed by the madness of the role I'd played in the great reckoning facing us all. Eli was alive because of me. Haven Valley was under terrible threat because of me. I was a bundle of nerves, avoiding eye contact with anyone, thankful I was still expected to keep to myself in penance. Not even Alice approached me, despite news of her pregnancy. She likely hated me for endangering her unborn child.

If they only knew! *Dear God, help me.* Like the crest of a wave torn by a gale-force wind, my emotions were frayed and divided. What was I doing? Doubt raged through me.

But I was also still caught up in my interaction with Eli. *Imagine living without fear for an hour. Then you could be like the brook. Wouldn't that be something?*

His way of being was peculiar, innocent, and terrifying. I felt the desire to both run to him and run away. I couldn't decide what would be better.

I knew where Bobbie stood on the matter — we'd talked all the way home yesterday. I should run, naturally. I should leave the boy alone and let him find his own way. And I should avoid Rose because she would see the guilt in my eyes. *Bow out and don't say a word to anyone about anything,* Bobbie had instructed. *If they are meant to find the boy, they will. If not, the boy will find a way to survive.*

Besides, what if the boy really was a wolf in sheep's clothing? I couldn't see it because I was already under his spell, Bobbie had suggested, which is why I should just take a deep breath and stay away.

And my promise to my father?

"What if Ben wasn't your father?" Bobbie said. "What if that was another Fury looking like your father?"

"That's possible?"

"I keep telling you, there are many different kinds of Fury. They can present as almost anything. Your only job now is to protect the unborn child in your womb. Please tell me nothing is as important."

I hesitated. "You're right."

"So you'll stay away?"

Another pause. "For now."

She frowned. "I can only help you if you let me."

I was lost in those thoughts when Andrew walked into the Chapel and headed to the pew where I sat with my mother and Jamie. The same unpleasant feeling that always bloomed in my chest opened as he approached. In the chaos of everything, I hadn't thought of my baby's father at all.

We hadn't shared a private moment since Rose had told him about my pregnancy. I'd hoped that carrying his child would change the way I felt about him, but I still hadn't chosen him.

"Good morning, Grace," he said, lowering himself beside me.

"Good morning."

He laid his hand on my knee. "How are you feeling?"

I wanted to move my knee but remained still as practiced. "Fine," I lied. My muscles and bones ached from the constant tension.

"That's good to hear. I was hoping you would join me tonight for dinner?"

It wasn't one of my nights to be with Andrew, so the question took me a tad off guard. And with all that was happening, how could I? I wasn't sure how to respond.

Noticing my hesitation, Andrew continued. "It's just that we haven't had a chance to talk since news of our pregnancy. I know things are chaotic, but it would be nice to celebrate."

Before I could answer, my mother placed her hand on my other knee. "The truth is, Andrew, Grace is putting on a brave face. So much has happened and she's rather ill."

She'd sensed my awkwardness and saved me. Something in her had changed since Ben and Eli's arrival. She was hardly the same woman I'd known a week ago, and I loved her even more deeply for it.

Andrew removed his hand and his eyes darkened with concern. "Should she see the doctor?"

"Oh, no," my mother said. "He's already

instructed her to take appropriate vitamins and rest. I'm keeping a close eye on her, don't you worry."

Andrew nodded. "Good. Thank you." He dropped his voice and shifted his gaze back to me. "Perhaps when you're feeling better then? We should discuss your move into my house."

I hesitated. "Yes, of course."

After a lingering gaze, Andrew stood and walked to sit on the front pew with the other council members.

I offered my mother a thin smile of appreciation, and for a moment we held each other in a knowing look. Things were different between us now that I was with child. For the first time in many years, she was mothering me.

She gave my knee a gentle squeeze, then turned her focus back to the stage. I glanced up and saw Rose taking the podium. Silence filled the room.

Rose faced us, her eyes focused. They lingered on me longer than the others. Or maybe my fear was making me see things.

"Is it not true that we have accepted Jesus, God's only Son, and him alone, as our Savior?"

The congregation answered in unison, "Yes."

"Is it not true that all forms of wickedness would drag us away from our inheritance of the kingdom of heaven, which awaits us all because of our decision to accept him into our hearts?"

Again, "Yes."

"And that we follow every word given us in his Holy Scriptures?"

"Yes."

"That word warns us about wolves in sheep's clothing, who come with a message of hope and love while drawing us into idolatry. This is the bride's great test. We have accepted our calling while the world has fallen prey to the Fury."

She paced to her right, eyes on her flock, drawing them into a holy passion for righteousness. I could feel it washing over me and I cringed, knowing I had desecrated the very holiness the word had led our community into.

"By now you all know that a man named Ben Weathers entered our haven. Many of you knew Ben before we were called to holiness, and because of that connection to our past he was permitted to stay within the perimeter as we sought to understand the meaning of his arrival. How could a man survive the Fury and make his way to us? Now we know: he was infected with the

Fury himself. A wolf in sheep's clothing. But the darkness swallowed him and took his life the day before last."

She let the statement stand as speculation whispered through the sanctuary. My mother sat perfectly still beside me. We were perhaps the only two in that room who wondered if Rose could be wrong about Ben.

Rose lifted her hand for silence. "As you also know, a young boy unknown to us all accompanied Ben. He too was permitted to stay. But much has come to light since their arrival. Now we know the darkness took Ben's life because his only role was to deliver the boy to us. And that boy is the darkness masquerading as light."

Silence.

Colin was the first to ask the obvious question. "How can you be sure? He's so young."

"I'm certain!" Rose snapped with enough conviction to make any man cringe. She continued in a more measured tone. "I have it from the highest authority that the great deceiver who would test us in the end has come. And our time is short. He may have seemed young and innocent, but if his full power as a Fury is allowed to manifest, you will wish you had never been born!"

311

I held my breath, taken aback by her strong words. Voices of concern erupted, but Rose silenced them quickly with both hands raised.

"The boy escaped us, almost certainly with the help of someone here. He walks free to stalk us in his deceptive ways. For the sake of our salvation and inheritance, I implore you to understand the gravity of this situation. The wolf is at large and must be apprehended at all costs."

A beat passed. To a man, woman, and child, we hung on her every word. She still hadn't answered Colin's simple question with any detail. How could she be so sure Eli was the wolf in sheep's clothing? Eli had done nothing to show himself as a threat. Sylous had said this?

My heart was pounding so loudly that I wondered if my mother might hear. Or worse, Jamie, who was watching the prophet, drinking in her words. He wouldn't hesitate to turn me in if he even suspected my involvement.

"Until the boy and any who might have assisted him are found, we are placing Haven Valley under high-alert protocols. All members of Haven Valley will be required to be in their homes by five p.m. sharp. All children will be kept at home during the day, watched and accounted for. No one is allowed outside alone. Groups of three must be maintained at all times. All able men over the age of sixteen will report to Harrison to participate in a search for the boy, which will now extend beyond the perimeter."

"Outside the perimeter?" Colin said. "If the boy's escaped our valley, then we're safe."

"We will not be safe until the boy is found!" Rose raged. "He will find his way in at night, in our dreams, in the very air we breathe! He must be found immediately."

I could see the veins bulging at her hairline. She was terrified of Eli. If she ever got her hands on the boy she would kill him without hesitation.

"What if he really is just a boy?" My mother's frail voice filled the room as she slowly stood. "How can you be so sure he's a Fury?"

I wanted to yank her back down. I wanted to stand and defend her, apologize for her outburst, claim exhaustion and insanity. But it was too late.

"Are you questioning my authority in this matter?" Rose demanded.

"No. I'm just trying to understand how we can be so sure he's not just a boy who longs to be protected. And isn't our charter to remain within the safety of the red line? Why are we risking our purity by breaking our own law?"

Rose pinned my mother with a terrifying glare, then moved her gaze across the rest of the community. "Who else among you doubts my knowing in this matter?"

No one answered, but others surely wondered the same. I exhaled the breath I'd been holding and hoped that the collective questioning would grant my mother some grace even as she sat back down, back stiff. I'd never seen her show such courage.

Rose stepped forward. "The one who was sent to us from God, who leads us and protects us, appeared to me. Sylous's warning was undeniable. If the boy is allowed to live five days among us, he will bring the end to all. Two of those days have passed. It is written that the darkness comes as light and the thief comes to kill and destroy. If we doubt Sylous, we will be consumed by the evil that stalks us and we will surely die."

Rose stood trembling. Not a soul stirred.

I glanced to my left and saw my mother sitting like a board, face drained of blood. No one, not even my mother in her new-found courage, would dare voice doubt now.

"What we face is beyond our understanding," Rose breathed. "But there can be no doubt: the boy must be found." With that, she walked unsteadily down the steps and sat in the pew.

Harrison let the silence linger before clearing his throat. "We have survived the wrath of the Fury by remaining true to the word given us." His voice echoed through the small auditorium. "Stand with me," he said, spreading his arms wide. "Stand with us against the evil that seduces us and threatens our pure standing before God."

Someone began to softly weep. Cries were joined by sniffles as Haven Valley's faithful tried to contain the heavy presence of holiness in that place.

"And if there is one among us who has conspired with the devil, may God have mercy on your soul. I beg you to come forward now before your defiance of God brings death to us all."

Fear swallowed me as the reality of my situation returned to me with those words. He was speaking about me. I wasn't only standing against my family, Rose, and the town; I was in defiance of Sylous. And of God.

And this to protect a boy who could bring about the end of the world.

God help me.

CHAPTER TWENTY-SIX

My mind was filled with images of Eli. Of his bright smile filling with gnarled teeth, his sweet voice turning harsh as he sneered and salivated, his blue eyes becoming bottomless pits of terror. But everyone knew I was given to flights of fancy. Like a child, they told me. So maybe it was only my overactive imagination filling me with wild thoughts. Was Eli leading me astray as Rose suggested? Was I really willing to continue to endanger Haven Valley to keep one boy hidden from a reckoning with truth?

Several hours had passed since we'd left the Chapel in a daze of holy terror. A new sense of desperation to find the missing boy was paramount in every hushed conversation. I was trying to rest as my mother had instructed, but how could I with such unrest everywhere?

I heard the search party called out as the flock descended the hill on which the small church sat. They would start searching outside the perimeter on the south side, sweeping north. By noon they would reach the train tracks and find Eli. I was sure of it.

I sat up on my bed and swung my feet over the side. If I did nothing, the search parties would find Eli with the backpack I'd left for him! It would quickly lead them to me.

If I risked trying to move him into the perimeter, I could get caught red-handed. Worse, I might be bringing the wolf into the sheep pen.

Either way, I was in terrible trouble. Bobbie had warned me.

But there was still the issue of Eli himself that battered my brain. Who was he? Why did he fill me with both fear and great calm at the same time? How could he be both a dangerous beast and an innocent wonder? By helping him escape and keeping him hidden, was I acting in mercy or in deception?

Surely the latter, but I couldn't bring myself to accept it.

Raised voices drifted through my door, which was slightly ajar. I lifted my head from my palms. Jamie and Mother were having words. Again. I stood close to my door to listen.

317

"Please, Jamie . . ."

"I just don't understand what would cause you to do such a thing," Jamie snapped. "Our family is facing accusations as it is, with Rose eyeing Grace. The intruder was your husband, for heaven's sake! Why would you draw more attention to us?"

"I don't know," Mother said, voice trembling. "I saw the boy when he first came, Jamie." She sniffled. "His eyes, blue as they were . . . I've only ever been that struck once before — by you and your sister, when you were born. Everyone told us your eyes would lose their shine, but they never did."

"And that was enough reason to stand publicly against our leadership?" Jamie demanded.

"Grace said your father mentioned the word *brother*. And after seeing him . . ." She faltered. "I've dreamed of him, Jamie. He's just a child."

"He isn't just a child!" Jamie spat. "He's dangerous! You're living proof of his deception."

"I haven't been deceived. I just believe he needs his family to protect him."

"Based on the color of his eyes?"

"Based on the way he made me feel. Based on the way I still feel!"

Jamie didn't respond, and a moment later

hard steps across the wooden floor echoed up the stairs.

"Jamie, please try to understand," my mother called after him, but it was too late. I heard the front door slam, followed by a desperate whimper. Soon my mother's whimpers turned to sobs, and I ducked back inside my room and pushed my door shut.

My heart was racing. I wasn't the only one who sensed something about Eli. My mother had connected with him the way I had. Were we both deceived, then? Or both his only hope?

I considered rushing out of my room and down the stairs to stand with my mother and tell her she wasn't alone. But there wasn't time for that. Emboldened by her hope, I knew if I was going to act, I had to do so now.

"Don't do this, Grace."

I turned to face Bobbie, who was standing a couple feet behind me, face drawn and pale. I knew what she was going to say before the words came out.

"You'll get caught."

"Yes, I might," I agreed. There was no point in denying what I knew.

"Then you would be insane to do what you're thinking," Bobbie said.

But it was already too late, because I knew

what I was going to do as if I'd always known. I wasn't willing for the boy to die before I understood who he really was.

Bobbie stepped forward and placed her hands on both of my shoulders. "Listen to me, Grace. If you're wrong . . . Do not do this! They'll crucify you!"

"Not if I don't get caught," I said. "That's a risk I'm willing to take."

Bobbie searched my eyes, deeply concerned. "He's dangerous," she finally said.

"And what if he isn't?"

"Why would you risk so much for a boy who might get everyone killed?"

"You told me to trust no one. That anyone could be the deceiver. Can you tell me without a shadow of a doubt that Eli is the darkness masquerading as light?"

She balked, because she didn't know.

"Me neither," I said. "And until I can, I'm not willing to sign his death warrant."

"I may not know what kind of Fury he is —"

"Or if he's just a boy," I interrupted.

"Or if he's just a boy," she acquiesced. "But I do know he presents a danger to you, and you're my charge. I beg you to reconsider. Please listen to wisdom. That would be me. Listen to *me*!"

"They'll find the backpack!"

She gave a nod. "Then get the backpack but leave him!"

I didn't respond.

"Grace, just the backpack."

I stared at her, then turned on my heels and walked out of my room.

For the second time in two days, I found myself slipping out through my bedroom window. My fear was still there, screaming in the background, begging me to stay in my room where it was safe. But a new determination nudged me onward.

Before I left I made sure to make an appearance before my mother, who was still crying at the kitchen table. I got some water, played the sick card, and announced I was retiring to my room for several hours, hoping to sleep through my nausea. My mother was so caught up in her own grief that she'd just nodded me off.

I knew my mother well. Her emotions often trapped her in dark places, and as much as I wished she didn't have to suffer, I was counting on that suffering now. It could easily be hours before she moved from her slump.

I dropped to the grass from the low branch and quickly hid behind the large trunk. Houses rose on either side of me.

Another neat row ran before me, and a third behind our house. It was the middle of the day, so I'd have to move with extreme caution, especially with the search teams out and about. They were surely still working their way north, outside the perimeter. So my best route was probably the most direct path, albeit out of sight. It would take me about ten minutes to maneuver along the south side of the homes, then north to the abandoned cars, keeping well clear of any occupied structures.

Bobbie's words still whispered through my mind, setting my nerves on edge. *Please listen to wisdom, Grace. Don't do this!* I inhaled deeply and tried to settle my mind. The only thing I knew for certain was that if Rose got her hands on Eli, she would kill him as she'd killed my father. So I focused on that thought alone.

I ducked low as I ran along the back of our house, stopped at the corner to make sure the coast was clear, then went on to the next house. My pulse pounded, and the occasional voice from inside the homes pushed me faster.

Bobbie wasn't with me, and for that I was grateful, but her warning clanged like a bell at the back of my mind.

I reached the last home, pulled up at the

corner, flattened my back against the brick, and took several deep breaths. So far so good. With a quick poke of my head around the corner, I saw that the coast was clear. The town had come to a virtual standstill — that was good. But anyone caught outside would stand out — that wasn't so good.

I drew my head back and let out a long breath. Just a quick sprint to the tree line, I told myself. Then north along the trees and west to the tracks. I could do this.

I pushed off the wall and raced toward the tree line, knowing that I was at my most vulnerable out here, in the open. Knowing that a voice would call out at any moment, demanding to know why I was running away from the town like a terrified rabbit.

But none came. And then I was at the trees and grabbing a trunk to stop myself. I collapsed to my knees in the shade, panting but safe. For the moment.

The breeze carried voices to me from the east, and I turned to listen. Nothing. It had probably been one of the search parties at the perimeter, less than fifty paces from where I hid. They were still a long way from Eli.

It took me at least ten careful minutes to reach the northern perimeter unseen. Then another five to pick my way west. Oddly enough, the silence bothered me as much as anything, because Bobbie's voice, despite her absence, was always in that silence, demanding I turn back.

But I didn't turn back. And when the tracks finally came into view, I was running again, desperate to be in the protection of the car that held Eli.

I raced along the tracks toward the car. *Please be here.* A quick glance south assured me I was still alone.

Then I was at the railcar, yanking myself up and in on my belly. Rolling to my knees.

"Eli?"

He stared at me with round eyes from the corner where he was seated. "Hi, Grace," he said, smiling.

"We need to go." I rushed over and began collecting the things I'd brought him the day before, which were now strewn about.

"Where are we going?"

"To some abandoned buildings east of town," I said in a rush. "They've been searched and cleared. The search parties are headed this way. We have to move!"

"Okay." No concern marked his voice. But I didn't have time to consider whether it was his naïveté or his way of deception. We were going, and that was that.

He reached for the backpack and held it

open so I could shove things inside. Soon we were packed up and he'd strapped the bag to his back. I nodded for him to follow and, as he always did, he moved without questioning me. This was another peculiar aspect of the boy, but not something I had time to dwell on. I dropped from the train car and turned back to help Eli down. I placed a finger over my lips, and he nodded.

I knew the abandoned buildings left by the mining company were marked as cleared, because Jamie had given my mother and me a full report after yesterday's search had come up empty. They'd placed yellow tape on all the outbuildings that had been cleared. Sure, they would probably return to search them again in the coming days, but for now, it was the safest place I could think of. And closer to me if I needed to reach Eli.

I had no plan beyond moving Eli, but that was enough for me now.

"Ready?" I whispered. "As fast as we can."

"Ready," he said.

And then we were off, he following close behind as I raced back the way I had come.

CHAPTER TWENTY-SEVEN

We reached the abandoned buildings without being seen except by the birds in the trees. Tucked out of sight along the tree line, I pulled up, breathing heavily. Eli stopped beside me and looked at the scene.

Tall weeds and dying grass covered the ground. The back of the building — either an old house or a store — was falling apart. The wooden planks, once white and clean, were gray and rotting. All the windows were boarded up. Where there should be three steps that led up to the back door, there were only two. But the yellow tape over the door was all I cared about right now. The words "Keep Out" were printed in black along the two-inch-wide strip.

But I was going in.

I motioned for Eli to follow and crossed through the tall grass to the stairs. "Watch yourself," I cautioned as I straddled the missing first step to the creaking second and then the third. The porch held my weight easily enough. Ducking under the tape, I pushed the back door open and stepped into the house.

"Close the door behind you," I whispered, studying the room. The moment he did, we were plunged into darkness. I waited, hoping my eyes would adjust, until a small beam of light cut through the darkness from behind me. I turned to see Eli holding out the flashlight I had brought him, smiling proudly.

"Good thinking," I said, and took the flashlight. "Follow me. And try to keep your feet in the prints that are already here, okay?"

"Okay."

The bottom floor of the house was as I'd expected. Thick layers of dust were scuffed from the boots of those who'd searched the building yesterday. The stench of mold hung in the air. The house was empty except for the tiny creatures that scattered into hiding as we entered each room.

A single flight of steps led up, and they creaked from age as we ascended. On the second floor, we found a narrow hallway with a small bathroom and two bedrooms.

I tried the knob over the sink in the bathroom, and not surprisingly, nothing happened. No toilet either. The place was about as homey as the train car Eli had been stashed in, but safe. For now. We moved into the farthest room — a simple square space with a double window boarded up.

Eli looked around and placed his backpack on the ground. "I'll take this room," he said cheerfully.

"You'll have to be careful with the flashlight at night," I said, handing it back to him. "You don't want to draw attention."

"Got it." He took the flashlight and flicked it off. A thin shaft of light broke through two boards at the window, giving us some light but not much. "How long will I stay here?"

"Until they're done searching for you."

"Who's searching for me?" he asked.

"Everyone."

"Why?"

I knew I didn't have a lot of time, but I wanted answers as much as he did. "Because they believe you're dangerous."

Eli considered this for a moment. "But you don't."

Truth was, I didn't know how I felt. "I think you're just a boy," I lied. That's what I wanted to believe, even though everything about him suggested he was more.

Eli grinned. "And you believe you're just a girl."

"Well, no. I'm a woman."

He stared at me and gave a funny chuckle, as if to say, *That's what I just said.* He turned and squatted beside the backpack. Unzipped it. Then began to take the items out and set them on the floor around him.

"Who are you, Eli?" The words fell from my lips before I could call them back.

He looked up at me over his shoulder. "Just a boy, right?"

I wasn't in the mood. Standing there in the dim room, I needed reassurance that I wasn't unwittingly enabling the darkness.

"Are you dangerous?"

He stood and faced me, his expression relaxed and innocent. "Is the sunlight a danger to the night?" he asked.

It was a strange question. "They don't exist at the same time, so no."

"But imagine all you knew was night and had never seen the sun. If a sun came up and chased the darkness away, would you feel threatened?"

"If all I knew was darkness? I suppose so, yes."

"Well, think of me as the sun," he said.

I shook my head. "But Haven Valley doesn't live in darkness."

"Then fear, which is the same thing. Does Haven Valley live in fear?"

"Fear isn't darkness," I said. "It keeps us from putting our hand in the fire."

"You don't have to rely on fear to keep you from putting your hand in the fire. You can make that choice without fear, only because you still want your hand. But I'm talking about deeper fears. The fear of failure or loss. Being afraid that you aren't good enough. Fearing evil. Understand?"

I didn't know how to answer.

"Are you afraid, Grace?" he asked sweetly. "A little fear is good for you."

"Because it keeps you safe."

"Yes."

"Because you can be threatened?"

"Yes."

"Because you're just a girl?"

"Yes."

I could feel my bottom lip quivering, though I couldn't explain why. There was something unnerving about the energy in Eli's tone, the look in his eyes.

"Like I'm just a boy." He flashed a grin, spun around, and grabbed something off the ground. "The truth is, you're the light of the world." He bounced back around to face me, now clutching something in his palm. "You've heard this?"

"That I'm the light of the world?"

"Yes."

It sounded familiar, but it wasn't a phrase I could pin down. What was I supposed to say? Light of the world. I wasn't even sure I understood what that meant. Besides, Jesus was the light, not me.

"But you're made in the likeness of God," he said as if hearing my thoughts, just like Bobbie could. "Like God. Do you think that means eyelashes and fingernails?"

I'd never considered the question.

"No," Eli said. "He's the light without darkness."

Warning bells issuing charges of heresy clanged through my mind, and in that moment I thought Eli really *was* the darkness masquerading as light. He was suggesting that I was like God?

"I was made like God, but we fell into darkness," I said, voicing what I'd been taught.

"Exactly. Into blindness of the light. Blindness to who you've always been. Darkness. But that doesn't mean you can't see again." His eyes brimmed with excitement. "Want to see something?"

I hesitated, leery of his naïve beliefs, but his enthusiasm was infectious. "All right."

He opened his palm, and in the center sat

a single match. He grabbed the match with his other hand and scraped it against his denim pants leg. The match caught flame and flickered between us.

"Even a small amount of light chases away shadows. What can threaten this light?"

"It's just a small flame," I said.

"Then let's make it bigger!" He swept his free hand around the front of the match, blocking it from my vision, then opened both hands so his palms were spread out like a tray. There in the center where the match had been hovered a ball of light.

I gasped and stepped back.

The ball was a perfect sphere the size of a baseball, slowly rotating in the air. Eli had turned a match into a ball of flames. But not like yellow or red flames I'd seen before. It almost looked electric to me. Like a powerful light bulb without the glass.

"Bigger light," Eli said. "Nice?" He smiled at me over the turning sphere.

"That's . . . that's impossible," I croaked.

"Yes," he said in a playful tone. "If I were just a boy."

I looked past the brilliant light sphere into his kind eyes and felt my pulse begin to slow. His face was filled with knowing and peace.

"Impossible," he began again, "if you were

just a girl. But if you're the light of the world, then not so impossible."

I shifted my eyes back to the light, drawn to its surface. I wanted to reach out and touch it, to let my fingertips feel its power.

"Go ahead," he said.

"It's safe?"

"Of course."

I stepped closer, losing myself in the wonder of it all. Usually it was me sharing wild stories with children; now a child was sharing one with me. Only this one was real. Right?

Eli watched as I reached my hand out. I could feel the warmth, but more, I felt it drawing me closer, closer, like a magnet drawing steel.

The moment my fingertips touched the sphere, they began to tingle just under the surface. And then, without warning, power swelled and shot up my arm and down through my body — into my lungs and deeper still into my very bones.

I gasped. But I wasn't afraid. It was comforting. Warm but not hot. Powerful but not painful. For a split second, I felt certain that the light and I were one. I belonged to it and it belonged to me. It was in me and I was in it. And in that moment, I wanted to fall deeper into the light and forget the rest of the world.

"Now tell me," Eli said. "What can threaten this light?"

What blots out light? I dropped my hand and looked at him. "Darkness," I said.

"You think? Well, let's see." He hurried to the farthest, darkest corner of the room. But the darkness was no more, naturally. It was now the brightest part of the room.

"Is the light threatened here?" Eli asked, turning back.

"No," I said. "But —"

"More darkness, then," Eli cried. "Bigger darkness!" He rushed from the room, calling over his shoulder, "We must find bigger darkness!" I'd never seen him so excited as he rushed down the stairs with the ball hovering above one hand.

"Eli!" I hurried to catch him, but he was already down and around the corner. "Be careful!"

I followed the light, naturally. It couldn't be hidden. It illuminated every dark space and danced across surfaces that had been cast in deep shadow. Through the kitchen, across the main room, and into what looked to be a storeroom. Windowless.

He stood in the center of the room, a couple feet from me. Slowly he extended the ball of light toward me, and as he did, the light grew. It reached out with long wispy fingers around us, then spread to all four corners. All traces of darkness were gone in its brilliance.

A room that had been encapsulated in darkness was now fully illuminated, and all from the sphere in Eli's palm.

"There can be no darkness where this light is," Eli said. "And its source is infinite, with no limit or end. What can possibly threaten that light?"

"Nothing," I said, my eyes fixated on the light still dancing in Eli's hands.

"Nothing. When you don't see the light, you feel threatened. Close your eyes."

I looked at him, then closed my eyes.

"Keep them closed," he said. "What do you see?"

"Darkness." Fear began to creep back into my chest, but I kept my eyes closed.

"You're blind to the light," he said with a small chuckle. "That's all. So you see darkness and feel fear, and so goes the whole world, lost in darkness. But the darkness isn't actually threatening you. Your blindness is." A beat. "Open your eyes."

I did, and light flooded my vision. I blinked, staring at the sphere. Tears sprang to my eyes. How beautiful the light was in that moment of seeing.

"The biggest lie is that fear will keep you safe in the darkness, but fear *is* the darkness. So round and round you go, fighting darkness with darkness. Better to open your eyes and see the light. In that light, there is no darkness. So you've always been safe. You just don't know it because you're blind to who you are as the light."

I stood there for a long moment, his words ringing in my ears. They defied all I believed about the world. About my identity. Could it be so simple? No, I thought, it didn't make sense.

But there stood a boy who seemed to know no fear.

Eli pressed his hands together and the ball of light vanished, plunging us back into darkness. In the space of less than a breath my familiar friend, fear, was whispering in my ear.

I had to get out and back home! This was all wrong, I could feel it in my bones.

Something touched my hand and I jumped. Eli's hand wrapped around my fingers and gently pulled me forward. Then out of the room into the deep shadows of the house. But at least I could see.

He smiled up at me and dropped my hand. I wanted to ask him questions. I wanted to understand how anything he'd just shown me could be true. I wanted to know he wasn't deceiving me. But all I could do was stare at him as he smiled at me.

"Cool, huh?" he said.

I nodded, but I wasn't so sure. "Cool."

"That's you, the light. So why are you afraid?"

I lay on my bed as darkness stole the light outside my window. I had been there for hours, although it felt like minutes.

I'd managed to get back home without being detected, and as I put distance between myself and the house where Eli was hidden, the buzz of the experience faded. By the time I sneaked back into my room, the experience itself was a distant memory, replaced by a logic that demanded I figure out what was really happening.

I remembered little Stephen saying Eli could do magic. And now I'd witnessed something like magic with my own eyes, something that shouldn't be possible. What other power did he have? What if that power was exactly what Rose and the rest of Haven Valley feared? Weren't they justified in that fear?

But I couldn't deny the way the light had called to me. The beauty it held, the joy and love it had given me. Deception? Truth? What had my father learned that he could no longer tell me? Who was Eli?

Round and round I chased in the same mental circles, from uncertainty to desire, from fear to peace and back into fear. My mind wanted to rationalize it all, but I couldn't, and my heart was torn between acceptance and rejection.

Bobbie had spent a good hour with me, sitting on the end of my bed, before finally leaving me alone. We'd fallen in and out of the same rounds of conversation, much like the rounds that were happening in my mind.

Bobbie: "You should be more afraid of him now than ever."

Me: "He said I was the light of the world."

Bobbie: "He's a dangerous child who will send you to hell. You can't trust him."

Me: "I want to believe him."

Bobbie: "That would be foolish. Use your wisdom. Think this through."

Me: "Can I be threatened?"

Bobbie: "Don't be ridiculous, of course you can! Have you forgotten what lies beyond the perimeter? Can you be threatened? *He* threatens you!"

Me: "What if he's right and I am what he says?"

Bobbie: "What if he's wrong? You'll lose

everything. Are you willing to risk that?"

Me: "I saw it with my own eyes."

Bobbie: "That's how deception works. He's defying everything your teachers have taught you from the Holy Book."

Me: "What if those teachers are wrong?"

Bobbie: "What if they're right? The devil is playing games with you. Use your logic, Grace. Use wisdom!"

Me: "So this is deception."

Bobbie: "You have to stay away from him."

Me: "You're right."

And then after a while, we'd start all over again to the point of Bobbie's incredulous exhaustion. Eventually, she'd given me one last warning and left me alone.

When I first heard the commotion downstairs, I nearly ignored it. But then I thought I recognized Rose's voice and sat up. There was no mistaking it. Rose was downstairs!

I rushed to my door and pressed my ear against the wooden surface. I couldn't make out what they were saying, but I recognized my brother's voice as well. And then my mother's softer tone. I took a deep breath and eased the door open a sliver.

"We have reason to believe you know more than you're letting on," Rose said.

"I swear I've told you everything I know," my mother insisted.

Then Jamie: "Mother, if you confess, amends can be made. If they force you, it will go badly. Please, for the love of God, tell them!"

Confess? Confess to what? I opened my bedroom door wider and stepped out into the hallway, listening intently.

"I have nothing to confess. I don't even know what you're accusing me of."

"We have evidence, Julianna!" Rose snapped. "You aren't doing yourself any favors by hiding the truth."

"What evidence?"

A long beat.

"We found signs of someone hiding in one of the old train cars north of the perimeter," Rose said.

"This," Jamie said.

The room fell quiet, and two thoughts dropped into my head — like two hand grenades. One, Eli and I must have left something behind. Two, it wouldn't take my mother long to realize that it was my doing.

My sins had caught up with me!

I considered rushing back into my room, locking the door, and scrambling back out my window to hide away with Eli. But how long could we actually survive? They would find us. They would find him. What had I been thinking?

"Do you have another explanation for how my old shirt ended up out there?" Jamie asked.

Panic lapped at my mind. I'd taken some of Jamie's old things to Eli. How stupid! And how could we have been so careless to leave something behind?

"I . . ." My mother faltered. She knew it wasn't her or Jamie, which meant it had to be me.

"Well?" Rose pressed. "Do you have any other explanation?"

"No," my mother finally whispered.

"No?" Rose demanded.

"No," Mother said. "I don't."

I didn't understand. I pushed off the wall, leaning closer but staying out of sight.

"So you confess to helping the boy escape?" Rose asked.

"He's just a boy, Rose," my mother said, her tone low and controlled.

Confusion spread across my chest. What was she doing?

"You have no idea what you've done here," Rose said, voice scalding.

"Tell us where he is," Jamie snapped.

"I won't," my mother replied.

No, I thought. *No, she can't do this!* I stepped forward and felt a hand grab my arm to pull me back. I spun to see Bobbie

341

standing beside me, shaking her head.

"That boy will be the end of Haven Valley!" Rose cried. "Tell us where he is or I swear you will be thrown to the Fury!"

"I can't let her do this," I whispered, tugging against Bobbie's hold.

She placed her other hand on my shoulder. "Yes you can, and you must."

"Think carefully about what your silence will cost you," Rose threatened.

"Mother, please," Jamie said. "I beg you, please —"

"I won't allow you to harm him," my mother said. "He's Ben's son."

"Take her!" Rose shrieked. "I swear it will be your life or his. Take her away!"

I struggled against Bobbie's hold, tears filling my eyes and spilling down my cheeks. I wanted to cry out that it was me they wanted, that I was the guilty party. But my voice was lost to my shock and grief. And to Bobbie's warning stare.

"Why are you holding me back?" I raged at her.

"Because you want me to," Bobbie said. And that crushed me, because deep down I knew she had to be right.

There were more mumbled words downstairs, more heavy steps, and then finally there was nothing but silence.

I fell forward into Bobbie's arms and she pulled me close as I wept, tortured by a single thought.

I didn't deserve to live.

I fell forward into Robbie's arms, and she pulled me close as I wept, undone by a single thought:

I didn't deserve to live.

CHAPTER TWENTY-EIGHT

I lay awake most of the night, vacillating between raw emotion and numbness. Back and forth, neither granting me any peace.

I'd heard Jamie come home a few hours before the sun came up. He plodded up the stairs, maybe in exhaustion, maybe in disbelief. He paused outside my door, and I feared he might come inside. What would I say to him if he did? Would he see the guilt written all over my face, drag me away to lock me in a cell with my mother?

I never found out, because he didn't come in. He just stood outside my door for a minute before walking back down the stairs.

The sun had come up an hour ago, and I considered moving from where I was but couldn't find the will. My mother had confessed to my sin. I could save her if I surrendered myself. If I turned Eli in. Him for her. A stranger for my mother.

But he wasn't a stranger anymore. And

I'd made a promise to my father. And my mother would be horrified to learn I'd sacrificed Eli. And maybe he was the hope we all needed in Haven Valley.

Bobbie was no help. Admitting to my role in Eli's escape would bring great trouble to me, she argued. Besides, I couldn't be sure Rose would actually harm my mother.

I heard a commotion downstairs. Jamie was up. Again he climbed the stairs; again he stood outside my door. This time he knocked.

"Grace?" he called through the door without opening it.

I didn't respond. What was I supposed to say?

"Grace, I'm headed back out to search."

They hadn't found him. I forced myself up and off the bed, then walked to the door and opened it. My brother forced a smile. Dark circles hung under his eyes. His face was pale, his facial hair untrimmed. He looked as if he hadn't slept in days.

I imagined I looked the same. For a moment, we just stood there, neither of us wanting the other to see what was really happening behind the masks we were wearing.

Jamie cleared his throat. "Are you going to be okay here alone today?"

"I'll manage."

He nodded and paused another moment as if he might say something else, but then seemed to think better of it and turned to leave. He was at the top of the stairs when I spoke.

"How is she?" I asked.

He stilled for a beat, and I saw him roll his hands into fists at his hips. He glanced over his shoulder, and I thought maybe I saw remorse in his eyes. Without a word, he turned back and descended the stairs.

My thoughts jumped to the worst scenarios imaginable. Worse than death. Images filled with pain and misery. My mother's body broken and abused, her mind torn, her will fading.

Because of me.

I stood in my doorway as Jamie's boots clumped across the first floor and out the front door. Fresh tears blurred my vision as thoughts of the beautiful woman who had raised me filled my mind. And with them, a terrible guilt strong enough to snuff me out.

I knew then that I couldn't let them harm my mother. It couldn't be her for my sake. It couldn't be her for Eli's sake. There was only one solution.

I had to turn Eli over to Rose.

I walked out through my back door and carefully made my way across the town toward the east side where I'd hidden Eli in the abandoned building. I was mindful of being seen but cared less than I had previously. In an hour, when I walked up to the Pierce home with the boy in hand, it would all be over anyway.

I'd expected my fear of the consequences of my sins to assault me, but I was either too numb or too resolved. I did fear for Eli, however, so I began to lie to myself.

Maybe Rose wouldn't kill Eli. Maybe if he showed her what he'd shown me, she would change her mind. Eli didn't seem to fear anything, so maybe he would find a way to save himself. Maybe there was hope after all. I needed to at least imagine that much so I could maintain the strength needed to save my mother.

As soon as the abandoned house was in sight, that hope began to fade. How could I really be considering this? I should just trade myself for my mother. Leave the boy out of it. Tell them that I'd helped him escape and he'd taken off into the forest. But what would that solve? Rose wouldn't rest until the boy was found.

I took a deep breath and made my way to the back of the house. Turning the corner I came to a stop, surprised. Eli was standing in the tall grass behind the house, basking in the sun as a light breeze pulled at his hair.

I glanced around to make sure we were alone. He shouldn't be outside!

He must have heard me because he turned around, smiling. I tried to politely return his smile but couldn't. The sight of him standing there — the sun washing over his round face, his eyes catching the light and shining like jewels — filled me with terrible guilt.

Eli walked toward me, his expression never wavering. He reached me, lifted his hand to wrap his fingers into mine and looked up at me. "It's okay, Grace."

Okay? What was okay? He had no idea just how not okay things were.

Tears filled my eyes. Surely he didn't know what was coming. But then maybe he did. Maybe he had always known.

"Can I show you something?" he asked. He doubled back in the direction he'd come, his hand still laced in mine, gently urging me to follow. "Come on, it's okay. Promise."

I went with him, wondering how I was going to break the news to him. Or if I could. Maybe I should just take him without any explanation.

We crossed the backyard and stepped into the forest.

"Where are we going?"

"You'll see. Hurry." The excitement in his voice only deepened my guilt. How could such an innocent boy be the subject of such rage and fear?

When we reached the red rope, I instinctively pulled back.

Eli paused. He glanced up at me without releasing my hand. "Don't worry. Nothing can hurt you here."

"He's wrong." I looked to my right to see Bobbie leaning against a tree. "You most definitely can be threatened here and everywhere." She pushed herself off the tree. "But confessing to Rose will bring you certain suffering."

What are you saying? Go past the red rope with him?

"If you refuse to abandon him, regardless of my advice, better to go with him than turn him in. Rose is a bigger threat to you now than the Fury beyond the rope." She shrugged. "Either way, you're playing with fire."

I looked back at the boy, who seemed oblivious to her. As I looked into his eyes, peace began to fill my chest.

Eli gave my hand a light tug. "Come on."

I stepped over the red rope and let him lead me forward. The forest was thick, but Eli deftly maneuvered us through the trees. I could see no path. After several minutes the trees thinned out. The grass was greener here and the sun was hot with so little shade. Still I followed, hand in hand with Eli, both of us silent.

We reached the base of a steep hill that rose above the forest. I knew it well because it was visible from Haven Valley, though I didn't know anyone who'd actually climbed it. There was a small game trail that headed up and out of sight. As a child, I'd often looked at the grassy knoll and thought of the Fury hidden in a lair here, waiting for me to wander away from safety so they could tear into me.

Eli dropped my hand. "To the top," he said.

"The top? I'm not sure that's a good idea."

"Come on," Eli said, starting for the small dirt path. "Up, up, up." He didn't glance behind to make sure I was following; he just left me standing there, uncertain.

I glanced behind me and could see the

roofs of the homes that ran along the edge of Haven Valley. I'd followed him this far, and going back now without him would be pointless. Without him, I had nothing to exchange for my mother.

Was he leading me into a trap? Bobbie had said it was okay to follow him. But Bobbie didn't want me to confess to having hidden Eli.

I swallowed and started up the path, hurrying now to catch Eli. The path was thin and steep, winding up and around the hill toward the top. The higher we climbed, the more tenuous the path became, falling off on the right to a deep ravine.

"Why are we climbing so high?" I demanded, now truly unnerved.

"Some things are best done in high places," he said. "Hurry!"

What things? I wondered. Things the Fury did? But Bobbie had said it was okay.

My lungs started to burn and my legs ached from the climb, farther and farther up. I tried to keep my mind off the danger we were placing ourselves in so far from safety. I tried to keep my mind off the fact that we would have to go back down the same way we'd come up. I tried to keep my mind off my mother.

But I failed miserably on all counts.

Eli stopped ten paces ahead of me, and I hurried the last few steps to his side. We had crested the grassy hilltop. At the center lay several large flat rocks. Eli ran to the closest and jumped up. "We're here!"

I walked to the rock and looked around. From up here so much was clear. As far as I could see in every direction, mountains rolled to the horizon. Forests stood guard, thick with Fury who remained hidden until called upon to consume the unfaithful.

But I was most interested in Haven Valley behind us. It was the first time I'd seen the whole town from this bird's-eye view.

I had lived most of my life inside this valley. Homes lined up in neat little rows to the south. The paved road up the middle between the outbuildings. The rise north, on which the little white Chapel was perched. The fields to the west, with barn and cows and goats and chicken coops. The schoolhouse and storage units to the east. I could see the large symbolic gate, the old train cars, everything. The entire town lay out before me in a perfectly maintained oval surrounded by the red perimeter rope, and beyond it, the trees.

Two search parties were still at it, one on either side of town. Rose wasn't giving up. From here, the people looked like tiny stick figures. One of them was likely Jamie.

"I've never seen Haven Valley from so high," I said.

"Or maybe you've never really seen Haven Valley at all," Eli said. "But that's why we are here."

I looked up at him standing on the rock, staring down the hill, face flat now. "It is? What do you mean?"

He shoved his chin at whatever had caught his attention. "See for yourself."

Immediately, a distant haunting cry shrieked on the wind, sending a chill up my spine. I slowly turned my head, following his stare.

Down below, along the tree line of a meadow, was a Fury half in, half out of the dark forest. A black shroud moved like a fog around it. I couldn't see its eyes or mouth, but I knew it was staring up at us from inside that dark hood.

My heart stopped and I inched backward. My calves bumped into the rock Eli stood on, and I spun. Grabbed his hand, near panic. "It's . . ."

"A Fury. Yes, I see it," Eli finished for me, his voice calm as ever.

"You see it?"

As the words left my mouth, another shriek — more like a whine — echoed below me and I twisted back, still clutching Eli's hand. Two more beasts stepped out from the trees to the far right of the first one, these clearly larger. And then several more, emerging from the trees like black fog. How many were in those trees? Too many! Even one was too many!

"Of course I see them," Eli said. "They're right there, aren't they?"

I could hardly breathe now. "They're between us and the town." *Breathe.* "How are we going to get out of here?"

A chorus of haunting cries echoed around me, to the left and right now. More Fury — I dared not look. We were surrounded by them!

"God help us," I whispered.

"They're pretty far from home," Eli said. "They normally stay much closer to their hosts."

"We have to get back!" I cried.

"To where? There?" He was looking directly at Haven Valley, and when I lifted my eyes, I couldn't at first comprehend what I was seeing.

The town I'd grown up in looked nothing like I knew it. A black fog hung low to the ground within the red perimeter. It rippled with long writhing cords or maybe snakes that stretched from building to building, as if they were some kind of plumbing system, only above ground. The same black fog was concentrated around each home, curling and coiling with long tendrils. All of this I saw in a single glance.

But it was the Fury in the fog that threw my mind into complete disarray. Hundreds of wraiths, thousands maybe, swirled around the search parties, hovered around the homes, drifted in and out of the walls, trailed by the fog wafting around them like a stubborn foul scent. So many Fury, smothering the town. Where there were some outside the perimeter, there were a hundredfold inside that rope.

Like a growing symphony, their sound reached me, distant at first, then growing in volume, a terrible high-pitched wail mixed with a soft, throaty, guttural roar. The sound was as horrifying as the sight. And it came from inside the perimeter.

Haven Valley was infested with Fury!

"What's happening?" I cried. "Why is . . ." I didn't even know what my question was because I was staring at the impossible.

"Shadows," Eli said.

"Shadows?"

"Darkness. Blindness. Fear. Fury. They're all the same thing."

"But . . . they're inside the perimeter?"

"Where they've always been."

"We have to tell them!" But my mind was immediately thrown back into the impossibility of what I was seeing. No, this couldn't be. We were protected from the Fury inside the perimeter! I was seeing something that wasn't there.

"This isn't real," I ventured, spinning back to Eli.

"Not really, no. No more than darkness is real. It's only the absence of light."

"No, I mean there can't be any Fury in the perimeter. They're out there, in the world, not here!"

"You're right, they are out there, smothering the world. But they are also here. In fact, there are many more Fury in Haven Valley than in most places. Sylous first opened your eyes to the same fear that's always existed in the whole world, then promised to hide it from you if you follow the law. He's a spirit of religion."

"How can the Fury be here? We're Christians! You're saying our faith is a failure?"

"It's not that Christianity has failed; it's that so few Christians have really tried it. If you were in the truth, you would know love without fear. You think you're saved from some future hell, but as you can see, it's all around you. Fear has invaded you and blinded you to the light."

Invaded me? Panic swirled around me, and as it did, I heard a shriek in the back of my mind. The Fury were inside of me? I scrambled up on the rock beside Eli and grabbed his hand, if only to still the terror now raging through me.

"Make it stop!" I cried, and covered my face with my hands, clenching my eyes shut. "Stop this!"

"Okay," he said, unconcerned.

Immediately the sound stopped, as if he'd pulled the cord that powered it.

"Look now."

I slowly opened my eyes and looked at the valley below. I gasped and jerked my hands from my face. Where only a moment ago Haven Valley had been smothered by a writhing darkness, now it glowed bright. Wisps of light strewn with vibrant colors — red, blue, green and gold — swirled around the buildings.

"She who has eyes to see, let her see," Eli said. "Nice, huh?"

"What happened?" I asked.

"Now you're seeing the truth beyond fear."

"What is it?"

"Light. Love. Sight. The kingdom of heaven. They're all the same."

"You mean the inheritance of the pure?" I asked, looking down at him. "But that's . . . It hasn't come yet." I turned my eyes back on the town. "And what happened to the Fury?"

"There's light and love seen in true sight, which we call the kingdom. And there's darkness and fear experienced in blindness, which we can call the world. Which do you prefer?" He was smiling, daring me.

And then the light was gone again, replaced once more by the dark fog trailing a thousand Fury. But they were silent now.

For a few seconds, I just stared. I didn't know if I dared believe him.

I glanced around, hoping Bobbie would appear to give me some guidance.

"She's not here now," Eli said. "I sent her away because I want you to listen to me before we go back to town."

He had that power over her? I felt exposed there, but maybe he did have some power over the Fury.

"We can't go back down there," I said, voice unsteady.

"Of course we can. You have to take me to Rose. But first, tell me who you are." He beamed beside me, daring me to tell him what was so obvious.

"You already know," I said. "Grace."

"That's your fear-based self. Who is the true you? Remember?"

I hesitated. "You mean the light?"

"The light of the world. So if you're the light, why are you afraid of the Fury, who are only darkness and can't exist in the light?"

Could it be true? Yes, it could be. I knew that in my bones, but it sounded far too good to be true.

"Because you cling to fear and darkness as your protector, that's all," he said. "But you can't serve two masters. You have to let go of one to serve the other. Deny one to know the other. Let go of your whole life bound in fear to awaken to who you are as the light. And that light shows itself as love."

Looking into his bright blue eyes so full of certainty, I allowed myself to believe him for a moment. It still sounded too good to be true, but surrendering to his words, even for a few moments, flooded me with a hope I had never known.

"So, you're saying that everyone in Haven Valley is the light of the world, but we've all been blinded to that light by the Fury?"

"Just like the rest of the world."

"Why would Sylous show us the Fury?"

"To increase your fear so you would follow him."

"Why?"

Excitement filled his eyes. "You'll see soon enough."

I couldn't wrap my mind around what he seemed to be suggesting, so I pushed back again. "That's the opposite of what Rose teaches. We're good Christians, so how can the Fury blind us?"

"Actually, you serve fear. You think it will save you, but fear can't save you. Only love can, and God is love. You can choose the light, which shows itself as love, or you can choose darkness, which shows itself as fear. Not both."

"But there can also be some wisdom in fear, right?"

"In the world's eyes, yes. It seems to protect you. Do this and you will be safe. Don't do that or you will be in trouble. Run, hide, attack, defend. But that keeps you in fear of the monster you run from. So does judgment. You can only judge what you fear. In blindness, fear sounds godly, but it's a false god. And that false god is the air most people breathe. Religion has given itself over to it. You understand this?"

His words set off a high-pitched ringing in my ears as he continued.

"Love, though . . . there is no fear in love. None. It's the light in which there is no darkness. It's the truth that makes no accounting of wrong, because that can only be done in fear. Until you awaken to this love, none of your confessions or beliefs mean anything. This was written thousands of years ago. It's not new truth. It's only been forgotten, you understand?"

I nodded, stupefied by the thought that if he was right, everything I had been taught was upside down.

Eli chuckled. "Yup. But if you have the courage to step beyond what you were taught, that can change." He took my hand in his and stared at the valley. "It's time."

"No. No, we can't go back down there." The town was still smothered by the black wraith-filled fog. "You have to change this."

"You mean close your eyes to the Fury?"

"I can't go down there like this." I grasped for more arguments to dissuade him. "And if I turn you over to Rose, she'll kill you."

"But I'm not afraid to die," he said. "Why would anyone who knows themselves as the light be afraid of the death of their body? The body is beautiful, but only a temporary tent to live through. Come on." He started down from the rock, giving my hand a gentle tug.

"Wait!"

He looked up.

"Can you just make the Fury go away?"

"That's what we're doing. But to do that, we have to go into it. Don't worry, I'll be right with you. Just remember that you're the light. When you know that, the Fury vanish like shadows." He paused, then added, "If it helps, call them shadows rather than Fury."

The guardians would soon be looking for me. My mother was being held for my sin. I had to get back.

I gave Eli a tentative nod. "Okay. Stay with me."

"I'll never leave you, Grace."

And then we were heading back down the declining game trail.

CHAPTER TWENTY-NINE

Fear raged through me as we hurried down, my hand in Eli's. And when he led me into the clearing where I could see the wraiths emerging from the trees, my heart was in my throat.

Shadows. They are only shadows. And I'm the light. The light of the world.

I don't think my recitations chased them away. I think Eli did that, because the moment we stepped into the clearing, those closest drifted back like dogs backing away from a predator. Then they faded and were gone, like shadows under a brightening sun.

Confidence surged through my chest. As long as I was with Eli, I was safe. And yes, I was the light of the world. Nothing could harm the light, only block it.

Eli and I shared a knowing glance. He giggled, then let out a triumphant whoop and raced forward, yanking me along behind him. Part of me was startled by his boldness — there were still shadows out there! But I staggered forward just behind him anyway, caught up by his courage. Across the field, the shadows vanished as we neared them. The power he had over the Fury was stunning to me. Why had I ever been afraid?

We didn't stop running until we reached the perimeter. I pulled up, panting. "Hold on."

He released my hand and spun back. "You see? Easy!"

But looking at Haven Valley within the perimeter, I thought it might not be so easy. The fog was everywhere, knee high and hovering and coiling around the buildings ahead of us. Only then did I notice there were no Fury, only the fog. It was like a stench that followed them. I could smell it now.

"The black fog you see is part of the Fury," Eli said. "Like their scent."

"What about the creatures?"

"They've retreated into their hosts."

"Are they demons?" I asked.

"No. Shadows, remember?"

"Shadows," I said.

"Come on." He started forward. "We aren't done yet."

I took another moment to stare at the scene before me, then stepped over the perimeter and entered Haven Valley.

As Eli approached, the fog parted, granting a wide berth for him to pass. Easy. The Fury couldn't stand against the light of who he was. The moment Rose saw his power, she would change her mind, surely. It was going to be a glorious day for Haven Valley! Eli had come to show us our inheritance, the kingdom of heaven, which was already here. They would set my mother free.

This is it, I thought. *The end has finally come!*

As we approached the houses, the fog twisted through windows and vanished inside, scurrying from Eli and me. We were like two prophets entering town with the power of God as our staffs. The light had come, and the shadow in the valley of death was no more.

Eli led us past the homes toward the main strip of stores, where we were certain to encounter people. I could feel Bobbie wanting me to worry about being seen, but I let her fears fall away.

Everything changed when we saw the first person. It was Judy Smithworth, a teacher whom I'd always loved dearly. A kind woman with bright eyes and curly blonde hair cut short as required. Her husband was a farmer. She stood not thirty paces before us, staring and stupefied. The boy was found.

The sight of her stunned me. Ropes of dense fog wrapped around her chest and neck, and the offshoots wove their way into her eyes, her ears, her mouth. She stood in a thin, shifting fog.

And she was clearly unaware of any of it. Unaware that she'd bound herself to fear, which blinded her to the kingdom of heaven, in which she was the light.

Her eyes were on Eli. "Grace?" she said.

I shifted my eyes to several others beyond her. The Martin family paused in a huddle of eight. Tyler Smith and his children watched from outside the general store. Margaret Holden stared from across the street. They were the same. All bound in the darkness, all staring at me and Eli walking through the center of town. At least half of them were covered in the rash that had first afflicted Evelyn, whispering among themselves. One of Tyler's boys took off running.

A group of children rounded the corner to our right — the Pierce children among them, including Evelyn. Like the others, the children were clouded in a thin fog, though the cords of darkness weren't as developed.

I stopped, reminded of just what awaited

us when we encountered Rose, which would be soon. She was likely already hearing the news.

Eli looked back at me, eyes bright, unconcerned. "Remember who you are. You can only serve one master." With that, he headed directly toward the children. They'd stopped and were staring, as were the adults. No one seemed to know what to do.

Rose would.

Stephen Pierce, the youngest in this group, pushed past the other children and smiled as Eli approached. I hurried to catch up to him, doing my best to still the nerves now buzzing on high alert.

"Hello," Stephen said.

"Hello, Stephen," Eli replied. The fog surrounding the boy retreated when Eli stopped not ten feet from him.

"Everyone's been looking for you," Stephen said. "Why have you been hiding?"

"I didn't mean to be hiding," Eli said. "I was just away exploring."

Stephen's small eyes lit with excitement and curiosity. "I've never been exploring."

"I could take you if you want."

Stephen beamed and nodded before another hand reached out, yanked him back, and stepped forward to block the boy from Eli's gaze. Evelyn, her eyes filled with terror and anger. Her hands were concealed with gloves. Cords of darkness were wrapped around her arms, chest and neck. They didn't retreat as Stephen's had.

"Hello, Evelyn," Eli said.

"Stay away from my brother," Evelyn spat.

"I see you've been having some trouble with your skin."

She stiffened. "You don't know anything about me."

"I know you're in pain," Eli said. "I know you cry yourself to sleep because it hurts so bad."

He stepped closer, almost close enough to touch her. The adults nearby inched back, clearly afraid of him. But the children remained, watching him carefully.

"I know you believe you deserve to feel this pain," Eli said, his voice hardly loud enough for me to hear.

Evelyn was shaking her head slightly, but her eyes misted with tears.

"I know you think this is all your fault. That you've failed your mother. That you've failed God. That you don't deserve forgiveness."

Tears slid down Evelyn's cheeks, and I swallowed the emotions rising from my chest.

Eli took another small step. "Do you

believe you've failed God?"

The girl sniffed and dropped her eyes. Eli reached out and took the girl's hand in his own. Almost immediately, the cords of fear retreated into her body. A quiet sob hitched her shoulders.

"You can't fail God," Eli said. "He can't be threatened. Nothing can compromise him. And in him you're already made whole."

Evelyn lifted her eyes and looked at Eli's face. "I'm not whole," she said. "I'm not what you say."

"Yes you are." Eli lifted Evelyn's hand up, carefully ungloved her fingers, and exposed the red, harsh rash that covered her skin. He studied her hand, turned it over gently in his own, then looked back up at Evelyn's face. "You are perfect," he said. And then he lowered his head and placed a kiss on the top of her blistered hand.

"Get away from my daughter!" Rose's warning cut through the stillness, and I turned to see her marching toward us, flanked by the guardians Morton and Ralph. Her face was red with anger as she ran toward her daughter.

I heard Evelyn's cries and turned back to see that Eli had stepped away from her.

"You monster!" Rose screamed, reaching

the children. "What have you done to her?" She yanked Evelyn out of Eli's reach and ran her hands over her daughter's face, down her arms, looking for whatever harm Eli had caused. "What did he do?"

Evelyn, still sobbing, raised her ungloved hand. We all saw it at the same time. The skin on her hand was clean, free of any redness or rash.

Rose pushed up the sleeve on Evelyn's arm to reveal more beautiful skin.

"He healed me," Evelyn said, staring at her skin. "He saved me."

Rose glanced from Evelyn to Eli. Behind her, two more of our guardians had arrived, staring with curiosity and caution. The children leaned forward to look for themselves.

Harrison arrived and knelt down to examine his daughter's skin. A larger crowd was gathering. News of the boy's appearance was drawing them like flies now.

"What happened?" Harrison demanded.

"The boy healed me," Evelyn said.

"Impossible!"

"I told you," Stephen announced from where he stood, grinning. "He can do magic."

"The devil's work!" Rose snapped, glaring at Eli. But he offered her a gentle smile, and I watched as her glare softened. Even she knew that something greater than the devil's work was happening, surely. Hope surged through me.

More people had gathered and were watching with some amazement, all looking from the softly sobbing girl to the boy who had just taken away her disease. Most of Haven Valley was here now, and I caught a glimpse of Jamie standing on the fringe of onlookers, his face darkened with anger.

All of them were bound in cords of fear, but no one more so than my brother, who looked to be choking in a cloak of writhing darkness. If they could see what I saw, they would be running for the hills. But it wasn't my place to speak.

Eli looked at the gathered crowd and started pacing. "There's a story about a boat caught in a terrible storm. All the passengers were terrified except one, who slept in peace even as the waves pounded the boat, threatening the lives of all on board. They called that one Yeshua. The others rushed to him and begged him to save them. He stood and asked them one question. 'Why are you afraid, you of little faith?' "

Eli looked at Rose, who appeared dumbstruck. "Why would this teacher not be afraid in the face of such a terrible threat?

Unless what he saw and what the others saw were two different realities. Where they saw a threat, he slept in peace. This was perhaps his greatest miracle, much greater than the healing of a rash."

Not a soul moved. His words held them in perfect stillness.

"Today Haven Valley faces a terrible storm of fear. But you too can see truth. You too can be freed from the blindness of fear and see with new eyes. In that new sight, you will see light instead of darkness. When you see the light, you will know love instead of fear because in love, there is no fear. In love, there is no record of wrong. Unless you know that love, everything you believe is worthless and gains you nothing, Christian or not. I come as a way-shower. But it's up to you to follow the way."

Peace settled over me. Emotion clogged my throat. They were listening! Eli really had come to save Haven Valley, and they were listening. How foolish of me to doubt.

As quickly as the peace had come, the atmosphere around me changed. I heard the clicking of his shoes on the pavement behind me, walking toward us from the south. Dread filled my chest and I was terrified to look.

To a man, woman, and child, all had torn

their eyes from Eli and were staring past me in shock. So then I had to look.

I twisted just as he came to a stop fifteen feet behind me. Grinning. Standing before us for the first time in ten years.

Sylous.

CHAPTER THIRTY

Sylous stood in silence, his white suit pristine, his dark hair slicked back, face sunken and pale, his green eyes carefully drinking in the scene. I couldn't take my eyes off him — it was as though he was looking through us rather than at us. As though his eyes were reaching past our flesh and stirring the fear in our bones.

Rose was the first to move, stumbling forward. "Sylous, you've come."

He raised his hand and silenced her. She pulled up near me, fingers trembling at her sides. Rose feared him as deeply as any of us.

"It appears you've all lost your faith to the deception of a little boy." Sylous cut his eyes toward Eli, who watched calmly.

"No," Rose said after a moment of silence. Her eyes were trained at Sylous's feet. "We are still faithful to your holiness. Always."

No one else dared to speak. But I could, I

thought. I could say what I had seen from the hilltop.

"Yet you seem to marvel at this Fury, who comes like a thief to steal and destroy."

"No," Rose said, lifting pleading eyes.

Sylous scanned the crowd and raised his voice. "Are you all foolish enough to believe lies of sight beyond fear?"

"Eli is magic," came a small voice. All eyes turned to see that little Stephen had stepped out from the children.

"Please, Sylous," Rose cried, face white with fear. "He doesn't understand what he is saying."

Sylous ignored Rose's plea and walked toward the child.

"Please," Rose tried again.

Sylous again held up his hand, and Rose stilled. He towered over the small boy, then bent over, hands on his knees. "Will you be honest with me, son?"

Stephen nodded, and Sylous dropped to a squat so he was nearly eye level with him. "Do you believe this boy has power?"

Stephen nodded again.

"Do you believe he is dangerous?" Sylous asked.

Stephen shook his head.

"So he's tricked you, then," Sylous said.

"No. Eli is my friend."

Sylous raised his pale hand and gently tucked a loose strand of hair behind Stephen's ear. "You are mistaken, boy," he said. "He isn't your friend. He's your enemy."

"But he doesn't feel like my enemy," Stephen said.

"That's because he's the most dangerous kind." Sylous patted Stephen's shoulder and stood.

Rose took a step toward him. "Sylous, please —"

"Enough!" Sylous roared, turning. He glared at Eli, who hadn't moved. I wondered why he wasn't defending himself. Was Sylous more powerful than him? All the peace I'd felt earlier had been replaced by a familiar fear that felt crippling.

"I warned you," Sylous bit off. "I warned you all." He was looking at Eli but speaking to us. "Didn't I tell you that the Fury would come as light? Didn't I make it clear that it would be your greatest test?"

"Yes," Rose said. "You did."

"And yet here he stands, twisting your minds with his lies." Sylous stepped past Eli, walked to the edge of the crowd, and turned to us with icy certainty. He raised his hands to either side and looked at us all. "You would like to see? So be it."

A beat of silence engulfed us. I heard them

before I saw them, a terrifying whine that grew into shrieks and guttural roars. I knew they were the same Fury I'd seen from the hilltop, and I spun in panic, hands at my ears, expecting them to rush in from the perimeter.

But they were already upon us, swarming, hundreds of the wraiths, screaming with pitiful wails that made my bones shrivel.

Even as I stared in horror, I realized what the others surely did not — the Fury hadn't come from outside the perimeter; they had always been in the town, only hidden from our view.

Long bony fingers with sharp nails lashed out. Faceless creatures of the most terrifying imagination, screaming at every soul in Haven Valley, came to life in form. Sharp fangs and white eyes cloaked in hoods revealed our deepest fears.

The sound was so loud and the sudden commotion so violent that I hardly noticed the screams of those around me. In a wild panic, men and women were running in every direction, but the wraiths were with them each step. Some were rushing for cover, others were grabbing loved ones and shoving others out of the way. Some fell to their knees and began to beg God for mercy. A few brave souls were fighting back, but the more they fought, the more Fury there were to fight. It was as if they had emerged from within us as much as from the air surrounding us.

I stood frozen for a few seconds, and then I was turning and running for my life. I made it two steps before realizing that the Fury were erupting around me as quickly as they had around the others. There could be no escape from the fears we carried.

I spun back and saw Eli standing in the midst of the chaos, undisturbed. I rushed for him, grabbed his arm, and fell to my knees before him. "Save us!" I cried. Surely he could, with the power I had seen him use.

He looked down at me lovingly and smiled. "Remember, Grace, you are the light!" he cried above the cacophony. "Just like me."

Fear rammed up into my throat and came out in a brutal scream. Roars and painful shrieks echoed around me. "Can't you see they will destroy us all!"

He spread his arms wide, eyes fiery. "What I do, I do for you. There is nothing to fear. Let it all go. All of it. Death means nothing. Follow me!"

I pushed away from him, suddenly terrified that this was his doing. That he was the source of the Fury. That I had indeed unwittingly brought this terror upon us all.

I felt the hot breath of a Fury as it screamed behind me, ready to tear into me. I fell to my side, curled up into a ball, held up my arms to hide my face, and hoped death would come quickly.

And then they were gone. One moment the air was filled with their shrieks, the next I could hear only the wailing of terrified men and women and children.

Trembling, I stayed on my side. The screams of those around me slowly subsided, replaced by whispered pleas to God.

I opened my eyes and peered over the crook of my arm, half expecting to see lurking Fury. There were none. Even the wisps of fog and coiling black cords were gone. Haven Valley had returned to its peaceful self.

I pushed up to look around me. People were gathering together, weeping, shaking, holding one another. The center street had claw marks etched into the pavement, windows shattered, doors broken and hanging on hinges. But no Fury. And from what I could see, not a scratch on anyone.

I heard the familiar clicking of shoes and twisted to see Sylous approaching. He scanned the scene and paused when his eyes connected with mine. I dropped my stare, aware of his power over me. A power we had called into question.

"The next time, they won't be so kind," he said. "I offered you a place of safety on the condition that you keep your hearts pure and free of deception. A way I still offer. Perhaps this small reminder will help you appreciate the evil that looms beyond this perimeter. A boundary I alone control for your own good."

I pushed myself to my feet, unsteady and deeply unnerved but otherwise unscathed.

"If you want to endure the full wrath of the Fury, then surrender yourself to this foolish boy and his ways of sight," Sylous cried. "But if you wish to remain under my protection, then you must retain your holiness and follow the laws of God."

People muttered around me, begging for protection.

Harrison, face pale and twisted with fear, his children and wife still trembling behind him, stepped forward and lowered himself to one knee in a show of submission. "Forgive us for straying. We will follow."

Sylous glanced over the crowd. "Anyone else?"

Nearly as one, the people of Haven Valley stepped forward and knelt. I glanced to either side, bent knees and bowed heads all around, then looked back at Sylous. *I should bow too,* I thought. But then I caught a glimpse of Eli, the strange, beautiful boy standing off to the left, watching as he always did, face filled with peace.

You are the light of the world. There is nothing to fear. I do this for you. Follow me.

He turned his gaze to me, and the moment our eyes connected, peace washed over me. Who was I to believe, Sylous or Eli?

Sylous's voice cut through the warmth gathering around me. "Without the shedding of blood, there is no forgiveness of sin. All who have betrayed God must receive their punishment unless they confess their sin and repent." He paused, face stern. "Also, the boy Fury must die at your hands before his lies can take root."

All eyes turned to Eli.

"You have until noon tomorrow to kill him, or the Fury will have their way."

Then Sylous walked up the street, rounded the corner, and was gone.

We watched him go, stunned and confused. At least I did. What he said made sense in my old way of being. Sylous was an angel, sent with the word of God to the elect. He had to be.

God had always killed those who stood in defiance of him. He'd sent many messengers to warn of the wickedness of the world. He would save us only if we agreed to his conditions, and those conditions began and ended with a confession of our own wickedness, our own worthlessness. This is what Sylous said.

Eli said the opposite. That Sylous was a religious spirit who inspired through fear of danger rather than love. Was Eli a heretic? A wolf? The great deceiver? Or was that Sylous?

And where was Bobbie?

"Right here," she said to my left.

I almost spoke to her out loud but caught myself. *Where have you been? I was almost killed!*

"Right here, protecting you. Didn't I tell you not to bring the boy? Now look at what you've done."

Protecting me? I didn't see you.

"Trust me, I was here in all the chaos. You suffered far less than most of them."

I decided to take her at her word.

"The question now is, are you going to make this better for yourself or worse? I strongly suggest you keep your mouth shut."

They saw me bring him in. They'll want to know how I knew to find him.

"Tell Rose he came to you. That's true. He's here of his own will, not yours."

But I can't let them kill Eli. I don't think he's evil.

She frowned at the boy. "You may be right, but he's not your concern. This is his own path to follow. Don't throw yourself on that same path."

Rose broke the silence that had swallowed all but me. "Take the boy," she said.

I glanced over to where Bobbie had stood, but she was gone. Now what?

Claude and Morton grabbed Eli by each arm and spun him around. The sight of such innocence being led away to whatever cruel demise awaited him proved too much for me.

"You can't!" I cried, stepping back. "He's innocent!"

They all looked at me. Me, the one who was speaking out for Eli in defiance of Sylous. Was I doing that?

"How dare you defy the truth after all we just witnessed!" Rose spat.

"She brought the boy in!" someone cried.

Rose glared at me. "This is true?"

"He led me in."

"How did you know where to find him?"

I hesitated, then tried to follow Bobbie's wisdom. "He found me." And then I betrayed myself. "He's shown me a way beyond darkness. He can save us."

The blood drained from Rose's face. If a pin had been dropped in that moment, we all would have heard it.

A hand grasped my arm. "Enough, Grace." I turned to see Jamie's blue eyes shadowed with anger.

"Please, Jamie," I begged, knowing I had already condemned myself. "Listen to me."

"I am listening to you! How dare you betray us?"

"No," I said. "I just wanted you to hear him. He . . ." But I ran out of words.

"*You* did this to us," Rose said, her voice dark and menacing. "It was you who brought the Fury into our holy sanctuary! You're as guilty as the boy!"

Jamie's grip on my arm tightened. Tears collected in my eyes.

"No," I whispered, knowing it was no use.

Someone moved out from the crowd and got my attention. I turned to see Andrew staring at me with disbelief. I wanted to rush to him for the first time since our wedding. I wanted to beg him to understand, to protect me, even though I'd never loved him. I'd been wrong! I needed him now.

"Please, Andrew. Listen to me . . ."

He glanced at Rose, then turned away

from me. And I knew then that no one would come to my aid.

"Lock them both away," Rose snapped. "We will cleanse our holy sanctuary of sin and repent. Our inheritance awaits us all in holiness and grace."

CHAPTER THIRTY-ONE

I wasn't even aware that Haven Valley had a prison until I was locked inside one. It was located in the basement of the security office, a building I'd never been inside.

There was no sign of Eli when I entered, and I didn't have time to ask because I was quickly forced down a flight of creaking steps into a dark basement.

I tried to ask what was happening then, but Marshall and Tanner, who held me by either arm, wouldn't speak. Tanner, who had always shown me kindness, wouldn't even look at my face. They shoved me into a small room with bars for walls, slammed the door shut, and retreated up the stairs.

I called out for Eli, wondering if they'd locked him down here as well, but all I heard was my own voice bouncing off the walls. I was alone.

A small amount of light drifted in through three small rectangular windows high up toward the ceiling. The cell reminded me of the Pierce basement, where all my troubles had begun.

It was longer than it was wide — maybe eight feet wide by ten feet in length. There was a single wooden bench along the back wall and a bucket in the corner. Otherwise it was empty. Cold. A dirt floor.

The hours slipped by slowly as I sat alone, tormented by my thoughts. Waves of nausea washed over me, and I threw up in the bucket twice. My head ached. I didn't know what lay in store for me, but Sylous had made one thing perfectly clear: I would have to confess and be cleansed or face terrible punishment. What did confession mean now? Was it only something I had to say with my mouth? What did repentance mean now? How would I show them my holiness? By saying and doing all the right things according to the law?

But that meant denying Eli.

I thought about what might be happening to him. Where were they keeping him? I couldn't fathom them killing a boy! And would Eli really let them take his life? He had the power to save himself, right? He wouldn't have come all this way just to be killed.

What did Eli hope to accomplish by allowing them to take him? It made no sense to me. In fact, the only thing that did make sense was that Eli really was a Fury who'd deceived me. Everything he said flipped the doctrines I'd been taught since childhood on their head.

But I just couldn't see how the love and wonder he'd shown me could be so wrong.

My thoughts slipped from Eli to my mother. Would they release her now that it was clear I was the one to blame?

As the daylight died and the sounds of night drifted into my cell, I tried to think back to what I'd experienced on the hill with Eli, but it all seemed so far away now. I'd seen the Fury that smothered Haven Valley — so had everyone else. The only difference was that I'd seen them inside the perimeter before Eli and I had come, whereas the others believed that Eli and I had brought the Fury.

I'd also seen the light, but I couldn't see it now in this dark place. Had it all been a trick of some kind? Was it true, or had I really just sacrificed everything for nothing?

In the darkness that came with night, I felt certain I would rot in this cell. Every time I closed my eyes I imagined the wraiths who'd torn through us all. Hooded, faceless ghouls with teeth and haunting eyes and long white fingers. Their shrieks. Eli said they weren't demons, so what were they? Fear, he said.

The same fear that was now coursing through my blood.

I eventually gave in to self-pity and let myself sob there in the dark cell.

By the time the first signs of daylight peeked into the basement, my eyes were swollen and my throat was raw. My chest ached and my mouth was dry. I heard the door at the top of the stairs open and a single pair of boots descending. I stood on achy legs and hurried to the barred door. Tanner came into view, still avoiding my eyes.

"Please, Tanner," I croaked. "What's going on?"

"Step back. Turn and place your chest and forehead against the back wall."

I did as he asked and heard him unlock my cell. A second later something clinked against the floor. Another click of the lock sounded, and then he left, his steps echoing. The heavy door at the top slammed shut and I was alone again.

He'd left a plate of food and jug of water in the corner of my cell. The water was lukewarm, as was the porridge on the plate. But I devoured it, thinking I needed nourishment for the baby.

Then I returned to my sulking. The light brightened outside and the day moved forward. It was eerily silent in the basement prison. I hadn't slept all night and was exhausted. Empty. Numb. At some point I fell into a merciful sleep, dead to my troubles in Haven Valley.

Voices woke me. I remembered where I was and jerked up. Pain coursed through my neck and back. I'd fallen to my side on the wooden bench, and everything was stiff. The light had brightened. It had to be midday. Sylous had given the town until noon.

The voices were outside. Many voices. I stood and turned to the small window. The town was gathering next to the security building. Why? We'd never met here before.

We'd never had an execution in Haven Valley before either. Were they actually going to follow through?

Rose's voice cut through the murmurs. "Family of Haven Valley, we have gathered here today to restore righteousness to our hearts. To right the wrongs of one of our own and to silence the deception of the wolf who comes in sheep's clothing."

Ice filled my blood, and I jumped up on the bench to hear more clearly.

"It's important to remember what we've been called to as the children of our Father God and his Son, Jesus Christ. The price we pay in turning away from the world and embracing holiness pales in comparison to the glorious inheritance that awaits us all. We must remember that we are all still vulnerable to punishment for any disobedience. It is crucial that with this act, we kill our doubt, return to the faith that protects us, and never waver again."

Then, in a softer voice, "Bring him forward."

My heart was racing. Him. Eli. Surely someone would stand up and stop this madness. Was everyone present? Were the children there?

"Without the shedding of blood, there is no forgiveness for sins," Rose cried. "Today we silence the heresy masquerading as the light that this boy has brought among us. Today we ensure our inheritance as the remnant of God's holy church."

Panic seized me. I grabbed the bars at the window and almost cried out, but I realized that no amount of begging on my part would dissuade them. Crying out would only worsen my own situation.

Emotion surged up my raw throat and burned in my chest. "Oh God, please, someone stop this!" I whispered.

Rose's voice came again, softer but biting. "You have been shown to be an agent of the devil." She was talking to Eli. I held my breath. "Do you deny this?"

A beat. Then his young voice came. "I always knew you would kill me. But a light will rise that will chase away all shadows." He paused. "And really, there is no death anyway. It's just a passing."

"So says the Fury," Rose bit off.

"Stop!" a tiny voice cried. Stephen! "Please stop."

"You can't do this, Mother," a second voice said. Evelyn.

And then as if they'd broken the dam, more soft voices filled the air. Emboldened by Stephen and Evelyn, the children of Haven Valley were calling out for mercy.

A loud crack stopped them all. A gunshot. Followed by the sound of a body collapsing on the ground.

Silence.

They had killed Eli.

I turned from the window, numb. Collapsed on the bench, dumbstruck. Rose had just executed my brother.

The children started crying softly, but it was all too late. Eli had come and Eli was dead. I couldn't think straight.

"Let the pain we are feeling be a reminder of the consequences of heresy," Rose said. "Burn this body and bring Grace to the sanctuary in three hours."

I slipped to the floor, laid my forehead on the packed dirt, and sobbed into the earth. Eli was dead, and with him, all the light he'd shown me. They would come for me next.

Nothing remained now.

A gentle nudge woke me. My cheek was pressed against the ground, my body shivering from the cold.

"I tried to warn you," Bobbie said.

I pushed myself up and slowly turned to where she sat on the corner of the bench, legs crossed, arms the same. But I didn't see how she could help me now. So I slumped back down and curled up on my side.

"They killed him," I whispered.

"He threatened them," she replied.

"He didn't deserve to die."

"Do you deserve to die, Grace? Does your unborn baby deserve to die? Because if you don't wise up, that's exactly what's going to happen."

I sniffed, a fresh round of tears filling my eyes. I had shoved the thought of my baby aside, but her words made me sick. Surely it wasn't that bad.

"I don't want my baby to die."

"You should have listened to me from the start," Bobbie said.

"Rose would never threaten my child."

"You heard Sylous. I was trying to protect you from this, but you ignored me. This is all your fault."

I pulled tighter in on myself, knowing everything she said was true.

"Why, Grace? Because a boy made you believe in something that felt warm and fuzzy? It didn't save him. You think it'll save you now?"

"He showed me things."

"And where are those things now? Can they save you or your baby? No, Grace, they can't."

She was angry with me and had every right to be. I had abandoned common sense. I'd ignored discernment and wisdom.

I heard her move, then she was kneeling beside me, resting her hand on my shoulder. "The boy can't help you, Grace, but I still can."

"It's too late," I whispered. "There's no out now."

"Yes, there is. You were deceived, but you can find your way back. It won't be easy and it will take time, but you are still a part of this community."

"You're saying I should trust Rose now, after what she did?"

"No. Trust no one. But you can repent. Do whatever it takes to realign yourself with them. Beg Rose for forgiveness from the congregation. Confess and beg for mercy. You have to show them you understand the error of your ways and swear you won't stray from the path again."

"Confess how?"

"Confess you were deceived. Denounce the boy and his lies. You have to prove your faithfulness to the Holy Family." Bobbie stroked the side of my head, her fingers warm and comforting. "Repent, Grace."

I shook my head and released a sob.

"I know it's hard, because a part of you loved Eli. He was a beautiful boy, and for all I know there was some good truth mixed in with everything else. But even a little poison spoils the batch, right? You have to take responsibility for what you've done and repent. It's the only way."

I sobbed quietly, knowing everything she said was true. I had wandered too far from what I knew, and it had cost me so much already. The only path now was to return.

"Repent," Bobbie said, her voice calm and sweet. "And I will be here."

"Always?" I asked in my misery.

"Always."

CHAPTER THIRTY-TWO

They came for me an hour later. I was still curled on the floor in my misery. Bobbie had stayed with me, stroking my head and shoulders, easing my loneliness, whispering the truth I needed to hear.

Repent, Grace.

Denounce Eli's heresy.

Return to the faith. It's the only way.

By the time Marshall and Tanner hauled me off my cell floor and yanked me up the stairs, I knew what I had to do to ensure my safety and the safety of the child inside me. No more wandering from the path, no more questioning the truths I already knew. I would wholeheartedly give myself back to the laws of God.

I was escorted across the town center. The single paved street was nearly abandoned. Thoughts of what the others had seen, watching Eli's death, made my stomach turn, and I forced myself to keep my gaze forward. Nothing could interfere with my resolve.

I was led to the church and through the double wooden doors. The pews were empty, a sight I didn't often see. Rose stood in the center, just before the stage, her fingers woven together in front of her. Her eyes were directed at me alone, her face cold.

Behind her, seated on the stage in six chairs, were the members of Haven Valley's council. Harrison and Andrew were among them. I dared a glance at Andrew only to see that he wouldn't even lift his eyes to look at me. I was suddenly aware of how filthy I was, having spent the night in their prison. Would Andrew ever be able to look at me again without seeing me like this?

Marshall and Tanner guided me to stand before Rose but held my arms in their firm grasp. Maybe they thought I was strong enough to make a run for it. Unable to look Rose in the eyes, I shifted my gaze to the hem of her skirt.

"You've been summoned here today to stand trial for the sins you've committed against this community and God," Rose said. "Do you understand what these transgressions are?"

I nodded, eyes still lowered in submission.

"You aided a Fury who nearly destroyed our holy community. You lied to all of us. You gave yourself over to his heresy and then stood by his side in defiance of the sound doctrine that protects us all from sin."

I swallowed, doing my best to maintain control of my emotions as she heaped on the judgment.

"Do you have anything to say for yourself?"

I lifted my eyes to her face but kept them trained on her cheek so I didn't have to look directly at her. I didn't know what to say, how to even begin to explain myself. Everything I thought of sounded like insanity.

Repent, Grace, Bobbie's voice whispered inside my head. With a quick flick of my eyes to the right, I saw her standing along the side wall.

Do whatever it takes to realign yourself with them.

I returned my gaze to Rose, but before I could say anything she spoke again. "This level of deception is truly something I never would have expected from you."

My eyes filled with tears. "I'm sorry," I whispered.

"We are far beyond sorry," Rose said. I could feel the sharp edge to her words. As if they could reach out and cut my skin.

Denounce the boy's heresy, Bobbie said. *You have to prove your faithfulness.*

"I was led astray by the boy's lies," I began. "That doesn't excuse my actions, but I see so clearly now how blind I was." Something switched inside me, and the instinct to protect myself rose up. It was as if Bobbie had taken over.

"He lied to me, led me to believe what I was doing was godly and good." I paused, letting myself accept my own words. "I see now how foolish I was to believe him. I don't even know why I did. He tricked me, and I feel deeply embarrassed and ashamed." My bottom lip was quivering and I could feel a cool tear slip down my cheek.

Good, Grace. Confess. Beg forgiveness.

"I betrayed you all and threatened our community. And I'll do whatever's necessary to show my repentance."

I looked up at the council. They were faces I knew and respected. Rebecca's aged brown eyes, Colin's hard thin mouth, brothers Peter and Donald with their matching stern expressions. I prayed they would remember me as I had been.

"I will face whatever consequences you deem fit. I wish to return to my faith here. To be made pure and holy again."

Andrew was finally looking at me, and I

400

addressed him directly. "I'm truly sorry for what I've done. I beg you to forgive me." The last few words barely made it out in a whisper, and I thought I saw empathy cross Andrew's face.

I kept my eyes on him, longing to return to the days when he looked at me with fondness. Reminded again how cruel I'd been to reject his desire for me. If given another chance, I would cherish his affection.

"What you're asking is difficult," Rose said. "The offense of heresy is an offense against God himself and requires punishment. Yes, he punished Jesus on our behalf, but that grace isn't free. You must align to the truth to receive it. And aligning to the truth is best assured if we fear punishment. We fear punishment when we've experienced it ourselves. Do you understand what I'm saying?"

"I understand," I said.

"Do you?" she questioned.

"I repent."

"Of course you say you repent. Anyone would. But true repentance only happens in great fear of God's holy wrath! Do you have any idea just how deep the Fury's deception runs already? Just a few words from that boy, and now it will take great vigilance to cleanse the hearts of our community."

"The boy, not Grace, was a Fury," Andrew said. "I won't defend her part in this, but falling victim to deception is different from being sin itself."

I wanted to rush to him and wrap my arms around his neck.

"Would you be so forgiving if she wasn't carrying your child?" Rose demanded. It was clear she was in no mood to show mercy. She turned back to me. "Do you believe you can align to the truth without being punished?"

I thought about it a moment, knowing my answer could get me killed. "I will do whatever is required to regain my good standing with God," I said.

Rose considered this, and after a moment she stepped forward until her face was only inches from mine. "I let you into my home, let you watch my children, and in the midst of it all you betrayed me," she whispered, her tone harsh and cruel. "Hear me clearly, little girl. If you ever betray me again, I will not hesitate to kill you, unborn baby or not. Do you understand?"

I was too terrified to reply with words, so I just nodded.

After another tense moment, Rose stepped back. "The punishment must be severe enough to deter others from even considering deception. We are nearing the end and must be more vigilant now than ever." A beat. "We will administer the cleansing ceremony."

I'd never heard of such a thing, but from the somber faces of the council members, I hated to think what it entailed.

"And what of the child?" Andrew asked.

"God will spare the child if it's his will," Rose snapped.

Rebecca and Colin shared a glance, then offered approving nods. One by one, the others followed suit. The last nod came from Andrew. My fate was sealed.

"Her mother, Julianna, will also be held to the same standards of accountability," Rose said. "She lied on behalf of her daughter, preventing us from discovering the truth. In my mind her crimes are just as severe."

My mother? I almost cried out in objection.

Say nothing, Grace, Bobbie said. *You'll only make things worse. It's out of your control now.*

So I said nothing.

"The ceremony will be held at dusk," Rose said. "Under the eyes of the council, Grace and Julianna will learn to fear God."

403

They came for me again an hour before sunset. This time Tanner and Marshall instructed me to strip. They doused me in freezing water and dressed me in a thin, coarse gown with sleeves that stopped at my elbows and a hem that skimmed the tops of my feet. I was filled with embarrassment and shame. These were men I knew. Men I had grown up with.

They led me out into the freezing evening air to the northern perimeter. The council was already there, as well as my brother, all standing beside Rose, eyes fixed forward. They'd erected a tall wooden frame — two thick round poles topped by a heavy cross-beam — just inside the perimeter. The frame was stabilized by weighted sandbags. Hanging from the top beam were two thick ropes, ending about five feet from the ground.

Red ropes.

It looked like they'd built the whole thing just for me and my mother.

Claude stood by the right post. He was holding something, but I couldn't see what. I was shivering in the wet gown, but fear of pain pushed the cold away.

"Leave her there, Tanner," Rose instructed with a nod. He stopped me five paces from her. Their eyes shifted to my right, and I looked to see my mother being steered toward me, dressed in a similar gown.

A chill washed down my back. The reality of our predicament was almost too much for me to bear. This was my doing. All of it! I should never have gone beyond the red rope!

My mother saw me and her face softened. She looked tired, eyes swollen, skin pale. Then she was beside me, facing the council.

"Mother, I —" I whispered.

"No, sweetheart."

"Silence!" Rose turned to face the council. "Tonight we witness the first cleansing ceremony, a measure put into place to correct the most dire offenses. For those gathered, let us remember the great cost of betraying the Christian faith and the pain it inflicts on those we love."

She faced my mother and me. "Let the wounds you receive tonight and the scars they leave remind you of God's wrath. May they instill in you forevermore a fear of straying from his righteousness."

She nodded at someone behind me. "Grace first."

Strong hands seized my arms and propelled me toward the structure. It was only then, as Claude stepped forward, that I saw what he held. It was a whip made from cord of the same red rope, bound tight at the end like a serpent's tail.

I don't know what I had expected, but the sight of that coiled red whip filled me with revulsion and I instinctively jerked back, digging my heels in.

"You can't!" my mother cried. "She's pregnant!"

"God's wrath plays no favorites," Rose said. But I could hear fear in her voice as well.

Tanner and Marshall pushed me forward. They yanked my arms up to meet one of the hanging ropes and began tying my wrists to it. Pain ran down my arms, but I could hardly feel it through my panic.

My mother was beside herself. "Please, you can't! The baby . . ."

"Gag her!"

I could hear my mother thrashing. "Please, you can't do this to her!" She issued a muffled cry, then broke free for a moment. "Wait, please," she cried. "Let me take her punishment!"

I jerked my head around. "No, Mother . . ."

"Let me take her punishment! I'm responsible. I'm her mother. I should have known. If I'd done my duty, she never would have gone to the boy!"

Rose held up her hand. "You believe taking your daughter's punishment will cleanse her? She has to be held accountable for her own sin."

"The memory of my pain will be punishment enough for her," my mother begged. "Please, show her mercy and let me take her place. It's the Christian way."

"Mother, no, stop this!" I cried out, but now I was the one being ignored.

"Taking Grace's punishment will not excuse you from your own," Rose said.

"I will endure both hers and mine," my mother said.

"No, I will take my own punishment," I cried.

"One more word from you and I'll have you both whipped to death!" Rose screamed at me.

This wasn't the Rose I knew. She was as terrified as she was enraged.

She turned back to my mother. "You understand what you're asking?" she clarified. "Forty lashes might kill you."

"Yes," my mother said. "But Grace is with child!"

The moment she spoke those words, I was

afraid that Rose would agree. She treasured the unborn and would protect them if there was a way.

Dear God. I was the only guilty party here, and now my mother, who would never harm a fly, was going to pay for my mistakes. This couldn't be happening!

"So be it," Rose barked.

Tanner quickly untied my wrists. He and Marshall spun me back around as two others dragged my mother forward.

"Mother . . ."

"Shh, shh. It's okay, sweetheart." Tears slipped down her cheeks. "This is for the best."

I just stared at her for a moment, unable to accept her sacrifice for me. I would rather be dead than watch her suffer for my sin. She couldn't possibly be thinking clearly.

I whirled around to face the council, ripping my arms free. Then I rushed up to Rose, who watched, face flat, as the guardians tied my mother's wrists to the dangling rope.

I fell to my knees. "Please, she doesn't understand what she's doing," I cried, tears blurring my vision. "I deserve to be punished for what I've done, not her!"

"You're right," Rose replied, voice steely. "You deserve the blame. And so you'll pay your own price." She turned hard eyes to Claude, who held the whip. "Bring it to me."

I twisted back to see my mother hanging from the rope, wrists secured above her head. Claude stepped up to Rose and held out the whip.

Rose snatched the long coiled cord and shoved it at me. "Whip her!"

The air around me stilled.

Rose grabbed my arm and pulled me to my feet. Shoved the whip into my belly. "Whip her or I swear I'll kill her!"

"No." Her intention was finally sinking into my skull. "I can't!"

"You can and you will if you have any hope of seeing your mother survive."

Grace, you must do whatever is necessary, Bobbie's voice whispered through my mind, and I knew she was close. *Whatever is asked of you.*

I couldn't do this. I couldn't inflict this kind of pain on anyone, much less my own mother.

If you don't it'll be much worse for both of you. Think of your unborn child. Think of the damage this could do.

"No," I said again, staring at the whip I held over my belly. "I . . . I can't."

"Look at me, Grace." My mother had twisted toward me. Light glistened in her eyes. If she was feeling fear, she hid it well. "Listen to me. I know what I'm doing. Do as Rose asks. It's alright."

"I can't hurt you," I wept. "You can't ask me to do this."

"It's all going to be alright. You must do what's best for your child, just like I'm doing for you."

Listen to your mother, Grace. Protect your baby. You have to do what is asked.

I glanced back toward the other council members as they watched. Surely someone would intervene. Rebecca? Colin? Surely someone would stop this insanity. My eyes fell to my brother, who was staring at the horizon.

"Jamie . . . Please, she's our mother."

He said nothing. I knew he was lost to me, that I was alone now. I looked at Andrew, pleading, but he lowered his gaze. My tragic reality was setting in. I had done this. Whipping my mother was my price to pay.

A sob escaped my mouth and I turned back to Rose. "Please, there has to be another way."

"There was another way," she snapped. "But you chose the path of deception instead. This is where that path has brought you." She closed my fist around the whip handle. "Do what must be done."

Do what she asks, Grace. It will keep you safe.

"Honey, look at me," my mother said, and I did, the whip heavy in my hand. "Let me take this burden for you." Tears streamed down her cheeks.

Listen to your mother.

"Now, Grace," Rose said, shoving me forward.

My mother gave me a confident nod, then turned around so only her back, barely covered in the thin material, was facing me. I stood frozen.

"Now, Grace!" Rose shouted.

With tears streaming down my face, I raised the whip over my head. "Forgive me," I whispered to the sky, to my mother, to God. "Forgive me."

I brought my arm around and watched the long cord strike my mother's back. She moaned, and blood immediately began to soak through the material over her back.

"Again," Rose said.

Again I raised my arm and brought it down. Another crack. Another bloodcurdling moan. The blood began to spread through her thin gown. The rest of the world faded from my view.

"Again!"

Again I brought the whip down. And again, and again, and again. My mind went numb as it retreated to protect itself.

By the sixth lash, my mother could no longer support her own weight, and she hung like a sack on the end of that rope.

"Again!"

"Please, I can't," I sobbed, falling to my knees. "I can't . . ."

Claude's large hand reached down and swiped the whip from my grasp. Without missing a beat the lashing continued, harder and with more intensity. Over and over, each blow landed against my mother's unresponsive body.

I wept on my knees, grasped chunks of earth between my fingers. "Please, you'll kill her," I cried.

But there was no relief. The forty lashes lasted for an eternity, and I knew then what eternal hell must be like.

And then it stopped.

I glanced up through my teary gaze and saw Rose had lifted her hand.

"Tie her up."

Tanner scooped me up and carried me to the second rope. He yanked my hands up and tied my wrists tightly to the rope. I didn't feel anything except torment for my broken mother. The world went dark as a hood was thrown over my head.

"You will spend the night out here in the dark contemplating your sins," Rose said close to my ear. "I hope in the morning you will understand the weight of your choices."

"My mother," I croaked. "Please, she needs help."

But there was no response.

"Please!" I called out again. I could hear them leaving.

I couldn't see anything. I couldn't feel anything.

I could only hang there and weep.

CHAPTER THIRTY-THREE

At some point during the night I heard my mother's fight to keep breathing end. I would carry that moment with me for the rest of my life. I screamed for help, but no one came.

I slipped in and out of consciousness after that. Each time I came to, I'd call for her. And each time her silence reminded me she was never going to reply again. My mother was dead.

When I heard the birds start their morning chirping, I dared hope that when I opened my eyes I would find myself in bed at home, waking from a nightmare. But I wasn't at home. I was hanging from a rope, paying the price for my deception.

They came to collect me when the sun rose over the horizon. They cut down my numb hands and pulled off the hood so I could watch as my mother's body dropped lifeless when they cut her free. I just stared, too broken and numb to react.

I was escorted back to the prison and locked back inside my cage, where Tanner told me I would be expected to repent before the congregation the following day, so I should prepare. I hardly heard his instruction. I curled up on the cold ground, pulling my knees close to my chest, hoping to block out the world and escape into darkness.

For the next few hours I just lay there, a single paralyzing thought consuming my mind and reminding me of who I was. I had murdered my mother. There was no way around it. Every path led me back to the damning conclusion. I had killed my own mother.

I was slightly aware of movement sometime later, but I didn't respond. There was a rattling of tin and locks, but I didn't raise my head from the floor to see. There wasn't any point. I was going to spend the rest of my life in this cell, and after what I'd done, I deserved to.

Eventually, a chill set into my flesh that had me shivering. I shifted to search for warmth and was surprised to see that it was night. I could make out a fresh plate of food and a water jug in the corner. And just beside it, a folded heap that looked like a blanket.

I pushed myself up, arms shaking. I crawled over to the blanket, pulled it across the floor, and wrapped it around my body. The material was rough, but it added a layer of warmth, and after a moment my bones stopped knocking against each other.

All I saw was darkness. All I felt was cold. I couldn't imagine warmth or light. I had been stripped of them both.

Can darkness steal your light?

The thought popped into the farthest corner of my mind, and I answered.

Yes. It has.

Has it? Or have you just forgotten who you are? Can the light be threatened? Another small question, followed by another automatic answer.

I'm not the light of the world. I was wrong. He was wrong.

Then who are you? This time the thought was stronger, stirring something in my chest.

I'm just a girl.

Who were you before you were born a girl?

I ignored that question.

"I'm just a worthless girl who killed her mother," I whispered.

Who was she before she was born a girl and became a mother?

I didn't know how to answer such a

strange question.

She is the light of her Father's eternal light. Death has no power over her.

"You're wrong," I said louder. "I watched her die."

What is death?

The thoughts were materializing, growing in volume and power. Taking on a familiar tone. I sniffed in the darkness, overcome by how real the conversation felt, even though I knew I was only talking with myself.

"I don't care what death is," I whimpered. "My mother's gone."

"She's always with you, more alive than she ever knew she could be. And now she knows love without fear in the same way I do."

The voice had taken form now. Whether it came from inside or outside of me, it filled my ears and disturbed the silence in the prison basement. I knew Eli's voice well. But it couldn't be the boy, because he was dead too.

I looked in either direction but saw only darkness. My heart started to pick up speed. All this time alone with my grief was messing with my mind.

"Careful, Grace," another familiar voice said behind me. I turned to see Bobbie sitting, legs crossed, on the wooden bench in my cell. "Remember the consequences of forgetting wisdom."

"The wisdom of the world dresses up as helpful protection while binding you to fear," the boy's voice said. I couldn't see him, but it was as though he was sitting beside me.

"Don't be foolish," Bobbie said. "He's dead."

Eli's voice answered. "Death is only a shadow. Is a shadow real? Can you pick it up?"

From the corner of my eye, I saw movement in the cell beyond the bars. I squinted, then gasped.

His blue eyes were bright, his round face and short stature clear. I scooted back, stunned as Eli stood before me, hands easy at his sides, watching me with a smile. Only a line of steel bars separated us.

I stared, unable to conceive of what I was seeing, strung between fear and hope. Fear, because people didn't come back from the dead. He could be a perversion of what he'd once been, a Fury manipulating me again. Hope, because my heart longed for the peace he'd shown me.

I pushed myself off the ground and let the blanket fall to my feet, eyes fixed on his.

"Hello, Grace," the boy said.

A hand grabbed my shoulder as if warning me not to accept what I was seeing. I knew it was Bobbie without having to look; I could feel the tremble in her fingers.

"This isn't right," she whispered. "Think about what you are seeing."

"You can't be here," I whispered to Eli, at a loss.

"Because I'm dead?" Eli asked.

"Yes. You're dead."

"But there is no death, remember?"

"Yes, but . . . your body . . ."

"Don't worry about this body." He smiled. "I only borrowed it. Your problem is that you worship the death of the body. You think it's the final watershed that determines everything. It's not. It's no more than the shedding of a costume."

"I worship death?" I was still trying to comprehend his appearance. Had I lost my mind?

"Yes," Bobbie cut in. "You've lost your mind."

"Better to lose your mind than to lose your identity," the boy said as if he'd heard her, which I was certain he had.

"My identity as the light," I said, already knowing where he was going.

"The light you've always been. Better to lose your whole life in body than to remain lost to the light that you are. But you cling to your experience of this life and fear loss. See? You've made an agreement with fear to keep you safe. It's your master."

I blinked as his words washed over me. Having faced my mother's death, I drank them in like water.

"And you can only serve one master," I whispered, the words bubbling up from deep inside my gut.

Eli gave me a nod. "Exactly. But don't feel so alone — most people place their faith in fear instead of love."

"In darkness instead of light," I said as understanding filled my mind.

"This will only bring you suffering!" Bobbie said, her tone fearful and panicked. "Remember what happened last time you listened to him."

"Surrender your attachment to safety, Grace," Eli said. "When you attach yourself to this life, you blind yourself to who you are, and in that blindness you believe you're separate from the light and can be threatened. You've unwittingly made an agreement with fear to keep you safe. It's time to awaken to the light in which you've always been safe."

"Follow wisdom," Bobbie said. "This boy's heresy will deceive you. Protecting yourself is the only way to ensure holiness."

"To say you need to be protected from darkness only empowers the darkness as a threat," Eli said. "Through your belief in it, you live in darkness."

"Fear," I said as it all came back to me. "But didn't I become evil at the fall?"

"You embraced the knowledge of good and evil, judgment, which blinded you to the light you are and have always been. You're the light, only lost in darkness, that's all. But you can be reborn into the perception of light. Jesus called that perception 'seeing the kingdom of heaven.' Like being born all over again into a different way of seeing and being. Becoming like a little child."

I blinked. Then was everyone the light, just blind to it? What about other religions?

"Why focus on others when you're blind yourself? The blind can't lead the blind, and I can assure you, you're quite blind just like most, regardless of religion. If you weren't, you wouldn't be in fear."

"This is madness!" Bobbie spat. "Heresy! Don't you see he is trying to deceive you?"

"Still, I'm already born again," I said, ignoring Bobbie. "Otherwise I would go to hell. I'm a Christian."

Eli gave me a patient smile. "Seems to me

421

you're already in a kind of hell called fear and judgment."

"I mean when I die."

"Being reborn is a lifelong journey from darkness to light, blindness to sight, that has little to do with the next life. Until you're born again, you can't perceive the light, which is everywhere — the kingdom of heaven. You see darkness instead of light and are lost in fear rather than in love. As you're reborn into the kingdom, you see light where you once saw darkness. Do you want to see?"

I could hardly imagine a more beautiful thing, but my mind was screaming danger at me. Or was that Bobbie?

"How?" I whispered.

"Simple. Surrender. Repent. But true repentance is changing what you've been taught to believe about reality. Everyone thinks they're right. So changing your mind is much harder than changing your behavior by following a set of laws and saying the right prayers. That means nothing unless it awakens you to love. Changing what you think feels like a kind of death to the old self who rules your life in judgment, but as you repent, you awaken to the light you've always been. Being born again."

"Enough of this!" Bobbie said. "He's

overturning everything you know!"

"And now you're feeling the fear of being wrong, which is another kind of hell."

"Heresy!" Bobbie hissed. "He's deceiving you!"

Eli stepped forward and passed through the bars so that he was now standing in my cell, not three feet from me. Bobbie quickly jumped to the corner behind me. I took a step back, dumbstruck.

"Can we be rid of her for a moment so I can show you something?" Eli asked.

A look of stark terror had paled Bobbie's face. Who was she, really? So wise in so many ways, but so full of fear. The opposite of Eli.

"Trust me," Eli said.

I turned back, heart pounding. Then gave him a shallow nod.

He lifted his arms and clapped his hands.

With that single clap, the world around us changed. The dark cell we were in vanished. I was in a white room, and I shielded my eyes as they fluttered and adjusted to the sudden shift from darkness to light.

I looked around, stunned. There was nothing but whiteness in all directions. White before me, behind me, above me, below me, and to either side. It was solid under my feet, but I couldn't tell the floor from the walls or ceiling. I just knew I was standing on something firm.

And there was me. And Eli. I could see my dark shoes on the white floor, and my hands . . . My hands and arms! They were somehow different. Part of me, but a translucent white, as if they were made from the same stuff as everything else.

"Beautiful, isn't it?" he said.

"I . . ." I couldn't get over how my skin looked. "Is this real?"

"You're here, so it must be," he replied, then gave a shrug. "Not the you that you thought you were, but the you that you've forgotten. The you that all your treasured beliefs have blinded you to."

"Are we still in Haven Valley?"

"We're still in the cell."

I rubbed my fingers together. They felt the same as always. "I don't understand. How's this possible?"

"I have stripped away everything you think you are so that you can discover who you actually are. The only thing I've left is your old questioning mind."

He smiled, clearly amused by the deepening confusion on my face.

"The only way to know yourself in and as the light is to let go of all your attachments to who you think you are in this world. You know the sayings: hate your entire life, deny yourself, take up the cross. All these mean the same thing. Let go of the meaning you give life in all your judgments of value based on the knowledge of good and evil. You've heard this?"

"Jesus said those things," I said, knowing the verses well. They were some of Rose's favorites, but she hadn't put it that way.

"Yes, Jesus, who made a way for all to see and be who they are beyond their blindness. This is the only way to know yourself in and as the light. You don't let go of the world because it's bad. You let go because your attachment to your fear-based self blinds you to who you are as the light. Simple."

He turned around in a circle, gazing at an invisible horizon. "Here, with so few distractions, letting go will be easier for you." His eyes were bright. "Ready?"

"For what?"

He spun around, waving me forward. "Come on!"

And then he was running, laughing. Caught up in his excitement, I took off after him. It was like running on air because there still was no definition to anything.

I glanced ahead, trying to see what was coming, but all I saw was more white. It hardly looked like an "ahead" at all, but I was moving, my feet smacking the hard surface under me.

I heard it before I saw it. Out of nowhere it appeared. I nearly stumbled, but I managed to stay upright as I pulled up and stared at the scene.

There, against the perfectly white backdrop, thundered a massive waterfall, fed by the sky and spreading out into a large crystal pool. The wall of beautiful green and blue water, roaring in its majesty, was the width of Haven Valley at least. I jerked my head up but couldn't see its source. It appeared to extend forever.

A waterfall out of nowhere in a place that seemed fictional . . . Amazement filled me. Eli had rushed all the way to the pool's edge and was on his knees, bending toward the glassy surface, watching it swirl. He looked back over his shoulder and waved me closer.

Drawn to the water, I hurried forward, dropped to my knees beside Eli, and stared at the crystal pool. Waves of light wove their way through the water just beneath the surface like thousands of glowing ribbons.

The water's alive, I thought. *It's not just water.*

"Think of it as love." Eli looked up at me with round eyes. "God is light, and in him there is no darkness at all. God is love, and whoever aligns to true love aligns to that light."

Knowledge returned to me in a flash, and I spoke what I knew. "The light of the world."

"All-powerful, all-consuming, infinite, having no beginning and no end. The same light that made you in its likeness. It is you and in you. It always has been."

But I'd been blind to it.

My fingers were trembling. It was as if a long-lost melody was coming back to me after a lifetime of deafness. As if my eyes were being opened for the first time since I'd been delivered from my mother's womb.

"Watch." Eli cupped his palm and dipped it into the water. He drew his hand back up, held it inches below his chin, and spoke, keeping his eyes fixed on the small pool of water in his hand. "Love, dear one. The love that knows no wrong like the light knows no darkness." Then he lifted his hand to his lips and tipped the water into his mouth. He spread his arms and beamed at the sky as his little body trembled with joy. "Love, daughter of heaven! Drink the light that is love!"

I turned back to the water as longing deep inside of me roared to life. Without another thought, I dipped my hand into the water. The power of the water tingled on my fingers and palm.

Daughter, light of the world, there is nothing to fear. Drink of my love. Let go of your whole life and become who you've always been.

Daughter? A lump gathered in my throat. Daughter of whom? The name came from beyond my memories and learned behaviors. Beyond my past and hopes for the future. I knew that name not with my mind but with my heart.

Father.

Without hesitation I brought my hand to my lips and drank the water. The moment it hit my mouth, everything around me shifted. There was no longer a waterfall, or a boy, or a pool, or Grace. The waters of love and light engulfed all I thought there should be and left me with only what was.

Father. The source of my being. Love. Pure light that filled every corner and cell of my body yet reached beyond me because it couldn't be limited. It couldn't be contained. And I was in it, fully braided with the light that held me in perfect love, free from all fear and trouble and darkness. Because in my Father there was no darkness.

In that moment, I knew who I was. Knew

beyond understanding. I was experiencing love all around me and in me. I was awakening to who I always had been.

I closed my eyes, tilted my head back, and began to shake with the power of it all.

My Father is light, and in him there is no darkness. I am the light of the world.

My Father is love, and as I experience true love I experience him, he in me and I in him, as one. There is no fear in true love, the love that holds no record of wrong. That love is the evidence of being in the light.

Overwhelmed, I hung my head and wept like a child. It was so simple. Tears of gratefulness and wonder fell from my eyes. I felt like I was being reborn into a whole new perception of all that existed. How could I have missed this?

For a long time all I heard was the thundering waterfall, which to me was like the thundering of love through my mind, my veins, my bones. I knew that love. I experienced it. I *was* it.

How long I knelt there, I don't know. Maybe an eternity. And then my weeping turned to sniffles and I gave a huge sigh.

Eli, I thought. *Where is Eli?*

I opened my eyes, and the moment I did, the thundering waterfall was gone. I blinked in the dim light of the cell.

I was back!

I started to stand, but my legs were too weak and I collapsed back on my heels, twisting to see the cell.

Eli was leaning against the bars, arms crossed, smiling at me. "Hello, daughter. It's so nice to meet you again."

Mouth gaping, I stared at him, then glanced around to see that Bobbie was gone.

"Was that real?" I stammered. "Did that really happen?"

"You tell me."

But I already knew. Nothing had ever been so real.

Eli pushed himself off the bars and stepped up to me, reached for my shoulder, and took a knee so we were the same height. "Now you know who you are," he said, searching my eyes.

I swallowed and let my experience fill me. "Yes." My voice came out thin, choked by emotion.

"In this world you will have troubles," he said. "It's okay. They are all only opportunities to let go and see yourself as you truly are. Be glad, because the light has overcome and all those troubles are only shadows."

I nodded.

"The first shadow you will face is Sylous."

I had forgotten about Rose and Sylous

and my terrible standing in Haven Valley.

My child! I placed my hand on my belly, and new questions filled my mind.

He gave me a nod. "Then ask."

I hesitated. "The Fury . . . Who are they?"

"They're the fear you and the whole world create in denial of the light, thinking that fear will protect you," he said. "But whatever's done in fear only creates more fear. Love creates more love. You see the Fury as monsters, but I see them as what they are. Shadows."

His revelation stunned me.

"Then why didn't you stand up to them?"

He smiled patiently. "Listen to what I said, Grace. They. Are. Shadows. There's nothing to stand up to."

"But they attacked us. You're saying our own fears attacked us?"

"Because you don't know who you are. Most of what you call the devil is actually your own fear manifesting. But they don't exist in the light. I can't force you to believe in the light, but now you know the truth."

Was it really that simple?

"Language makes it hard to understand, but yes," he said, eyes twinkling. "It really is that simple."

"What about Sylous?"

"Sylous is different. A religious spirit not

made by you, but still a shadow. The world is full of his kind, they just remain hidden behind the fear they feed on. You'll understand much more soon, I promise."

"Why didn't you use your power to stop him?"

"But I am. Right now, through you." He beamed like a proud teacher. "Just remember, he only has the power you give him through your fear."

It really did sound simple. And yet . . .

I lowered my eyes as the memory of my mother being whipped flooded me. I could feel the shadow fall over me. I'd seen her body as it fell to the ground. How could I live with her death? A knot filled my throat and I tried to fight my emotion, but the more I did, the more I sank.

"I have nothing left in this world," I whispered.

"That's a perfect place to start," Eli said. "You were born into the world of shadows to rise past those shadows, just like everyone. To find the light in the darkness. Nothing else matters."

I looked past him to the dark hallway beyond the bars. Dark, cold, so very real now. How could I have gone from such wonder to such worry in the space of just a few minutes?

"Because you're still clinging to who you thought you were," he said.

"But my mother . . ."

"Isn't who you thought she was either. She's alive and well."

A gentle breeze brushed across my shoulders there in that basement cell, and my heart leaped. The draft caressed my face, warm and easy, smelling of lilacs and roses, wrapping itself around me in a loving embrace.

Daughter.

I recognized my mother's voice immediately, and tears sprang to my eyes. "Mother?"

Do not be afraid, Grace. There's nothing to be afraid of.

My spirit soared in response to her voice, because I knew then that the boy was right. My mother had not died. In a strange way I couldn't put my finger on, my concern for her vanished. I wasn't thinking of her anymore.

I was thinking of the waterfall and the voice I'd heard there as my Father's love thundered through me. My body started to shake again from my shoulders to my ankles. It could hardly contain the power the memory of his voice brought.

Light of the world, there is nothing to fear.

As I knelt there on the cold floor, lost in his presence, I suddenly wanted to weep and dance at the same time.

Drink of my love. Remember who you are, daughter.

"I will," I breathed, barely able to speak. "I will." And I thought, *Not my will but yours, because I'm one with you in truth.*

My last resolve to cling to the way I had known myself — as Grace in Haven Valley — broke with that thought. As though I was once more by the crystal lake, my Father's love crashed through me. There were no words to describe the unity I felt with my Father in that moment. Perhaps it was more profound here than in the white place, because I was experiencing truth while in a dark cell.

Joy that I couldn't contain boiled up inside of me, and suddenly I was leaning back on my knees, laughing at the ceiling, letting tears of joy stream down my cheeks as the gentle breeze that had brought my Father's voice swirled around me.

My mother was in that breeze.

I impulsively jumped to my feet and began to spin, arms stretched wide.

Eli was laughing like the child he was, though he wasn't really a child. He mimicked me, twirling. "Yes, yes, yes! She knows! She knows!"

Anyone peering into the cell would surely have concluded that we'd both lost our minds. But the ways of the spirit were insane to blind minds. If knowing the Father was insanity, we were celebrating that insanity.

Eli and I danced, laughing, caught up in boundless joy and peace. I had no thoughts of the past or what would come. I was just there with my Father, Eli, and the clarity of who I truly was.

Much later it occurred to me that I hadn't heard Eli's voice for a while. I settled and looked around. The cell was dark and empty except for me and the pot in the corner. Not a sound could be heard.

He's gone, I thought.

But no, Eli was never gone.

CHAPTER THIRTY-FOUR

The first thing I saw when I woke up was the light. Not the light from my dream, but daylight coming in through the window.

I sat up and the reality of that dank cell crashed into my awareness. Eli had been here. Or had that all just been a dream? No, not a dream. I'd been awake with Eli, who'd shown me who I was. Who my Father was. Where my mother was.

And yet here I was, imprisoned and in terrible trouble.

I stood and walked to the bars between me and the next cell. The basement was empty. My heart raced as slivers of doubt cut into my mind.

"Eli?"

No response.

I moved back to the bench and sat, then closed my eyes. A tremble had taken to my fingers. I began to whisper Eli's truth out loud, desperate to feel the love and warmth from before.

There is no fear in love.

"Is that really what you believe?"

I opened my eyes and saw Bobbie standing on the other side of my cell door, arms crossed.

"All because some little kid came to you in your dreams and said so?"

But this was Bobbie, who I now knew had to be a Fury, because she was full of fear — the wisdom of the world, desperate to protect me.

"You're a Fury, aren't you?"

She blinked. "Yes, but deep down you've always known that, haven't you? And not all Fury are the same. I'm only here to help you. That's what wisdom does."

Maybe I always had known.

"That's what the wisdom of the *world* does," I corrected her. "And what I experienced with Eli wasn't a dream."

"Are you sure? Is that what you're going to tell Rose when they come for you? That Eli came back from the dead, showed up in your cell, and told you there is no fear in love?"

I didn't respond.

"It sounds insane," Bobbie said. "Because you can't begin to believe that it's possible to live without fear. Does that mean no one knows how to love? Because everyone lives in fear of something. Fear of being ridiculed, fear of heresy. Even God fears, for goodness' sake. He fears for you!"

"My Father fears nothing, including my failure."

"Not true," she snapped. "What *is* true is that soon they'll come to collect you, and we need to make sure you don't mess this up." She eyed me, clearly annoyed by my apparent dismissal of her. "Even if the boy is right, you won't do anyone any good locked up here. Play their game. To the Romans, be a Roman. Speak their language. Repent. It'll set you free to teach them all this love stuff over time."

She made good sense, though what she meant by *repent* was very different from what Eli meant by it.

A thought blossomed in the back of my mind as I stared at Bobbie. *You manifest what you believe. You create it.* Whatever I did in fear only created more fear. Fury. But if I was in the love that held no record of wrong, more of that love would come. Regardless of what I did, I didn't want to do it in fear.

Bobbie tilted her head slightly and gave me a questioning look. "What nonsense are you trying to believe now?"

The door at the top of the stairs creaked open. Bobbie and I both turned to watch as heavy boots started down the stairs, one pair and then another. Tanner and Marshall. They were coming to collect me for my appearance before the community, just as Bobbie had said.

"It's time," Tanner said.

Bobbie had moved to the side, her eyes still trained on me. "Use common sense," she said. "It is the only way to ensure your protection."

Marshall unlocked my cell and ushered me forward.

Bobbie was still present and speaking. "Protect yourself, Grace. Please, for my sake."

For her sake, because her existence depended on me remaining in fear. She was of my own making, a Fury.

Tanner and Marshall kept me close as they guided me up the stairs and out of the basement. I squinted against the bright sun. It was already hot. The streets were empty as they led me to the Chapel.

Bobbie was suddenly in front of me, eyes drilling into mine. "Think of your baby!"

The air of peace and truth that had started collecting around me stilled. Yes, what of my baby? Didn't I have an obligation to fear for my unborn child?

Tanner and Marshall ushered me in through the double doors of the Chapel, and the eyes of the Holy Family shifted to stare at me. Some of them looked sad. Others looked as though they pitied me. Who wouldn't, after what I'd suffered? After what my mother had suffered?

Most watched me with uncertain, shifting eyes. I felt sorry for them. They were only slaves to what they'd been told and believed, like all in the world. And I saw in their eyes the power that the whole world, regardless of creed or religion, had bound itself to.

Fear.

I remembered standing on the mountain with Eli beside me, looking down on this city and seeing it drenched in thick darkness. Fear tucked into every nook and cranny, every corner, every plank of wood.

Fear.

Fear.

Fear.

Jamie caught my eye as they led me up the center aisle. He showed no emotion. Whatever had happened to him on the mountain had changed him. But I already knew what had happened to him. He'd been filled with more fear than he'd ever known, and that fear was manifesting as anger, because anger was just another form of fear. A reaction against the fear of loss.

Andrew sat two seats over from Jamie, watching me with a pitying frown. He was fearing for both me and how my fate would reflect on him.

The children were looking at me with round eyes, fearing the unknown.

Colin, the most vocal of the council members, scowled, fearing that what he disapproved of would be allowed and bring harm.

Everywhere I looked now, all I saw was fear. All darkness was fear, and much of what my religion had taught me was based in that fear. How could we all have missed such an obvious observation?

But I didn't blame them. I was in fear as well. It was as if we were all in a storm and we were all cowering, trying to be saved by giving in to the demands of fear. But now I knew: whatever was done in fear only created more fear.

Rose pointed to the top of the stage, and I obediently climbed the steps and faced the crowd, alone and high for all to see. She looked up at me, mouth set in a hard line. Fear.

"Today you confess your sins and deny the boy's heresy before the church in a display of repentance. In doing so you take the first step to finding forgiveness. Do you understand the deception you've allowed to threaten God's elect?"

This was it. It all came down to this moment. And I was trembling.

"Repent, Grace," Bobbie said. She appeared at the side of the stage. "Save yourself today and we'll figure everything out later."

Rose waited, watching me carefully.

"Denounce Eli's heresy," Bobbie snapped. "Think of your baby."

My mother's death was evidence of what Rose was capable of under Sylous's guidance. What would she do to my baby? Standing there before them all, I was terrified.

There is no fear in love. Only love casts out fear. A beat passed, and then, *See the shadow.*

And with that, my vision changed. As if someone had removed dark glasses that were distorting my view, the scene before me transformed into a terrifying picture. Thick cords of darkness crept along the walls and the ceiling, smothered in a wispy black fog. It was whispering and clicking, speaking its own language of fear.

The cords grew like vines from the floor,

crawling over the pews, clasping the ankles of every member, winding tightly around their chests and necks, penetrating their ears and eyes without their knowledge.

It was the fear Eli had shown me before, part of the Fury. Like their scent. The wraithlike beings I thought of as the Fury were still hidden from my sight, but the whole place was surely filled with them, thicker here than anywhere.

I inched backward. Rose looked at me with confusion. The others stared, oblivious to the dark cords of fear that enslaved them.

There are two kingdoms, daughter. Choose love over fear.

The words hit me like an anvil dropped from the sky, and I began to shake. I was seeing fear coiling around the children and covering their mothers' faces. That same fear was also in me, and I looked down to see black cords sliding up my legs and coiling around my belly like a snake. I could feel them slipping into my ears.

I started to panic, but the words whispered again.

It's only fear, daughter. It's a lie.

"Speak!" Rose snapped. Wafts of fog escaped from her mouth as she spoke. "Do you understand your sin and repent?"

I blinked a couple times to clear the darkness from my view, but it remained. I was shaking as I stood there, seeing our creations. I closed my eyes, ignored the thoughts begging me to end it all with a few words of confession, and spoke what I knew to be true despite my fear. This was my true repentance.

"There are two kingdoms, two paths, two choices," I began. "Love and fear. Light and darkness. Sight and blindness." A surge of power filled my chest and spread through my body. "We have given ourselves over to fear, but fear is a lie. Only love can set us free from fear."

The surge of power running through me grew and heated my chest, and I opened my eyes. A glow hovered around me. The tentacles of fear clinging to my body were writhing and softening their grip.

The cords of fear choking Rose were tightening, slithering frantically. The jungle of fear in the sanctuary was hissing loudly now, as my words evoked more fear in those who'd been deceived by it.

Darkness was here, but so was the kingdom of heaven, seen in the light.

I spoke quickly, ignoring Rose, who was opening her mouth to cut me off. "God is love," I said, louder now. "And whoever abides in him abides in love, and he in them."

People were shifting uncomfortably in their seats, still oblivious to the Fury's black cords of fear.

"A love that isn't provoked, a love that records no wrong, a love that is unconditional and casts out all fear."

With those words, the back doors of the church slammed shut. The windows crashed down, sealing us in our own prison of fear.

As if from nowhere, Sylous was standing at the back of the sanctuary, glaring at me with dark eyes. The auditorium turned to him in shocked silence. They'd felt his presence.

And with his presence, fear seeped back into me. The coils tightened around my chest and throat again, demanding I remain silent.

The hissing and clicks grew louder as many cords — hundreds of them, like rushing lovers — slithered across the room and up Sylous's legs and ran into his torso, his chest, then his neck and temples. It was as if Sylous was energizing the fear in that room.

Or feeding on it.

And still, none of the others could see what I was seeing.

He spoke, voice low and gravelly. "It appears you've let the Fury poison one of your own."

That was a lie, but I couldn't find the courage to speak it aloud. Sylous was more than just a Fury, but he fed on fear, and the room was full of it. Seeing him in his greatest power, I dared not resist him.

"I thought I was clear," he said, speaking to all but staring at me. "There is no remission of sin without the shedding of blood. And yet there stands sin, speaking lies to deceive you all."

The rest heard only Sylous, but I heard the Fury, like a million insects now covering every bare inch of the wood in that sanctuary. I stood trembling from head to foot.

Then Sylous lifted one hand, and my sight of the fear ended. The black cords were gone, as was the fog. I now saw what they all saw — Sylous dressed in white, saving his sanctuary from the hells of sin.

"Perhaps the extent of my power isn't understood," Sylous said, walking down the aisle, eyes on me. "I am the principality who was sent to save you from hell. I chose you, gave you true sight, and called you to live in the protection of my kingdom. And all I asked in return is that you confess your loyalty to God and heed his laws. Was it too much to ask? It appears you would rather suffer the fate of all who refuse to confess their sin to God."

"You should have listened to me," Bobbie sneered. Her gaze condemned me. "I would have saved you. Now you'll pay."

Sylous reached the stage, took the steps in one long stride, and unceremoniously wrapped his hand around my neck. Then he hauled me down off the stage as if I were a doll. He stopped at the front of the main aisle, fingers gripping the back of my neck like a vise.

"I don't have time for games," Sylous hissed. "For ten years I've kept you safe from the Fury. Five days ago, this poor wretch sold her soul to the boy who came to deceive you all. Eli is dead, but his spirit lives on in the one he's possessed. She must now suffer the same fate as the boy. Anything less and I will be powerless to protect you from the Fury you yourselves witnessed when the boy came. The choice is yours."

Frantic, I clawed at his fingers. He only squeezed my throat harder, and I cried out.

He lifted me off the ground so the tips of my shoes barely touched the floor, then tossed me forward. I crashed to the floor on my knees and elbows, gasping for fresh air. I heard a click followed by several gasps, and I twisted back to where he stood.

Sylous's arm was extended toward me. In his hand he held a gun.

It was pointed at my head.

CHAPTER THIRTY-FIVE

Jamie watched as Sylous calmly pulled the gun from behind his back, cocked it and pointed it at his sister. Part of him wanted to rush forward and save her, but his better discretion held him in place. She was poisoned; there was nothing he could do for her now. Really, she wasn't his sister anymore. She was only one more soul destined for eternal hell.

He'd hoped having the blood of their mother on her hands would bring her back to the law, but it seemed to have no effect. She was completely lost.

All that remained was making sure she didn't drag all of Haven Valley into the depths of hell with her. He would mourn her because she used to be his sister. But now she had given herself over to the devil. If God could kill those in Sodom and Gomorrah for their sin, why would he or any of them offer mercy to one soul who had known the truth only to trample on it?

Can you do what is needed? a voice whispered in his head. *Would you set aside your selfishness and do the will of God?*

Jamie twitched, unnerved. But he knew the wrath of the Fury all too well. And he had no desire to feel the wrath of God again.

He would do whatever was required.

My mind felt like it was being torn apart, but in that chaos I was certain of one thing. If I stood and spoke about love I would die. And my baby would die with me.

"Make your choice," Sylous demanded.

"Kill her," Rose whispered.

Sylous turned to her, eyes hard. "What did you say?"

Her voice was strung like a piano wire. "I said kill her!" she cried.

"I could have saved you," Bobbie said from the place where she still stood, looking on like a disappointed mother. "You did this."

Sylous scanned the flock at Haven Valley. "And you? Will you fear God and follow his commandments?"

Whispers of "yes" rippled through the auditorium, growing in voices of agreement. But my mind was on Sylous's last word. Commandments.

A new commandment I give you, that you love one another as I love you. This is how they will know that you follow me, that you love one another.

And there was no fear in love.

Sylous flipped the gun on its end so he was holding the barrel. He turned and held the gun out to someone on my right. I looked up into my brother's wide eyes.

"Then we'll let Jamie do what is needed," Sylous said.

Jamie glanced around, then stepped into the aisle. He walked forward and took the gun from Sylous. Held it unsteadily and slowly pointed it at me.

"Kill her," Sylous said.

Stand up, daughter. Stand and show them what you've seen.

My heart was hammering like a drum and my arms were shaking, but I pushed myself up and staggered to my feet. I faced my brother, who'd taken a step back and was sweating. His eyes were dark and his jaw was clenched, but he wasn't pulling the trigger. Not yet.

And if he did? Then I would be with my mother. And Ben. And Eli. And my baby. It was really that simple. What did I hope to gain by saving myself? What good was it to live this life if I had lost my soul? My only purpose was to find my soul and do it now, even if I lost my life. My fear of dying was my own creation.

With that realization, a new thought filled my mind. *Show them.* I had the power to show them, didn't I?

"Kill her!" Rose shrieked.

I held up my hand, still afraid but knowing why I stood in that storm. "Before you kill me, do you want to see what I see?" I faced the pews. "Do you want to see how the Fury have infected me?"

"Don't you dare do this to me!" Bobbie shrieked.

"Pull the trigger, boy," Sylous snarled. He was afraid as well.

I lifted my other hand in a sign of surrender. "I know how to get rid of the Fury, Jamie. They're in here now, all around us. They're feeding on us. On me."

"You're lying," Jamie spat. But his whole face was quivering and I knew he was fighting himself.

"Watch," I said, and I turned to Bobbie. "Show yourself."

She took a step back, terrified.

"You're my creation," I said. "And I say show yourself!"

In the eyes of the rest, it probably looked like I had lost my mind and was speaking to empty space. But in the next moment, the space wasn't empty. All who had followed my stare saw Bobbie appear.

Gasps peppered the sanctuary. She looked around, stunned. *Show them,* the voice had told me, and this was what I knew to show them.

Bobbie, dressed in black and white, blonde and beautiful, stood like a statue, eyes round and confused. But her bewilderment fell away as she jerked her head to me, face red. "How dare you betray me?" she growled.

"Show yourself as you are," I said.

I watched as my close friend slowly shifted from a beautiful woman into a wraith. A faceless, black-hooded ghoul with long white fingers and blue eyes. She was different from the other Fury I'd seen, because there were many kinds of fear. She was the kind known as the wisdom of the world. But fear was fear, and as Eli had said, all fear was darkness.

I lifted my hands and looked at my fingers, then my body. "Show yourselves, all of you."

Ten or twelve other wraiths appeared around me. Some materialized close to me out of nowhere. Some emerged from my body. All were intently focused on me, eyes piercing, jaws wide, a few weeping. Some had yellow eyes, others black, most white.

They weren't spirits or demons or entities. They were fear — the same kind everyone in the world hosted without knowing it. The only difference was that on two occasions Sylous had given us the capacity to see fear more clearly than others — once thirteen years ago when he'd first appeared among us, and once after Eli had healed Evelyn. And Sylous did this to increase our fear.

Now my fears were showing themselves in fullness for all to see what they truly were. My creations.

My Fury didn't have faces, but if they did, they would all be versions of me, and for the first time I truly understood them for what they were. My self-pity, my anxiousness, my anger, my hopelessness, my judgment, my self-criticism, my worthlessness, my victimhood, my self-righteousness, my disapproval of others, my fear of being deceived, my need to control any situation, my guilt . . .

Yes. My guilt, which was the largest Fury of them all, twice the size of the others, hovering over me and glaring with yellow eyes, arms crossed like a disgusted god.

And in that moment, I understood not only my fears but the fears of the world. A man jealous of another man who took his wife. A mother upset at her child for disobeying. A truck driver worried he wouldn't be able to feed his family. A country putting up defenses at its borders to keep enemies out. A pastor worried he wasn't serving the flock well enough. On they went — a million fears that blinded humanity to the light of love. None of the fears were less damaging than others, I saw. Anger was as destructive as murder.

The world had made an agreement with fear to keep it safe, but that safety was a lie wielded like a sword, turning the world into a sea of blood. Humanity had been murdering itself for a very long time. Only love could cast out that fear.

Yea, though I walk through the valley of the shadow of death, I will fear no evil, because it's only a shadow.

I stood still, letting my Fury be, surprised by how obvious they were. They were silent but desperate, and I was sure that if I'd been in a different state of being, they would have been able to tear into me as they had Jamie on the mountain. But I wasn't giving them that power anymore.

Most of the people in the room were still glued to the far corner, where Bobbie had just unveiled herself as a black-hooded Fury. A symphony of alarm and terror had filled the auditorium.

Those screams were cut short when a gunshot echoed through the room. Jamie had seen Bobbie morph and impulsively turned his gun on her, firing into her body. Could a Fury be killed?

I slowly turned to Bobbie, doing my best to ignore the other wraiths now plucking at my gown and pulling at my skin, clamoring for my attention. The bullet had passed through Bobbie and slammed into the wall. Jamie shot again. Bobbie stood unaffected, looking at me with round, shocked eyes.

"How could you do this to me?" she asked in a pathetically desperate voice.

By now the whole assembly had seen the other wraiths emerging from me, doubling back and spreading their fanged jaws, silently roaring in my face or cowering and whimpering.

I felt fear, enough to make me tremble, but I also knew the truth. So I looked directly at the wraiths circling me and held up one hand. "No," I said.

As one, they all slowed as if caught in thick air. Some stopped altogether and stared back at me.

"I am the light. There is no darkness in light. The light is love. There is no fear in love. I am love, so there's no place for you in me. So . . ." I searched for clever words, but found none. "So, no."

I watched as my fears faded, one by one. Black to gray to nothing. They didn't leave me, they simply vanished. But of course. Fear was of my own making, fueled by me, and I had pulled the plug through the full awareness of who I was.

To me, their departure was as though a thousand-pound weight I didn't know I'd been wearing had been suddenly cut free. For a moment, I was sure that my feet lifted off the ground. A wave of peace rose through me and filled my chest, my mind, the air. I felt like I could walk through walls.

My fears were gone.

And Bobbie?

I turned back to the corner where Bobbie remained, staring at me, looking utterly abandoned and forlorn.

"I don't need you either," I said.

"Please, I can't live without you," she begged.

"I'm sorry."

With a last mournful whimper, she faded into nothing. Like a fog under a hot sun, Bobbie was no more.

Lift your eyes, Grace. The kingdom of heaven is the perception of light. If your perception is clear, you will see that your whole body is full of light. Only blindness keeps anyone from seeing it.

My mind filled with a knowing that set my bloodstream on fire and transported me to a different kind of awareness. With my eyes open to the kingdom of heaven, I saw.

Where there had once been darkness, now there was only light. Warm, brilliant, washing through and over every surface. The floorboards, the chairs, my fingers. I caught my breath.

All around me were the faces of Haven Valley I was so familiar with — Rose, Stephen, Evelyn, Levi, Colin, Jamie, who held the gun by his side — all of them shining with light from their very souls, exploding in a prism of soft colors. I knew they just saw me in flesh and blood — Grace, the girl who was a heretic — but I was seeing them as they really were.

They too were the light of the world; they were just blind to how their Father saw them. I was seeing with the eyes of Christ. They were seeing with the eyes of fear.

In the chaos, Sylous had left us. To where, I didn't know yet. I still wasn't sure how he was different from the Fury, but I had an idea.

And then I was seeing normally again and every eye was on me. For a long beat, they stared in stunned disbelief.

I took a deep breath and said what I knew to be true. "God is the light in which there is no darkness. And we are made in his likeness, light like him. But the world turned to darkness and we were blinded to our light."

"Blasphemy!" Rose cried, her finger stabbing at me.

"No, Rose." I took a slow step toward her. "Didn't you see the Fury right here in the sanctuary?"

"You brought them!"

"That's not true. They've always been here, feeding on us. They live in us and hover around us. Sylous opened our eyes to our own fears manifested in form and told us it was God's cleansing, which only filled us with more fear. There's now more fear concentrated in this valley than anywhere in the world."

"Lies," she bit off. Then to Jamie: "Kill her!"

"You saw my Fury," I said. "And you saw how I as the light let them go. How could I have that power if I was lying?"

The room was perfectly still as they considered my blasphemy in the face of their sacred beliefs.

"Where did he go?" Andrew asked, looking around for Sylous.

"I suspect he couldn't take the heat," I said.

"Why would the angel lie to us?" Jamie asked.

I faced him, courage coursing through my veins. "Because he's a demon, not an angel." It was my best guess, but I was pretty sure. "And he did this because he lives on fear. He feeds on it. He manipulated us into supplying him with an endless source of fear to feed on."

But Jamie wasn't hearing me. I couldn't see the darkness or the light as I had moments earlier, but I knew that his Fury were screaming in his mind, and his eyes were turning dark again.

"Kill her now or I swear there will be hell to pay!" Rose cried. "And I mean real hell, like none of you have ever known. Sylous has always protected us! How dare any of you listen to these lies? The demon comes as the light to deceive us." She glared at Jamie. "Now kill her!"

Jamie knew that Rose was right — every ounce of discernment in his bones told him that Grace had been taken over by the devil. Only a devil could do what she'd just done.

The voices in his mind hissed to life.

Can you do what is needed?

Can you save them from her?
Do it, do it, kill her.

Trembling, Jamie lifted the gun. "Without the shedding of blood, there is no remission for sin," he said, tightening his grip. "Repent now or I have to kill you."

But Grace didn't repent. Instead, she walked up to him. Right up to the gun, only a few inches from the barrel, which hovered before her chest. She smiled at him.

She's the devil. Kill her! Kill her!

"Do you want to die?" Jamie heard himself ask.

"Death is just a shadow, Jamie. I'm not afraid of shadows anymore. You can live with fear if you like, but it only draws more fear. Everything I said is true. All of it."

Her eyes showed not a hint of concern. Her face seemed to glow. The frightened sister he had always known had become a warrior, he couldn't deny that. And her new calm unnerved him as much as any Fury might.

But what if she was right?

Grace raised her hand and placed it against his cheek, a forbidden act. Warmth spread from her touch, and he nearly pulled the trigger then. But he hesitated, feeling the heat spread over his face.

"There is another way, Jamie," she whispered. "You don't have to be afraid."

Rose took a step toward them. "Pull that trigger, you coward!"

"I see you, brother," Grace continued. "You are the light. There is no trouble here. He has already overcome."

"Shoot her!" Rose screamed.

Who will you be without your protection?

The thought of releasing the laws that Jamie knew kept him safe made his bones groan. She had gone mad!

Do it, do what needs to be done!

Do it!

The warmth on his cheek spread down the side of his neck and onto his shoulder. He couldn't rip his eyes from hers. They weren't the same eyes he knew from before. There were certainty and affection in them. How could she love him now after all this? How dare she!

"It's okay," Grace whispered. "Let go, Jamie. Let go."

Jamie felt a warm emotion swell up his chest and into his throat. The voices continued to hiss in his mind, demanding he save the world by killing his sister, but the wonder in her eyes was swallowing him. Was it possible?

"I love you, brother," Grace said.

Like an overwhelmed dam, something

inside Jamie broke.

Suddenly he wanted nothing more than to believe her. To be rid of the fear that had guided his life in a promise to keep him safe. To know the kind of love she knew without judgment or condemnation. Without fear of punishment or consequence.

With that thought, the warmth from her touch swallowed him whole, and he knew he couldn't do what he was meant to do.

Jamie lowered the gun, hung his head, and began to weep.

The moment Jamie hung his head, Rose knew he'd fallen under Grace's deceitful spell. Her words, like honey, had filled the auditorium and enthralled them all, including her to some extent. For a moment, she wondered if there might be some truth, however small, in what Grace was saying. In how she was being — fearless and gentle.

But that would mean everything Rose had based her life on was wrong. The fear she felt from that thought shoved all deception aside, replacing it with a holy wrath of God.

Sylous had insisted that Jamie be the one to kill Grace, but Jamie had failed. And Sylous had vanished. The others were looking at Jamie and Grace now, some tearing up, some lost in confusion, some incensed —

but not nearly as many as she would have expected. How could they be so easily wooed by the lies of the wolf in sheep's clothing?

Even her children. Perhaps they more than the others, staring in wonder. So innocent and good. What if they were seeing something she couldn't? What if . . .

I will leave you to face hell on your own.

Sylous's words swept through her, and fear mushroomed in her gut. But it was immediately joined with courage. He was still here, watching over her like a constant lover.

I cannot serve you if you do not serve me. The Fury will tear you to pieces.

"No," she whispered. "Please . . . I can fix this."

I was wrong to put my faith in you. I was mistaken to think I could save you.

"No!" Rose screamed, balling her hands. She looked at the congregation, all eyes on her. But her mind was on Sylous. "Please, don't leave me. I need you. I'll do whatever you ask. Please, don't leave me."

You know what has to be done.

Rose shifted her eyes to the gun hanging in Jamie's limp hand as his shoulders shook in silent sobs. Grace stood with her back to Rose, hands on her brother's shoulders.

Now!

464

His voice came as a snarl, propelling her forward. Fear washed through her in great waves, numbing her mind. In four long steps, she reached Jamie, ripped the gun from his hand, and jumped to the side. Gun now in both hands, aimed at Grace. Finger on the trigger.

But Grace had turned, and the calm in her blue eyes reached into Rose, inviting her to surrender to a new lover. To peace and rest.

"Kill her!" Sylous's voice shook the rafters. He was there in person, right behind her. And his hand was around the back of her neck, squeezing like a vise. Then he spoke softly in her ear, so that she could feel the heat of his breath and smell wafts of lilac. "Be a good lover and do as I ask, Rose."

His arm slid around her chest, and he pulled her body back against him. She could see his strong hands, feel his muscle.

"Kill the girl now," he whispered in her ear.

"I am," she gasped. The gun was shaking like a leaf in her hands. "I am!"

But she wasn't.

Before her was Grace, the one Sylous seemed powerless to stop. The one he was terrified of. The one who had no fear.

Behind her stood Sylous. All eyes were

fixed on him now. Somewhere a child was crying, but she didn't know whose child. It sounded a bit like Levi. No one was hushing him. They were concerned with something far more urgent: Sylous, the one who had saved her from the hell of her father and led them into a sanctuary where the Fury couldn't harm them. She'd lived to please him, loving him as no other.

And in that moment, she had no doubt he would rip her head from her shoulders if she didn't surrender to him now. He was the one who protected them, not threatened them. So why was he so afraid?

"Because he needs our fear," Grace said in a soft voice. "He feeds on our fear. He's a religious spir—"

"Blasphemy!" Sylous roared, body shaking behind Rose. He was breathing heavily. Full of fear. And for a moment, speechless.

Grace was still looking directly at Rose, fearless, ignoring Sylous. "Love is the evidence of truth," she said. "A love that holds no record of evil and blesses those who persecute. Isn't that what Jesus himself taught?"

Sylous shoved Rose and she staggered to her left, on the edge of panic.

He straightened his coat and spread his arms, addressing the congregation. "Do I look like a cruel taskmaster to you? If not for me, you would all be dead. Dead and in hell!"

They stared, drinking in his words.

"I am your lover! I am the one who puts you to bed at night!" His rage was leaking through again, and now he set aside his composure altogether, shoving a finger of accusation at them all. "I am the one who leads you to Jesus and saves you from hell! I am the one who shows you how wretched you are! But for my sight, you would make yourselves God in defiance of his holiness! I am the one who keeps you humble and on the narrow path. I am your only hope now!"

"No," Grace said calmly. "You're the father of lies who uses fear to keep us blind to who we are. If we surrendered to love, all fear would be gone and you would search out another valley to seduce with your lies."

She scanned the church, beaming. "Imagine an infinite love that is unconditional. That can't be provoked or threatened. In that love you'll see fear for what it truly is: a shadow." She was beside herself with joy. "Imagine that! Shadows that we've gone into agreement with. But in love, the Fury vanish, because there is no fear in love, just like there's no darkness in light."

"God cannot fathom, much less express,

unconditional love!" Sylous bit off, face red. He paced, glaring at them all, unable to hide his rage. His fear of losing their loyalty.

Rose blinked with a new thought. How could such a powerful being be so terrified? And how could a God who was infinitely powerful be afraid of losing anything?

"God demands a response from you, all good Christians know that!" he continued. "That's his condition! If you don't say yes, you will spend eternity in hell, and if you want to test that, be my guest. Take a gamble." He flung an arm out like a spoiled child. "Throw caution to the wind and risk never-ending torture. Or say yes to God now and throw out the wicked one who's tempting you to believe her lies!"

Rose stood back, mind fractured, gun at her side now. Grace didn't even acknowledge Sylous. She was still fixed on the flock. Rose's flock.

Sylous's flock.

"Eli said we are the light, but Sylous says we're not the light," Grace said. "Who are you going to believe? Fear has blinded all of humanity. We call it the fall from the garden. The fall from the kingdom of heaven. But today we can all see again."

Rose stood aghast. Stunned, because somewhere in Grace's words, she saw a sliver of truth. And in that sliver, light. How could a loving being ever threaten any harm for any reason? Was Sylous not loving?

Sylous began to tremble, glaring at Grace with hatred. From head to foot he shook, fists clenched. Rose had always found his wrath oddly attractive. But why?

She took a step back, suddenly terrified of him in the worst possible way.

No one spoke. No one moved.

"I know you're afraid, Rose," Grace said, voice tender. "I know you believe you're nothing without him. But he only keeps you blind to eternal life, which is living free from fear right now, not after you die. Choose life, Rose. Choose love."

The veins were thick on Sylous's neck. With a sudden roar, he turned and rushed at Rose, eyes red, lips quivering.

He was coming for her. He was going to force her to shoot Grace. He was going to tear a gash in her neck.

She acted as much from some deeply hidden instinct as from that sliver of light that Grace's words had opened up in her mind. She jerked the gun up and fired when he was halfway to her.

The gun thundered and bucked in her hand. A hole appeared in Sylous's forehead, and Rose immediately thought, *Oh no, what have I done?*

Stopped in his tracks, Sylous stared at her, stupefied. But he did not waver. Instead, his lips slowly twisted and peeled back, revealing a jaw with fangs. His body began to morph, arms lengthening, eyes narrowing into slits, claws extending.

He tilted his head back, spread his long jaw and roared at the ceiling. The windows rattled and the congregation cowered.

Sylous, who was now as much beast as man, lowered his head, chest rising and falling in great breaths. "I've always despised you." His voice was low and guttural, popping with phlegm. "Now I will kill you."

He flinched and came like a bolt of lightning. Rose's blood turned to ice.

"Leave," a voice said to her right. Grace, standing with head tilted down, staring at Sylous with bright and certain eyes.

The word seemed to have its own power, slamming into the onrushing beast like a wave. As if hitting an invisible wall, Sylous came to an abrupt halt. Jerked his head around to stare at Grace. Confusion overtook his fanged face.

"Leave us now," Grace said.

The beast who was Sylous blinked once, then began to smolder. His flesh turned to fog, and with a shriek that faded with his body, he returned to where he had come from.

Sylous was gone.

Rose gasped as his presence left her. But it didn't feel like a simple leaving. It felt as though a heavy, debilitating disease had been dragged from her lungs, ripped from her heart. Her mind cleared and she stared at the empty space before her.

Gone.

The gun fell from Rose's hands and thumped loudly on the wood. She slowly turned to Grace, who was smiling.

"Fear," Grace said, "or love. Darkness or light. Religious judgment or Christ. You can only serve one master."

Rose fell to her knees and began to weep.

Grace turned to the elect in Haven Valley as soft sobs and sniffles whispered through the sanctuary. "Eli opened my eyes to see the light. Do you want to see the world the way he sees the world?"

"Yes," Rose breathed. Then with all the strength left in her body, she lifted her head to stare up at the rafters through tearful eyes. "Yes!"

"Then see," Grace said.

And they saw.

471

EPILOGUE

Two Weeks Later

We sat in the tall grass, maybe fifty souls in all, less than half the population Haven Valley had recently been. The sun was bright overhead and children darted about, caught up in a game of tag. Blankets had been laid out for people to come and sit. This place that had once been off-limits was now a beautiful meeting ground where we could fellowship and remember we were the light.

Haven Valley had been transformed. After the glorious day in the Chapel, when our eyes had been opened to the kingdom of love and the Fury had been exposed as only shadows, nothing had been the same. The first thing to go was the red rope.

But we all had many red ropes in our minds: the boundaries made of fear that we believed would keep us safe — a false salvation born in fear. And not everyone had received the idea of freedom with the same enthusiasm.

Seeing truth, it turned out, is often deeply disturbing to the mind that is deeply invested in the prisons it thinks will keep it safe, a system of security that provides comfort, even if it's an illusion created in fear. Freedom always comes at the cost of the old.

Some saw and longed to know more. Others saw and were afraid, unable to believe. Still others saw and were deeply offended by having been deceived for so many years. Free from Sylous's law, Harrison, Levi, and others, including Andrew, had left to find their own way. They had no interest in seeking out the light.

But I was certain that the light would continue calling them home. Love was simply too powerful not to cast off all shadows in time.

For me, the calling had come through the voice and presence of a sweet boy named Eli, and I had surrendered to his love in the chaos of deep suffering. Others might choose prolonged suffering, but eventually every knee would bow in wonder and every tongue would sing the glory of that light. Or so it was written.

I didn't blame those who had left. I considered leaving myself. In fact, I did leave, if only for two days. Jamie and I simply had to know what the outside world really looked like. So we'd taken the trip four days after Sylous had been cast out of Haven Valley.

What we found was a world that was ten years older than the one we'd last seen but otherwise hardly different, except for the kinds of technology that had emerged in our absence. We stood on a hill overlooking the city before daring to venture in, stunned by the vastness of it all. People hustling and cars zooming every which way — it was a sight to behold.

The Fury were there, naturally. Not in the way we had seen them in Haven Valley, but if our eyes had been opened to see fear personified, we would have seen them everywhere, hovering about and feeding on nearly everyone, surely.

Along with me, Jamie and Rose were among those who'd chosen to stay. Jamie's heart had been taken by darkness quickly in the forest, but it fell more quickly into light. Now, understanding his fear, Jamie shone as brightly as I'd ever seen him.

Rose couldn't deny her deep agreement with fear or how love had shown her a way out of that fear, but her road was different from Jamie's. She would soon have to face the authorities, and we all knew that once the public found out what had occurred in Haven Valley, there would be an outcry. The world's version of justice would demand punishment to satisfy its fear.

But I didn't think those impending consequences were at the top of Rose's mind. Her struggle was more due to the guilt she felt for having fallen so far from the truth despite her intentions to follow a pure Christian path. Even now, as many talked quietly among themselves, Rose stood off to the edge of the grassy field, lost in thought.

I placed my hand on Jamie's shoulder to signal I would be back, then stood and walked toward Rose. Evelyn and Stephen, running on the grass, waved as I passed, and I waved back.

The ability to believe and see the light was easier for most of the children than for any adult. Stephen had recently told me he was going to start practicing flying. "The light of the world can surely fly!" he'd said excitedly before rushing off to find Evelyn. She was one of the only children to remain unsure in the wake of Sylous's demise. She'd committed herself deeply to her mother's guidance, and fear still lingered in her mind.

I placed my hand on my lower stomach,

reminding myself once again to make sure my child learned love rather than fear in every situation.

Rose glanced at me as I approached. Tears on her cheeks glistened in the sunlight. My heart felt her pain. In her position, I would surely have been as deceived as she'd been. In fact, I had been. She believed what she'd been taught, and so had I. Wasn't the whole world the same way? In punishing Rose, the world would only be doing what it thought it should do to protect itself. And that impulse to protect itself was born in fear.

The whole world was lost in fear. Only a direct encounter with love could save it.

I stopped beside her and we stood in silence for a long moment, letting the breeze whisper through our hair. I decided I liked mine short, but Rose was going to try growing hers out, long like her beautiful daughter's.

"Do you think we could forget love enough to end up enslaved to the Fury again?" she asked.

"I think we're enslaved often, whenever we cling to this world in fear of losing something. Fear's always available to us, just like love is. We have the opportunity to choose love over fear with every breath we take, and each time we choose love, it becomes more natural, until it becomes our breath."

She nodded and sighed. "Sometimes I think I still feel him," she whispered. "He manipulated me for so long . . ." Her words trailed off, and I stayed quiet as she processed. Rose didn't use Sylous's name anymore — it was too hard for her to say. "His words rang so true to me. I never saw what he really was."

"No one did."

She nodded thoughtfully, staring at the horizon. "Sometimes I think I can hear them in the night."

"The Fury?" I followed her stare. "Maybe that's a blessing. At least you know what they are. Most don't even know their fear has the kind of power it has."

Rose remained silent for a few beats. "I miss Harrison," she whispered, eyes misted once again.

I placed my arm around her elbow and pulled her close.

She looked up at me and shook her head, then lowered her eyes. "How can you be so kind to me after everything I've done?" she asked.

"Love holds no record of wrong, remember? Bless your enemies. It's easier on some days than others, but I'm learning."

Rose gave me a sideways glance. "So I'm your enemy?"

I saw the corner of her mouth pull up into a smile, and I started to laugh, joined by her.

As our laughter faded, we fell into an easy silence. Rose finally broke it. "So what now?"

I shrugged. "We learn to rest in love, no matter what happens. And we share that with whoever has ears to hear. What a story you have to tell the world! Maybe they will listen to you more than anyone else."

"Well, then," Rose said, turning to join the others. "No time like the present. Guess I should get back and do that now."

I watched her go, then turned to follow, and as I did, I heard a soft giggle on the breeze. I glanced around, knowing I wouldn't see him. At least not in person. In my mind's eye, I could often see his bright blue eyes and his charming smile. His presence seemed to follow me wherever I went.

I hadn't actually seen Eli in the flesh since he'd appeared to me in my prison cell. I doubted I ever would. Who was he, really? They'd thrown his burned body over a cliff, but it was now missing, maybe taken by animals. Had he been a real boy? He had to be. Or had he been an angel? Or something else I hadn't considered yet?

The mystery would remain until I died, I supposed. But it really didn't matter either way. Eli would be with me always, because no matter who he was, he was the embodiment of love, which knew no fear.

Indeed, Eli *was* love. And beyond all of my blindness, so was I.

I smiled and headed toward Jamie, who was now laughing with Colin about something. What a difference the truth could make! Yes, our mother was gone. Yes, Ben was dead. Yes, we had all endured the hells of fear for far too long.

But Jamie and I and the others were alive, more alive now than any of us had ever been. So were Eli and Ben and my mother and little Lukas.

It was going to be a beautiful day in Haven Valley.

It already was.

ABOUT THE AUTHORS

Ted Dekker is the award-winning and *New York Times* bestselling author of more than forty novels, with over ten million copies sold worldwide. He was born in the jungles of Indonesia to missionary parents, and his upbringing as a stranger in a fascinating and sometimes frightening culture fueled his imagination. Dekker's passion is simple — to explore truth through mind-bending stories that invite readers to see the world through a different lens. His fiction has been honored with numerous awards, including two Christy Awards, two Inspy Awards, an RT Reviewers' Choice Award, and an ECPA Gold Medallion. In 2013, NPR readers nationwide put him in the Top 50 Thriller Authors of All Time. Dekker lives in Nashville, Tennessee, with his wife, Lee Ann.

Rachelle Dekker is the Christy Award–winning author of *The Choosing, The Call-*

ing, and *The Returning* in the Seer series. The oldest daughter of *New York Times* bestselling author Ted Dekker, Rachelle was inspired early on to discover truth through the avenue of storytelling. She writes full-time from her home in Nashville, where she lives with her husband, Daniel, and their son, Jack. Connect with Rachelle at www .rachelledekker.com.

The employees of Thorndike Press hope you have enjoyed this Large Print book. All our Thorndike, Wheeler, and Kennebec Large Print titles are designed for easy reading, and all our books are made to last. Other Thorndike Press Large Print books are available at your library, through selected bookstores, or directly from us.

For information about titles, please call:
  (800) 223-1244

or visit our website at:
  gale.com/thorndike

To share your comments, please write:
Publisher
Thorndike Press
10 Water St., Suite 310
Waterville, ME 04901